The Crime and the Criminal by Richard Marsh

Richard Bernard Heldmann was born on 12th October 1857, in St Johns Wood, North London.

By his early 20's Heldmann began publishing fiction for the myriad magazine publications that had sprung up and were eager for good well-written content.

In October 1882, Heldmann was promoted to co-editor of Union Jack, a popular magazine, but his association with the publication ended suddenly in June 1883. It appears Heldman was prone to issuing forged cheques to finance his lifestyle. In April 1884 He was sentenced to 18 months hard labour.

In order to be well away from the scandal and damage this had caused to his reputation Heldmann adopted a pseudonym on his release from jail. Shortly thereafter the name 'Richard Marsh' began to appear in the literary periodicals. The use of his mother's maiden name as part of it seems both a release and a lifeline.

A stroke of very good fortune arrived with his novel The Beetle published in 1897. This would turn out to be his greatest commercial success and added some much-needed gravitas to his literary reputation.

Marsh was a prolific writer and wrote almost 80 volumes of fiction as well as many short stories, across many genres from horror and crime to romance and humour.

Index of Contents

BOOK I - THE CRIME

CHAPTER I

THE OPEN DOOR

I ran down to Brighton for the Sunday. My wife's cousin, George Baxendale, was stopping there, with the Coopers. The wife and I were both to have gone. But our little Minna was very queer—feverish cold, or something—and Lucy did not like to leave her with the nurse. So I went down alone.

It was a fine day, for November. We drove over to Bramber—Jack Cooper and his wife, Baxendale, and I. When we got back to Regency Square it was pretty late. I was to go back by the 8.40. When we had dined I had to make quite a rush to catch the train. Jack and George both came up to see me off. As the Pullman carriages all seemed full, I got into the compartment of an ordinary first-class carriage.

"You'll be better in there," said Jack. "You'll have it to yourself."

I did, till just as the train was off. When the train had actually started, a woman came hurrying up the platform. A porter threw open the door of my carriage, and she got in. I let her have the seat by the door through which she had entered. I went to the other end of the compartment. I did not feel too much obliged to the porter who had shown her in. Although it was not a smoking carriage, as I had expected to have had it to myself, I had intended to smoke all the way to town. In fact, I was smoking at that moment. I hardly knew what to do. The train did not stop till it reached Victoria. There would be no opportunity of changing carriages. I did not relish the idea of not smoking, while I scarcely knew if I might venture to ask permission to smoke of the new-comer.

I made up my mind that I would. I had only just lighted a cigar. I had not looked at her as she came up the platform, to notice what kind of person she was. I had been too much engaged with Jack and George. I turned to her, raising my hat as I did so.

"May I ask if you object to—"

I had got so far; but I got no farther. She looked at me, and, as she did so, and I saw her face clearly, and met her eyes, my blood went cold in my veins.

The woman at the other end of the carriage was either Nelly, or Nelly's ghost. If she was her ghost, then she was the most substantial ghost I had ever heard of. And yet I had to stare at her for some moments in stupefied silence before I could believe that she was not a ghost. Before I could believe that she was genuine flesh and blood.

She struck me as being as much surprised at seeing me as I was at seeing her—and, at first at any rate, not much better pleased. We stared at each other as if we were moonstruck. She was the first to find her voice—she always was quicker, in every sense of the word, than I am.

"Tom!" she said. Then gave a sort of gasp.

"Nelly!" It was all I could do to get her name to pass my lips.

I am not going to enter into details as to what I said to her, and as to what she said to me. Nothing pleasant was said on either side. When a man meets a woman, even after a separation of seven years and more, who has wronged him as Ellen Howth, as she was named when I first knew her, had wronged me, he is not likely to greet her with sugared phrases, especially when he has had every reason to suppose that his prayers have been answered, and that she is dead. When I saw that she had tricked me, for the thousand-and-first time, and that she was not dead, as I have written, my blood went cold. When it warmed, it was not with love for her.

We quarrelled, as we had done many and many a time before. She had been drinking. She was always bad enough when sober; when not sober she was infinitely worse. Every moment I expected her to assail me with personal violence. She threatened to, over and over again. I feared that there would be some outrageous scene in the railway carriage. Fearing this, and the scandal which such a thing would necessarily entail, I formed a wild resolution. I determined that, even while the train continued to fly through the air, I would leave the compartment in which she was, and at any and every risk seek refuge in an adjoining one.

The resolution was no sooner formed than I proceeded to put it into execution. There was no necessity to lower the window; the handle was inside the carriage. Turning the handle, I rose from my seat. Whether she mistook or designed to frustrate my purpose, I cannot say. No sooner did I rise, than she came rushing at me. The violence of her assault took me by surprise. The handle escaping from my grasp, the door swung back upon its hinges. She had me by the shoulders. I endeavoured to wrest myself free. There was a struggle. In the struggle, unconsciously certainly to me, we must have reversed our positions, because, suddenly loosing her grasp of me, before I had the faintest suspicion of what was about to happen, she had fallen backwards through the open carriage door, out into the night, and the train was going at express speed to town.

It was some moments before I realised what had actually occurred. When I did do so, I sat down on the seat in a sort of stupor. I was roused from it by the banging of the carriage door. It was being swung backwards and forwards by the momentum of the train. I shut it, almost mechanically; as I did so I noticed that the glass was shattered. It might have been broken by the banging of the door, or she might have broken it by striking it in her frantic efforts to clutch at something.

What was I to do? My eyes wandered to the alarm-bell. Should I ring it and stop the train? To what purpose? She might not be dead. Indeed, the probabilities were that she was, at least, not quite dead. In such a case I knew her well enough to be aware that nothing was more likely than that she would at once denounce me as her attempted murderer. Then in what a plight I should be! To the best of my knowledge and belief she had brought her fate upon herself. I had nothing to do with it. Undoubtedly, I had not opened the door to hurl her through. It is easy enough after the event to say that at all hazards I ought at once to have stopped the train, and explained what had occurred. I should have done so had I been able to foresee the events which followed. I should have been willing to have given a great deal to have saved myself from bearing what I actually have borne. But, at the moment, I foresaw nothing. My wits were woolgathering. I was confronted by the thought that, in face of her allegations of my guilt, my protestations of innocence might avail but little. I had suffered too much on her account already to have any desire to suffer more.

As I sat there thinking, something struck me a severe blow in the face. It was a piece of glass from the broken window which had been loosened, and which had been forced out of its place by the pressure of the wind. I lowered the window, lest the remaining fragments should also be driven from their places. The sharp edge of the piece of glass had come into contact with my cheek. It had cut me to the bone. I put up my handkerchief to stop the bleeding. As I did so I noticed that my overcoat seemed to have been torn open in the struggle; the top button appeared to be missing.

The blood flowed freely from the open wound. The piece of glass seemed to have cut me like a knife. My handkerchief was quite inadequate to stop the flow. It was becoming soaked with blood. While I was wondering what I should do if the bleeding did not shortly cease, the train drew up at Victoria.

The distance between Brighton and town had never before seemed to me to be so short.

CHAPTER II

THE MAN WITH THE SILK HANDKERCHIEF

Now that I had reached Victoria I did not know what to do. I continued to sit in a sort of bewilderment, wondering. Should I speak to the guard, or should I not? Should I walk out of the station as if nothing had happened? I was, or it seemed to me that I was, between the devil and the deep sea. Whichever path I took was the path, not of safety but of danger.

While I sat hesitating and apparently incapable of anything but hesitation, the carriage door was opened. I supposed that, seeing me, a porter had opened it for me to alight. But it was not a porter who stood there looking in—looking in, as it struck me, with eager curiosity. It was an individual in a top hat and an overcoat ornamented with fur cuffs and collar. Even in my state of confusion, and in that imperfect light, I was at once struck by the fact that both hat and overcoat were the worse for wear. The face under the hat was also the worse for wear. The cheeks were ruddy, with a ruddiness which suggested alcohol. The moustache and whiskers were too black for nature. The eyes, which were at once both impudent and shifty, in colour almost matched the whiskers. There was something about the man which reminded me of some one I had seen before. Who it was, at the moment, I could not think.

He addressed me with what he probably intended for an ingratiating smile, "This is Victoria." I told him I was aware of it. "All get out here." I added that I was also aware of that.

His eyes, which had been travelling round and round the carriage in an eager, searching fashion, which, for some reason, made me curiously uneasy, finally rested on my face. He at once noticed the blood-stained handkerchief which I still was holding to my cheek.

"Nose bleeding?"

"No; I've cut my cheek."

I don't know why I sat there speaking to the man as I did.

"Permit me to offer you my handkerchief; yours seems soaked with blood."

Taking out a red silk handkerchief, the corner of which had been protruding from the outside pocket of his overcoat, he held it out to me. I was reluctant to take it. One is reluctant to accept the loan of a silk handkerchief from a perfect stranger, more especially, perhaps, from the sort of stranger he appeared to be. But what was I to do? I was in want of a handkerchief. My own was worse than useless. It was reeking wet. Great gouts of blood were commencing to drop from it. My cheek was bleeding as profusely as ever. I was beginning to wonder if a blood-vessel had been severed. One cannot buy handkerchiefs on a Sunday night. I should have to borrow from some one. So I borrowed from him. Unwillingly enough, I admit. As I applied his handkerchief to my cheek, turning, I threw my own through the open window at my side.

He rushed forward, as if to stay my arm. He was too late. The handkerchief had gone. "Good God!" he exclaimed, "what have you done?"

He seemed unnecessarily excited, considering that, in any case, the handkerchief was mine.

"I've thrown it away. You don't suppose that, in that condition, I could carry it home." He looked at me with his eager eyes.

"Was your name upon it?"

"I believe so; why?"

Leaning over, he laid his hand upon my shoulder. He spoke in a tone of voice which, in spite of myself, sent a thrill all over me.

"Man, supposing they find it? It may be a question of life or death. Let's get out of this—come!"

It was time that we left the carriage. I had noticed a porter staring in, as if wondering why we remained its occupants. But that was no reason why the stranger, thrusting his arm through mine, should have almost dragged me out on to the platform. As he continued to cling to me when we were on the platform, I remonstrated—"Be so good as to release my arm."

Paying no attention to my request, he made as if to hurry me on.

"Come to a little place I know near here. I am a bit of a doctor. I'll soon make that cut of yours all right."

I did not budge. I repeated my request—

"Be so good as to release my arm. I am obliged to you for your suggestion. I, however, prefer to go straight home."

"Quite right; there is no place like home. Let's go and find a cab."

Not at all nonplussed, he again made as if to hasten on. I still declined to budge.

"Thank you. I can perform that office for myself. If you will give me your address, I will forward you your handkerchief. Or, if you prefer it, I will deposit with you its value."

"Sir, I am a gentleman." He drew himself up with an assumption of dignity which was so overdone as to be ludicrous. The two last words he repeated—"A gentleman!"

"I do not doubt it. It is I who may not be a gentleman."

"I, sir, can tell a gentleman when I see one." He laid a stress upon the personal pronoun, as if he wished me to infer that such clearness of vision might be a personal peculiarity. "I will give you my address in the cab."

Willing to humour him, I suffered him to stroll up the platform at my side. I held out my hand to him when we reached a hansom.

"Your address?"

"I said I would give you my address in the cab." Leaning towards me, he spoke in that curious tone which had impressed me so unpleasantly in the railway carriage. "Get into the cab, man; I travelled from Brighton in the next compartment to yours."

I was foolish. I ought, even at the eleventh hour, to have addressed myself to an official, to have made a clean breast of it, to have told him of the accident, the unavoidable accident, which had happened on the line. I know that now too well. I knew it, dimly, then. But, at the moment, I was weak. The fellow's manner increased my state of mental confusion. In a sense, his words overwhelmed me. I yielded to him. I got into the cab. He placed himself at my side.

"Where shall I tell the man to drive?" he asked.

"Anywhere."

"Piccadilly Circus!" he shouted. The cab was off.

We sat in silence, I in a state of mind which I should find some difficulty in making plain. I will not attempt it. I will only say that I should have dearly liked to have taken my friend, the stranger, by the scuff of his neck and to have thrown him out into the street. I did not dare.

When we were clear of the traffic I asked him, in a voice which I scarcely knew to be my own, it was so husky and dry—

"What did you mean by saying that you travelled from Brighton in the next compartment to mine?"

"Mean? My dear sir, I meant what I said. It was a coincidence—nothing more." He spoke lightly; impudently even. I felt incapable of pressing him for a more precise explanation. He added, as a sort of afterthought, "I'm a detective."

I turned to him with a start. "A detective?"

He pretended to be surprised by my surprise.

"What's the matter, my dear sir?" He paused. Then, with a sneer, "I'm not that sort. I'm the respectable sort. I'm a private detective, sir. I make delicate inquiries for persons of position and of means." He emphasised "means." "Have you a cigar?"

"I gave him one; he proceeded to light it. I was conscious that, since I had admitted him to a share of the cab, a change had taken place in his bearing. It was not only familiar, it was positively brutal. Yet, strange though it may appear—and I would point out that nothing is so common as that sort of wisdom which enables us to point out the folly of each other's behaviour—I found myself unable to resent it.

"I've been down to Brighton on business; to make inquiries about a woman."

"A woman?"

"A woman who is missing—women are missing now and then—Louise O'Donnel. I suppose you never happen to have heard the name?"

"Louise O'Donnel?" I wondered what he meant; there was meaning in his tone. Indeed, every word he uttered, every gesture he made, seemed pregnant with meaning. The more I saw of him, the more uncomfortable I became. "I do not remember to have heard the name Louise O'Donnel."

"Yes, Louise O'Donnel. You're quite sure you never heard it?"

"So far as I remember, never."

"Perhaps your memory is at fault; one never knows." He puffed at his cigar—or, rather, he puffed at my cigar. "I don't think I'll give you my address. I'll call for the handkerchief at yours. What is your address?"

I hesitated. I was quite aware that to give him my address would be to commit a further act of folly. But, at the same time, I did not see how I could avoid giving it him without a row or worse.

"My office is in Austin Friars?"

"Austin Friars? You don't happen to have a card about you?"

I did happen to have one of my business cards in my letter-case. Taking it out, I gave it to him. He looked at it askance, reading the name on it out loud.

"Thomas Tennant. Rather an alliterative kind of name. Almost like a pseudonym." I sat in silence. "However, there may be some one about with such a name." He slipped the card into his waistcoat pocket. "I shall have pleasure, Mr. Tennant, in calling on you, for my silk handkerchief, in Austin Friars; possibly to-morrow, possibly next week, or the week after—but that I shall call for it, sooner or later, you may rest assured." He looked at me with a grin. "Now that we have transacted that little piece of business, I don't think there is any necessity for me to inflict my company upon you any longer. I may as well get out."

I was thankful for the prospect of a prompt deliverance. But I was not to be rid of him so easily, as his next words showed. He was drumming with his finger-tips on the front of the cab.

"By the way, you were good enough to mention something about a deposit for my handkerchief. I think that, after all, I will trouble you for one."

I advanced my hand towards my pocket.

"With pleasure. If you have no objection, I will buy the handkerchief right out at a liberal price?"

His reply was a sneer.

"Thank you; I am obliged; the handkerchief is not for sale. I prize it too greatly—as a present from my late lamented greatgrandmother. But something on deposit I don't mind."

"How much shall we say?"

"Say—we'll say ten pounds."

"Ten pounds!" I stared at him. The fellow's impudence was increasing. "You are jesting."

He turned on me quite savagely—his black eyes glared.

"Jesting? What do you mean by saying I am jesting?"

"I shall certainly deposit with you no sum approaching ten pounds."

He continued to regard me as if he were taking my measure. I met his glance unflinchingly. I wished him to understand that I was not quite the simpleton he seemed to take me for. I think he grasped something of my meaning. His tone became sullen.

"Make it five pounds, then."

"I am more likely to make it five shillings. However, under the peculiar circumstances, as I don't know what I should have done without your handkerchief, I don't mind going as far as half a sovereign, which is about four times its value."

His reply, though scarcely a direct answer to my words, still was sufficiently plain.

"You and I, Mr. Tennant, will spend the night together."

"Again, I ask you, what do you mean by that?"

The fellow smoothed his clean-shaven chin and grinned.

"I mean, Mr. Tennant, that I am beginning to suspect that it may be my painful duty to thrust myself on your society until I have ascertained what became of the woman who got into your compartment at Brighton, but who was not in it when we reached Victoria."

A creepy, crawly feeling went all over me. This came of not having told the truth, the whole truth, and nothing but the truth, directly the accident had happened. Already I was suspected of the worst. And by such a fellow! Already, to a certain extent, I was in his power.

I did not give him the five pounds he asked. I did not make quite such an idiot of myself as that. But I gave him much more than his ancient rag was worth. He rattled the coins, gold coins, together in the palms of his hands; he chuckled at the sound of them; he called out to the cabman, "Stop!" Standing on the pavement, he took off his hat to me with a sweeping flourish, saying, with a laugh—

"The handkerchief itself—that priceless relic of my late lamented greatgrandmother!—I will call for at your office in Austin Friars."

CHAPTER III

THE NAME ON THE SCRAP OF PAPER

I was quite conscious, as I drove home the rest of the way alone, that I had made of myself, doubly and trebly, a fool. But, if possible, still worse remained behind.

How the African gentleman, of whom I read the other day, manages with 999 wives, I, for one, am at a loss to understand. When a man is on good terms with one wife—and I had rather be on good terms with one wife than on bad terms with 999—occasions do arise on which he experiences little difficulties.

For instance, I had been in the habit of telling my wife everything—or, perhaps, it would be more correct to write, practically everything. It would have been well for me if there had been no reservations. As a matter of fact, I had said nothing about two or three little incidents of my pre-nuptial existence. Notably, I had said nothing about Ellen Howth—though that, perhaps, was rather more than an incident.

The result was that when I reached home I was in something of a quandary. The wife plied me with the usual questions, to which I was unable to supply the accustomed copious and satisfactory answers. She wished to know how my face came to be cut in that terrible fashion. I rigged up some cock-and-bull story about a broken window—a window had been broken, but not altogether in the manner I led her to infer. Then she found that a button was missing from my overcoat. Another cock-and-bull story had to be manufactured to account for that. It did not require a woman's keen eyes to discover that there was something amiss about my general demeanour—that I "wore a worried look." In endeavouring to satisfactorily account for that I blundered fearfully. We went to bed with a shade of coolness perceptible on either side. I felt that I had been ill-used generally, and Lucy felt that I had ill-used her.

The wife had bound up my face with a sticking-plaster. In the morning the sticking-plaster was much in evidence. I had not had a good night's rest. I should like to know who would have done, after my adventures of the evening! I got up, not so much in a bad temper as oppressed with gloom. Lucy, as a matter of course, plied me with her questions all over again. We had a fencing match while dressing. The match was continued at breakfast, till the buttons almost came off the foils. I had resolved, in the small hours of the morning, to screw my courage to the sticking point, and to make a clean breast of it to some one. I told myself that the first plunge would be the worst, when I had taken that all would be well. But, by the time I started for the City, I had become so aggrieved with Lucy that my resolution, as it were, had assumed a different hue. It was irresolution again.

I bought all the papers. I searched them to learn if anything or any one had been found upon the Brighton line. I did not see very well how there could have been, in time for the fact to have been printed in the morning papers. But a morbid anxiety constrained me to the search. Pilbeam, who always travels with me to town, displayed almost as much interest in the papers as I did. He wanted to know why I had bought them. He became facetious in his way—which is his way, and, thank Providence, his way only. I listened to Pilbeam's facetiæ while I was mentally asking myself if it would be better—for me—for her to be found living or dead. In the one case I knew that she would denounce me at once to the police, and I should sleep that night in gaol—and then, what could I say or do? In the other, the odds might be slightly in my favour. Under the circumstances, I naturally enjoyed Pilbeam's jokes. They were so funny, and so suited to my mood.

That was a dreadful day. There was no business doing. Had there been I might have been saved from thinking—and from drinking. As a rule, I never drink anything in town. But that day I had to. I was too invertebrate to keep going without it.

Soon after midday I was sitting in one of the City bars—one of those in which men play chess and draughts and dominoes. I was leaning on one of the little marble tables scribbling aimlessly upon a sheet of paper. Some one, standing in front of me, addressed me by my name. I looked up. It was a man with whom I had occasionally done business—a man named Townsend, a tall, well-built fellow, with what one sometimes hears called the "beauty of the devil." He had always been something of a mystery to me. Although I had done a good deal for him at one time or another, he had never given me an address at which, in case of necessity, I could find him. His reference, which hitherto had been a sufficient one, had been a City bank. He used to give me instructions, and then would call at the office to see what I had made of them. He certainly seemed to get hold of reliable information, principally about mining securities; but that he was no City man I was persuaded. There was about him an indefinable something which irresistibly suggested the West End. He struck me as some butterfly of fashion with opportunities and tastes for punting of various kinds. That he confined his transactions to me I never for a moment believed, and in spite of his being the best dressed and the handsomest man I ever saw, whenever he gave me anything like a large line, before I operated I was always careful to have an eye for cover.

"I've been looking for you," he said, as I glanced up at him. "They told me at the office I should probably find you here. I want you to do a little deal for me." He dropped into a chair on the other side of the table. "What's this you've been scribbling here; anything private?"

He referred to the piece of paper on which I had been allowing my pencil to scrawl, I knew not what. "It's nothing; only rubbish."

He picked the piece of paper up; I was watching him as he did so. As his eyes fell on it, not a little to my surprise a most singular change took place in his countenance. Although his face was clean shaven, and, therefore, as one would have thought, likely to give visual evidence of any passing shades of feeling, it had always seemed to me the most inscrutable of masks. Neither success nor failure seemed to make the slightest difference to him. His expression was ever the same. The change which now took place in it therefore, was all the more surprising. In an instant there came into his face a look of the most unmistakable terror. His eyes dilated, his jaw dropped open. He sat staring at the paper as if paralysed by horror.

"What the devil's this?" he gasped, when his attitude and his continued silence were beginning to make me conscious of discomfort, and, goodness knows, I had been, and was, uncomfortable enough without his help!

I had not the faintest notion what it was which had had on him so singular an effect. I took the paper out of his momentarily nerveless hands. So soon as I saw what was on it, I too had something like a fit of the horrors. "Goodness gracious!" I exclaimed.

It showed in what sort of groove my mind had been working. Unconsciously I had been scribbling the name of the woman whom the stranger, when we had been together in the cab the night before, had told me he had been searching for in Brighton. There it was, "Louise O'Donnel, Louise O'Donnel," scrawled all over the paper, perhaps fifty times.

"What an extraordinary thing," I murmured.

And, indeed, it seemed to me to be a very extraordinary thing; and by no means a pleasant thing either. Very much the other way. It showed what I was capable of doing without being aware of it. I did not like it at all.

By the time I had regained some of my composure Mr. Townsend appeared to have regained some of his. He had called the waiter, from whom he was ordering brandy. I ordered brandy too—a shillingsworth; what they give you for sixpence would have had no effect upon me. We both drank before anything was said. Then Mr. Townsend looked at me over the top of his glass.

"May I ask, Mr. Tennant, what you know about Louise O'Donnel?"

The effect which the discovery of that name upon the sheet of paper—my sheet of paper—had had upon me was sufficiently capable of explanation. Only too capable. Why it should have affected Townsend surpassed my comprehension. I hardly knew what to answer when he put his question.

"Know! I know nothing."

"Is that so? Then how came you to write the name upon that scrap of paper?"

"I know no more than the man in the moon."

"Indeed. Then are you suggesting that its presence there is an illustration of the new kind of force which promises to be the craze—telepathic writing, don't they call it?"

This was said with a sneer. Something about the tone, the manner in which it was uttered, reminded me forcibly of some one I had heard quite recently elsewhere. The resemblance was so strong that it came to me with the force of a sudden shock. To whom could it be? It came to me in a flash; the stranger of the night before. Directly he had appeared at the carriage door he had reminded me of some one. Now I knew of whom. He was sitting in front of me at that moment—Mr. Townsend. His tone was the stranger's, his manner was the stranger's; even his face, in some strange fashion, was the stranger's too. The stranger wore side-whiskers and a moustache, he was older, he was not nearly so good-looking, he lacked Mr. Townsend's peculiar air of polish, but in spite of the differences which existed between them, there was the resemblance too. The more I stared—and I did stare—the more the resemblance grew. Mr. Townsend leaned towards me across the table. The attitude was the stranger's.

"Are you trying to think of where you heard the name before? I see that you have heard it."

"Yes; last night."

"Last night!"

He was holding the glass in which the waiter had brought his brandy in his hand. As he echoed my words he brought it down upon the marble-topped table with a crash. It was strange that it was not splintered.

"Last night, as I came from Brighton."

Mr. Townsend must have been in an oddly clumsy mood. As I spoke it seemed to me that he deliberately knocked his glass off the table on to the floor. When he bent over it, it was to find it shivered into fragments. From the waiter, who came to remove the broken remnants, he ordered a fresh supply of brandy. I had my glass replenished too.

"Have you a double, Mr. Townsend, moving about the world?"

He was raising his glass to his lips when I put the question. He spoke before he drank. "A double? What on earth do you mean?"

"Because it was from the lips of your double I heard the name of Louise O'Donnel."

"My double?" He put down his glass, untasted.

"I came up with him in the same train last night from Brighton."

"You came up with him in the same train last night from Brighton? With whom?"

"Your double."

His face was absolutely ghastly. He had gone white to the lips, and a curiously unnatural, sickly white. I could not make him out at all. I suspected that he could not make me out either. I know that something about him had for me, just then, a dreadful sort of fascination.

"I do not know, Mr. Tennant, if you are enjoying a little jest at my expense. I am not conscious of having a double, nor am I conscious of having come up with you last night in the same train from Brighton. By what train did you travel?"

"By the 8.40 express."

"By the train, that is, which leaves Brighton at 8.40?"

"Yes; and which arrives in town at ten."

Unless I was mistaken, a look of distinct relief passed over his face.

"Oh, then, you certainly never came from Brighton with me. It occurs to me, Mr. Tennant, that you are not looking well. You almost look as if you had had a recent serious shock. I trust that it is only my fancy."

He looked at me with eager, searching eyes, which reminded me very acutely of the stranger's.

"I am not feeling very well to-day, and that's a fact."

"You don't look very well. By the by, how came this double of mine to mention the name?"

Mr. Townsend nodded towards the sheet of paper, almost, as it seemed to me, as if he were unwilling to pronounce the name which was upon it.

"He merely mentioned that he had been down to Brighton to look for a woman named Louise O'Donnel."

Mr. Townsend's glass came down on to the table with the same startled gesture as before. If he was not careful, he would break a second one. And, since he glanced our way, so the waiter seemed to think.

"Been looking for her? What had he been doing that for?"

"That is more than I can tell you."

Mr. Townsend sat and stared at me as if doubting whether I spoke the truth.

"May I ask you, in my turn, what you know about this mysterious Louise O'Donnel?"

He looked down, and then up at me. He smiled, his smile striking me as being more than a little forced.

"That is the funny part of it. I, too, know nothing of Louise O'Donnel—no more than you do."

"It seems odd that you should take so great an interest in a person of whom you know nothing."

"Does not the same remark apply to you?"

"Not at all. I heard the name mentioned last night, casually, for the first time. It seems to have lingered in my memory, and I appear to have scribbled it, in a fit of abstraction, and, certainly, quite unconsciously."

Taking out a cigar, Mr. Townsend commenced to light it with an appearance of indifference which was, perhaps, a trifle too pronounced.

"Very odd, very odd indeed, that both you and I should seem to evince so much interest in a person whose name we have merely heard casually mentioned. It occurred to me that, when you found the name confronting you, you appeared—shall I say startled?—as if it or its owner was connected in your mind with disagreeable associations. Perhaps, however, that was simply a consequence of the general ill-health from which you say you suffer. And, I must say myself, that you don't look well. I hope that, next time I see you, you will be better."

He carried it off with an air. But I did not believe him. I felt persuaded that he knew more of Louise O'Donnel than he chose to confess. What he knew was more than I could say. But I felt equally persuaded that he wished that he knew less. He went off without saying anything further about the little deal which he had said that he wanted me to do for him. It had, apparently, escaped his recollection. I, too, had forgotten it till after he had gone. I had never felt less inclined for business in my life.

Scarcely had I returned to the office than the door opened, and, wholly unannounced, the stranger of the night before came in. He might, almost, have been waiting and watching for my return.

CHAPTER IV

BLACKMAIL

Again I was struck by the man's resemblance to Mr. Townsend. It was obvious even in the way in which he advanced towards me across the room. It was almost as if Townsend had slipped on some costume of a masquerade, and reappeared in it to play tricks with me. The fellow, going to the centre of the room, crossed his arms, in theatrical fashion, across his chest, and stood and stared at me—glared at me would be the more correct expression. Not caring to meet his glances, and to return him glare for glare, as if we were two madmen trying to outstare each other, I fumbled with the papers on my table.

"You have called for that handkerchief of yours? I am obliged to you for the loan of it; but I had to leave home for town so early this morning that my wife was not able to get it ready in time for me to bring it with me. If you will give me your address I will see that it is sent to you through the post."

There was a considerable interval before he answered me—an interval during which he continued to glare, and I to fumble with my papers. When he did speak, it was in one of those portentous and assumed bass voices, which one inevitably connects with the proverbial "Villain at the Vic."

"I have not called for my handkerchief."

"Then, may I ask to what I am indebted for the pleasure of your presence here. I have only just come in, and I have some rather pressing business which I must do."

"Your business has nothing to do with me."

"Probably not; but it has with me."

He came a step nearer, still keeping his arms crossed upon his chest. This time he spoke in a sort of a hiss. It seemed obvious that at some period of his career he must have had something to do with the stage.

"Do you not know what has brought me here. Does your own conscience not tell you, man?"

I began to suspect that he had been drinking. I looked up at him. He was eyeing me with a scowl which, to say the least of it, was scarcely civil.

"How should I know what has brought you here, if it is not a desire to regain possession of your property? I take it that you hardly intend to suggest a further deposit."

I do not think that he altogether relished the allusion. His scowl became less theatrical, and a good deal more natural. He seemed, for a moment, to be at a loss as to what to say. Then a word came from between his lips which startled me.

"Murderer!"

That was rather more than I could stand. I sprang to my feet.

"What do you mean, sir, by addressing me like that? Are you mad?"

My assumption of indignation did not seem to impress him in the least. He returned to the basso profundo.

"Have you seen the evening papers?"

At the question something began to swim before my eyes. I had to lean against the edge of the table.

"No; what is there in the evening papers to interest me?"

"I will show you."

He began to unfold a paper which he took from his pocket. Laying the open sheet before me on the table, he pointed to a column of leaded type.

"Read, mark, learn, and inwardly digest that, if you can."

The heading of the column was enough for me. It was headed, "Tragedy on the Brighton Line." I could read no farther. I dropped down into my chair again. The stranger continued to regard me with accusatory eyes.

"What's the matter with you? You don't seem well."

"I've not been feeling well all day."

"So I should imagine. Else you had been more or less than human. Since you are not able to read the paper yourself, at which I am not surprised, I will read it for you. The paper says that the body of a woman has been found on the up side of the Brighton line, just before Three Bridges Station."

"Dead?"

"Dead—murdered."

I was speechless, tongue-tied. The whole hideous folly of which I had been guilty rose in front of me, and paralysed my brain. I saw, too clearly, and too late, the dreadful nature of the error I had made. I realised the awful something which, owing to my own cowardice, now stared me in the face. It might have been bad enough if I had played the man; but it would have been better than this.

The stranger kept his eyes fixed on my countenance. I have no doubt that on it was seen some of the horror which racked me. His voice sounded to me like an echo from far away.

"That explains how it was that I saw a woman get into your carriage at Brighton, and that she was not there when we reached Victoria. You had left her on the line."

I made an effort to shake off the stupor which oppressed me. It was out of the question that I should continue to sit there passively, and allow this fellow to jump, in his own fashion, at his own conclusions. Better late than never! There might still be time for me to play the man. I took out my handkerchief to wipe away the moisture from my brow. I looked at the man in front of me.

"May I ask you for your name, sir?"

"My name is immaterial."

"Excuse me, but it is not immaterial. You thrust yourself upon me last night, you thrust yourself upon me again to-day. If I am to have anything to say to you, I must know with whom I am dealing."

"You are dealing with the witness of your crime."

"That is not the case. I have been guilty of no crime."

"Why do you lie to me? Don't you know that I could go straight from this room and hang you?" He raised his voice in a manner which told upon my nerves. I looked furtively about the room. I had to wipe the moisture from my brow again.

"Is it necessary that you should speak so loudly, sir! Do you wish to be overheard? There are clerks in the adjoining room."

"Then send them away; or don't try to hoodwink me—me!" He struck his hand against his chest, accentuating the second "me," as if he were an individual altogether separate and apart. "If I were to follow the promptings of my bosom, I should go at once to the police, and leave you to dangle on the gallows."

"You are under a misapprehension, sir. I give you my word of honour that you are. I may have been guilty—I have been guilty—of an error of judgment, but not of a crime."

"Do you call murder an error of judgment?"

"There has been no murder—I swear it!"

He held up his hand to check me. "Let me tell you how much I know about the business before you go out of your way to lie to me." Seating himself on the edge of my writing-table, he brought his right hand down upon it now and then to emphasise his words. "Directly the train started I heard two voices in the compartment next to mine—in your compartment. The voices were raised in quarrelling. I had, by the purest accident, seen a woman get into your compartment just as we were leaving Brighton, and I knew that the voices were yours and hers. The quarrelling got worse and worse. I feared every moment that something dreadful would happen. I was just going to sound the alarm, when there was silence. Immediately after a door banged—the door of your carriage. I was afraid that something dreadful had happened. And yet, I told myself, if nothing had happened I should look foolish if I stopped the train. Unable to make up my mind what to do, I did nothing. When on reaching Victoria I made a bolt for your carriage and found that the woman was not there, I saw that my worst fears were realised. Then I understood the sudden silence, and the banging of the door."

"She had fallen out."

"Fallen out?"

"Yes."

"Who opened the door for her to fall?"

"I did." Seeing the slip I had made I endeavoured to correct myself. "That is, I opened the door with the intention of leaving the carriage, in order to escape her violence. In trying to prevent my leaving she herself fell out."

"If, as you say, the whole thing was an accident, why did you not sound the alarm?"

"I ought to have done; I know I ought to have done. I can only say that it was all so sudden and so unexpected that I lost my head."

"To whom have you mentioned a word about the—accident, until this moment I have charged you with your crime?"

"To no one. My reticence, unfortunately, is the error of judgment to which I referred."

"You call that an error of judgment! Then, let me tell you, it was an error of judgment of a somewhat peculiar kind. A mere outsider would say that reticence was the best course you could possibly pursue."

The fellow's way of looking at the matter made things look blacker and blacker. The moisture accumulated upon my brow so fast that I could scarcely keep it from trickling down my cheeks.

"It might have been the best course to pursue had I been guilty, but I am not guilty; I swear it. I am as innocent as you are. It was my misfortune that there were peculiar circumstances connected with the matter which I wished to keep private. I feared to be misunderstood."

"You were not misunderstood by me, I do assure you. I understood, and understand you only too well. The point is that you still seem unable to understand me. You still appear to be unable to realise that I was in the next compartment to yours, that the divisions between the compartments are thin, and that you shouted at the top of your voice. I distinctly heard you threaten to kill the woman—yes, and more than once, and in a tone of voice which sounded very much as if you meant it."

He was wrong, and he was right. That was the worst of it. Undoubtedly, there had been strong language used on either side, uncommonly strong language. A listener who was not acquainted with all the circumstances might have supposed that some of it was meant. I can only protest that, so far as I was concerned, I had never meant what I had said half so much as she had meant what she said. No, nor a quarter as much. Nor, for the matter of that, an eighth. She had aggravated me to such an extent that I undoubtedly had said something—and perhaps in rather a loud tone of voice—to the effect that I should like to kill her. But I said it metaphorically. Every one who knows me knows that in practice I am the least bloodthirsty man alive. I never could kill a cat. Even when there are kittens to drown I have to leave them to my wife. Instead of the woman having killed herself I would infinitely rather she had killed me.

But it was no use trying to explain these things to the man in front of me. I saw that plainly. So far as he was concerned, my guilt was as if it were written in the skies. Taking up a position in front of the fire, he assumed what he possibly intended to be a judicial air, but which struck me as being a mixture of truculence with impudence.

"When a man threatens to kill a woman, and she is killed immediately afterwards, one asks who killed her. I do not ask, simply because I know. My impulse is to let the world know too. When I do get into the witness-box my evidence will hang you."

I thought it possible, nay, I thought it probable. If I had only made a clean breast of it when the scoundrel had first accosted me the night before!

"The thing now is, what am I to do?"

"I should have thought," I gasped, "that the thing now is what am I to do."

"Nothing of the sort. You have placed yourself outside the pale of consideration. It is myself I must consider." He said this with a lordly wave of the hand.

Crushed though I was, I found his manner a little trying.

"It is my misfortune that my ears are ever open to the promptings of mercy."

"I had not previously supposed that a characteristic of that kind was a misfortune."

"It is a misfortune, and one of the gravest kind. It is one, moreover, against which I have had to battle my whole life long. The truly fortunate man is he who can always mete out justice. But the still, small voice of mercy I have ever heard. It is a weakness, but it is mine own. My obvious duty to society would be to take prompt steps to rid it of such a man as you."

That was a pleasant sort of observation to have addressed to one.

"It strikes me that you take rather a strained view of your duty, sir."

"That would strike you. It doesn't me. But I will be frank with you. Why should I not be frank—although you are not frank with me. Though perhaps I can afford to be frank better than you can."

He threw his ancient overcoat, faced with ancient mock astrachan, wide open. He tilted his ancient silk hat on to the back of his head. He thrust his hands into the pockets of his ancient trousers.

"The plain fact is, Mr. Tennant, that I am a victim of the present commercial depression."

He looked it, every inch of him. Though, at the moment, I scarcely cared to tell him so.

"The depreciation in landed property, and in various securities, has hit me hard."

"To what securities do you allude?"

I fancy he made an effort at recollection, and that the effort failed.

"To South American securities, and others. But I need not particularise." He repeated the former lordly gesture with his hand. "The truth is that my income is not only seriously crippled, but that I am, at this present moment, actually in want of ready cash." I believed him, without his protestations. I judged from his looks. "Now, if I do something for you, will you do something for me?"

"What will you do for me?"

"Keep silence. I am not compelled to blurt out all I know. If I show mercy to you, what return will you make me for my kindness?"

I did not quite like his way of putting it. But that I had to stomach.

"What return will you require?"

He looked at me; then round the room; then back again to me. He was evidently making up his mind as to what it would be advisable for him to say.

"I should require you to make me an immediate, and, of course, temporary advance of £100—in gold."

"A hundred pounds? I am not exactly a poor man; on the other hand, I am emphatically not a rich one. To me a hundred pounds are a hundred pounds. Say ten."

"Say ten! I'll be hanged if I say ten! And you'll be hanged if you try to make me."

"Twenty."

"Nor twenty."

"I'm afraid I could not go beyond thirty."

"Then the discussion is at an end."

"Suppose—I only say suppose, mind—that I was able to find fifty."

"I won't take a penny less than a hundred pounds—not one centime."

"Would you undertake to go abroad?"

"Go abroad! I'll be shot if I would. You might go abroad. I have my business to attend to. You forget that I am a private detective in a very extensive way."

"For how long will you keep silence?"

"A month."

"Then, in that case, I must decline to advance you even so much as a hundred pence."

"Two months."

"No—nor in that case either."

"Three months."

"If you will undertake to keep silence until you are compelled to speak, I will give your suggestion my most careful consideration."

"Give it your most careful consideration! Oh, will you? It strikes me, Mr. Tennant, that you are as far from understanding me as ever. If you don't put the money down upon that table at once I go to the police."

He straightened his hat. He began to button up his overcoat. He looked, and, it struck me, sounded as though he meant it. I hesitated. If the woman who hesitates is lost, so also is the man. I was lost before; I was lost again, because I hesitated. I was conscious that still the bold part was the better part; that I should be wise to go to the authorities and tell them the whole plain truth, although so tardily. I knew that this man was a mean bloodsucker; that he would spend my money, and then come to me for more and more, and, after all, would hang me if he could. But I dared not face the prospect of being handed, there and then, to the police; of being delivered by him into their clutches, with his evidence to hang me. I wanted to see my wife, my child, again. I wanted, if I could, to prepare them for the cloud which was about to burst in storm upon their heads. I wanted breathing space; time to look about me; to make ready. I wanted to postpone the falling of the hammer. So I gave him the hundred pounds which he demanded, bitterly conscious all the while of what a fool I was for giving it.

He would not take my cheque. Nothing would do for him but gold. I had to send a clerk to the bank to get it. He thrust the washleather bag in which it came, as it was, into his pocket. He was good enough to say that he would not insult me by counting it; he would treat me as one gentleman should always treat another. Then, with a triumphant grin, and an airy raising of his hat, he left me to enjoy my reflections— if I could.

CHAPTER V

THE FACE IN THE DARKNESS

I did not go home even when he had left me, though shortly afterwards I started to. As I was going along Throgmorton Street I met MacCulloch. He was jubilant. He had pulled off a big stake over some race or other—upon my word, I forget what. It was one which had been run that day. He asked me to have a small bottle with him. While we were having it three other fellows joined us. Then MacCulloch asked the lot of us to go and dine with him. I knew that I ought not to, but I didn't care. I seemed to care for nothing. The moral side of me seemed dead, or sleeping. I was aware that, instead of plunging into dissipation with MacCulloch and his friends, duty, not to speak of common sense, required that, without further loss of time, I should prepare Lucy for the worst. Instead of following the path of duty, I went to dine, and that without sending to Lucy a word of warning not to wait for me. When the usually good husband does misbehave himself, it strikes me that he is worse than the usually bad one. I speak from what seems to me to be the teachings of my own experience.

We went down, all of us, in two hansoms to the West End. I rode upon MacCulloch's knees. We began by playing billiards at some place in Jermyn Street. I know that I lost three pounds at pool. Then we dined in a private room at the Café Royal. I have not the faintest recollection of what we had for dinner, but I am under a strong impression that I ate and drank of whatever there was to eat and drink, and that of both there was too much. My digestion is my weak point. The plainest possible food is best for me, and only a little of that. I was unwell before the dinner was half way through. Still I kept pegging away. I never did know why. By the time it was over I was only fit for bed. But when I suggested that the next item on the programme should be a liver pill or a seidlitz-powder and then home, they wouldn't hear of it. Their idea of what was the proper thing for men in our situation was another couple of cabs and a music-hall.

I am not certain what music-hall it was. Something, I can scarcely say what, leads me to believe that it was one at which there was a ballet. So far as I was concerned, as soon as I was in my stall I fell asleep. They wouldn't let me sleep it out. Some one, I don't know who, woke me, as I understood the matter, because I snored. When sleeping my breathing is a trifle stertorous perhaps; at least, so Lucy has informed me more than once. Then we went for a turn in the promenade. So far as I am able to recollect, MacCulloch who, I suspect, in common with the other men, had been since dinner making further efforts to quench his thirst, wanted to introduce me to some one whom he didn't seem to know, and who certainly didn't seem to want to know me. I fancy Kenyan, one of the fellows who was with us, trod upon somebody else's toes, or somebody else trod upon his. At any rate there was an argument, which in an extraordinarily short time began to be punctuated by blows. Some one hit me, I don't know who, and I hit some one—I am disposed to think MacCulloch, because his back was turned to me, and he happened to be nearest. Then there was a row. The next thing I can remember was finding myself on the pavement in the street—sitting down on it, if I do not err. They did not lock us up; personally, I should rather have preferred their doing so; it would have relieved me of a feeling of responsibility. Having, I believe, helped me up, MacCulloch, slipping his arm through mine, suggested that we should go upon the spree. I did not, and do not, know what he meant, nor what he supposed we had been doing up to then. Anyhow, I strenuously objected. I insisted upon a cab and home. He, or some one else, put me into one, and off I went.

The presumption is that directly the cabman started I fell asleep. When I awoke I found him bending over me, pulling at the collar of my coat.

"Now then, sir, wake up; this is Hackney."

I stared at him. I did not understand. "Hackney! What do you mean?"

"The gentleman told me to drive you to Hackney, and this is Mare Street. What part of Hackney do you want?"

I supposed the man was joking. I had never been to Hackney in my life. I did not even know, exactly, in what part of town it was situated. My house is in West Kensington. Why he imagined that I wished to pay a first visit to Hackney at that hour of the night I was at a loss to understand. I told him so. In return, his bearing approached to insolence. He wanted to know if I was having a lark with him. I, on my side, wanted to know if he was having a lark with me. He declared that the gentleman who had put me into the cab had instructed him to drive me to Hackney. Then it dawned on me that MacCulloch, or his friends, might have been having a little joke at my expense, and not the cabman.

When I desired to be taken to West Kensington in the shortest possible space of time, Jehu did not altogether appear to see it. He observed that his horse was tired, that he ought to have been in the stable before now, and that the stable was on the Surrey side of Waterloo Bridge. We compromised. He was to drive me to the Strand. When there, I was to find another cab to take me the remainder of the distance. When we did reach the Strand the man demanded a most extortionate sum for his fare. But, as I did not feel in a fit frame of mind to conduct another heated argument, I gave him what he asked, none the less conscious that I was enjoying myself in a most expensive kind of way, as I was aware that Lucy, if she ever came to hear of it, would think.

I was wide awake during the remainder of my journey. Having found another cab, I made a point of seeing that its driver did not go wrong. I did not want this time to find myself, say, at New Cross or

Hampstead Heath. When he drew up in front of my house—at last!—I was looking forward, with a morbid sense of expectation and a bad headache, to the sort of greeting I might expect to receive inside. But—I repeat it—I was wide awake.

Directly the cab stopped, I got out. As I stepped upon the pavement, something came at me, through the darkness—a woman. It was a dark night—it all happened very suddenly. The details of the figure and the costume I could not, or at least I did not, make out. That I own. But about the face I have not the slightest doubt. I saw it as plainly as ever I saw a face in my life. It looked at me with wide, staring eyes. There was a look in them which I had never seen before. The lips were parted—I saw that the teeth were clenched. It was very white, and it struck me, just in the moment during which I saw it, as looking strangely white.

But it was none of these things which made my heart stand still, which made me, with a gasp of horror, reel backwards against the cab. I cared nothing for what the face looked like. What I did care for was that I should have seen that face at all. That it should have come to me, like an accusing spirit, all in an instant, out of the darkness of the night. For it was the face of the woman whom, like a coward, I had left lying dead on the Brighton line. It was the face of Ellen Howth.

CHAPTER VI

A CONFESSION

"He will be all right now."

The voice seemed to come to me out of the land of dreams. I seemed to be in a dream myself. What I saw, I seemed to see in a dream. It was some moments before I realised that the man bending over me was Ferguson, our doctor; that I was lying undressed in bed; that my wife was standing by the doctor's side. When I did realise it, I sat up with a start.

"What's the matter?" I asked. "Have I been ill?"

It struck me that, as he replied to my question with another, the doctor's eyes were twinkling behind his glasses.

"How are you feeling?"

I felt, now that I was once more conscious of any sort of feeling, very far from well. My head was splitting. Everything was dancing before my eyes. I sank back on my pillow with a groan. The doctor laid his hand upon my brow. It felt beautifully soft and cool. He said something to my wife; then he went. Lucy went with him, I presume, to see him out.

Presently my wife returned. She did not even glance at me as she passed. Going straight to the other side of the room, she began busying herself with something on the dressing-table. I might not have been there for all the notice she took of me. I could not make her demeanour out at all. Indeed, the whole proceedings were mysterious to me. She was wont to be so solicitous when I was ill.

"What's the time?" I asked.

"Half-past four."

That was all she said. She never turned her head to say that. The silence became oppressive. "How long have I been lying here?"

"It's an hour since the cabman rang the bell."

"The cabman?" It all came back to me with a rush. The appearance of the apparition—the face I had seen gleaming at me through the darkness; the sudden blank which followed. I half rose in bed. "Has she gone?" I cried.

Then Lucy did turn round. Words came from between her lips as if they were icicles.

"Mr. Tennant, to whom are you alluding as 'she'? Have you not yet grasped the fact that you are in the presence of your wife?"

Then I perceived that I was misunderstood. I lay down again. Seldom had I felt so ill. I closed my eyes; even then I saw things dancing about. This unkindness of Lucy's was the final straw. I could have cried.

"My dear, why do you speak to me like that? What has happened?"

"I will tell you what has happened. I can quite understand how it is you do not know. You came home, Mr. Tennant, in such a condition that when you got out of the cab which brought you, you could not stand. Had the cabman not been a good Samaritan you might have lain in the gutter till the milkman came. If the milkman had found you it would, of course, have been pleasant both for your wife and family. I thought you were dead. I sent for Dr. Ferguson; but, when he came, he informed me that you were only"—what a stress she laid upon the adverb!—"drunk."

I knew that she misjudged me—that she had not even an inkling of the situation I was in. But at that moment I could not even hint at it. She went on—

"I don't know, Mr. Tennant, how much money you went out with. You have come back with 1s. 3d. in your pockets."

That "Good Samaritan" of a cabman must have robbed me. I felt sure that I had more than 1s. 3d. when I got into his cab.

"You have broken your watch; you have spoiled your clothes, and you appear to have either given away or lost your hat. The cabman said that you were not wearing one when you engaged him."

That I could hardly believe. What could I have done with it? It seemed incredible that I could have driven to Hackney and back without a hat.

"I may add that, if you take my advice, at the earliest possible moment you will have a bath." She moved towards the door. "I am going to try to get some sleep in the spare room."

I could not bear to think of her leaving me like that. I called to her, "Lucy."

"Well?"

"You are hard on me. I have been dining with MacCulloch."

"I don't know who MacCulloch may be, but next time you dine with him if you give me warning I will keep a doctor waiting on the premises ready for your return."

"Lucy! You would not speak to me like that if you knew all. I am in great trouble."

Her tone changed on the instant. She came towards the bed.

"Tom! What do you mean!"

"I know that I have been a fool, and worse. Even you don't know how great a fool I have been. To-night I have been trying to drown thought."

She knelt on the floor beside the bed, stretching out her hands to me across the coverlet.

"Tom! You're not playing with me, as they say some husbands do play with their wives? Tell me what you mean?"

I found this tone harder to bear than the other. A shudder went all over me. I closed my eyes. What did I mean? How could I tell her? My throat went dry and husky—a condition which was not owing to the potations of the night.

"I've been a good husband to you, haven't I? I've tried to be."

"My darling, you've been the best husband in the world. That's what makes this seem so strange." She alluded to the events of the night. "Why have you been so silly?" Putting her arms about my neck, she drew me towards her.

"You have no conception how silly I have been."

She laid her cool cheek against my fevered one. "Tell me all about it. Is it money?"

"Money would be nothing."

Her voice sank. "What is it?"

"It is something which happened last night."

I felt her shiver. "I knew it. I felt there was something wrong when you came in, although you would not own there was."

"I was afraid to tell you."

She drew closer to me. Again her voice dropped to a whisper. "What was it, Tom?"

"It was something which happened in the train." I paused. My tongue seemed to stick in my throat. "When we left Brighton a woman got into my carriage."

"A woman?" She withdrew herself a little. Then I felt that I could not tell her who the woman was; at least, not then.

"She had been drinking. At least, so I suppose. As soon as the train started she began to quarrel."

"To quarrel?"

"Yes. I was afraid there would be a row. You know the express does not stop between London and Brighton. I did not know whether to pull the alarm-bell or not. I made up my mind to try to leave my carriage and get into the next."

"Do you mean while the train was moving?"

"Yes. I thought it better to run the risk than to stop the train, and have a scene, and, possibly, a scandal. One never knows what may come of being mixed up in that sort of thing with a woman."

"Well?"

"She tried to stop me leaving the carriage, and in trying she fell out."

"Tom!" Taking her cheek away from mine, Lucy looked me in the face. "Fell out?"

"Yes."

"While the train was moving?"

I nodded.

"How awful! She might have been hurt! What did you do?"

"That's where my folly began. I did nothing."

She continued to stare at me, evidently not comprehending. My task was getting more and more difficult. After all, I almost wished that I had not begun it.

"It was all so sudden, and I was so bewildered that I lost my head."

"Then don't you know what became of her?"

"I did not know till the evening papers appeared. She was killed."

"Killed!" Lucy's arms were still about my neck. I felt them give a convulsive twitch. "What did you do when you knew she was killed?"

"Went with MacCulloch to dine. You see, it seems that the body was found on the line. They appear to have jumped to the conclusion that there has been murder done. It struck me that if I went and told my story the odds were that I should be arrested as her murderer. I had not the courage to face the situation, and so by way of a compromise I went with MacCulloch to dine."

Lucy removed her arms from about my neck. She put her hand to her forehead as if perplexed.

"Tell me, plainly, just what happened. How did she fall out? Was there a scuffle?"

"In a sense there was. To prevent my leaving the carriage she took me by the shoulder. In trying to maintain her hold she got her back to the open door. She must have stepped backwards before either of us realised how near to the open door she really was, because, before I had the faintest suspicion of what had happened or was about to happen, she had disappeared."

There was silence. I did not feel equal to meeting Lucy's eyes, but I felt they were on my face. At last she spoke.

"I see. No wonder I saw that something had happened. No wonder that you found it difficult to tell me what it was." Rising to her feet, she went to the fireplace. Leaning her elbow on the mantelshelf, she stood in such a position that her face was turned away from me. "Is there any probability of their being able to connect the affair with you?"

"Given certain conditions, there is an absolute certainty. To my shame be it said, that is really the reason why I went with MacCulloch to dine."

Then I told her about the fellow who had been in the adjoining compartment. How he had forced himself upon me at Victoria; how he claimed to have overheard all that had taken place; how he had arrived at his own conclusions; how he had levied on me blackmail. Lucy listened quietly, putting a question now and then, but never looking at me all the time.

"And am I to understand that this person believes that you committed murder, and is prepared to go into the witness-box and swear it?"

It was not only the question, it was, more than anything, the way in which she asked it, which made me shiver.

"The fellow is a scoundrel."

"Is that why you gave him the hundred pounds? If he is such a scoundrel as you say, why did you not show him the door, and defy him to do his worst?"

The calmness with which she spoke made me writhe. My tone became dogged.

"I have no excuse to offer. I was, and am, quite conscious of my folly."

"I don't wish to say anything unkind to you; I quite realise how you stand in need of all the kindness one can show you; but I don't at all understand your story as you tell it. Why did you quarrel with this woman?"

"I did not quarrel with her; she quarrelled with me."

"But it takes two to make a quarrel. Why did she quarrel with you?"

"I tell you, she had been drinking."

"But, even then, what did she say to you, or what did you say to her, which could have caused such a disturbance? Because, I can see, from your own statements, that both of you had lost your tempers."

I was silent. I knew not what to answer.

"I suppose that the woman was a stranger to you—that you had never seen her before?"

What could I say? I felt that if I did not tell the truth then it would come out afterwards. Better, while I was about it, make a clean breast of everything.

And yet I found it hard. Lucy's ideas are narrow. She has her own views of things, and strong views some of them are. She thinks, for instance, that there ought to be the same standard for a man as for a woman: the same moral standard—that a man ought to come to his wife with clean hands, in the same sense in which a woman ought to come with clean hands to her husband. I am afraid that I had been rather in the habit of finding favour in her eyes by endorsing her opinions. It seemed hard that the only real peccadillo of which I had been guilty should be cropping up against me after all this lapse of time. I had repented of it, and put it behind me, long ago; and yet here it was, as fresh and vigorous as ever, rising to confront me from its tomb.

Lucy seemed struck by my continued silence. She repeated her question in an altered form. "Had you seen her before?"

"Many years ago."

"Many years ago? You knew her, then?"

"I used to know her, to my sorrow, once upon a time, long before I knew you, my dear."

The final words were intended as a sort of propitiation—I saw that she was getting roused at last—but they failed in their effect. She stood straight up, facing me, her fists clenched at her sides.

"Who was she? What was her name?"

"Her name was Ellen Howth. I assure you, my dear, that there is no necessity for you to get warm. I have heard and seen nothing of her since I married you. Indeed, these many years I have thought she was dead."

"Why did you think she was dead? What did it matter to you if she was dead or alive? What did you know of her?"

"Really nothing, I am afraid, to her advantage."

"What do you mean? Tell me the truth, Tom, if you have never told me it before. What was she to you?"

"She was nothing to me. My dear, she was a person of indifferent character."

"Do you mean—" She paused. She came close to the bed. She leant over me. "Was she—"

I knew what she meant too well. My heart and my voice sank as I replied. I did not know how she would take it.

"I'm afraid that she was."

She stood straight up. She drew a long breath. She looked down at me. When she spoke her voice trembled—half with passion, half with scorn.

"I see! Now I understand your story very well, and just what happened in the train. And you are the man who has always held himself up to me as different to other men—as a model of what a man should be. And all the time you have had this story in your life; and how many more besides?"

"You are very hard on me, my dear. I assure you, this is the only one."

"So you tell me now. Not long ago you told me there was not one."

"I have always meant to tell you all about it."

"Indeed? Then how skilfully you have concealed your meaning! I suppose that, like other men, when you wearied of your light-o'-love you cast her from you. Years afterwards she meets you in the train. She takes advantage of the opportunity—probably the first opportunity which has offered—to tell you what she thinks of you. Your coward conscience plays you such tricks that you try to flee from her, even at the peril of your life. She will not let you off so easily, so you threw her from the train."

"I did not. I never laid a hand on her. So far as I was concerned, it was pure accident. I swear it."

"Whether that is true or not can only be known to your God, and you."

Lucy turned on her heels. Without another word she left the room.

CHAPTER VII

A VISITOR

These might be a silver lining to the cloud. If there was, I should have liked to have had a peep at it. Just then it would have done me good. I could not see much promise of happiness either in the near or in the distant future. I had been reading a good deal lately about the "ethics of suicide." If my wife believed me guilty, I should find it difficult to convince a judge and jury of my innocence. I might as well commit suicide as hang. I should be the victim of a judicial murder if they did hang me; but I did not see how my situation would be materially improved by that.

Such reflections did not tend to make me sleep. As a matter of fact, I never closed my eyes. The consequence was that, when the time came for me to rise and start for the City, I was ill—really ill. My head burned. It felt every moment as if it would burst. I could not see out of my eyes. The paroxysms of indigestion from which I suffered bent me double. My wife came and found me in this condition.

"You are not looking well," she said.

I was aware of that without her telling me. I could not see how it could be otherwise, suffering as I was suffering then. If ever there was an object of pity, I felt that I was one. But there did not seem to be much pity either in her voice, words, or manner. I said nothing in reply to her remark. I only groaned.

"Will you have your breakfast in bed?"

"I don't want any breakfast, thank you."

"Shall I send for Dr. Ferguson? Though I don't know if he is an authority on dipsomania."

"Lucy! don't talk to me like that!"

"Why not? I merely made a statement of fact. And, of course, you are suffering from the after effects of overindulgence."

That was a charming fashion in which to endeavour to smooth the pillow of an invalid. I changed the subject.

"How is Minna?"

Minna is my little girl—a little fair-haired darling she is. With all her father's tender-heartedness; more— with, I hope, some of that father's power of forgiving injuries.

"I am going to send her away to-day."

"Send her away?"

"Certainly. I have not yet made up my mind whether I shall go with her myself or send nurse with her alone. Are you well enough to enter into a discussion?"

"No," I said; "I'm not."

Nor was I. At that moment I was neither mentally nor physically her equal. Since, at any time, Lucy has about nine-parts of speech to my one, I had no intention of measuring myself against her, conversationally and argumentatively, when I had none.

I was ill four days. So ill that I could not leave my bed. At least, I was clear upon that point, if no one else was. I am almost inclined to suspect that Lucy had her doubts; or she pretended to have them. I am disposed to believe that she would not have allowed me to have stayed in bed at all if she had had her way. She threw out hints about the necessity of attending to matters in the City; though I explained to her, as clearly as my illness would permit me, that in the City things were absolutely stagnant. Then she dropped hints upon more delicate subjects still; but to these I resolutely turned a deaf ear. I vowed that I was too ill to listen.

However, on the afternoon of the fourth day things reached a climax. Facts became too strong for me. I had to listen. Lucy came into the room with an envelope in her hand.

"There is some one who wishes to see you."

I supposed it was Parker, my senior clerk. He had been backwards and forwards bothering me two or three times a day.

"Is it Parker?"

"No. It is a stranger to me. I believe you will find his name in that envelope. He would not give it me."

I opened the envelope which she handed to me. It contained half a sheet of paper, on which was written, "The gentleman who travelled in the next compartment to yours." At sight of those words I sat up in bed—rather hurriedly, I fancy.

"Good gracious!" I exclaimed; "where is he? I hope you haven't let him in."

"Jane let him in. At present he is in the drawing-room waiting to see you."

"It's that blackmailing ruffian."

I gave her the sheet of paper.

"I guessed he was something of the kind. So this is the man who holds you in the hollow of his hand? I see."

She might see, but I didn't. There was about her vision a clearness and coolness which made me shudder. It was dreadful to hear her talk in that cold-blooded way about anybody "holding me in the hollow of his hand." She continued to regard me in a manner which I had noticed about her once or twice of late, and which, although I said nothing about it, I resented.

"Perhaps now I may be allowed to talk to you as if you were a reasonable man. During the last few days I have hardly known whether you wished me to regard you as a child."

"My dear!"

"You have been lying there, pretending to be ill, doing nothing, and worse than nothing, while your fate and my fate has been hanging by a hair. I had not thought that my husband could be so contemptible a thing."

"Really, Lucy, I wish you wouldn't speak to me like that."

"Possibly. I have discovered, too late, how you dislike to hear unpleasant things."

"I don't know that I am peculiar in that respect."

"I don't doubt that there are other backboneless creatures in existence besides yourself—unfortunately for their children and their wives."

"Lucy, I won't have you talk to me like that—I won't."

"Then get up and play the man! Do you know that the hue and cry is out all over England for you?"

"For me?"

"For the man who threw the woman from the train. 'The Three Bridges Tragedy,' they've christened it. The papers are full of it; it is the topic of the day. They have found the carriage from which she was thrown. It seems that it was all in disorder and stained with blood, and that the window was broken. You said nothing about that to me. They have found the porter who saw her into your carriage. Who was it saw you off from Brighton?"

"Jack and George. Why do you ask?"

"Because the porter who admitted her to your carriage declares that you were talking to two gentleman. They are looking for them now."

"Surely they will never make Jack and George give evidence against me."

"You may be sure they will. A porter has come forward who says he saw you in the carriage at Victoria. He has given a description of you, which is sufficiently like you to show that he will probably recognise you if he sees you again. It seems that the only thing they are in want of is your name."

I sank back in bed, appalled. The prospect, in my weak state, was too terrible for contemplation. It seemed incredible that a wholly innocent man could, by any possibility, be placed in such a situation.

My wife went on, her voice seeming to ring in my ears almost as if it had been a knell of doom—

"Play the man! I have been playing the part for you up to now. Now play it yourself. I need not tell you what it has meant to me to learn that my husband has been, as it were, a living lie. You know how I have believed in you, and what you have been to me because I believed in you. To have the object of one's faith collapse, like an air-pricked bladder, into nothingness, and worse than nothingness, is calculated to give one something of a shock. But I realise that this is not a moment for reproaches—that it is a time for deeds, not words. I realise, too, that I still owe my duty to you, as your wife, although, as my husband, you have failed in that which you owe to me. If you will take my advice, you will get up, and you will go at once to a first-rate lawyer; you will tell him the truth—the whole truth, mind—and you will place yourself entirely in his hands, even if he counsels you to surrender yourself to the police. I should do so without a moment's hesitation."

"It's all very well to talk about surrendering to the police. It's easy enough in theory. It's I who shall hang, not you."

"Tom, don't deprive me of all my faith in you; leave me something of my belief; try to be a little of a man. Don't add blunder to blunder—blunders which are worse than crimes—simply because you have not courage enough to be frank. As for the man who is waiting to see you in the drawing-room downstairs—"

She was interrupted by a voice speaking from behind.

"As for that man, is it not Paul Pry who says in the play, 'I hope I don't intrude?'"

The speaker was my friend, the blackmailer. He had forced himself into my bedroom unannounced.

CHAPTER VIII

MORE THAN HIS MATCH

Yes, unannounced. I am sure that if I had had the least suspicion of his approaching presence I should have kept him out by the simple expedient of turning the key in the door. As it was, there he stood, as bold as brass, holding in one hand the handle of the door which he had closed behind him, and in the other his hat, the brim of which he was pressing to his breast.

A striking change had been effected in his appearance since I had seen him last. He had expended a portion of my hundred pounds to advantage in a tailor's shop. He was newly clad from top to toe. The overcoat which he had on was new, and so also was the astrachan which made it glorious. Thrown wide open, it revealed the fact that the gloss of newness was still upon the garments which it covered. A gold watch-chain ran from pocket to pocket of his waistcoat. Beautiful kid gloves encased his hands. Spats adorned his brand-new polished boots. His silk hat shone like a mirror. Even the dye upon his hair and whiskers had been renewed; it gleamed a beautiful blue-black. In his new splendour his resemblance to Mr. Townsend was more pronounced than ever. Even in the state of agitation which, ill as I was, his sudden appearance caused me, I could not but be struck by that.

He showed not the slightest sign of discomposure at the manner in which I greeted him. He stood grinning like a mountebank, not only as if he was sure of a hearty welcome, but as if the whole house belonged to him.

"Sorry, Mr. Tennant, to hear you are unwell—really grieved. I can only hope that it is nothing serious."

His impudence was a little more than even I could stand. I let him see it.

"What the dickens do you mean, sir, by entering my bedroom?"

In reply, he only smiled the more.

"My dear sir, I am here out of pure consideration for you. When I heard of your ill-health, I could not bear the thought of subjecting you to the inconvenience of coming down to me. So, instead, I came to you."

"Then, having come, perhaps you would be so good as, at once, to go again."

He turned towards me with a movement of his eyebrows, as if to express surprise.

"Gently, sir! Surely you presume upon the presence of a lady. Is that the way in which you should speak to me? I have no desire to keep you. My business with you ought not to detain me more than half a minute."

He seated himself on a chair, which he drew up towards the fire. Placing his hat upon his knee, he began to smooth the nap with his gloved hand. Unbearable though I felt his insolence to be, I saw that, unless I employed actual violence, I should not be able to induce him to budge. I looked at my wife. I should not have minded so much if she had not been there. I had borne with the fellow's insolence before; I might have borne with it again. But I was conscious that Lucy's eye was upon me, and that, unreasonably enough, she was expecting me to show the sort of stuff of which I was made. I say that this attitude of hers was an unreasonable attitude, because, what could she expect of a man who was recovering from a severe attack of illness, and whose nervous system was a shattered wreck. I temporised.

"What do you want with me?"

I fixed my gaze upon him. Avoiding it, he flicked his gloved fingers in the direction of my wife.

"At your service! Pray do not let me inconvenience the lady."

"You do inconvenience the lady greatly."

Both my tone and my manner were severe—as severe, that is, as they could be—considering that I was in my night-shirt sitting up in bed.

"I trust not. I would not wish her to leave the room one moment sooner on our account."

Then I saw what he was at. He wanted to get me alone and without the aid of my wife's moral support to back me. I looked at Lucy. She was standing very straight, looking alternately at both of us, as if she were making up her mind which she ought to admire most—or least. I caught a gleam from the corner of her eye. It was the one I sought.

"I have no secrets from my wife. What you wish to say to me you may say in her presence, and be so good as to say it quickly, sir."

Leaning back in his chair, thrusting his thumbs into the armholes of his waistcoat, the fellow looked at Lucy with a smile upon his impudent face for which I could have struck him—and no doubt I should have struck him, had my health permitted it.

"No secrets from your wife? What a model husband you must be! Permit me, madam, to tender you my most sincere congratulations—you have secured a prize."

My wife said nothing. But I saw her lips curl.

"Do not address yourself to my wife, sir; address yourself to me."

Still lolling back in the chair, the fellow turned, with the same impudent smile, to me.

"To you? Certainly I will address myself to you. I am here to address myself to you, though my address will not occupy more than half a dozen words. I want from you a hundred pounds. That is the only remark which I wish to address to you."

"What!"

I was reduced to gasping.

"Surely what I say is plain enough. And don't I say it plainly? I want from you a hundred pounds."

"This is Friday, and you only had a hundred pounds from me on Monday."

"Yes, and this, as you say, is Friday. A hundred pounds are but a hundred pounds. In the hands of a gentleman they fly. Especially when he has to provide for what may be called preliminary expenses of a certain kind, which, in themselves, make a hole in a century."

I knew to what he referred. He meant that he had replenished his wardrobe. As though that had anything to do with me.

"Do you imagine that I am a bank at which you have a large current account on which you can draw at sight."

He laughed—or pretended to.

"That is precisely what I not only imagine, but fervently believe."

"Then your belief is a very foolish one. I assure you that you were never more in error in your life."

He glanced at a gold watch which he took out of his waistcoat pocket.

"Why should we waste time over these small quibbles? Are we children, you and I? I have an engagement shortly. If you have not the sum in the house in gold I will take what you have in cash, and the balance in an open cheque to bearer."

"You will have neither cash nor cheque from me. I will not give you one single penny."

"Do you mean it?"

He replaced his watch in his pocket. He rose from his chair. There was, in his bearing a return to the manner of "the Villain at the Vic." The fellow was theatrical all through. All his moods were equally unreal. At the same time there was something about the change which I did not altogether relish.

"Of course I mean it. You don't suppose that I am going to be robbed and plundered with impunity by you."

"You prefer to hang?"

"You know that I am as innocent of crime as you are, and probably much more so."

"Don't lie to me, you hound!" He turned with a sweeping gesture towards my wife. "You must excuse me, madam, but you will do me the justice to remember that I suggested your departure from the room. I cannot allow your presence to debar me from plain speaking." Directing his attention again towards me, he began to button up his brand-new overcoat, with a deliberation which was, doubtless, intended to impress me. "As you have been lying in your bed, like a cur hiding in its kennel—because pray don't suppose that you can make me believe that you have been sick with anything else but terror—I don't know, my man, if you are aware that all England is on tiptoe, watching for your capture. If I were to point you out, at this moment, in any street in England, the people would tear you limb from limb. The whole country is thirsting, righteously thirsting, for your blood."

"It is false!"

"Is it? Refuse to give me what I ask, and I will prove to you if it is false."

"I won't be robbed by you."

"Then you'll be hung by me instead." He raised his hat, as if he was about to put it on his head. "Once more, and for the last time, which is it to be—the gallows or the hundred pounds?"

"You'll get no hundred pounds from me. I swear it."

"Then it will be the gallows. In ten minutes the news will be flashing through the land that justice has its hands about the murderer's neck."

He clapped his hat upon his head. He moved towards the door. I went all hot and cold—anybody would have gone all hot and cold with such a prospect as the scoundrel pictured in front of him. Whether, with a view of appealing to his better self—if he had one, which I doubt—I should have prevented his leaving the room, is more than I can say. I might have done. After all, self-preservation is nature's first and greatest law. I had, and always should have, an incurable objection to being hanged by such a rascal. As it was, it was my wife that interposed.

"One moment, sir, before you go."

He removed his hat—with a flourish which, as usual, was reminiscent of the transpontine drama.

"Madam, ten thousand, if you wish it."

"Are you the person who travelled in the next compartment to my husband's from Brighton?"

"Madam, I am."

"You look it."

The fellow might be excused for looking a little startled—which he certainly did do. I have found that particular tone of Lucy's, now and then, a little startling myself. The man did not seem as if he quite knew what to make of it.

"I look it, madam—how do you mean?"

"You look the sort of character."

"To what sort of character, madam, do you refer?"

"You look like the sort of person who would wear another man's clothes."

He drew himself bolt upright, as if his backbone had suddenly been straightened by a spring.

"Madam! I would have you to know that I wear no one's clothes but my own."

"You are wearing my husband's clothes at this present moment."

"Your husband's clothes?"

"Were they not purchased with his money?"

"Madam! you have a very extraordinary way of putting things. Is it possible that you intend to be offensive?"

"Is it possible to be offensive to such as you?"

"I, madam, am a gentleman, born and bred."

"That you are a gentleman of a certain kind I have no doubt whatever."

The man began to look badgered, as if he were growing conscious of a feeling of tightness about the region of the chest. He commenced to smooth the nap of his hat, violently, with his gloved hand.

"I take it, Mrs. Tennant, that you don't quite realise the position in which your husband stands."

"And I take it that you don't at all realise the position in which you stand."

The fellow ceased brushing his hat, the better to enable him to stare.

"I stand?"

"Yes, you."

"And pray, madam, how do I stand?"

"Have you ever heard of such a thing as an accessory after the fact?"

"An accessory after the fact?"

"Because that is the position in which you stand—in the position of an accessory after the fact."

The man looked unmistakably uneasy. He continued to suspend the operation of smoothing his hat.

"You are pleased to be facetious."

"You will find that that view will not be taken by a judge and jury."

It was with a distinct effort that the fellow returned to an attitude of defiance—squaring his shoulders and tugging at his moustache.

"I have no wish, and no intention, to chop phrases with a lady. I imagined, madam, that you desired to say something pertinent to your husband's terrible position—with the gallows already shadowing him. Since it appears to be otherwise I can but proceed to do my duty."

"By all means do your duty. But you understand that when my husband is arrested you will be arrested too."

"Pooh, madam—you cannot frighten me!"

"But I can, and will, get you penal servitude for life."

"Can you, indeed, madam? May I ask how you propose to do it?"

"By telling the plain and simple story of your connection with my husband. That will be sufficient, as you know."

"I know nothing of the sort; tell your story, and be hanged!"

Thrusting his hat upon his head, the fellow marched out of the room in a couple of strides. His exit, whether consciously to himself or not, was marked rather by haste than by dignity. When he had gone I looked at my wife. Lucy, on her part, looked at the door through which he had vanished.

"Now you've done it," I observed.

Lucy turned to me with a smile hovering about her lips, which, under the circumstances, I thought was a little out of place.

"I have done it, as you say."

"You don't seem to be aware of what you've done. What's the good of talking to him like that? Do you suppose that you can frighten him—that you can take him in? He knows very well that whatever happens to me he'll go scatheless. He's the one witness whom the prosecution will not be able to do without."

"I think you are mistaken. With a man of that type the high horse is the only horse you ought to ride. He desires nothing less than to get into the witness-box, or I misjudge the man. I suspect that his own record is not of a kind which he would care to have exposed to the cross-examining light of day."

Hardly were the words out of her mouth than there came a tap at the panel of the door. Lucy shot a glance towards me.

"Who's there?" she asked.

Whom should it be but our friend the scoundrel. He came in with quite a dove-like air of mildness, mincing, like a dancing-master, on his toes.

"Excuse me, but even on the front door steps my heart got the upper hand of me. I could not do what seemed even to approximate to cruelty. I could not hang anybody—I judge not, so that I may not be judged. My one aspiration is, and always has been, to be a friend in need. I cannot help it, but so I am."

Producing a parti-coloured silk handkerchief—brand new—he manipulated it in such a manner as to diffuse an odour of perfume through the room. My wife looked him up and down. Her tone was dry.

"Your sentiments do you credit."

"They do, I know it; but, such as they are, they are mine own." He coughed. "So far as I am personally concerned, financial considerations are as nothing. It is circumstances which weigh me down. Instead of one hundred pounds, suppose we say seventy-five—in a cheque and cash."

Lucy took upon herself to answer him—

"I am afraid we cannot say seventy-five."

"Merely as a temporary advance, till Monday. I expect remittances on Monday, very large remittances, from my agents."

Lucy's tone was even drier than before. "I am glad to hear it."

"Yes, quite so." The fellow glanced towards me. He came sneaking towards my bed. He spoke to me under cover of his hat. "I think, Mr. Tennant, if you were to ask your good lady to withdraw, and were to allow me to have one word with you, between ourselves, in private—just one—I know we should understand each other; I am sure we should."

I looked at Lucy. She also looked at me. I am bound to admit that what I saw in her eyes supplied me, to a certain extent, with the moral stamina in which, owing to the severe illness from which I had recently been suffering, I was temporarily deficient. I spoke to the fellow plainly—

"No, sir. As I have already told you, I have no secrets from my wife, and whatever you wish to say to me must be said while she is present."

"You are—you are"—I suspect that he was going to say something the reverse of complimentary, only Lucy's presence and attitude induced him to change his mind—"a husband in a million. Now, Mr. Tennant, allow me, as one gentleman speaking to another, to ask you if, considering all things, you are not disposed to advance me, on unimpeachable surety—that of my word—the sum of seventy-five pounds."

"I am not, sir."

"You are not? Strange! I confess I had not thought it possible. However, I will not utter what may seem a word of reproach. We will make it fifty pounds, then."

"We will not. At least, I won't."

"Then, since fifty pounds is insufficient to supply even my most pressing needs, it is useless for me to attempt to carry the discussion further. You are compelling me, Mr. Tennant, to take a step which, when it is taken, we shall both of us regret. But, remember, whatever comes of it—and ill will come—the act is yours, not mine. I wish you good-day, sir; a last good-day! Also, madam, I wish good-day to you." He marched to the door in a fashion which, this time, made up in dignity what it lost in haste. With the handle of the open door in his hand, he turned to me again, "I will concede still one more point. We will make it forty-five."

"We won't."

"Then nothing remains." He vanished, to immediately reappear; his head and shoulders were inserted through the partly open door. "Shall we make it forty?"

"Nor forty."

Instead of taking the rebuff as final, he brought his legs and body into the room after his head and shoulders. He addressed himself to Lucy.

"I am conscious, madam, that in this matter yours is the controlling voice. May I ask if you quite realise the responsibilities of your position? Your husband's life hangs in the balance. My necessities urge me on. Were it otherwise, I shall be only too happy to give that assistance of which, at present, I stand in need. Even as it is, you shall find in me no huckster. In proof of it, I need only state that I am willing to accept the loan of a paltry five-and-twenty pounds."

"You won't get it."

"Then what shall I get? I find it hard to believe that a man can be reduced to the position of a mendicant! I ask again—what shall I get?"

"Nothing."

"That is not only foolish, madam, it is cruel. Shall we speak of such a bagatelle as fifteen pounds?"

"No."

The fellow made a grimace as if he ground his teeth.

"Ten?"

"No."

He threw out his arms as if appealing to the gods of the gallery.

"Confound it; is a gentleman to be reduced to ask for the loan of a trumpery five-pound note!"

"Though he asks, he will not get it."

He looked at Lucy, as if he could not believe she was in earnest. Then he sighed, or groaned. His hat, which he had been holding in his hand, he replaced upon his head. Throwing his overcoat wide open, he began to examine his pockets, methodically, one by one, as if he searched for something. He did not find it, whatever it was.

"Bare, absolutely bare! This is awful. 'To err is human, to forgive divine!'" He raised his hat about an inch from his head, possibly under the impression that it was a text which he was quoting. "I came into this house with my heart beating high with hope, filled with the milk of human kindness, and it ends in this. It seems absurd to pawn a watch within four-and-twenty hours of buying it, though I certainly never should have bought it had I foreseen that I should receive such treatment. Might I ask you to oblige me with the loan of a sovereign to keep me going till I receive my remittances on Monday?"

"Better not. Your request would only meet with a refusal."

"Would it? That does finish it, that does. I'm off." I thought that this time he was off finally, but scarcely was he off than he was back again. He came hurrying towards me across the room. "I say, Tennant, I'm actually without a cab fare. Lend me five shillings, there's a trump."

"I will not lend you fivepence."

"You won't, won't you? Now we do know where we are." He glared about in his best tragedy style. "Perhaps you will give me back that handkerchief you borrowed."

Lucy interposed. "I shall not."

"You won't? Do you mean to steal it? Is it your intention to add theft to the rest of the family crimes?"

"I mean to keep it as evidence."

"As evidence? What do you mean?"

"As evidence of your being an accessory after the fact. If you take my advice, with the proceeds of the pawning of the watch which you purchased with my husband's money, you will remove yourself as far from the reach of the police as you conveniently can."

He put his hand up to his chin, as if pondering her words.

"If you will lend me—"

Lucy cut him short. She threw the door wide open.

"I will lend you nothing. Now go—unless you wish me to send for the police."

He looked at her, not seeming to like what he saw. He scowled his finest scowl.

"Go? Oh yes, I'll go." He cast his eyes up towards the ceiling. "Ingratitude, thy name is woman!" Then down to me—"Not to mention man." He began to button up his overcoat as if in a hurry. "I'll be even with some one over this, you see if I don't."

Then he went finally. We heard him stamping down the stairs; then we heard him shut the hall door behind him with a clatter and a bang as he went out into the street.

CHAPTER IX

FOR THE SECOND TIME

Lucy turned to me as soon as it was quite clear that the fellow had gone.

"Now get up and dress, and go at once to some great lawyer and tell him everything. To whom shall you go?"

"My dear! At this time of day? By the time that I reach town they'll have all gone home."

Lucy looked at me in that freezing fashion which has always struck me as being so singularly unsympathetic.

"What do you propose to do?"

"Well, my dear, I think I'll get up and dress, if you don't mind, and have a little dinner."

"Dinner?"

"Yes, dinner. It's easy enough for you to sneer, but if you'd been living on toast and water, which, to some extent, during the last four days, I practically have been doing, the prospect of a little decent food would even appeal to you."

She shrugged her shoulders.

"And you're a man? As, I suppose, is the individual who has just taken himself out of the house."

"I should be obliged, Lucy, if you would not institute comparison between that vagabond and me. I don't like it. In the morning I will follow your advice. I will go to a lawyer, and I will place myself unreservedly in his hands. Just now the thing is out of the question; I shouldn't find one, to begin with; and, in the second place, I'm hungry."

We had dinner. Or at least I had dinner, and she looked on at me while I was eating it. Her companionship did not tend to increase one's appetite. She sat in front of me, bolt upright on her chair, her hands clasped in her lap, eating nothing, and saying nothing either. She seemed to be counting every mouthful which I took, as though I was doing something of which I ought to be ashamed. I don't know what there was to be ashamed of. I don't see why a man shouldn't eat, even if he is going to be hanged, especially if he is innocent as a babe unborn, and is about to be made the victim of a judicial murder, as I bade fair to be.

A knock which came at the front door just as I was finishing came as a positive relief. I should have had words with Lucy if she had continued to sit, like an unblinking statue, in front of me much longer. The servant announced that the knocker was Mr. Keeley. Adolphus Keeley and I on Fridays play chess together, all through the winter—one week at his house, the next at mine. Owing to my illness, and the preoccupation of my mind and body, I had forgotten that this was Friday, and that it was his turn to come to me.

When Keeley was announced Lucy looked inquiringly at me.

"Shall I tell Jane to ask Mr. Keeley to excuse you?"

"Certainly not." I had not been by any means looking forward to the pleasurable prospects of a tête-à-tête. Keeley came as a relief. "Tell Mr. Keeley I will be with him in a minute."

Adolphus Keeley, to be frank, and to use an idiom, is not so wise as they make them. He is well intentioned, but dull. I have known him pretty well my whole life long, and I can stand as much of him as any one. But that night I found him particularly trying. He persisted in keeping the conversation in a groove for which I had a strong distaste. One of his weak points is an inability to see a hint in time to take it. I not only dropped hints, I threw them at him as hard as I could; but I threw them all away. I had a dreadful time. In preferring his society to Lucy's I had stepped from the frying-pan into the fire.

He began as soon as I was in the room.

"Well, Tennant, what do you think about the murder?"

"Murder? What murder?

"The Three Bridges tragedy; isn't it a dreadful thing?"

At the mere mention of the subject a shiver went all over me. I tried to make him see that it was a topic for which I had no relish. I might as well have tried to put two heads upon his shoulders.

"I have heard scarcely anything about it. I've been ill—very ill."

"I heard that you'd been seedy. Got a bit fluffy on Monday, eh?"

It is true that Mrs. Tennant was not in the room at the moment, but she might have been just outside the door; and, in any case, the insinuation was of an unwarrantable kind.

"Got chucked from the Empire, eh? Went home Hackney way, without a hat. I know. Shouldn't be surprised if you have been a little queerish; you look puffy even now. I tell you what, Tennant, you ought to go in for training. I could get a couple of stone off you, and you'd be all the better for it. But about this murder. I'm not a bloodthirsty creature, as a rule, but I should like to have the fellow who did it all alone to myself for about five-and-twenty minutes."

Keeley is one of the large army of muscular maniacs. He stands six feet three in his socks. He spends most of his spare time in a gymnasium, and the rest in what he calls "keeping himself fit." He could kill me with a single blow of his fist. Just then Lucy came in.

"Sorry to hear that Tom's been seedy, Mrs. Tennant."

"He's been in bed."

"So I hear. And what do you think of the murder?"

Lucy had brought some work in with her. Seating herself by the fire, she began busying herself with it.

"Do you think it was a murder?"

"I should think it was a murder. What else could it have been?"

"The woman might have fallen out of the train by accident."

"Accident? A lot of that!" I have told Lucy over and over again that, in the presence of ladies, Adolphus Keeley is sometimes brusque to the verge of rudeness. "Do you think that if there had been any accident about it, the fellow who was with her wouldn't have given the alarm? He knew better."

I had been setting out the chessmen on the board, and turned to Keeley with a pawn in either hand.

"Which hand will you have?"

"Left."

The white pawn was in the left hand. We sat down to play. Still he continued to prose. "Fred Courtney wanted to bet that they wouldn't have the fellow in a month. I should be almost inclined to take short odds that they'll have him within four-and-twenty hours."

He had moved to king's pawn. I was about to give the usual reply, but when he said that my hand faltered on the piece.

"Within four-and-twenty hours? What makes you think that?"

Keeley winked.

"I've heard something, that's all. It's your move."

I moved.

He brought his knight out. I fancy that I brought mine. But I am not sure. I found that, after all, I was not sufficiently recovered to do myself justice over a chessboard. I am more than his match as a rule. I have played him three weeks in succession—one night a week—without his ever winning a game. But on that occasion I was not a foeman worthy of his steel. He beat me with even ridiculous ease. And directly he had won he began again.

"You're fond of murders, aren't you?"

"Fond of murders, Keeley! What do you mean?"

"I've heard you say more than once that you like a first-class murder."

"I don't remember ever having said anything of the sort. It seems incredible that I could have done. It would have been in direct opposition to all my principles."

"Come!—I say!" He looked at me as if to see if I was joking. I emphatically was not. "I've heard you say that you'd like to be in the position of a murderer yourself, just for the sake of a new sensation."

"Keeley!"

"I have! And when the Putney mystery was on you took as much interest in it as if it had been a personal matter. Why, you have even talked about starting as an amateur detective to see if you couldn't ferret out the business yourself. You used to declare that the fellow who did it deserved flaying alive; and, when I suggested that there might be extenuating circumstances, you used to get quite mad with me."

"My dear Keeley, the Putney mystery belongs to ancient history. Won't you have another game?"

"But it seems to me that this Three Bridges business is quite as pretty a puzzle. What did he kill her for? They talk about getting up a sweepstake in the office. The possible reasons to be put down on pieces of paper, and whoever draws what proves to be the right one when the fellow comes to be tried and hung, to take the sweep. Now, what should you say he killed her for?"

"Would you mind changing the subject, Keeley. You forget that I have been ill, and still am very far from well, and that the topic is hardly one which is likely to appeal to an invalid's brain. I think I'll have a little whisky, Lucy."

I had a little whisky. In fact I had a fairish quantity; I had to, since I had to bear the burden of Keeley's conversation. That particular topic seemed to be the only one he had inside his head. He harked back to it nearly every time he opened his mouth. Had I not known the man I should have concluded that he was doing it out of sheer malignancy. But I did know him. I knew he was thick-headed. Lucy was not of the slightest use. She went on sewing in silence, as if all subjects were indifferent to her.

I was glad when Keeley rose to go. I went with him to the front door to see him off the premises. After he had gone I remained standing on the steps to get a mouthful of fresh air. It was a dark night; there was no wind, and there was a suspicion of fog in the air. I was standing on the bottom step but one. The nearest lamp-post was some distance down the road. What with the darkness and the mist I could not see any of the lamps on the hall doors on the other side of the street. It was very quiet. There was not a sound of footsteps nor of any sort of traffic.

Suddenly, while I was thinking of nothing in particular, except that Keeley had been making rather a greater ass of himself than he generally did, I saw something begin to shape itself in the air in front of me. It did not come all at once, but by degrees. First a dim outline, then feature after feature, until the whole was there. It began to take the shape of a face. It was a face—a woman's face—her face—Ellen Howth's. For the second time it had come to me, unwatched for, undreamed of, unawares, a visitant from the dead—come to me with its awful, staring eyes. There could be no question this time about my having drunk too much. I was as sober as I ever was in my life. I can give no adequate conception of the havoc with which I realised that this was so, and that the face was there. It came slowly towards me. The idea of a closer contact was more than I could endure. As it advanced, I retreated, backwards, up the steps. Still the face came on. I got into the house, and banged the door, as it seemed to me, just in time to shut it out. I staggered against the wall. Lucy came to me, as I stood there trembling.

"I was coming to tell you to come in. You will catch a cold." Then, perceiving my state of agitation, "Tom! What is the matter?"

"Lucy, I have seen a ghost."

"A ghost?"

"As I live and breathe, I have seen a ghost. Oh, my God!"

"Tom!"

"This is the second time I have seen it. I have a premonition that the third time will mean death."

There came a knocking at the door. Lucy looked at me.

"It is Mr. Keeley back again. The servants have gone to bed. I will open and see."

It was not Keeley. It was a short, broadly-built man, with a bushy beard. Other men were with him, though I could only just see them standing in the shadow at the foot of the steps. The bearded man addressed himself to me—

"Are you Thomas Tennant?"

"That is my name."

"I am a detective. You are my prisoner. I arrest you for wilful murder."

Then I saw that the men who had been standing at the foot of the steps, and who now, uninvited, were entering the house, were constables.

CHAPTER X

THE HONOUR OF THE CLUB

I had not a notion that it would be Louise, that evening at the club—not the very faintest! How could I have? I did not know that the lot would fall to me. I was the first to draw. When I saw that the card which I had drawn was black, and that on it were inscribed, in gleaming crimson letters, the words, "The Honour of the Club," it gave me quite a start. Of course I knew that the odds were equal. But, somehow or other, I had never expected to draw the thing. I held it up in front of me.

"Gentlemen, the Honour of the Club is mine."

Pendarvon, in the chair, stood up. The others all rose with him.

"Gentlemen of the Murder Club, charge your glasses to the brim." They filled them with neat brandy. Pendarvon turned to me, holding his tumbler above his head.

"Mr. Townsend, we offer you our most sincere congratulations."

The others all chimed in—

"We do!"

They emptied their glasses, with inclinations of their heads towards me. I don't fancy that, ordinarily, they would all of them have been quite equal to drinking half a pint of brandy at one swallow, neat. Some of them did not like it even then. As young Rasper-Stenning, who was in front of me, put down his glass, he pulled a face, and caught at the table. I thought he was going to be ill.

Pendarvon went on—

"The Honour of the Club, Mr. Townsend, rests with you. We do not doubt that, this day month, you will return it to us, as untarnished as when it came into your keeping." They sat down. I rose.

"Gentlemen, I thank you. I give you my word that, with me, the Honour of the Club is safe. I will wear it next my heart. At our next meeting I will return it to you with its crimson of a still more vivid hue. I will show you that it is possible to paint even scarlet red."

I put the Honour of the Club into my pocket-book. I went away with Archie Beaupré. He wanted to know if I had any one in my mind's eye.

"Not any one—unless it's you."

He was lighting a cigarette. He laughed.

"It's against the rules to kill each other. Have a light?"

I had one.

"I'll kill some one, never you fear. What is likely to afflict me is not a poverty of choice, but an embarrassment of riches. The difficulty will be to know, not whom to kill, but whom to leave alive. Think of one's creditors. How they cry out for slaughter."

But Louise O'Donnel never occurred to me. I was too fond of her. The little witch had twined herself about my heart. When I thought of her, I thought of nothing else but kisses. I don't know how many women I have loved in my time—I hope that, as becomes a gentleman, I have loved them all! I never loved one better than, at that period of my career, I loved Louise.

True enough, later on my love grew fainter. The fault was hers. My experience, a tolerably wide one, teaches me that, when a man's love does grow less, almost invariably the woman is at fault. The days went by. The Honour of the Club remained in my pocket. I could not make up my mind whom to choose. When it came to the scratch, I found the task harder than I supposed. I thought of my scamp of a brother. Goodness knows he would be all the better for killing. I might have pitched upon him had not another choice been positively thrust upon me. None of one's other relatives seemed worthy serious attention. The Depehurst people are a nuisance. But one scarcely felt justified in killing one of them, just by way of a joke, except it was Harold, who, what with his temperance fad, and his anti-gambling fad, and his social purity fad, and all the rest of his fads, is one of the most obnoxious prigs I know. On the other hand, if one commenced killing men simply because they were prigs, slaughter would know no ending.

Then Louise began to worry me. The usual story—her character at stake. As though it mattered! But, try as I would, I could not induce her to take my point of view. Never was a girl more unreasonable. I had always foreseen that she was the sort with whom one might have trouble. But then I had always supposed that she loved me. I made at least a dozen suggestions—delicately, and almost inferentially, as it were, because she was in a state of mind in which a slip on my part might have made her dangerous. Nothing would do for her except that I should marry her, which, of course, was absurd.

Then it happened. Up to the very last moment I was undecided. The fault was hers all through.

She was staying in lodgings at Brighton—really at my expense. I had enough expenses of that kind upon my hands just then! Her tenancy was up on the Monday. I told her to leave instead on the Sunday. She was to meet me at East Grinstead. She might have been under the impression that, having met me, she was to stay with me—if so, again the fault was hers. Leaving town early, I met her at East Grinstead Station. We lunched at a tavern near the station. After lunch we walked over to Turner's Hill. At the inn we had a hybrid sort of meal. Afterwards we started, as she supposed, to walk back to East Grinstead Station.

In so supposing, she was wrong.

She had been affectionate all day—too affectionate—with a sort of affection which suggested what a good wife she would be to her husband. When we left the inn, instead of going in the direction she supposed, I turned towards Paddockhurst, intending to walk through Tilgate Forest to Three Bridges Station, distant some four or five miles. She was a stranger in that country. I knew every inch of it—a lonely one it is at night. I made up my mind to put the issue plainly to her on the road. And that then, if she did not promise to be reasonable, I would do something for the Honour of the Club. The month allowed by the rules was up on the Thursday following. At the meeting I should be called to account.

Louise continued to be as unreasonable as ever—if anything, she was more so. She talked about my promises—as if they were anything! She cried, making quite a scene—or rather, a succession of scenes. She kept stopping, as we were going down Whitely Hill, accusing me of all sorts of things. I fancy she was rather taken aback when I turned into Tilgate Forest. It was pitch dark, and the walking was not too smooth. The game seemed wide awake. We could hear the rustling of unseen feet, the hurtling of unseen wings. Once we flushed a pheasant right from beneath our feet. A startled cock-pheasant is not the quietest of birds, but I don't think I ever heard one make such a noise as that bird did then. It startled even me. Louise was frightened out of her wits. I felt her trembling as she clung to my arm.

All the way along I kept saying to myself, "Now! now!" And I should have done it in the forest, only just as I was bringing myself to the sticking point, my eyes were saluted by a crimson glare. I thought for a moment we had gone further than I supposed, and had reached Wrench's farm. Then I thought of the charcoal-burners. You will find them somewhere in Tilgate Forest all the year round. Sure enough it was them. Their furnace was glowing blood-red—they had built it close to the path. They had raised a barricade of faggots to screen it from the wind. Louise wanted to stop and look at it, I believe, because she wanted the encouragement of its companionship. But I would not agree; I hurried her on. I had no desire to be seen just then, even by a charcoal-burner. As I was congratulating myself that we should get past unnoticed, a short, stunted figure, starting out from behind the barricade, glared at us through the gloom.

Little was said by either of us, as, leaving the forest, we went across the fields. Reaching the railway, we passed under the arch. I helped Louise over the stile. We paused by the gate. About half a mile off were the village and the station. I resolved I would give her another chance; then if she was obstinate, I would do it.

She was obstinate, even, as it seemed to me, in a positively ascending scale.

"You promised to marry me. I have your letter. I trusted you. If you are going to leave me to face my shame alone, there is nothing for me but death."

That saying of hers finished it; there was nothing for her but death. Only it came a little sooner than she quite bargained for. Just at that moment a train went thundering over the bridge towards town. As it went a cloud must have parted, because, suddenly, the moon came out. It shone upon us two. Louise looked up at me through the moonbeams. Although she had been crying—and I never knew a woman's face which was improved by tears—her prettiness, revealed, all at once, by the moonlight, particularly struck me. She looked prettier even than when I first saw her at the Coliseum. Her beauty went to my heart. She put her hand upon my arm—a tiny hand it was.

"Reggie, has your love for me all gone? Don't you love me still?"

"Oh, yes," I said; "I love you still."

Then, putting my hands round her neck, I began to choke her. Hers was a slender neck, so that I was able to put my hands right round and get a good, firm grip. I don't think that at first she realised what I was up to. She was thinking more of love than of death. At any rate she did not attempt to scream. She looked to me as if she was startled. She looked more startled as I increased the pressure. Appetite came with eating. I had not altogether relished the business until I tackled it. But, as I got a tighter and tighter hold, and felt her convulsive writhings and her life slipping through my fingers, I began to feel the joy of killing, for the killing's sake. I began to be filled with a sort of ecstasy of passion—the sort of sensation which I had been in search of when I joined the club. After all, it was worth feeling. Lifting her up, I bent her backwards over the gate. She took longer to die than I should have supposed. When she had ceased to move, and went all limp in my grasp, I dropped her. My fingers were rigid with cramp. For some seconds I could not move them. When I could, the pain was excruciating. I found, too, that I was not only breathless, I was damp with perspiration.

She lay in an ugly heap on the ground. I arranged her draperies and straightened her. In her pocket was a purse—one which I had given her, so I was only regaining my own—some letters in an envelope, which, I guessed, were also mine, and a handkerchief. I knew that she was in the habit of wearing a portrait of mine, which I had been ass enough to give her, in a locket round her neck. Opening her dress at the bosom—which I had a job in doing—I found the locket tied to a piece of ribbon. Tearing it off, I put it, with the other things, into the inside pocket of my overcoat. Not wishing to leave the body lying there for the first passer-by to find in the morning, picking it up I carried it a few feet along the hedge which bordered the railway embankment. On the other side of this hedge shrubs were growing on the sloping banks. Raising the body above my head, I threw it, as far as I could, among these shrubs. I distinctly heard it fall. Then, immediately after, I heard a sort of rustling—exactly the sort of rustling which the body might have made had it been alive and was rising to its feet. I knew well enough that it was not alive; I had taken care of that. But the sound was, in one sense, so apposite, and, in another sense, so very much the other way, that it filled me with an unreasoning panic terror. I started off running across the open meadow as if I had been running for my life.

I had meant to keep along the Brighton line to Three Bridges Station. It was only when I struck the stile which leads to the footpath across the Horsham line that I realised what an idiot I was. Then I pulled up, and only then. I was in a muck of sweat. Sitting on the stile, I began to mop myself with my pocket-handkerchief. I was exhausted—all of a quiver. Something of my absurd attack of terror was with me still. I actually thought that I had seen a face rise up from among the bushes and stare at me—white in the moonlight. As I recalled my folly—even though I was conscious it was folly—I shut my eyes and shivered.

As soon as I felt myself presentable and in a condition to move, I went along the Horsham line into the station. I gained the platform unobserved. I made at once for a refreshment-room. I was aware that it was not the part of wisdom to expose myself too much, but I felt that I must have a drink, even though directly after I was hanged. There being two refreshment-rooms on the up platform, I had two drinks at each of them.

The return half of my East Grinstead ticket was available to town from there; so I had no concern on that account. As I came out of the second refreshment-room, feeling that the stuff which they had sold me for brandy had done me good, I tackled a porter about a train. The next, and last, to London was at 10.20. Glancing at my watch, I found that it was just past the hour.

A woman, coming up to me as I moved from the porter, asked me the question which I had just been asking him. I noticed what a pleasant voice she had—few things in a woman appeal to me so much as that. Something in her bearing suggested that she might not resent a desire on my part for sociability. I gave her the information she required, with additions of my own, thrown out by way of feeler. She responded; we began to talk. The long and short of it was that I travelled with her in the same compartment to town.

Possibly I had at the moment an unconscious craving for congenial society—I am a gregarious animal. Certainly, she did appeal to what I take to be my instincts in an unusual degree. She was not in her first youth, but she was still good-looking, and she was not made up. I hate a woman who paints and powders; after all my experience I have never got over a feeling that a woman who does that sort of thing can't be clean. She was good style; if she was not exactly a woman of our world, then she was either very clever or very near it. She had seen the world, and it had not spoilt her. She was well dressed, and by the right people. I would not have minded doing a turn in the Park with her any day of the week.

She was frankness itself—it was that which made me shy a little. With strangers our women are not so frank, though that I have a sympathetic, not to say fascinating, way about me, I make no doubt. It is not a question of conceit; I know it. I ought to, considering it is the leading article of my stock-in-trade.

She said she was a widow. We got so thick that she gave me her card—Mrs. Daniel J. Carruth, with an address at West Kensington. She herself was English, her husband was American, which explained the name. She had been out of England several years; had returned to find herself alone. She felt her loneliness she said. I had no reason to suppose she lied.

"Have you no children?"

"No. I have scarcely known whether to be glad or sorry. There is something to be said on either side of the question." Looking down she began pulling at the pile of her sealskin coat. "You must know that my husband was many years my senior." I nodded. "It would have made a difference if he had been young."

Though I did not quite see the sequence, I nodded again. She had given me permission to light a cigarette. I was at my ease. I was conscious of feeling a really curious interest in Mrs. Carruth.

She glanced up at me. Hers were fine eyes, though about them there were two peculiarities—they seemed to be looking, not at me, but at something far away, and they always smiled.

"It seems so odd. When I left England, though I was poor, I had troops of friends. Now I have come back I am rich, but all my friends seem to have vanished into air. I have not one."

"That is a state of things which is not likely to continue long."

"Perhaps not; I hope not—one does not like to be friendless. But it is all so different to what I had looked forward to. When one has been absent a long time from home, and is able to return at last, one dreams dreams. Only those who have experienced it can know how"—she hesitated, as if for a word—"strange it feels when one is forced to recognise that those dreams have been but dreams." She glanced down; then up again. "I have many acquaintances; they are not friends."

I agreed with her, asking myself at the same time what she might happen to mean. Was she dropping a hint to me? If so, I might be more than half disposed to take it. Mrs. Carruth appealed to me strangely, every moment more and more. The minutes sped; before I knew it we were in town.

I saw her into a hansom at Victoria. She asked me to call on her; to renew and improve the acquaintance made in the train. I said that I would. What is more, when she was gone, I told myself that I would keep my promise.

Her voice lingered in my ears.

CHAPTER XI

WHAT MR. TENNANT HAD WRITTEN

There were several letters by the morning's post. One's creditors, at any rate, seemed to be in town. Do those sort of people ever go away? Lily Langdale wanted me to look her up. Confound little Lily Langdale! I had looked her up too much already. Chirpy Mason, writing from Monte Carlo, wanted to know if I could do him a hundred or two. Would I wire? No; I would neither do the one or the other. I knew Chirpy. He had probably made the same request to half a dozen more of us. There were only two letters among the heap worth looking at. One contained just two type-written words, "Buy Boomjopfs." No address, no signature, no nothing. I put that aside. It would entail my going into the City as soon as I could. The other letter was from Haselton Jardine:—

"SLOANE GARDENS.

"DEAR TOWNSEND,—If you are in town and this catches you, and you have nothing else to do, come round to-morrow (Monday) and dine en famille. Only Dora! I have something which I rather wish to say to you.

"Yours,

"H. J."

I was to go down to them at Cockington on Friday. What had he to say to me which would not keep till then, I wondered. But I had nothing else to do—and there was Dora! So, scribbling a line of acceptance, I told Burton to take it round. When I opened the paper I found that Sir Haselton was leading for the defendants in the great diamond earring libel case—Mrs. Potter Segundi against Lady Lucretia Jenkyns. I should not have minded being in court to see the fun. They say Mrs. P. S. has brass enough to start a foundry. I know, of my own knowledge, that Lady J. is fairly well equipped. When I am in Queer-street I hope that Sir Haselton will be briefed for me.

It was past one when I got out. I ought to have gone straight to the City. Instead, I dropped into the Climax, and had just one rubber. I cut Pendarvon against Graeme and Bicketts. Pendarvon and I had the luck of the devil: we scored a bumper. Altogether, with bets, I walked off with about a pony. When I reached the City it was not very far from four. I made for a broker in Austin Friars—a man named Tennant, Thomas Tennant—as steady a file as ever I saw. I have done a good deal of business through him at various times. I don't fancy that he has much nose of his own; but he keeps quiet, asks no questions, and follows instructions to the letter.

Tennant was out. He was not in the House. A clerk thought that he was at Danby's; he would go and see. I knew where Danby's was—it is one of those City restaurants where there is more drank than ate—so I saved that clerk his trouble, and went myself.

I spotted Tennant directly I got inside the place—a plump little fellow, with round, pasty face, and hair which always looked to me as if he soaped it. A mild, unassuming neat-as-ninepence sort of man. He had a table to himself. As a rule, in a mild sort of way, he is jolly as a sandboy. Just then it appeared to me that he seemed hipped. Taking a chair on the opposite side of the table, carelessly, thoughtlessly enough, I took hold of a scrap of paper on which he had been scribbling. When I glanced at it a thrill went down my back. It was a bolt out of the blue. I do not think that in all my life before I was ever so taken by surprise.

Tennant had been scribbling all over the sheet of paper a woman's name—"Louise O'Donnel." That my appearance on the scene at that particular moment was a pure coincidence, I had, of course, no doubt. It could not have been otherwise. But how came he to have been writing that name? I could scarcely believe my eyes. I stared at the paper, and then at him.

"What is the meaning of this?" I asked.

"The meaning of what?"

When I showed him what he had been writing on the piece of paper he seemed to be as much taken aback as I was. At first he wanted me to believe that he had been writing a name over and over again without having an idea of what it was that he was doing. I could not make him out at all. He made me feel uneasy.

So far as I was aware, I was the only person in England who had been acquainted with the girl's real name. She had always assured me that such was the case, and I had believed her. Everybody, except myself, knew her by her stage name—Milly Carroll. Her father was the only relative she had in the world, and he was in Colorado. Father and daughter had fallen out. Coming to England with a burlesque company from New York, she had left him on the other side of the world. If this story of hers was true— and I did not, and do not, believe she lied—she was not that sort of girl—how did Mr. Thomas Tennant come to be in possession of her name?

I put the question to him point blank.

"What do you know about Louise O'Donnel?"

"Nothing."

"Nothing? Tennant, I say!"

"I heard it mentioned for the first time in my life last night."

"Last night?" The coincidence made me shiver again.

"As I was coming up from Brighton."

"Brighton?" I had to gasp for breath. "Did you come up last night from Brighton? By what train?"

"The 8.40."

I figured it out in my mind. I should not be surprised if that was the identical train which had rattled over the arch while Louise and I had been leaning against the gate, just before I did something for the Honour of the Club. And Tennant was in it. "Was the long arm of coincidence going to make things pleasant for me?"

"What did you hear about Louise O'Donnel as you were coming up from Brighton?"

"Nothing. The name was casually mentioned in my hearing, that was all. It seems to have stuck in my head."

It did seem to have stuck in his head—and it seemed to have crept unawares from the ends of his fingers. That something had been said or done to fix the name in his memory, I did not doubt. What had been said or done was another matter. Somehow I did not seem to care to question him too closely. Generally, in his own placid, fish-like fashion, Tennant is as cool as you please. Then he was as fidgety as if he had been sitting on hot bricks. He said he was ill, and he looked it—if his ailment was not more mental than physical I misjudged him.

I clean forgot all about the Boomjopf shares, which I had come up to instruct him to buy. I left Tennant in Danby's without having mentioned them to him from first to last. Indeed, I never thought of them till I pulled Groeden's tip out of my pocket when I got home to dress for dinner. Seeing the girl's name upon that sheet of paper made me all of a fluster.

Scarcely had I left Danby's when I all but cannoned into my scamp of a brother. He seemed as little pleased to see me as I was to see him, but as I had seen and heard nothing of him for the last two years, I thought that I might as well do the fraternal. He looked seedy enough, and cad enough to boot. The cad was in his face and bearing; the seediness was in his clothes. He had on what looked like, not a second, but a fourth-hand overcoat, trimmed with the usual imitation astrachan. If he had his way, I believe that he would be buried in imitation astrachan.

"Not in prison then?"

"No." He fidgeted inside his clothes. "I'm not in prison."

"Recently come out?"

"Nor have I recently come out."

"Or just going in?"

"Not unless, my dear Reginald, it is to visit you."

Alexander was cheeky; he must be in funds, although he did not look it.

"May I ask, my dear Alexander, what means you are at present taking to increase your fortune?"

He blew his nose with an old silk handkerchief and a flourish. Did he ever do anything without a flourish—even pick a pocket?

"I don't know, my dear Reginald, that it much matters to you what I am doing, but I don't mind telling you, in confidence, that I am at present devoting my energies to the detection of crime."

"To what?"

The idea seemed too funny.

"To the detection of crime. In other words, I am a private detective, on, I think I may say, a considerable scale."

"The deuce you are! That is something new."

"And you—may I ask what you are doing?"

I stared at Alexander. He certainly was coming on.

"I'm talking to you."

"I trust that the occupation gives you satisfaction. I regret that I am compelled to cut it short. My time is valuable. In fact, at this moment I have a pressing appointment with a gentleman well known in City circles."

"A bailiff or a policeman, Alexander? They are both of them well known in City circles."

"Probably, my dear Reginald, they are better known to you than they are to me. Good-day."

"Good-day!"

He raised his hat about three feet; I raised mine about three inches. We parted, I do believe, for the first time in our lives, on the most affable of terms.

CHAPTER XII

SIR HASELTON JARDINE

Sir Haselton Jardine was a man whom I had rather been in the habit of holding in awe. One never could be certain how much he knew. A man could scarcely rise to the forensic heights which he had reached without knowing something of almost every one. He was so quiet and so self-contained that it was impossible to gauge the extent of his knowledge until too late.

He was rather short, and he was very thin, and he stooped. He had colourless grey eyes, which you scarcely ever saw, though, if you had your wits about you, you felt that they all the time saw you. He had a peaked grey beard, too straggling to be Vandyke, and sandy hair, which he parted low down on the right-hand side. His voice was as soft and gentle as any girl's—when he was asking a jury to hang a man he was always the very pink of courtesy, and I wonder how many he had sent that way in his time. He had beautiful hands, and he either braced his trousers too high or else it was a principle of his to have them made too short. Jardine's trousers were a standing joke—he always looked as if he had got into his younger, and distinctly smaller, brother's. He was a widower, and Dora was his only child.

I always had had a tenderness towards Dora Jardine. I suspected that, under certain circumstances, she might not be ill-disposed towards me. It was Sir Haselton that I felt shy of. He had the reputation of being rich, apart from his practice at the bar, and that was supposed to be worth fifteen thousand a year. Dora was pretty; he might very well have eyes for an altogether bigger man than Reginald T. But somehow of late I had begun to fancy that he himself had a partiality for me. He had become quite fatherly. I was in a measure free of the house. On Friday I was to go down to his country place at Cockington to shoot; he had quite made a point of my making an indefinite stay.

Now there had been his note of the morning!

Sir Haselton was not visible when I arrived. I found Dora alone in the drawing-room. Very nice she looked. Not one of the new order of tall girls, but tall enough, and straight as a dart. Brown hair, which, in certain lights looked golden, and which had a natural crinkle. Pouting lips—very pretty ones—good nose and chin. Her eyes were her most remarkable feature, as was the case with her father. Blue eyes—laughing blue eyes I have heard them called—and innocent and girlish too. But to me they were something else besides. I never knew a man or a woman with eyes like that who was deficient in grit. I will go further. If the women who have gone to the devil, and smiled when they met him face to face, could be polled, I should be disposed to wager that the majority of them had eyes like Dora Jardine's. I am not insinuating anything against her—quite the other way. Only I am a student of women's eyes.

She was standing by the fire as I went in. She turned, holding out her hand.

"I am glad you have come," she said.

I felt as I took her hand in mine—and I felt it not for the first time—that she and I were kindred spirits, and that, girl though she was, she was stronger than I. I said something; I don't know what. Then I looked at the fire. I felt that her eyes were on my face.

"What a strange face you have, as though, in you, were the makings of a man."

I don't know how she was in the habit of talking to other men; she was always saying that sort of thing to me. I laughed. "What sort of man?"

She did not answer my question. She ran her conversation on lines of her own.

"What have you been doing since I saw you last—killing time?"

"Unfortunately, Miss Jardine, I have nothing else to do."

"Would you like to have something?"

"That depends."

"On what?"

"On the something."

"I see. I suppose that you will be doing something else on Saturday; you are going to kill papa's pheasants?"

"You speak as though that was an improper thing to do."

There was a slight movement of her shoulders.

"I suppose that some men kill pheasants, and that other men rule empires. I might like to do both things, but I confess that if I had to choose I should prefer the empires."

I looked at her. Quietly, and without any ostentation, she gave me back glance for glance. Something from her eyes seemed to get into my veins.

"Suppose it was not yours to choose?"

"It would be were I a man."

"It certainly has never yet been mine."

"Then you certainly are not a man."

Her high-faluting amused me. That the little, brown-haired, blue-eyed thing should talk in such an inflated strain! And yet I felt that if she had been a man she would have gone for the gloves—nay, that though she was a woman she might go for them still.

She went on—

"That is the very essence of being a man; that he can choose what he will be and do."

"You are on the wrong track. He might choose to win the Derby—plenty of them do—but the odds are he will fail."

"He might try."

"And come a cropper. Men of that sort get posted every settling day. If he is a cautious man he will limit his range of choice to things which are within his reach."

"Are you a cautious man?"

As I met her eyes I could not have told her. I seemed to see so clearly in them something which was not caution, something which thrilled and kept time with a pulse of mine. While I hesitated Sir Haselton appeared—his dress shoes making the shortness of his trousers still more conspicuous. Immediately after, dinner was announced.

They always feed you well at Jardine's, and it seems to me that lawyers generally do. And, though to look at him you might not think it, Jardine can drink with any man—perhaps to counterbalance the dryness of his profession. And he has some stuff worth drinking. His guests can do as they please; he himself is old-fashioned—he sticks to the cloth when the women are gone. That evening, bearing the hint in his note in my mind, I stuck to it with him.

I was curious to know what it was he wanted to say to me; it took me aback when it came.

I lit up when Dora had gone—Jardine does not smoke—post-prandial wine-drinkers seldom do. As he leaned back in his chair a lean, dried up, insignificant little chap he looked; but whoever, on that account, would have liked to have tried a fall with him would have done well to get up early. The fingers of his left hand grasped the stem of his wineglass, but, used though I was to his trick of peering through his half-shut eyes, I could not make out if he was looking at me or at the glass.

"Townsend, I want to say something to you in confidence."

I nodded; though I don't mind owning that I felt a bit uneasy. He might have wanted to say all sorts of things to me in what he called confidence—and he was the sort of man to say them too. His next words, however, reassured me.

"I am not a man of strong likes or dislikes"—I should rather say he wasn't, being about the most bloodless creature going!—"but I like you, if you will excuse me, Townsend."

"Excuse you, sir? You flatter me too much."

He smiled—if the wrinkling of his thin lips could be called a smile.

"Flatter you? I hardly think I flatter you. I will tell you why I like you, Townsend."

He paused. I waited. The old fox kept twisting the stem of his wineglass round and round between his thin white fingers.

"I like you, Townsend, because, although you are out of the common run, you are not sufficiently so to be unpleasantly conspicuous. You have what I lack, passion. You are as likely to ascend to the top of the tree as to the top of the gallows. I hardly think I flatter you."

"You at least credit me with having aspirations."

"I believe, Townsend, that your wealth scarcely exceeds the dreams of avarice—eh?" The remark had so little connection with anything that had gone before, that I think I stared. He favoured me with one of those lightning flashes which are among the tricks of his trade—then you can see what eyes he really has. "I said I wanted to speak to you in confidence."

"Precisely. You only flatter me too much."

Again that wrinkling of the lips which he, perhaps, intended for a smile. I wondered what the dickens he was at.

"You see, Townsend, things reach my ears which do not come to other men. May we take it, Townsend, that you are not a millionaire?"

"You may certainly take it, sir, at that."

"Pressed, now and then, for ready-money, perhaps."

What was he driving at? Was he going to develop into a sixty per cent. and offer me a loan?

"I believe that most men are."

"Yes—they are." It struck me that there was something about the pause he made which was anything but complimentary. I was beginning to feel like throwing something at him. "You have a brother, Townsend." How did he know that? "Have you seen him lately?"

"This afternoon."

"So recently? Is he doing well?"

"He said he was."

"There is nothing clogs a man so much as a brother of a certain kind."

"I take care that my brother does not clog me."

"I believe, Townsend, that you do." What did he mean by the inflection with which the words were uttered? "You are wondering why I talk to you like this. I will explain."

He took a sip from his glass. Then held it up in front of him, connoisseur fashion.

"I am something of a curiosity. I have lived my own life. In my way, I have enjoyed it. But I have one thing with which to reproach Providence. He has not bestowed on me a son." He emptied his glass. "Townsend, why don't you drink? I can recommend this port. Drink up, and let me fill the glasses." I let him. "That a son is not always an unmixed blessing I am aware. On the other hand, Dora has been a model child. Still, a daughter can hardly do for a father what a son can. So I still am hoping for a son."

What did the old beggar mean? He was still so long that I thought he had forgotten to go on. But I did not feel that it was my cue to break the silence. And at last he condescended to remember.

"You have in you the makings of the sort of son that I should like to have."

"I? Sir Haselton, did I not say you flattered me?"

"I hardly think I do. I think I know you pretty well. Dora seems to think she knows you even better." Now I began to see his drift.

"Townsend, what do you think of Dora?"

"I have sometimes feared, sir, that I have thought of her too much."

"Indeed." The word, as it came from between his lips, was a gently murmured sneer.

"I should not have imagined that you were that kind of man. Townsend, would you like to marry?"

"It has been my constant dream."

"Has it? And about Lily Langdale and others?"

What did he know about Lily, and the rest of them? I would have given something to have learned just how much the old sleuth-hound did know about everything or anything. I felt all the time that he had me at a strong advantage. When I am in his presence I always do feel like that.

"You yourself, sir, have been a bachelor."

"True—I have. I take it, Townsend, that when you marry you will cease to be a bachelor."

"Undoubtedly."

"What would you say to ten thousand pounds a-year?"

"Sir!"

"When Dora marries she will have that income to commence with. Should her marriage prove a happy one, it will be increased."

He paused, as if for me to speak. I deemed silence to be the better part of wisdom.

"The man who marries Dora will have to have a clean slate, if it has to be cleaned for the occasion. I shall require him to give me a correct statement of his position. I will see that his house is set in order. He will have to take my name; Dora shall always be a Jardine. He will have to enter public life."

"Public life?"

"Have you any objection?"

"It depends upon what you mean, sir, by public life; it is an elastic term."

"He will have to enter Parliament. Means will be furnished to enable him to do so. As a country gentleman he will have to take an interest in local and in county government. He will have to play a prominent part on the stage of national politics. He will have to aim at the top of the tree. Dora has ambitions; her husband must have them too."

When he paused I was silent again. There was a cut-and-dried way about his fashion of settling things which nettled me.

"Have you no ambitions, Townsend?"

"I have such ambitions as a poor man may have."

"A poor man is entitled to have the same ambitions as a rich one—if he is strong enough. I was poor once upon a time. I did not allow my poverty to hamper my ambition. What do you think of the programme which I have drawn up for Dora's husband?"

"I think it an alluring one."

"For a strong man it has possibilities. You may take it from me that, properly backed, you are strong enough to be able to say, with truth, that few things are beyond your reach."

"I think myself that, given the opportunity, I might find the man."

"I think so too. You shall have the opportunity. You have heard on what conditions. That is what I wanted to say to you. We shall see you at Cockington at the end of the week. Perhaps, before you leave us, you may have something to say to me."

"I trust, sir, that I may have something to say to you that will be pleasant to us both."

CHAPTER XIII

AN AFTERNOON CALL

"You're sleeping it out. Are you going to lie in bed all day?"

I opened my eyes. I looked up. Somebody was shaking me—Archie Beaupré.

"You don't mean to say that you're awake? I admire your hours."

"Is it late?"

"I don't know what you call late. It's nearly one. Do you generally sleep to this time?"

"Made rather a night of it, my boy. It was five when I left the Climax."

"Oh, you went to the Climax, did you, after you left Jardine's? Win?"

"A trifle. What brings you here—starting in the early-calling line?"

Archie seated himself on the bed, murmuring—

"He calls this early."

Beaupré is the third son of the Duke of Glenlivet—one of the duke's famed thirteen. Not a bad sort—stone broke, like all the rest of us. Archie was born in two different sections—one-half of him makes all for wickedness, and the other half makes all the other way—and, whichever half of him is to the fore, he's thorough. Jardine and I had found him in the drawing-room with Dora when we had finished our hobnobbing—at which I was not sorry. When a man has had the sort of talk with the father which I had had, he is not, on the instant, all agog for a tête-à-tête with the child. He wants to straighten things out inside his head a bit. We had left the Jardines together, Beaupré and I. He had gone to some twenty-third cousin of his great grandmother—the man's relations are as the sands of the sea for multitude, and he keeps in with every one of them—and I had gone on to the Climax Club. Now, I wondered what he wanted on my bed.

When Burton had brought me my coffee, and Archie had put himself outside a soda, tempered, he began.

"Don't laugh at me, old chap." Of course, when he told me not to laugh, I was at once upon the grin—it's human nature. But he went on, "I am a miserable wretch, I swear I am."

"Who says you aren't?"

"What a muck I've made of things!"

"Who denies it? Give me the rascal's name?"

"And I might have been a respectable chap once, if I had liked."

"My dear Archie! When?"

He was too woebegone to heed my chaff. He went and leaned his elbow on my mantelshelf, and his head upon his hand.

"Reggie, I've been thinking that you and I ought to cut the Jardines."

"The deuce, you have!"

"For their sake. It is not fair to them that we should let them run the risk of being contaminated by even a remote connection with the shadow which, I suppose sooner or later, is sure to fall on us. It will come specially hard on me—because I don't mind telling you, between ourselves, that Miss Jardine's society to me means much." I stared; things were coming out. "But the knowledge that this is so has come too late. Unless the whole business of the club—I won't give it a name, but you know the club which meets once a month in Horseferry Road—is a ghastly joke."

"That is what it is."

"What?"

"A ghastly joke."

Beaupré looked up at me. I don't know what he saw in my face, but a funny look came on his own—a look almost of fear.

"Sometimes, Townsend, I don't know if you're a man or a devil."

"The devil was a sublimated sort of man, and I expect he still is. This coffee is just a trifle too sweet."

It was my second cup. I was sitting up in bed and stirring it.

"Of course, you have done nothing."

He said "Of course"; but I saw he was uneasy.

"Of course, I have."

"Townsend!"

The man gave quite a jump. He brought the back of his head with a bump against the wall, without seeming to notice it.

"I hope, as I said, on Thursday to have the pleasure of returning the Honour of the Club with its scarlet a more vivid hue."

He was glaring at me as if I had been some sort of hideous wild animal.

"You don't mean that you have killed some one?"

"Certainly. What else should I mean? Though I don't perceive that there is any necessity for you to announce it from the tiles."

He staggered to a chair, plumping down in it with the stiffening all gone out of him.

I laughed.

"My dear Archie, you had better have another drink. You don't seem quite the thing."

He looked me straight in the face, I giving him look for look. When he had sustained my glance for a moment or two he shut his eyes and shivered. I saw a shudder go all over him. I drank my coffee.

"You're sure that you're not joking?"

"Some men joke most when they are most in earnest. Perhaps I am one of them."

"Who was it?"

"A little girl I knew."

"A girl? My gracious! When was it?"

"Sunday evening."

He turned to me with a sort of gasp.

"Was it near Three Bridges Station?"

"Within half a mile."

"My God! It's in the paper! Townsend, what have you done?"

"It is in the paper, is it? May I ask what is in the paper?"

"They've found the body." He sprang from the chair.

"Reggie, I wish that I had died before you did this thing, and before ever I heard of that accursed club."

"That is rather good, from you—the club having been a suggestion of your own."

"I had been on the drink, hadn't I? I was mad. I swear, before the living God, that I never dreamed that you fellows would take the thing up in bitter earnest."

"My dear Archie, respect the proprieties, if you respect nothing else—not quite that sort of language, if you please." He stared at me and laughed—a queer laugh it was. "You remember the rule which directs what course the members shall pursue towards a colleague who, for any cause, turns tail and rats. That also, I believe, was a suggestion of your own."

"Are you afraid that I shall turn tail and rat? You need have no fear. That I shall never do, especially now. If we are to go to the devil, we'll all travel the same road. But there is one thing on which I do insist. I insist on your ceasing your connection with the Jardines."

"You insist?"

"I beseech you, then."

"I don't wish to say anything which may sound at all unkind, but don't you think, my dear Archie, that you are taking rather a liberty in intruding yourself into my affairs? The accident of our both being members of the same club gives you no warrant for anything of the kind. It certainly gives you none which I am likely to recognise even in the faintest degree."

He began to pace about the bedroom like a caged wild cat. Presently he made an announcement:

"It strikes me that I had better go home."

"I trust that you will allow nothing which I have said to deprive me of the pleasure of your society, but perhaps it might do you good if you were to toddle home and take a pill."

"Good-day!" he shouted.

Snatching up his hat and stick from the couch, he banged out of the room without another word.

I don't mind owning—since, in these pages, at any rate, candour is the order of the day—that when Beaupré had gone I did not feel quite up to concert pitch. Things were going contrary. The club did bid fair to be a bit of a failure. Although the suggestion, as I had said, had been Archie's, it was Pendarvon who had put it into shape.

I don't quite know how Archie first came to think of the thing. Some of us had been playing poker in his rooms. Pendarvon had been losing. He began to tell us about a story which he had been reading in which there was a suicide club. He said that he had half a mind to start such a club himself. Archie at once suggested that he should go one better; instead of a suicide, let him make it a murder club. Let the members draw lots, and whoever drew the lot, instead of suicide let him go in for murder—for the Honour of the Club. Pendarvon took up the idea in a way which startled us. We had all been drinking; there and then drawing up a sort of rough outline of the club, he got us all to promise to join. There were to be thirteen members; the club was to meet once a month; lots were to be drawn; whoever drew the lot was to kill someone, not a member of the club, within the month. On this basis Pendarvon had actually got the thing into shape. We had had one meeting. The lot had fallen to me.

I can safely say that if I had had the slightest inkling that old Jardine was going to say what he had said I should have given Pendarvon's pretty little plaything the widest of wide berths. I might easily have succeeded in keeping Louise quiet by the use of some less drastic means; at any rate, until I was sure of Dora. On Sunday I had cared for nothing. The very next day I had something for which to care. A golden future dangled before my eyes.

It was like the irony of fate.

Still the game might not be lost. I yet had time. I might, at any rate, make my hay and enjoy it while the sun was shining. To-morrow—whose to-morrow it was, or what weather it might bring, no man could tell. I would live out to-day.

I looked at the newspaper. It was as Archie had said; how funny that he should be touched by Dora! They had found the body—but that was nothing, if that was all—and it was all. I had not supposed for a moment that the body could stay hidden. It had all happened just as I expected. A platelayer, walking along the line, had seen something lying among the bushes—Louise. There was some sensational rubbish to catch the pennies of the mob, but the whole thing merely amounted to this, that Louise was found.

Queer stick, old Jardine! Fancy his having taken to me, after all! He was a keen judge of character; I have seldom met a keener, and, as he said, there was that in me which differentiates strength from weakness. I had known, I had felt it, all along. I have, to begin with, the courage of the devil. Give me something of a chance, and my foot in the bottom niche, it should not be my fault if I did not reach the top of the pillar of fame.

The mischief was, my affairs were in a muddle. It was not money so much; I could manage for that, and, if things went as they ought to go, not impossibly Jardine would stand by me there. I had a shrewd suspicion, from the remarks which he had dropped, that he knew as much about my pecuniary position as he cared to know. It was other things, and one of those things was Lily Langdale. It is extraordinary how I always have managed to get myself mixed up with women. The teachings of my experience I should sum up in something like a bull—the best thing that can happen to a man is for him to be born sexless.

While I was dressing Burton imparted a piece of information which brought me to a rapid resolution.

"Mrs. Langdale was here after you went out, sir. Made rather a noise. Talked about stopping for your return."

"Did she?" That settled it.

I went straight off to Miss Lily. I was plain with her. She did not like it—she was equally plain with me. What home truths one does get from women! A woman in a temper is ten thousand times more candid than a man. But she had sense enough to understand that she could scarcely expect to score, on those lines, off me. I explained that what would be done for her depended upon how she behaved herself, but I did not explain that it depended much more upon Sir Haselton Jardine.

Lily's place was in the Hammersmith Road. As I was leaving it, something like calm having followed the storm—never, if you can help it, leave a woman in a rage, it is cruel—whom should I encounter but Mrs. Daniel J. Carruth, my acquaintance of the train. Very nice she looked, with a natty little toque on her clever head, and a fluffy fur thing round her throat. I have seen many uglier women ten years younger— yes, and as far as appearances went, further gone in the sere and yellow.

She came sailing up when she saw me.

"I hope, Mr. Townsend, that you are coming to give me a call, and that I am just getting home in time."

I was not going to give her a call. I had forgotten that the address she had given me was at West Kensington. Her very existence had escaped my memory. But when she asked me, why, I went.

A decent house she seemed to have, in a street at the back of St. Paul's School. An old fellow was in the drawing-room when we got in. I say old, though I daresay he was not more than fifty. He reminded me, somehow, of some one I had seen somewhere before, and known intimately, as it seemed to me, but I could not for the life of me think whom. He was tall and thin, and stooped, though he looked as tough as leather and sinewy and strong. He was bald on the top of his head. What hair he had, and the fringe of whisker on his chin, was grey. He wore an undertaker's frock-coat, and in his open shirt-front was a diamond as big as a pea.

Mrs. Carruth introduced us.

"Mr. Townsend, this is an old friend of mine, Mr Haines."

The old chap did not stay long. I fancy he did not altogether relish my intrusion, or what he took to be such. When he had gone I told Mrs. Carruth that he seemed to remind me of some one I had known.

"Is that so? One does sometimes fancy that one sees a resemblance. I think that in your case it is only fancy. Mr. Haines is an American, a Westerner. He has only recently arrived in England. He was my husband's friend for many years."

I found Mrs. Carruth very pleasant. Friendly—but not too friendly. She seemed to do everything in fairly good style. The room in which we sat was not only prettily furnished, it was distinctly that sort of prettiness which costs money—it had no connection with the "How to furnish a twelve-roomed house tastefully for £200" kind of thing. Tea was served with the accompaniments of silver and Wedgewood china, by a maid who knew her work. Altogether Mrs. Carruth and her way of doing things favourably impressed me.

She alluded to the queerness of our meeting.

"I hope, Mr. Townsend, that you will not allow the informal fashion of our introduction to each other to prejudice me in your eyes."

"Quite the other way. Chance acquaintances are sometimes the pleasantest one makes."

"You speak from the man's point of view. From the woman's, I think that you are wrong. I have had my share of moving about in the world. I have found that, generally speaking, chance acquaintances are things to be avoided."

"It is I, then, who must warn you that both prejudgment and prejudice begin with a 'P.'"

"I promise, for my part, that I won't judge you until I know you better. Only you must give me a chance. Were you really coming to see me when we met?"

"No, I wasn't. Frankly, I was not at all sure that you would care to see me. I know, as you have said, that my view of chance acquaintances is a man's; and how was I to know that your words as you rattled off in your hansom were not merely intended as a courteous dismissal?"

She put down her cup and saucer, seeming quite distressed.

"Oh, I hope you won't think that of me! I assure you, Mr. Townsend, that if I had wished to dismiss you I should have done so. I hope you won't mind my saying—since you have yourself said so much—that as I left you my feeling was that, for once in a way, I had made a chance acquaintance which it might be worth one's while to cultivate. And, as I told you, I was practically alone in this big town, and when one is alone one does want friends, and—I think that that's all."

That might be all, but I understood. When I left I felt that I liked Mrs. Carruth even better than I had done at first. She interested me in a really curious way.

CHAPTER XIV

SELLING BOOMJOPFS

The newspapers on the Wednesday and Thursday were beyond my understanding. I had never before so clearly realised how great a stir a little thing might make. The little incident at Three Bridges had assumed the dimensions of an event of national importance. Had one of the great decisive battles of the world just been fought it could scarcely have seemed to occupy a greater space in the public mind. Everywhere the words stared you in the face, everywhere you heard the words slipping from somebody's tongue—Three Bridges Tragedy! At least the thing received a magnificent advertisement. What a heap of money would have been required to procure a similar advertisement for Pickemup's Pills.

They appeared to have got the business into an elegant muddle. Either the luck was on my side, or some one had blundered. People seemed to have leaped to the conclusion that Louise had been thrown from a passing train—my pitching the body over the hedge on to the railway embankment, read by the light of after events, amounted to a stroke of inspiration. The papers were full of observations on the dangers of English railway travelling. Why were not our carriages all thrown open to the world? Our present system of horse-boxes rendered it possible for the innocent A. to be cooped up with the dangerous B. through sixty miles of country. The means provided for inter-communication, the alarm-bell, and all the rest of it, were fatally insufficient, as witness this most horrid instance. As I read I stared.

From my point of view the most extraordinary part of the affair was that there actually seemed some excuse for the public blundering. Immediately after the arrival at Victoria of the 8.40 from Brighton, it had been discovered that the window of one of the first-class carriages was smashed to shivers, the compartment was stained with blood, and bore every appearance of having been the scene of a recent struggle. That was the very train which had passed while Louise and I had been arguing at the gate—had another little argument been taking place on board the train? But what capped the record was a statement which had been volunteered by a Brighton porter. He declared—or was stated to have declared—that he had shown a lady into the identical compartment in which the window was smashed, just as the train was starting; that the only other passenger the compartment contained was a gentleman, whom, if he saw him again, he thought he should recognise; and—mirabile dictum! he had seen the body which had been found on the line, and in the dead woman had instantly recognised the lady he had shown into the carriage. The question now was—all the world was asking it—where was the gentleman?

Yes—where was he?

On the Thursday I received another line from Groeden—"Sell Boomjopfs." This recalled to my mind the fact that, by the Monday morning's post, he had counselled me to buy them. I had started Citywards to act on his advice. The curious coincidence of finding Mr. Tennant scribbling Louise's name all over a sheet of paper had prevented my putting my intention into execution.

Groeden's latest advice sent me to the money article. Since Monday Boomjopfs had gone up fourteen. What an ass I had truly been! A pretty pile I had thrown away! What little game Mr. Groeden and his friends at Johannesburg were up to, I was not sufficiently in the know to be able to say. I took it that, the bulls having had an innings, the bears were to have their turn. The top price having been reached, the word was "Knock 'em." So off I went to sell what I had been fool enough to just miss buying.

I thought that I would give Tennant another try. When I reached Austin Friars I was informed that he was ill—had been away from the office since Monday. While I was hesitating what I should do—whether, that is, I should give a commission to his managing man, or go elsewhere—I heard a voice in the inner office which rather made me cock my ears.

The voice was my rascally brother's. He was not speaking in a whisper. His words struck me as queer ones.

"If Mr. Tennant takes my advice, he'll see me though he's dying."

"I shall see Mr. Tennant at his private address to-night. I will tell him what you say. What name shall I give?"

"Name? Tell him the gentleman who came up with him on Sunday night from Brighton."

I went out into the street, still not clear in my mind as to what I should do. Presently, along came Alexander. But what a change had come over him since Monday! Then he was a faded ruin; now he was a vision of splendour. He was arrayed in new garments from top to toe—and not garments which had been procured at a slop-shop either. Alexander must have come into a fortune. The glory of him made one blink one's eyes.

Again, at sight of me he did not seem glad.

"Still out?" I began.

"Sir!" He pulled his hat more over to the side of his head. "Allow me to point out to you that the fact of your being my brother does not entitle you to insult me. May I ask what you mean by saying 'Still out'?"

"My dear Alexander, is it possible that you can think me capable of insulting you? I am only too glad to see that you still are out. And in such gorgeous apparel! What universal provider have you been inspiring with confidence?"

He drew his imitation astrachan cuffs further down over his wrists.

"I believe, my dear Reginald, that I informed you on Monday that I am a private detective on a considerable scale. As such, it is part of my business to wear disguises. You saw me in one of them on Monday. At this moment I am in my usual attire."

"Indeed! and excellently it becomes you. Almost anybody might mistake you for a respectable person. Alexander, by the way, what was that you were saying about your having come up with Mr. Tennant on Sunday night from Brighton?"

Alexander looked at me for a moment as if my question had knocked the sense right out of him. Then, without a word, turning into a narrow passage which was on our right, he walked off down it at the rate of a good five miles an hour. I let him go, though what had sent him off in such a style at such a pace was hidden from me.

I did sell Boomjopfs, but not through Mr. Tennant's managing man.

That night was to be the second meeting of the club. I dressed when I got home: then I put my proofs into my pocket. After a solitary dinner I started off to give back to the Club its Honour.

CHAPTER XV

THE CLUB

The club held its meetings in Horseferry Road. I had never been there in the daytime, but by night the approaches, the surroundings, the place itself did not strike one as being particularly savoury. One wondered what the deuce one was doing in that galley.

We were instructed to tell cabmen to pull up at the Gas Light and Coke Company's Offices. Since it was not deemed expedient to let even jarveys know exactly where in that salubrious locality men with the price of a cab-fare in their pockets happened to be going, the rest of the distance was to be walked.

I fancy that in the daytime the lower part of the house was used as offices. When I reached it the street door was closed, the place seemed deserted, not a light was to be seen. Each of us had been provided with a pass-key. Letting myself in, I found myself in a pitch-dark passage. Striking a match, I used it to light me up two flights of stairs. At the top of the second flight I was confronted by another door. On the left-hand side, against the wall, was an electric button. I pressed it twice, then counted three; pressed it once, counted another three, then pressed it twice again. Almost immediately afterwards a gong was struck within. While the sound was still vibrating in the air, I sang out—

"Reginald!"

As I uttered my Christian name the door was opened and Pendarvon received me on the threshold within.

"Welcome, Reginald! You are the first-comer," he said.

We turned into a room on the right. The room was plainly furnished, the walls were painted red, a red carpet was on the floor. In the centre stood a good-sized oval-shaped mahogany table. Thirteen chairs were placed round it. In front of each was a decanter of brandy and a glass. In front of one was a manuscript book, bound in crimson morocco, pens, ink, a crimson velvet bag, and a small heap of red cards, of the size and shape of ordinary playing-cards.

As Pendarvon had said, he and I, up to the present, had the place to ourselves. Cecil Pendarvon was fairly tall and fairly broad—the florid type of man. He had fair hair, fair beard, and light blue eyes. Your first impression of the man was that he was always laughing. When you came to study him a little closer you began to doubt if his laugh suggested merriment. I knew him well. I had come to understand that the more he laughed the worse it would be for some one.

He stood, stroking his long fair beard, laughing at me now.

"Pendarvon, I don't quite see what's the use of the counting, and the ornamental ringing, and all the rest of it outside the door."

"You mayn't see it now. One of these days you may. There may come a time when it will be advisable that we should know that the person at the door is not a member of the club."

"If you mean that one of these days we are likely to receive a visit from the police, you don't suppose that we should be able to keep them out, if they had made up their minds to enter. We should be trapped like rabbits in a warren."

"I think not. That door is of sheet iron. It is held in position by four steel bolts which run into a wall made of solid Portland cement. By the time the police got through it we should be miles away."

I looked round the apartment.

"Is this room then not what it seems? Is there a hidden door?"

"There is not. But there is something quite as good. There is a fireplace."

"A fireplace?"

"And likewise a chimney, which is a chimney. When I took this place I had an eye to all the possibilities. Look here."

He went to the fireplace, a huge old-fashioned one, probably over six feet wide. The stove occupied not one-third of it. He stepped inside, I following. There was ample room for both of us. He pointed upwards.

"Stanchions, which will make excellent steps."

I saw that there were stanchions, rising one above the other, set in the side of the chimney.

"Where do they lead to?"

"Climb up twelve, put your hand out to the right, you will find a bolt. Draw it, push, a door will open. Go through it, you will find yourself upon the roof."

"The roof, at night—I thank you!"

"The chimney-stack will be on your left, between you and a fall into the street. Keep it on your left, go straight forward—you will find yourself upon the edge."

"The edge! Of the roof? Pendarvon, my thanks increase!"

"If you feel for it on your right you will find a rail. This is the rail of a bridge which crosses from this house to one in the street behind. When I took this room I took that house. It will remain empty. Cross the bridge. Close to your hand, on your left, you will find an iron ladder set straight against the wall. Descend it, you will land yourself on the flat roof of an outhouse. Within a foot of you, still to your left, there is a window. It will be always left unlatched. You have only to raise it, enter the empty house, strike a light, and walk downstairs into the street. To reach that particular house, in that particular street, by road, a policeman will have to walk two miles."

"How long is this bridge of yours?"

"Under twenty feet."

"And how wide?"

"Perhaps ten inches—it is a single plank. The rail by which you hold is firmly fixed and bolted at either end. What the whole arrangement was intended for originally is a puzzle I have not attempted to solve. I heard of it. I thought it might suit us."

"Don't you think we ought to do what the firemen do—have a full dress rehearsal? I, for one, should hardly care to seek that path to safety without having had some practical experience of the peculiarities and perils of the way."

Pendarvon laughed.

"You fellows can have a rehearsal to-night, if you like—only you will get yourselves into a deuce of a mess. I don't guarantee that you will be able to keep yourselves clean. I only guarantee that that way, at a pinch, you will be able to save your necks."

As he finished speaking, the electric bell rang twice; there was a pause; then a single ring; another pause; then twice more. Pendarvon went to a gong which was suspended from the ceiling outside the room. He struck it, not too loudly. A voice on the other side of the other door exclaimed—

"Gustave!"

As Pendarvon opened the door, he turned to me.

"Gustave Rudini."

It was Rudini—an undersized, ill-dressed little fellow, more like a waiter out of work than anything else I know. Pendarvon had had some difficulty in completing the tail of his thirteen. He had insisted that there must be thirteen members. In order to make up the number he had had to bring in three fellows who, to say the least of it, were not in society. Of these three Rudini was one. According to Pendarvon, he was a Swiss anarchist. Since he killed on principle, he was not likely to hesitate to kill for fun. His was not a pleasant personality. He addressed every one as "Citizen "—as he did me now.

"Well, citizen, the good work begins." I asked him what he meant. "Have you not seen about the bombs at Saragosa—that is what I call good reading."

I shuddered. I felt more than half disposed to knock the creature down. Some demons had thrown bombs among a crowded audience at a theatre. No end of people had been killed and injured. The brute called the account of the affair good reading.

I suppose he read my feelings in my face. He stretched out his hands in front of him—with a snarl which was perhaps meant for a grin.

"Do you not agree with me, citizen, that it is good reading? If it comes to killing, why kill units instead of tens? It is only a little matter of arithmetical progression."

The next comer was a madman out and out. He was a religionist of a sect of which, I suspect, he was the first member and the last. He believed, it seemed, that death meant annihilation. Annihilation, to use a paradox, was all he lived for. But it had been revealed to him—I never heard by whom, or how—that he himself never could attain annihilation until he had killed some one, as it were, to clear the way. So he had joined the club, in order that his destiny might the sooner be fulfilled. His name was Shepherd— Henry Shepherd. He was a lanky, loosely-built man, with long iron grey hair, and sailors' eyes—eyes, that is, which were calm and deep. As he entered, he seated himself at table without uttering a word. He was the second of Pendarvon's gathered and garnered three.

The fellows now came hard upon each others' heels. Unless I was mistaken, they had for the most part, been quenching their thirst. Their eyes shone; their speech was inclined to be erratic; about some of them there was a joviality which they had found in their glasses. Teddy Hibbard, for one, was distinctly drunk. He came with Eugene Silvester, who was not much better. The pair staggered up to me.

Teddy tried to steady himself by a somewhat close attachment to Silvester's arm.

"I say, Reggie, old fellow, Eugene and I have been making up our minds whom we'll slaughter. Whom do you think we've decided on?"

"My dear Teddy, I haven't the faintest notion. Don't you think you'd better take a chair?"

"Thank you, old boy, I think I will." He took one just in time. "We've decided on slaughtering the first chap we meet of the name of Jones—there are such a lot of them about, you know."

Archie Beaupré came across to me. He was among the last to arrive. He also had been drinking. But liquor did not affect him as it did Teddy Hibbard. He never lost his equilibrium. There never came a stammer into his speech. Nor, in Iago's sense, did it steal away his brains. When drink entered into Archie, the devil went with it. When he had drunk enough to stupefy an ordinary man, he was very near to genius. In that condition I have known him write lines which no poet need be ashamed to own; and I have known him do things which must have set all the imps of Satan chuckling.

As he advanced to me, a casual acquaintance might not have supposed that he had been exceeding in the slightest degree. But I knew better. I knew it by something that was in his face, and in his eyes; by the ring that was in his voice, when he spoke; by the very way in which he clasped me by the hand.

"Here's luck!" he said—"I'm with you all the way."

CHAPTER XVI

DRAWING THE LOT

When we had taken our places, Pendarvon commenced proceedings. He looked round at us and laughed, as if the whole proceedings had been some mighty joke.

"Gentlemen, the usual preliminaries, if you please."

He had the crimson-covered book open in front of him. He read aloud the oath by which we all had bound ourselves. As he did so, men sobered down a little. The oath which he had evolved from his mischief-making brain was calculated to make one sober. It was the rule that, at each meeting, the oath was to be re-sworn. Having recited it, with his right hand resting on the open page, Pendarvon affixed to it his signature. The book went round. Each man recited the oath, his hand resting on the page, and signed.

By the time Pendarvon had the book again, a change came over the spirit of the scene. The suggestion of frivolity which had been in the air had vanished. Hibbard and Silvester, in spite of the assistance which they had received from outside sources, did not look happy. Pendarvon read out the signatures. When he came to one he stopped.

"Teddy, have you signed?"

Hibbard was indignant—or feigned to be.

"Signed? Of course I've signed! Can't you read it?"

Pendarvon tugged at his beard and laughed.

"Be shot if I can! I can see a smudge, and that's all I can see. In a matter of this importance a signature should be writ as plain as copper-plate, so that all who run may read. Teddy, would you mind signing again, this time a little clearer? and Silvester might follow suit. You would not care to take us at an advantage, and be the only two among us to keep your names dark."

Pendarvon went to Teddy with the book in his hand. Placing it on the table in front of him, he leaned over his shoulder while he wrote.

"That's better, Teddy; that's plain as print. 'Edward Hibbard,' that's something like a name. Now, Silvester, if you won't mind."

Silvester leaned back in his chair, and frowned.

"I don't understand. That's my usual signature. What else do you want?"

"We want it a little plainer; nothing more."

Silvester grumbled, but he did what he was asked to do. He signed again, and plainer. That was like Pendarvon. If he had made up his mind that a man should do a thing, the odds were that the man would do it, although against his own will.

Pendarvon returned to his seat in triumph. As he talked to us he kept on laughing. The ugliest thing about him was his voice; it was harsh and strident—sometimes it seemed to strike one like a whip.

"Gentlemen, we have all of us been looking forward with pleasurable anticipations to this, our second, meeting. I need not tell you why. A month to-night our Honour was committed to the hands of one of us. We are here to ask for its return."

With a laughing gesture, he turned to me.

"Reggie, our Honour is in your hands."

As he sat down, I rose, and as I rose a sound which was almost like a sigh went round the room. I fancy that some of the fellows were preparing themselves for what might be to come, by taking in a good supply of breath. That all eyes were fixed on me I was well aware—fixed on me, I mean, with a curious, unusual kind of stare. They looked at me as if they would have almost rather not, and yet could not help but look. I took out my pocket-book; I laid it on the table. Every little movement which I made was followed by their eyes. I doubt if ever a man had a more attentive audience.

"Gentlemen of the Murder Club, I greet you."

I bowed to each individual. As I did so I noticed how pale they seemed to look.

"I occupy, on this occasion, a unique position. I take it that no man ever stood in such a pair of shoes as mine before. There have been murder clubs, which have been called by other names. They have concerned themselves with revolutions—with religious, social, political reforms. A murder club, the object of which has been amusement, pure and simple, I doubt if there ever before has been. To our founders I owe a special, a peculiar gratitude. Beaupré, I bow to you—the original suggestion of our Club was yours."

I bowed to Archie. In return he waved his hand to me.

"And a devilish good suggestion, too!"

"Beaupré, the words you use could not be bettered. They exactly describe the theme. Mr. Chairman, I bow to you—it was you who clothed with flesh the dry bones of the suggestion, breathed on them, and gave them life."

I bowed to Pendarvon. Laughing, he bowed again to me. He knew I hated him, and I knew he hated me.

"I owe these special thanks to our founders, gentlemen, because, during the month which is past, they have provided me with such great, such unwonted sport. So soon as I knew that the Honour of the Club was indeed entrusted to my keeping, I became like the old-fashioned sportsman, who had to do his own beating and flush for himself his birds. In my case there was this marked peculiarity, that I did not even know where to find the cover in which a bird might happen to be hiding."

Pausing, I looked each member in the face in turn. Odd spectacles they most of them presented. The majority of them shifted their eyes as they saw mine coming, as if they were unwilling, or unable, to meet my glances.

"Gentlemen, I found the cover and the bird. I have had the gratification of being able to fulfil the promise which I made to you. I return the Honour of the Club, dyed a more vivid crimson stain."

As I spoke, two or three fellows gasped. I don't know who they were, but the queer sound which they emitted caused me to smile. Taking out the Honour of the Club from my pocket-book, I held it up in front of me. There was silence. Then Pendarvon spoke—

"Are we to take you literally?"

"In the sense that the Honour of the Club has, literally, been dyed a more vivid crimson—that, in other words, it has been dipped in the sacrificial blood? No. My meaning, there, was metaphorical. There was no blood to dip it in."

I handed the Honour of the Club across the table to Pendarvon. As he took it, he looked at me askance.

"That is not all you are going to tell us? The rules require you to furnish full particulars."

"Those particulars, Mr. Chairman, I am now about to furnish. The bird I flushed, marked, and bagged was a hen."

"A hen?"

"A woman, Mr. Chairman. Name, Louise O'Donnel. Age, turned twenty. Date, last Sunday. Scene, Three Bridges. Cause of death, strangulation."

Pendarvon leaned towards me over the table.

"Are you responsible, then, for what the papers have christened the Three Bridges Tragedy?"

"I am."

"Did you throw the woman from the train?"

"I did not. I threw the woman from the field, over the hedge, on to the railway embankment. I should explain to you, gentlemen, that it seems not unlikely that I may become the subject of a curious coincidence. I killed the bird under the railway bridge. As I was doing so a train passed overhead. This must have been the train of which you have read in the public prints. I cannot pretend to predict the course of events, but I can assure you that whoever smashed that window and had that little rough and tumble in the railway carriage had nothing to do with the Three Bridges Tragedy. For that I am responsible, and I alone."

Silence followed my words. I glanced round. Various expressions were on the fellows' faces, and among them was one which suggested doubt. I noted, with amusement, that what I had anticipated had taken place. They doubted if I had done what I had declared I had.

Pendarvon gave this feeling voice.

"The case is a little delicate, dear Reggie. A man say that he has done a thing, and then when B, on the strength of what A says, goes and does likewise, he may find that A has been having a joke with him—don't you see my point?"

"You want proofs."

"You say that this Three Bridges business is yours. Suppose that some one else is arrested for it, and—we will go so far—is hung, what shall you do?"

"Do? Why, let him hang."

"I see. Of course. You would."

"In a matter of this sort proofs are rather difficult to give, unless you were all to come with me to see the fun. I will tell you my story."

Then I told them exactly what had happened on the Sunday evening, as it is written. At the close I took two letters from my pocket-book.

"Mr. Chairman, I have here two letters. The first is the one which I wrote asking the lady to meet me at East Grinstead—that I took from her pocket after she was dead. The second is the one in which she promised that she would. I have pleasure in submitting them to the attention of the club."

I passed the letter to Pendarvon. From one of my tail pockets I produced a small parcel.

"You will have observed, gentlemen, that it is stated that nothing was found in the woman's pockets. That was owing to the fact that I had previously taken the precaution to empty it. I hold the contents of her pocket in my hand: a letter—that the chairman has—a purse, some keys, a pocket-handkerchief. This scrap of silk ribbon suspended this locket to her neck; in the locket you will find my portrait. That also I took from her after she was dead. I offer it, with the other items, for the inspection of the club."

Pendarvon read the letters carefully through; then, without remark, he passed them to the man who sat beside him. After examining my relics, he passed them too. The batch went round. One or two of the men carefully examined each separate item; most just glanced at them in passing; some seemed to shrink from touching them, as if afraid of coming into close contact.

When they had gone round, Pendarvon rose.

"I think, gentlemen, that our friend's statement has given general satisfaction."

Rudini tapped with his finger on the table.

"It was a woman; it is not a man's work to kill a woman."

Pendarvon laughed.

"There, Rudini, you must excuse me if I differ. I think that it is essentially a man's work. The women are always killing us. It is just as well that we should take our turn at killing them. Indeed, were it not too late I should almost be disposed to suggest that it should always be a woman who was killed."

Budini brought his fist down with a bang.

"Then I shall go."

"It will be soon enough, Budini, for you to talk of going when the suggestion's made. I repeat, gentlemen, that I think that Mr. Townsend has satisfied us that he really has done something for the Honour of the Club. As he himself says, in cases of this sort, the ocular proof it is almost impossible to give. But he has given us proofs, as it seems to me, of a sufficiently convincing kind. Are you content? Those of you who are will please stand up."

All rose—Rudini after a moment's hesitation.

"I see, gentlemen, that we are all content. We have excellent cause. Be so good as to charge your glasses. We thank you, Reggie; we appreciate the good deed which you have done, and we drink to your next fortunate adventure."

They drained their glasses—not, I suspect, before some of them were in need of what was in them. They would have sampled the brandy before had it not been a rule of the club that nothing was to be drunk except in response to the chairman's toasts.

Pendarvon continued—

"There only remains one thing for our friend to do."

He wrote something in the book in front of him. Then he passed the book to me.

"We have to ask you, Reggie, to put your name to that."

I saw that he had put the date of the preceding Sunday, and then—

"Louise O'Donnel—For the Honour of the Club."

"If I put my name to that it may be tantamount to a confession of murder."

"Precisely—it is in accordance with our rules—for our general protection—we shall have to sign a similar memorandum in our turns."

"May I ask where this book is kept? One does not like to think that such an interesting volume is left lying about."

Pendarvon pointed to a safe which was fitted into the wall.

"At present it is kept in there. It is as good a safe of its sort as you are likely to find. I have the only key But I agree with you that the proper custody of the book is a matter of importance. I would suggest that a safe be obtained with thirteen different locks and thirteen different keys, which it will be impossible to open except without common consent."

"Your suggestion, Mr. Chairman, is a good one."

"Then, by the time we meet again such a safe shall be obtained. In the meantime—sign."

I signed. Outwardly, I believe, that I was calm enough. In my heart I wished that, before I had ever heard of him or it, Pendarvon and his club had been at Timbuctoo, and stayed there.

As he blotted my signature, Pendarvon laughed. I felt, as I heard, that I had been a fool not to have exchanged him for Louise. To my ear, everything about the man rang false—and always had.

"Townsend, what an excellent hand you write! If only every one wrote as clearly! I wish I could. As you are aware, it now becomes my pleasant duty to inform you that the Honour of the Club which you have returned to us to-night will be framed in gold, and will be awarded to you as a diploma of merit."

"You may keep it."

"Reggie!—the idea! As though I would rob you of what you have so fairly earned!" He closed the crimson-coloured volume. "Our next business, gentlemen, is to ascertain the fortunate individual to whose keeping the Honour of the Club is to be now entrusted. Since you, Townsend, have won our diploma of merit, it becomes my duty, as a mere postulant, to resign to you the chair. You will conduct the drawing, in which, of course, you yourself will not take part. Gentlemen, Mr. Townsend will be our chairman, until some equally fortunate colleague has gained his diploma."

He rose from their seat, beckoning me towards it with his hand. As I accepted his invitation, there was some tapping of hands upon the table, and Archie called out, "Hear, hear!" I took up the little heap of cards which was on the table in front of my new seat, counting them so that they all could see.

"As you perceive, here are eleven." Kendrick sat on my left. I handed the bag to him.

"Colonel, will you be first to draw?"

Kendrick was the oldest man among us. His hair and moustache were white as snow. He was rich, respected, with troops of friends. Why he had joined us was more than I could say. I guessed that it was to gratify some private grudge. However that might be, I saw that his hand trembled as he thrust it into the bag. He took some time in choosing. When at last he drew his card, glancing quickly at both sides of it, he threw it down upon the table.

"Blank!" he said. "Not yet."

Rudini sat next to him. He made a little speech before he put his hand into the bag.

"If I am what Mr. Pendarvon has called the fortunate individual, it will be no woman I shall kill. I would sooner kill a thousand men. It is for that I joined the club."

But he was not the "fortunate individual." He drew a blank. He was shortsighted. He had to peer at it closely before he saw it was a blank.

"As the Colonel says—not yet. My time will come."

Poindexter sat by Rudini—the Honourable Jem. I always thought it was rather a shame to drag him in. He was only a boy, just out of his teens. He said nothing when he got the bag; he made up in eloquence of looks for paucity of words. There was a white, drawn look about his face which made him look as old as any one of us. He fumbled with the mouth of the bag, as though it was not large enough for him to get his hand in. When he did get one hand in, he dropped the bag from the other. Pendarvon laughed.

"Upon my word, you're shivering, Jem; is it with joy?"

The Honourable picked up the bag.

"What's it to do with you what I am shivering at?"

He stared at the card he drew. Then he gasped, "Thank God, it's blank!"

Pendarvon laughed again. I believe that the laughter which they say is heard in hell must sound like his.

"Why, Jem, one would almost think that you were glad."

The Honourable said nothing. He tried to stare at Pendarvon. But it was a failure. He put his head down on the table. And he cried. He was only a lad.

Old Shepherd came after the boy. When he saw that it was his turn he did a very curious thing. He got off his chair and he went on to his knees, and he said—

"I am going to pray."

He closed his eyes, and he clasped his hands in front of him. I suppose he prayed. I know we stared. Pendarvon was shaking with laughter—it was with soundless laughter for once in a way. I suppose that the man prayed for at least five minutes. I wonder that we were still so long. I was on the point of politely requesting him to cut it short when he rose from his knees. He put his hand into the bag. He drew a blank.

"My prayer," he said, "has not been answered. I fear, sometimes, that it will remain unanswered to the end."

What he meant it is not for me to say. It was plain that, as I have observed already, he was stark mad. In the next chair was Teddy Hibbard. He turned to Shepherd—

"I say, old chap, what was it you wanted?"

"The Honour of the Club. I am waiting and watching and hoping for the end."

"Are you? Then if I get it I'll give it you; a beginning's more my line."

He also drew a blank. When he perceived what it was he held it out towards Pendarvon and winked, "I'm not sorry." With a dexterous movement he threw it across the table, so that if Pendarvon had not put up his hand and stopped it it would have struck him in the face. "Put that in your pipe and smoke it, see."

When Silvester took the bag he began to shake it.

"We're getting warm." He turned to Shepherd. "I echo what Teddy's said. If I draw the Honour of the Club I'll pass it on to you."

Shepherd shook his head.

"That will not do. I must draw the lot myself."

Silvester held out the bag to him. "Would you like to have another try?"

"I must draw it, in due order, in my proper turn."

"It strikes me that you're not quite so anxious as you make out. I don't mind owning that my anxiety is all the other way. I should like to have a little longer run before I earn my diploma."

He drew a blank. Next to him sat Archie. Silvester passed him the bag, with a laugh—a queer laugh, which had in it a hysteric note.

"Try your luck, Beaupré—three shies a penny!"

Archie looked him in the face.

"There is no necessity for me to try my luck, Silvester. I know it before I try. I knew it before I came into this room. You fellows drawing was but a mere matter of form. I am to draw the Honour of the Club. It is written in the skies."

His voice rang through the room. I noticed that Pendarvon tugged at his beard, and stared at him, as if he could not make him out. But I, knowing the man as I did, knew his mood. Slipping his hand quickly into the bag, in an instant he drew it out. Without glancing at the card which he had drawn he held it up to us between his fingers. "See! The Honour of the Club!"

It was.

There was silence. Approaching the card to his face, Archie touched it with his lips.

"Welcome, thou dreadful thing!" He half rose to his feet. "Gentlemen, did I not tell you? As you perceive, the fortune of war is mine!"

I stood up as he sat down.

"Bumpers, gentlemen." They filled and rose. "Beaupré, feeling, as we must, that the Honour of the Club could not possibly be in better or in more deserving hands, we tender you our best congratulations on your good fortune as you know full well."

Then they all said in a sort of chorus as they drank, "We do."

"You have the prospect, nay, the certainty, of good sport before you, Beaupré—sport of a rare and of a most excellent kind. I speak from my own experience. That this day month you may have as pleasant a story to tell as mine—Beaupré, I can wish you no better wish than that."

Then Archie spoke. He held the Honour of the Club out in front of him while he was speaking.

"Mr. Chairman and gentlemen, I have not words with which to thank you. I would I had. They would indeed be warm. Mr. Chairman, to you I would particularly say that your good wishes strike me deep. They cut into my heart. For my fondest hope as I listen and as I look at you, with this piece of pasteboard held in my safe keeping, thinking of all that you have done on behalf of its twin brother, is that I may play half as well the man." He bowed round the table. "I thank you."

And he sat down.

CHAPTER XVII

A LITTLE GAME

Six or seven of us were in the street outside the club when the meeting was over. Where the rest had vanished to I do not know. There was not a cab to be seen. I doubt if a cab ever does ply for hire in that locality. Besides, what would be one cab among so many? The night was fine. Archie put his arm through mine.

"Come along, lets pad the hoof, my dears."

Off we went, the lot of us abreast. We had not gone a dozen yards before we came upon a policeman coming along as if the pavement had been in his family for years.

"Now, officer," cried Silvester, "make way!"

The officer slowed. He thrust his thumbs into his belt. He surveyed us with a genial grin which might almost have suggested that we were friends of his.

"What are you gentlemen doing here? This isn't the sort of place for the likes of you. If some of the chaps caught sight of those shirt-fronts of yours they might rumple 'em a bit."

Silvester pulled up the collar of his coat.

"My dear Mr. Policeman, how you frighten us! Could you tell us where we are or which is the way to anywhere?"

The officer jerked his thumb over his shoulder.

"If you go straight on, through Strutton Ground, it'll take you out into Victoria Street, but you'll find it a roughish way."

We did find it a roughish way. We also found that there were some roughish people thereabouts, especially the proprietors of the costers' barrows. It must have been at least eleven, but they were carrying on a market in the gutter as briskly as if it had been the middle of the day. I said to Archie, as soon as I saw what sort of place it was, that we had better sneak through in single file, and thank our stars when we found ourselves out of it. But the others didn't seem to see it. They were bent on improving the shining hour. And they improved it. When I did begin to understand that I was in Victoria Street, at last, some gentleman had borrowed my hat, and I had to tie a handkerchief under my chin to keep the rest of my hair on my head.

"A lively five minutes," observed Teddy, picking what were either pieces of a potato or of an onion from his eye.

I moved a little from him. Owing to his having been upset among the dried fish on a coster's barrow he smelt a bit strong. Silvester held up something in the air.

"I've got a cabbage, and, by jove, I believe some one's got my watch."

There was a roar of voices issuing from the street through which we had come.

"Here they are again!" I cried. "I've had enough of it. I'm off. Hi! cabby!"

Two hansoms were prowling by. I jumped into one. Two or three of the fellows followed me. We drove away from our friends of Strutton Ground with a parting yell, the rest of the fellows in the second hansom bringing up the rear.

They would not let us in at the Criterion. The individual at the door seemed to think that there was something in our appearance which was not exactly what it ought to be. Silvester presented him with the cabbage for which, quite unintentionally, he had exchanged his watch. But so far from allowing that handsome contribution to the family larder—it had cost Eugene perhaps fifty pounds—to melt his heart, the stiff-necked Cerberus actually threatened us with the police. So we adjourned to the tavern at the corner till they turned us out. Then we went for a quiet stroll along Piccadilly, seven abreast, which soon landed us in the thick of a row. It was a fight of giants while it lasted. But the police were one too many. They bore the Honourable off in triumph. We followed him in a body to Vine Street Station, where every one was most polite. But they wouldn't hear of bail. A policeman had a most dreadful eye, and he made out that it was Jem. So we had to leave him in the hands of cruel strangers to spend the night. Poor Jem!

When we got outside, being all of us so clear-headed and in such a thoroughly judicial frame of mind, Archie proposed that we should adjourn to his place and have a hand at cards. We belonged to perhaps two dozen clubs between us, but they were none of them sufficiently cerulean—though blue enough— to have admitted us without our first having gone through the ceremony of going home and washing ourselves and changing our clothes. So, as that sort of thing would have been an awful bore, we snapped at Archie's kind invite. And some uncivil policeman coming up and suggesting that it would be well for our own health and for the health of the neighbourhood if we stood not on the order of our going, we tumbled into a couple of cabs and went.

Archie's rooms were in Wilton Street. As the cabs drew up at his door, Pendarvon came strolling up. He pulled up at the sight of us. He stared. He appeared surprised. As every one who had been favoured with a near view of us during the last hour or so had appeared surprised, however much we might feel wounded, we could scarcely openly resent such an exhibition on the part even of a friend.

"What on earth have you fellows been doing?" he inquired. "You don't seem to me to have a whole suit of clothes between you."

Archie explained—

"My dear Pendarvon, if you had been doing what we have been doing, you would look as we are looking. Come inside!"

So Pendarvon entered with the rest of us.

When we were in we found that with Pendarvon we were six. We had been seven without him. The Honourable we had dropped at Vine Street, and Lister, for anything any one seemed to know to the contrary, was a clear case of lost, stolen, or strayed. Of the six, Gravesend was obviously no good for cards. He fell asleep as soon as he had found a chair to do it on. It did not seem to rouse him to any appreciable extent even when he tumbled off. The best we could do for him was to put him comfortably to bed on the hearthrug in Archie's bedroom. There was no fear of his doing himself a mischief if he rolled about.

Of the five who were left, Teddy was not exactly fit. But as the idea of leaving him out, filled him with nothing else but wrath, we cut him in. Silvester had quenched his thirst, but I do not think I ever saw him too drunk to play. He presented a truly remarkable spectacle as regards attire. The gentleman who had borrowed his watch, or some of his friends, had taken away the large portion of his shirt to wrap it up in. His coat was slit right down his back. Waistcoat he had none. And he had tied his braces round his waist in order to retain possession of what was left him of his trousers. However, with the assistance of one of Archie's dressing-gowns, he managed. The more Archie drinks, the more he's in the vein. As for me, I was ready to play for my boots. And Pendarvon was as sober as a judge.

Beaupré made it poker—poker is his pet game. We began with a ten shilling ante, and a ten pound limit. It made a pretty game, while it lasted. In the first jack-pot, when it came to threes, Silvester declared that all his cash was gone. It was he began the IOU's. Teddy's luck was wonderful. Before very long very nearly all our ready-money had gone his way. I had ten tenners and gold when I began. They soon paid a visit to Teddy. Pendarvon seemed to have a pocket full of money. He brought out a whole sheaf of bank-notes to give our appetites a twist.

Teddy had just taken another plump jack-pot when Beaupré ran dry. He replenished his pockets at his desk. When he came back, Pendarvon was about to deal.

"Don't you think," he said, "that this is a little slow? Suppose we double the limit. Teddy, I suppose you don't object."

Teddy said he didn't. More than half drunk, and fancying himself in the vein, he was not likely to object. I took it that Archie had already lost a hundred and fifty. I saw that he had only brought about another century to table. I guessed—for reasons—that he was squeezed for funds. I suspected that he might not care to plunge deeper than we were already. And so, to save him, I struck in.

"So far as I am concerned, I am content to go on as we are. It's good enough for me."

To my surprise, and to my amusement, Archie was quite vehement upon the other side.

"Rubbish! This sort of thing's only fit for babes, not men! Reggie, where's your courage—make it twenty."

So we made the limit twenty pounds.

Luck began to slip away from Teddy—small wonder either! He did some outrageous bluffing, against Pendarvon, too, who is one of the hardest men to bluff there is about. Teddy waxed wild. He and Pendarvon were the only two left in. They raised each other till there was, perhaps five hundred in the pool. Then Pendarvon saw him. Teddy threw down his cards with a curse.

"Ace high."

"Fours."

Pendarvon showed four sevens. Teddy had paid for his whistle.

After that, the luck, and, for the matter of that, the play too, went dead against him. He kept on drinking—he was not in the least fit for poker, but he would keep on playing. Archie, too, kept on the shady side. Silvester about held his own. I had an occasional hand worth backing. Pendarvon and I bid fair to share the spoils.

One round we all came in. I was first bettor. Silvester was blind. I opened with the limit. Each man went the limit better in his turn. When there was four hundred in the pool Silvester went out. Another round or two and Teddy went. There was over five hundred in the pool. Pendarvon had raised the limit over Archie. It was sixty pounds for me to come in. I had a straight, knave high. I saw the sixty. Archie saw it, and went twenty better. Pendarvon raised him twenty. I saw the forty. Archie scribbled another IOU— he had been reduced for some time to paper. He had raised again. Pendarvon followed suit. I thought that it was enough for me, and went. The two kept at it. There must have been over a thousand in before Pendarvon saw. Archie laid down his hand, with a smile, as though he felt sure that, this time, the luck was his.

"A full—queens high."

Pendarvon laughed.

"Not good enough! I take this pool—I pip you."

He also had a full—with three kings on top. Silvester spoke.

"Will somebody kindly stick a penknife into Teddy."

I looked up—poor Teddy was asleep. When, however, we charged him with it, he endeavoured to wake up and call us names. He insisted on continuing to play. It proved to be as much as he could do to pick up his cards—more than he could do to see them when picked up. The very next round, when asked if he proposed to cover the ante, he threw down his cards face upwards on the table, observing that it was no good coming in on a hand like that. He had held three queens! I struck. I declined to go shares in a robbery.

"Teddy," I remarked, "if you'll take my advice you'll go home to bed. Just now poker's not your line."

"I'm not feeling very well," he said. "I hate this game; it makes me ill. Let's play something else."

"We will. We'll sing 'Rock-a-by, baby,' and play at going to sleep. Come along, Teddy, let me offer you the temporary loan of my arm."

Archie interposed.

"Hang it, Reggie, you're not going! Put the beggar to sleep alongside Gravesend on the rug."

"I'm not going to sleep on the rug," said Teddy, "I hate the rug."

We compromised, putting him to bed on the couch in Archie's bedroom. It seemed unlikely that he would fall off, since he was asleep before we had the whole of him laid down. While we were together in the bedroom, I said a private word to Archie.

"If you'll hearken to the wisdom of the wise, old man, you'll cut it. You're not in the vein."

He chose to misunderstand my meaning.

"Do you mean I'm drunk?"

"I think I am—at least too drunk for poker; and too sleepy, also. If you'll allow me, I'll get home."

Archie looked at me in the way I knew, all his Scotch temper in his eyes.

"Are you afraid, or broke? Or what the devil's up?"

Pendarvon called from the next room.

"Are you fellows having a little game by yourselves?"

I jerked my thumb towards Pendarvon as Archie and I went in together.

"That's just what is up—the devil."

We four went at it again. I reckoned that at that time Archie had lost about two thousand pounds—nearly the whole of it to Pendarvon in IOU's. His heavier losses all came afterwards. Silvester also lost. He made a very nasty loser. He allowed things to escape his tongue which, under other circumstances, might have brought the sitting to a prompt and a turbulent close. Pendarvon, to whose address Silvester's little observations were principally directed, seemed to take it for granted that the fact of his being three-parts drunk covered a multitude of sins. For my part, on the whole I won. By degrees, as Silvester's sulkiness increased, the game resolved itself into a sort of triangular duel. Archie went for Pendarvon, and Pendarvon went for me. As he found, for the most part, that his assaults were unavailing, and that my mood was beatific, Pendarvon began to follow Silvester's lead and lose his temper. Not, however, on Silvester's lines. The more enraged he grew, the more he laughed. I knew the gentleman so well.

Archie began to play like a lunatic. Once Silvester declined to come in. I had four knaves; it was the second four hand I had had within a very few minutes. Of course, I started to back it for all I was worth. What Archie and Pendarvon had was more than I could guess; I did not much care. I felt that, whatever they had, I was about their match. I had taken one card, wishing them to suppose that I had drawn to two pairs. Archie had had two. I took it that he had started with a triplet. Pendarvon had had three; apparently he had opened with a pair. It seemed from the betting that they had both improved their hands, for neither seemed disposed to tire. The pool crept up to a thousand. Then Archie found fault with the rate of progression.

"Confound this limit! It's child's play; we shall be at it all night. Will either of you see me for £500?"

Pendarvon hesitated, or appeared to.

"Having fixed a limit, isn't it rather against the rules to travel outside? But, so far as I am personally concerned, I don't mind seeing your five hundred, and raising you another five. What do you say, Townsend?"

"I object. At this point of the game to change the points in such a fashion would simply be to plunder you. I hold the winning hand."

Archie became excited, and not quite civil.

"That's rot. I say ditto to Pendarvon, Reggie. Will you pay a thousand to see our hands?"

"I will do this. I will agree to each man tabling a thousand, and showing his hand."

"Done!" Archie scribbled an IOU. "Now, Pen, down with your thousand."

Pendarvon counted out a heap of Archie's IOU's, laughing as he did so.

"I hope that's good enough."

I drew a cheque on a sheet of paper.

"Now, Archie, if you please, let us see your hand."

He faced his cards.

"A straight flush!" he cried.

For a moment he took my breath away. That he could have drawn two cards for a straight flush had not entered into my philosophy. My next feeling was that the thing looked ugly. For a man with a straight flush in his hand to propose to increase the stakes was—well, not the thing. While words were coming near my lips, Pendarvon leaned towards him.

"Where is your straight flush? Show it us?" Then, with a laugh, "That's not a straight flush."

Archie stared at his cards.

"What do you mean?" Then, with a shout, "I'm damned if it is!"

As he recognised the fact, he seemed to me to turn quite green, and he swore. In his haste, giving only a single glance at his cards, he had let himself in. It was all but a straight flush—a case of the miss which is as good as a mile. His hand was four, five, seven, eight, and nine of hearts. It was a flush, but not a straight flush—he had overlooked the absence of the six. The curious part of the thing was that he should have drawn to such a hand.

Pendarvon faced his cards.

"I fancy, Archie, that I am better than you."

He was. He had a full. Three aces and a pair of kings. No wonder he had been willing to back his luck. I don't know what his feelings were when he found that I could show still more.

"Fours. I think that takes it."

It did.

As I scooped the plunder, Silvester rose.

"Show four whenever you like—eh, Townsend?"

His tone was disagreeable, and meant to be.

"I wish I could."

"I should say that your wish was gratified. It occurs to me that this is distinctly a game at which the soberest wins."

We looked at him. He looked back at us. He was evidently in a state of mind in which he was disposed to pick a quarrel with us, either separately or altogether. The thing to do was not to gratify his whim. He treated Archie to a peculiarly impertinent stare. "That was an odd mistake of yours. I'm drunk, but I'm not drunk enough for that, and I never could be." He gave Pendarvon a turn—"You didn't choose your cards badly. But it's only a question of courage. Take my tip, next time you make it fours." He lurched away from the table. "I'm off. You're welcome to what you've got—cut it up between you."

He staggered from the room. Archie rose, intending, as host, to see him off the premises. Pendarvon caught him by the arm.

"Let the beggar see himself out. If we have luck he may break his neck as he goes downstairs. He's made a bid for it." It seemed that he had. We could hear him stumble down two or three steps at a time. We listened. There was the sound of another stumble. Pendarvon laughed. "Bid number two."

Directly afterwards we heard him fidgeting with the handle of the front door. Archie grew restless.

"He'll raise the dead if he goes on like that much longer. Let me go down, and let him out."

We heard the door open, and immediately afterwards shut with a bang.

"He's let himself out. I fancy a little more rapidly than he intended. I'll bet an even pony that he's gone face foremost into the street. Let's hope it." Pendarvon picked up a pack of cards. "It's my deal. What are we going to do?"

Getting up, Archie helped himself to another soda and whiskey.

"Who'll have some?" We both of us did. "Let's play unlimited. I'm sick of this." Pendarvon raised his glass.

"Here's to you, Archie; you're a gambler."

"I thank the stars I am. Have you any objection, Reggie?"

I shrugged my shoulders, perceiving that remonstrance would be thrown away.

"I'm at your service."

"Then we'll play unlimited."

And we did.

It was a warmish little game. There is something about unlimited poker which appeals to one. The spirit of the gamble gets into one's veins like the breath of the battle into the nostrils of the soldier. One feels that it is a game for men, and that the manhood which is in one has a chance to score. Archie evidently meant going for the gloves. He never bet less than a hundred, and a thousand—in pencil on a scrap of paper—was as nothing to him. If we wanted to be in that game we too had to treat thousands as if they had been sovereigns. At the beginning the luck went round to him—possibly because it took some little time to make his methods ours. He bluffed outrageously. With a pair one was not disposed, at the commencement, to pay a thousand to see his cards. The result was that he scooped pool after pool. When he had made it plain that, if we wanted him to show, we should have to pay, we began to pay.

And luck began!

The ante was fixed at a tenner. I was ante. The other two had come in. Making good, I drew three to a pair of sevens, without improving my hand. Pendarvon opened with a hundred, Archie promptly making it five. I had not had a sight—I had had no cards—for the last five hands. This time, the devil entering into me, I made up my mind that I would find out what sort of game Archie was playing, and have a view if it broke me. I saw his five hundred. Pendarvon saw it too. Then Archie turned up a pair of knaves. I yielded without showing, and to my surprise, Pendarvon did as I had done. A pair of knaves seemed hardly worth fifteen hundred pounds. It looked like easy earning.

The same thing went on time after time. Archie could not be induced to see a man while he could keep on raising. The very next hand, when we had both come in, Archie started with a five hundred bet. So Pendarvon and I let him have the entries. And we had a twenty pound pot.

We had gone right round and come back again to pairs, when Pendarvon announced that he could open. He made it a hundred to enter. Archie and I went in—though, so far as I was concerned, I had an empty hand. Pendarvon took two, Archie stood pat, and I drew five, finding myself in possession of a pair of aces. Pendarvon started with five hundred pounds; we seemed to be getting incapable of thinking of anything under. Archie raised him nine thousand five hundred pounds, tabling his IOU for a round ten thousand. I retired; a pair of aces was not quite good enough for that. If I was to be broken, I might just as well be broken for something better. Pendarvon looked at Archie as if he would have liked to have seen right into him.

"Have you the Bank of England at your back?"

"What are you going to raise me?" inquired Archie.

"Nothing. I go. The courage is yours. I opened with a pair of jacks."

Pendarvon showed them. I doubt if he had anything more. I doubt if Archie had as much. But, still, ten thousand. The average man is not inclined to go as far as that upon a pair of jacks. I could see that Pendarvon felt that he had been bluffed. It put his back up. He meant to be even with Archie—and he was.

"Let me clearly understand what unlimited poker means. Does it mean that I'm at liberty to put half a sheet of notepaper on the table and say I raise a million?"

Archie fired up at the innuendo Pendarvon's words seemed to convey.

"What do you mean by half a sheet of notepaper? Do you suggest that my IOU is nothing but half a sheet of notepaper?"

"Not a bit of it. Why should I? My dear Archie, don't get warm. Only we are none of us millionaires. I know I'm not. Ten thousand pounds is a considerable sum to me. We, all of us, are playing on the nod. Before you go any further suppose we name a date by which all paper must be redeemed."

"I'm willing."

"Suppose we say that it must be redeemed within a week?"

"I'm willing again."

I also acquiesced. I saw the force of what he said, and I saw the pull which it would give him over Archie. Where Archie was likely to find such a sum as ten thousand pounds within a week was more than I knew, and, unless I greatly erred, more than he knew either. Pendarvon is a man of substance. His stannary dues alone are supposed to average thirty or forty thousand pounds a year, and if it came to a question of ready-money not improbably he could buy up Archie lock, stock, and barrel, and scarcely feel that he had made a purchase.

Archie must have been possessed by the very spirit of mischief. He entirely refused to be out-crowed on his own dunghill—even though he knew his rival to be the larger and the stronger bird. Almost immediately afterwards Pendarvon started the betting with a thousand pounds. Archie retorted by raising him fourteen thousand, laying on the table his IOU for fifteen thousand pounds. I went. I had two pairs, but the atmosphere promised to grow too hot for me. Pendarvon laughed.

"I'll see your raise."

He placed his own IOU on Archie's.

"Three kings."

Archie faced them. Pendarvon laughed again. He threw his cards away.

"Too good!"

He had supposed that Archie was bluffing—and had paid for his supposition.

The game fluctuated. Pendarvon had Archie once or twice upon the hip, paring down his winnings. At last we came to what proved to be the last, and hardest-fought-for pool of the sitting. It was a pot. We had gone right through the hands. In the second round Archie opened when it came to two pairs or better. He made it a hundred to go in. I went in, though I had only queens. I kept the pair and an ace, and took two—two more queens. Pendarvon and Archie both stood pat. I perceived that the scent of a big battle was coming into the air—when I saw my four queens, and made sure that they were four queens, it did me good to smell it coming.

Archie began, for him, very modestly—with a five hundred bet. I turned it into a thousand, which Pendarvon doubled. Then we went at it, hammer and tongs. As I raised Archie, and Pendarvon every time raised me, it made it impossible for Archie to even the bets, and force a display. At last it grew too hot even for him. I reckoned that I had thirty thousand in the pool. Pendarvon had made it another four thousand for Archie to come in. Although he was beginning to look as if he was not altogether enjoying himself, in he came. I raised him. Pendarvon raised me. The betting went on. I had IOU's for sixty thousand in the pool. The fates alone knew where the cash was to come from if I lost—unless it came from Sir Haselton Jardine, against which possibility the odds seemed pretty strong. Pendarvon raised me five thousand more. Archie realised at last that he could not see us unless we chose to let him—and that we did not mean to let him. He threw down his cards with a curse—it being a bad habit of his to use strong language when, if he only knew it, milder words would serve him at least equally well. One can damn so effectively with a softly-uttered blessing.

When Archie went I saw Pendarvon.

"Fours," he said.

I felt a shudder go all down my back.

"Four what?"

"Tens."

"Queens."

As I faced them, in its holy of holies my heart sang a loud Te Deum. Pendarvon stood up, still laughing.

"That's enough for me."

When I heard the peculiar something that was ringing in his laughter, knowing the man as I did, I knew that Mr. Pendarvon would watch for me and wait. His turn would come.

"I'm hanged!" cried Archie, "if I haven't thrown my money clean away!"

He certainly had—that is, if his IOU's represented money, which his best friend might be excused for doubting.

CHAPTER XVIII

DAMON AND PYTHIAS: A MODERN INSTANCE

"WEST KENSINGTON.

"DEAR MR. TOWNSEND,—Will you come and dine with me one evening next week? I am always free.

"I want to ask your advice on a small personal concern. You know the world so much better than I do.

"Truly yours,

"HELEN CARRUTH."

The next morning, when I woke from dreams of poker, this was the first letter which I opened. It was nicely written, in a small, round hand, as clear as copperplate—somehow it did not strike me as being the writing of a woman who did not know the world. Mrs. Carruth seemed friendly. With a background of intentions, as usual? What was the "small personal concern?" An excuse?—only that and nothing more? I wondered.

I had to go down to Cockington by the afternoon train—to Dora, and to Haselton Jardine. I should probably stay there till Tuesday or Wednesday—it depended. I might make it Thursday with Mrs. Carruth—if anything turned up at the last moment I could always send an excuse. Something about the woman attracted me. A tête-à-tête might prove amusing. There and then I scribbled an acceptance—appointing Thursday.

I was conscious of the possession of a head—the adventures of the night had left the flavour of brandy behind. We had made up accounts before we parted. There had been diversions! I had a nice little pocketful of money. Pendarvon owed me seventeen thousand odd, Archie owed him over four thousand, and me over thirty-five thousand. As I surveyed Archie's heap of IOU's I felt that I had better make early inquiries into the prices current of waste paper. Pendarvon's seventeen thousand I would get within the week, or mention it.

No need to trouble myself about Pendarvon. While I still was fingering his paper, Burton brought me an envelope on which I recognised his handwriting.

"Mr. Pendarvon's servant waits for an answer, sir?"

The envelope contained a cheque and note.

"ARLINGTON STREET.

"Friday.

"DEAR TOWNSEND,—Enclosed find a cheque for £17,450. Short reckonings make long friends. Please give IOU's to bearer.

"Yours,

"C. P."

I packed up his IOU in an envelope, with a word of thanks, and handed them to Burton. Pendarvon was the sort of man one liked to play with—when one won. He might not prove so pleasant an opponent when one lost, and owed one's losings, and was pressed for cash. Asking for no grace, he gave none. Archie would have to find that four thousand in a week.

Poor dear old Archie!

What was I to do? I had as much chance of getting thirty-five thousand pounds out of him as out of the first beggar I might meet in the street. Well, I could afford to be magnanimous. I was like unto him that expecteth nothing. I might let him off—if his beggarly, but proud, Scotch blood would suffer it. It might be worth my while to put him under an obligation.

He came in just as I had finished dressing—looking as if he had been spending the time since I had seen him last in trying to find that five and thirty thousand pounds. His eyes were bloodshot. His face was white and drawn. He was a vivid illustration of the night it must have been. Vouchsafing no greeting, sitting down without a word, leaning on the handle of his stick, he stared at nothing with his bloodshot eyes.

I opened the ball.

"Are you coming down with me to Torquay by the three o'clock?" Silence. "I suppose you haven't forgotten your engagement with Jardine?"

"I can't keep it. For a sufficient reason."

"What's that? Feel seedy? The run down will do you good. You'll feel as fit as a fiddler by the time you get to Cockington."

"That's not the reason."

"What is it then? I suppose you're not going to throw them over—they'll want your gun."

"The reason I'm not going is because I have not sufficient money with which to pay the fare."

I stared. I had not supposed the thing was so bad as that. Yet it was characteristic. In one of his moods he was just the man to play for his boots, and not miss them till he wanted to put them on.

"I suppose you're joking."

By way of reply he relinquished his stick, stood up, and solemnly turned out his pockets one by one. He held some coins out towards me in his hand.

"Six-and-ninepence. That represents my cash in hand. Of course, there is always the pawnshop."

"Stuff. You can always borrow."

"I am glad to hear it. From whom? Give me the gentleman's name. He is not known to me, I'll swear. I must be unknown to him, or he would never lend."

"Can't you do anything on a bit of stiff?"

"I repeat—give me the gentleman's name."

"If it comes to that, I'll lend you a hundred or so to go on with myself, as you very well know."

"I owe you five and thirty thousand pounds already."

"Look here, Archie, I don't want to make myself disagreeable, as you believe, but when you like you can be about as much of an idiot as they make them. Your proceedings last night would have been more appropriate at a symposium in the county asylum. As to what you say you owe me, we'll postpone the settling day, with your permission, to when your ship comes home."

"The arrangement was that all paper was to be taken up within a week."

"Rubbish. You and I know what those sort of arrangements are worth."

"Are you suggesting that I'm a thief?"

"I'm doing nothing of the sort. I'm asserting that you're a fool."

"Reggie!"

"Archie?"

He glared at me so that, for a moment, I thought that he was going to give further proof of the truth of my words upon the spot. But he changed his mind. He dropped on to a chair with a sort of gasp.

"What you say is correct enough. I have no right to cavil. I thank you for the word." He sat silent. Then he added, "But it's not only you I owe, I owe Pendarvon."

"If you take my advice, you'll pay Pendarvon."

"It's not advice I want; it's money. I owe the man, in round numbers, four thousand five hundred pounds. I don't know where to turn to raise four hundred."

"My dear Archie, you must excuse my saying, that's your affair. You would punt—although he gave you warning. The man lost heavily himself. This morning he's sent me round a cheque to settle."

"He has, has he? He is an honest man. My God! what it is to have money!"

"That's nonsense. If you were made of money you would not be justified in playing as you played last night."

"That's right. Give it me. I deserve it all. I wonder what my father will think when he finds out, once more, what sort of son I am."

"He'll think of the days of his own youth. When they are confronted with similar revelations, all our fathers do."

"I doubt it. I don't think my father was ever such as I am. Certainly, he never bound himself to commit murder within a month. I suppose that you have not forgotten that the Honour of the Club is in my keeping."

I had not. I had very clearly understood that it was that fact which had caused him to make the spectacle of himself which he had done. I stood contemplating the fire, twisting Mrs. Carruth's note between my fingers. He repeated his own words bitterly—"The Honour of the Club."

"It's a pretty club."

"My faith it is!"

"Your only bantling."

"Don't say that. It's Pendarvon's. You know it is. It's the biggest part of the debt I owe him. When I think of it, I feel like killing him."

"Why don't you?"

"It's against the rules. You stood by the rules, and so will I."

"Who are you going to kill?"

"For one thing, I shall kill my father. It will be as good as his death-blow when he hears of the sort of thing I am."

"That sort of murder won't come within the scope of the definition. If it did, possibly seven men out of ten would be entitled to the diploma of the club. Archie, I'll make you a proposition. I'll give you the money to pay Pendarvon, and I'll cry quits for what you owe me, if you'll agree, since you must kill some one, to kill any person I may nominate."

"Reggie!—what devil's game are you up to now?"

"At present, none. At this moment I have not the faintest reason to wish myself rid of any living creature. But before the end of the month the situation may be altered. Is it a deal?"

He hesitated; rose, and began to walk about the room. I watched him as he did so. I noticed how he clasped and unclasped his hands. He turned to me.

"I agree."

I sat down, then and there, and wrote him an open cheque for five thousand pounds.

"The balance will enable you to rub along for a time. If you take my tip, you'll let Pendarvon have his coin at once—before leaving town."

He took the cheque. Scanning the figures, he began to fold it up with nervous fingers. A smile—of a kind—wrinkled his lips.

"What things we may become! If ever there was blood money, this is it. And I'm a Beaupré. And do you know, Townsend, that for ever so long I've been dreaming dreams." He looked up at me, with a sudden flashing of his eyes. "Dreams of Dora Jardine."

I turned again to the fire—smiling in my turn.

"You told me so before."

"But I never told you what sort of dreams I had been dreaming. I never told you how she fills all my veins till, in all the world, I see nothing, think of nothing else, but her. I never told you how she is with me by day and by night, sleeping and waking; that, wherever I am, and whatever I do, I am always repeating to myself her name. I never told you that the dreams which I have dreamed of her have driven me mad. I never told you that."

"With all due respect to you, I should hardly have believed you if you had."

"Why? Because I am the thing I am? There's the pity of it! I have been so conscious of my unworthiness, so conscious that I never could be worthy, that, constrained by some madness which I verily believe is in my blood, I have become more unworthy still." He came closer to me. His voice dropped to a sort of breathless whisper. "And yet, Reggie, do you know, I believe that, in spite of all, she cares for me."

"I think not."

He became, all at once, almost ferocious.

"You think not! What right have you to think? How can you tell what grounds I may have for my belief?"

I turned to him. I had purposely kept my back towards him while he had been indulging in his hysterical ravings. Now I was surprised and amused to see what a change his hysterics had produced. His cheeks were flushed. His eyes were flaming. He seemed to have increased in stature. He seemed to have lost all traces of the hang-dog air with which he had entered the room.

"I ought, Archie, to have stopped you. If I remember rightly I did stop you on a previous occasion. I have, I assure you, good cause for thinking that your belief is an erroneous one; that cause is, that I have reason to believe that she cares for me."

"For you—Reggie!"

"I will be frank with you. With her father's express approval I am going down to Cockington to-day in the character of Miss Jardine's suitor."

"You!—My God!"

"Very shortly I hope to receive your congratulations on the confessedly undeserved good fortune which has dowered me with such a wife."

"But"—the man was trembling so that he could scarcely speak—"you're—you're a murderer."

"I am as you will shortly be. Let us hope that my man is not listening to these plain truths. What then?"

He began fumbling in his waistcoat pocket.

"I won't have your money. You can't buy me body and soul—no, not altogether. She shall know what manner of man you are."

He threw my cheque from him on to the floor.

"I see. Having led me into crime, you are going to tell of me. Is that sort of conduct in accordance with the Beaupré code of honour? Are you sure that you are not proposing to play Judas merely because I have conquered where you have failed?"

"No! No! I won't tell! I won't tell! You know I won't! But—that you should be going to marry Dora Jardine!"

He sank in a heap on to a chair, looking once more as pitiable an object as one would care to see.

"Come, Archie, pull yourself together. Have a drink, and play the man. Pick up the cheque, run down with me to Cockington, and wish me luck upon the road. Surely your own experience has taught you that love's transferable. So long as one has an object it does not much matter what it is, or whether it's in the singular or plural. Between ourselves, I believe that Miss Whortleberry, the American millionairess, is with the Jardines. You marry her—and her millions—I promise you I won't tell."

My words did not seem to brighten him up to any considerable extent. He sat staring with wide open eyes, almost like a man who had been stricken with paralysis.

CHAPTER XIX

THE PROMISE

But he went with me to Cockington. More, he picked up the cheque, and cashed it, and let Pendarvon have his money before he went. He struck me as not being very far from drunk when we started. Having commenced to drink, he kept at it like a fish. He was in deliriously high spirits by the time we reached our journey's end. I began to suspect that there was literal truth in what he had said; that there was a strain of madness in his blood; and that, consciously or otherwise, he was in actual training for a madhouse. The more I considered it, the less his conduct for some time past smacked to me of sanity.

It was past nine when we reached Jardine's. At the door they told us that dinner had been kept waiting for our arrival. It was ready to be served as soon as we appeared. Making a quick change, I hurried down into the drawing-room. As I entered Dora Jardine advanced to meet me.

"We expected papa by the same train by which you came, but he is detained in town. I have just had a telegram from him to say so. He says that he hopes to be here for the shoot, so perhaps he will come down by the mail—it gets here in the middle of the night, just before four." I bowed. She added, in a lower tone of voice, "Isn't it odd how some people have too much to do, and others have too little?"

"I am afraid, Miss Jardine, that such inequality is characteristic; while, if you are referring particularly to me, I assure you that very shortly I hope to be overwhelmed beneath the pressure of innumerable engagements."

She turned to the others. I knew them all. There was her aunt, Mrs. Crashaw, fat, not fair, and more than forty, a childless widow, who was understood to be rich. Lady Mary Porteous, the Marquis of Bodmin's sister, who was not so young as she had been. And there was Miss Whortleberry, the daughter of Asa Whortleberry, late of Chicago, and the present possessor of all his millions. Miss Whortleberry was one of those young women who seem to be America's most peculiar and special product. To look at she was a graceful, slender little thing, with big eyes and a face that was almost angelic in its innocence. An unsuspecting stranger might have been excused for taking it for granted that in the frame of a delicate girl there was the simple spirit of a child. A more prolonged inspection would, however, have revealed to him the fact that her costume was, to say the least of it, more suggestive of Paris than Arcadia. But it was when she opened her mouth that she gave herself away. Her voice, quite apart from its nasal twang, always reminded me, in some queer way, of Lancashire streets; it was hard and metallic. Her conceit was simply monumental. You could not talk to her for half an hour without discovering that there was only one heaven for her, and that was the heaven of dollars, and that, in her own estimation at any rate, she was its uncrowned queen.

She was lolling back in a corner of a sofa as I advanced to her. She vouchsafed me the tips of her fingers.

"Ah, it's you."

That was all the greeting she condescended to bestow.

There were four men. George Innes—Lord George Innes—who, on the strength of being one of the finest shots in England, is in hot request wherever there are birds about. I believe Innes is one of the cleanest living men I know. He is not rich, but, I take it, he lives within his income. He is fond of a modest gamble, but he won't play for big stakes, and he will only sit down where there's ready-money. His manner is a trifle suggestive of a poker down his back, but if I had been run in a different mould I could have fraternised with Innes. The man to me rings true—he is a man. He dislikes me—it is perhaps, just as well for him that he should.

Then there was Tommy Verulam, an ass, if ever there was one. I suppose he was there because of his father. I don't know what other recommendation he has. Then there was Denton, the man who writes. Personally, I have no taste for men who write. They may be all right in print, but generally they are nothing out of it, and the worst of it is, they are apt to think they are. And Silcox, M.P. I am told that he is very popular in his party, as being the only man in the Radical gang who is a fool, and knows it.

Presently Archie appeared. He was flushed. I thought he looked uncommonly well. He is a handsome beggar in his way. Dora received him with a something in her air which made his flush mount higher. I guessed how she set all his pulses tingling. Even Miss Whortleberry extended to him a welcome which, for her, was quite affectionate—he was a son of the Duke of Glenlivet.

Dora went in with Innes, as being the biggest there. I came in with the tail. We would change all that!

After dinner I made straight for the drawing-room. Something seemed to tell me that I had better make the running while I could. It was the pace which would win. Besides, the consciousness that I was once more in Dora's near neighbourhood had on me the same queer effect which it evidently had on Archie. I found her talking to the Whortleberry. Presently the millionairess went off with Mary Porteous. I had Dora to myself.

It was odd how the recognition of this fact gave me what positively amounted to a thrill. And yet, for a moment or two, neither of us spoke. She sat opening and shutting her fan. I sat and watched her performance. And when I did speak at last, my voice actually trembled.

"I have been thinking of what you said to me the other evening."

"What was that?"

"Have you forgotten?"

"Haven't you?"

"I could scarcely have been thinking of it if I had forgotten."

"What did I say?"

"You gave me courage."

"Courage?"

"Yes."

"Were you in want of courage?"

"Of that particular sort of courage. Some men only get that particular sort of courage from a woman. I know you gave it me."

She glanced up with those strange eyes of hers.

"Tell me what you mean."

"It would take me an hour to explain. Don't you know?"

"You never struck me as being in want of courage of any sort or kind."

There was an ironic intonation in her voice, which, in some subtle fashion, recalled her father.

"Is that meant as a reproach?"

"No." She hesitated, as if to consider. Then went on, "It is not so much your courage which I should have questioned, as the direction in which it has been shown. It is a sufficiently rare quality to make it unfortunate that any of it should be wasted. How much of it has been wasted you know even better than I do."

"I understand you. I thank you, not only for what you say, but also for what you leave unsaid. I am not only going to turn over a new leaf, Miss Jardine; I am going to commence a new volume. Though I shall always feel, myself, that you have commenced it for me."

"I am content, so long as it is a volume of a certain kind."

What did she mean? I seldom knew quite what she did mean. She puzzled me almost as much as her father. She was not like the average girl one bit. As she looked at me with her curiously smiling eyes, with the suggestion of strength which they conveyed to me, I felt that it was probable that she knew much more of the contents of my volume, the one which I claimed to be just closing, than I was likely to know of hers.

"Do you know, Miss Jardine, that you are making of me a proselyte."

"In what sense?"

"I have never, hitherto, believed in the influence of women. You are making of me a believer."

"That certain women have influence over certain men I think there can be no doubt whatever. I have influence over you; you have influence over me. Only"—she stopped my speaking with a movement of her fan—"I should be on my guard against your influence over me until I felt that my influence over you had produced certain results."

"I suppose that any attempts on my part to guard against your influence would be vain."

"You would not attempt to make them. You are not that kind of man."

"Miss Jardine!"

"You are not. You would not attempt to resist the influence of any woman. You would rather welcome it as a sort of study in sensation, as far as it would go. But it would not go far. It would soon reach a bed-rock of resistance. As soon as it reached that rock it would vanish into nothing."

"You flatter me by making so close a study of my peculiarities."

"I do not flatter you. I take an interest in you, because, for one reason, you take an interest in me. Now, Mr. Townsend, I am sure that I should find that bed-rock of resistance at a greater distance from the surface. If ever you welcomed my influence you might find it go much farther than you had at first intended. So I warn you in advance."

I was silenced, not so much by her words as by her bearing. Her eyes had an effect on me which no eyes had ever had on me before. They mastered me, and made me conscious of a sense of satisfaction at being mastered.

"You make me afraid of you."

"Just now you said I gave you courage."

"The two things are compatible. Fear of you might give me courage."

"You mean fear of appearing contemptible to me?"

"Exactly."

"Then that sort of courage I should like to give you." A gleam came into her eyes which was almost like a flash of lightning. "Perhaps I will."

"Do I not tell you that you have given me a taste of it already?"

We might have reached delicate ground. When a man and a woman deal in personalities, and persevere in them, a situation of some sort is apt to ensue. Archie's appearance postponed the crisis which I was beginning to think was nearer even than I had supposed. Archie seemed in a condition of almost feverish exaltation. In the look with which he favoured me there was something which certainly was not altogether friendly. Dora did not seem to notice it. She welcomed him with a smile. As he sat down on the other side of her I got up. I left them together.

"Poor chap!" I told myself as I strolled off, "let him have his innings. He must be badly burned or he would make a more strenuous endeavour to avoid the fire."

Lounging into the little drawing-room beyond, I came into collision with the aunt. She had the place to herself. She appeared to be just waking up from the enjoyment of forty winks. I daresay if I had not come upon the scene she would have had another. At the sight of me she roused. She beckoned me to occupy an adjacent chair. She was the aunt, and I still was unattached. I sat beside her.

"What do you think of Dora?" Her tone was confidential. She spoke to me under cover of her handkerchief. Seeing that I was puzzled, she explained—"I mean, how do you think she's looking?"

"I think she's looking very well."

"Isn't she! Wonderfully well! Don't you think she's lovely?"

I hardly knew what to say. She could scarcely expect me to be ecstatic.

"Indeed I do."

"Of course you would!" She smiled—such a smile. "And she's all she looks, and more. She is good as she is beautiful, and so clever. Extraordinarily so! She's a wonderful girl!" She closed her eyes, as if the wonder was too great for visual contemplation. "I often think that it is unfortunate that she was not born a man."

"You can scarcely expect me to agree with you there."

"You wicked creature!" She prodded me with her fat fingers in the arm. Mrs. Crashaw was one of those old women who, whenever they can, punctuate their remarks on the persons of their listeners. She arranged her bracelets on her wrists. "Haselton tells me that he has a very high opinion of you, Mr. Townsend."

"I am very glad to hear it. I only hope he does not think more highly of me than I deserve."

"I hope not. Young men nowadays are so wicked. They deserve so little. As you probably are aware, Mr. Townsend, I am Haselton's only sister. He reposes in me his entire confidence. He has no secrets from me."

I believed her! She might be his only sister, but Sir Haselton Jardine was as likely to repose his entire confidence in a woman of Mrs. Crashaw's type as in the first town crier. Whatever he told her would probably be told with, at least, one eye to advertisement.

"My brother Haselton is a man of peculiar gifts. A remarkable man. A man of genius if ever there was one. He is, of course, respected by all of us, by his country and his Queen. He has a marvellous knowledge of the world, and a great esteem for those sacred things which are too often disregarded. And when I learn that he has a high opinion of any person I know that that person must be all right upon the moral side. I am glad, Mr. Townsend, to be able to think this of you."

I looked down. I could not help but smile.

"Thank you, Mrs. Crashaw; you are very good."

"In this age of flippancy, the most shocking things are suffered. I hear, I assure you, of things which would astound you. I have made Haselton's hair stand up on end. It always gives me pleasure to hear of a young man who is not only clever but good. For my part, let them say what they will, I think it is better to be good than clever. I hope, Mr. Townsend, that you will always bear that in mind."

Again she prodded me in the arm. I could but bow my head.

"The man who marries Dora will be a most fortunate man. She has money of her own. She will have money from her father. She may have money from me—mind, I make no promise—I say she may have. It depends." Mrs. Crashaw smoothed out her ample skirts in front of her. "Then there is the family influence and position. With a clever girl like Dora for a wife nothing ought to be impossible to her husband."

The dear old thing might be prosy, but it did me good to hear her talking. Such observations, coming from such a quarter, carried weight and meaning. They meant that my position looked already as if it was assured. They meant that the whole thing—spontaneously, so far as I was concerned—had been threshed out in family councils, and that then the decision had been given for me. The thing seemed too good to be true; and yet it was true—here was the living witness. I was in for a stroke of fortune so stupendous as to seem to verge on the miraculous.

If only I had known of it before last Sunday! If only I had suspected that the thing was even possible! Why had I been so blind? Why had I not seen it coming? Why had Sir Haselton not dropped a hint in time? Oh, if he only had!

But the game was not yet lost. Lost?—it was all but gained! I had but to breast the tape, and win. The riding would do it. Luck was on my side.

I turned in early. I had had little enough of bed the night before. I wanted to get up fit, with a clear eye and steady hand. I did not want Innes to beat me too badly with the birds. One likes to hold one's own, whatever is the game.

In the corridor, as I was making for the sheets, who should I meet but Dora. She thought that I was going to make changes in my costume, to fit me for the smoking-room.

"Going to change your coat?"

"Not I. I'm going to bed."

"Really?"

"Really. I want to make some additions to to-morrow's bag. Sir Haselton won't thank me if I don't."

She looked at me as if she was trying to read my face. When she tried to do that I felt, in some occult fashion, that she succeeded. I would have been prepared to wager that she had her father's power of reading faces—and more.

"I want you to promise me something."

"What is it?"

"I want you to promise to top Lord George's score."

"You ask a hard thing, Miss Jardine. I do not profess to be Lord George Innes's equal as a shot."

"I believe, if you like, you can do anything."

"You believe too much of me. Honestly, for my sake, I wish you would believe a little less."

"Will you promise?"

"I promise that I will try my hardest, that I will do my best; and, as the archer says in 'Ivanhoe,' no man can do more."

"You will hare to do more for me; you will have to promise, and you will have to keep your promise."

It seemed an unreasonable request to make—especially in that insistent fashion—such a promise no man could be sure of keeping. A thousand things might be against him. I might shoot better than I had ever shot in my life, and yet not be certain of topping the score. Yet, when I saw the something that was in her eyes, I cast caution to the wind.

"I promise."

She held out her hand.

"Good-night."

She allowed me to retain her hand for a moment in mine.

"I know you will keep the promise you have made."

She was gone. I turned into my room. And, when in it, I reflected.

"If she knows that I will keep the promise I have made she knows a good deal more than I do. I wonder what will happen if I don't. I can, as a rule, see pretty straight along the barrel of a gun, but I do hope to goodness the birds will be good enough to cross my line of fire. She's the sort of girl to take the miscarriage even of such a promise as an omen. I want the omen to be all the other way."

Some one knocked at the door. It was Archie. He had a smoking jacket on.

"Aren't you coming down into the smoking-room?"

"I am not. And, if you take my tip, you won't go either. You must be almost as much in want of a trifle of bed as I am."

"I am obliged to you. I make my own sleeping arrangements." His tone was snappy. He seated himself on the arm of a chair. "Were you in earnest in what you said to me this morning?"

"To what are you referring?"

"To what you said about Miss Jardine."

"Certainly I was in earnest."

He fixed his glance upon me in a fashion I did not relish.

"Haven't you a grain of pity? Is there nothing human about you, Townsend?"

I felt strongly that that sort of thing must cease. The idea of Lord Archibald Beaupré's mentorship was an idea not to be endured.

"There has been a good deal about your manner towards me lately, Beaupré, to which I have objected, and with good cause. You have presumed on the friendship which exists between us in a manner of which I should have thought you, of all men, would have been incapable." He flushed. I saw I had struck home. "You must excuse me saying that if you consider that the fact of our being acquainted with each other entitles you to unwarrantably interest yourself in my private affairs, I must request that that acquaintance shall cease."

"You don't understand me—or you won't."

"I understand you better than you imagine. You are not the first jealous man I have known."

He went white and red.

"It isn't jealousy; I swear it isn't."

"It is a matter of complete indifference to me what it is. I object to it in any case."

He was silent for some seconds. He stared at his toes.

"Tell me one thing—have you proposed to her?"

"I shall tell you nothing. After the tone which you have used towards me I decline to allow you to ask me questions."

He got off the arm of the chair.

"Then God help her." He went to the door. At the door he turned again. "I don't believe that He will suffer it."

Then he went

If Archie went on like that much longer, he and I should quarrel. Vicarious morality is a variety of the article to which the most liberal-minded inevitably objects.

CHAPTER XX

THE NEWS FROM TOWN

I woke up feeling as fresh as a daisy. When Burton drew up the blinds the sun came gleaming through the bedroom windows.

"There's been a slight frost, sir, but I think it's going to be a clear day."

From where I lay in bed the sky looked cloudless.

"It seems just the morning for a shoot."

"I think it is a shooting day, sir—there's no wind, and a good light."

As Burton said, it was a shooting day. When I had dressed I went straight down on to the terrace. There was a slight nip in the air, and the faintest whisper of a breeze. It was the sort of day which makes one feel that it is good to be alive. I seemed to be the first one down. I never felt more fit. I stood there drinking in great draughts of the clear, cool air, with greater relish than I ever drank champagne. If one always lived in such an atmosphere, with plenty of money in one's pockets, one could afford to be a model of all the virtues.

Some one spoke to me from behind. It was Dora.

"You are the first on the scene."

I turned. She was standing at the open window of the morning-room.

"Am I the first to whom you have wished good morning?"

"The very first. Good morning, Mr. Townsend."

She held out to me her hand. I retained it in mine. A wild impulse seized me to kiss her on the lips. It was all I could do to hold my own against it. Her eyes were so provoking, her mouth so tempting. She allowed me to keep her hand in mine, though she might surely have seen my desire showing through my face. And I have no doubt she did, for she smiled at me.

"Well—good luck."

"I will keep my promise."

I released her hand. A gleam of colour was glowing on her cheeks. I doubted if she was not making fun of me.

"After all, papa cannot come. He wishes you to shoot without him. He says that he will certainly be down tonight."

We shot without him. I do not think that he was missed. I had never seen Sir Haselton Jardine handling a gun, but I should not fancy that he was much of a performer. He did not strike one as being built that way.

I spoke to Innes as we were strolling to cover.

"Innes, I'm feeling in first-rate shooting trim to-day. I don't pretend, for a moment, to compare my shooting to yours, but would you like to have a sporting wager?"

"How?"

One peculiarity of Innes's is that he never uses two syllables where one will do.

"Bet you a pony that I kill more birds than you."

"Birds? or all in?"

"All in if you like."

"Done."

That decided it. I had not expected that he would bet. I had a sort of suspicion that he rather avoided making bets with me, but now that he had bet, if I did not win his pony and keep my promise, luck would have to be against me with a vengeance.

There were seven guns—the house lot, and a local. Innes, Archie, I, and the local had the best places. The local was a man named Purrier. He seemed to be something in the gentleman farmer sort of line. He could shoot, though he was a pot hunter if ever there was one. Sport did not seem so much to his taste as killing. He potted ever so many of his birds before they had a chance of getting up. Archie shot wildly. He evidently had not taken my advice and gone to bed when I did. When he is in form his gun can be relied upon. At his performances on that occasion, I saw Vicary, the head-keeper, more than once pulling a face. Innes, as usual, performed like a book. And his luck was better than mine. The birds would rise his side. I never missed a chance. Yet, by lunch-time, he was nineteen pheasants, two rabbits, and a hare to the good—twenty-one in all.

I was a bit surprised to find that luncheon was done in swagger fashion. It was the first time I had shot at Jardine's. I had not been aware that they did things in quite such style. There was a portable kitchen, and a tent, and a regular table, and a lot of servants, and there were the ladies there. One doesn't care, if one is at all keen, for lunch being made a feature, when one is shooting. But I did not object so much just then. Dora's face was welcome, though I had such a pitiful tale to tell. We sat down anyhow. I planted myself beside her.

"I haven't kept my promise."

"Pray, how is that?"

"The stars in their courses have fought against me. The enemy is twenty-one ahead."

"That is nothing. You will keep your promise before you have finished. I know you will."

How she knew is more than I can say. She knew better than I did. And she knew quite right. I kept my promise. After lunch, I made up for all my ill-luck of the morning. Her words may have had something to do with it—and the tone in which the words were uttered. I believe they had. Anyhow, I wound up by beating my friend, the enemy, with more than two score birds in hand.

The local made all the running at the start. He shot like a keeper, for the larder, or like a dealer, for the shop, grassing bird after bird before it had a fair chance to stretch its wings. Some of the birds seemed a trifle tame; they were either weak on the wing or else they had been overfed. They would not rise until they were compelled. Some of them had to be driven right on to our guns before they would get up. This was nuts for the local. When he had a chance to stop them they never got up at all.

I began catching Innes all along. But it was in the last cover the trick was done. The bag for the day was close upon two thousand. Of these over seven hundred were winged in that last cover. Vicary had kept his bonne bouche for the finish.

When we reached it Innes and I were about equal. When the slaughter began he did all he knew. But I did better. I brought them down as fast as I could get the guns; and I fancy that my guns were loaded quicker than his. While it lasted it was as hot a bit as one could wish.

When it was over Innes came to me.

"You win."

"I think I do. What do you make your total?"

He told me. I told him that I made mine forty-seven more.

"I did not know that you were quite so many as that. But I knew that you were in front. The birds have broken on your gun in a crowd."

I owned that was so.

"I know that the luck has been mine. Of course, as a shot I am not to be compared to you. It was like my cheek to back myself. But, somehow, I seemed to know, in advance, that I should have the luck."

"It has not, by any means, been all luck. You're a good shot, Mr. Townsend."

Archie came slouching up. He had lost his temper—as he was wont to do when he had been making an ass of himself.

"Did you ever see anything like my shooting? I can't hit a haystack."

He was looking at Vicary, but whether he was speaking to him is more than I can say. Vicary chose to think that he was. Evidently Jardine's head man knew his business—he had given us a first-rate day. But he was one of those keepers who like to see their birds shot. When they were missed, and the principal offender gave him such a chance as that, he was not likely to let it pass him.

He looked at Archie. His face assumed an expression of rustic stupidity—it was a distinct assumption. Nature had made him look as sharp as a ferret.

"Well, sir, I did understand from Sir Haselton as how you could hit haystacks."

Archie went red all over, then went white to the lips.

I take it that last spinney was a good four miles from the house. So we drove home. It had kept clear, but it had again turned frosty. There was a keen bite in the air. They had sent our coats in the brake. The ladies were having tea when we got back. When we had changed we joined them—all but Archie, who, I imagine, stayed in his room to sulk. Innes and I got in together. The others were already in evidence, including the local, who was to stop and dine.

Mary Porteous called out as we came in—

"So you've had a good day?"

I answered. Innes, if he could, always saved his words.

"First-rate."

"And I hear that you've gained all the honours, Mr. Townsend."

"I've had a good deal of luck, Lady Mary—more than my share. But, I believe, as a matter of fact, that Mr. Purrier heads the score."

Mr. Purrier disclaimed the soft impeachment.

"I doubt it. I never saw better shooting, Mr. Townsend, than yours."

"It's very good of you to say so. You all seem very nice and complimentary."

Mary Porteous laughed.

"How modest we are!"

People went into the billiard-room after tea. I stayed for a moment or two behind with Dora. I had not had a chance of a word with her at tea. She had been entertaining Silcox and Purrier—it was she who sent them to billiards. The rest trooped after them. We were left alone. I had been sitting a little in the shadow, on the other side of the room. I crossed to her.

"I've kept my promise."

"Thank yon. It is almost as if you had done me a special and a most particular favour. But I knew you would."

"You seem to know me very well."

"I know you much better, perhaps, than you imagine."

"But, I assure you, I do not always necessarily keep promises which I make."

"Of that I am certain. But, before you make a promise to me, I shall know—know, mind!—if you will keep it. And I shall never ask you to make a promise which I do not know that you will keep."

"Are you a seer?"

"So far as you are concerned, I am."

She touched my arm lightly with her hand. I protest that she set me all a-trembling. There was a pause. She removed her hand. I do not believe that I could have spoken while she had it there.

"Papa has telegraphed that we are not to wait dinner for him, so we shall dine at eight. Papa says that he will dine alone, as he is bringing work with him from town. It seems to me that life is coming to mean, more and more, to him, nothing but a synonym for work."

I made up my mind, on the instant, that I would—if I could—put the matter to the touch before Sir Haselton Jardine appeared upon the scene. I felt that I could not hold myself in much longer, even if I tried. I was beginning to feel a longing for this girl such as I had never felt for a woman before—and I own that, in my time, I have longed for particular women now and then. Apart from all other considerations, I yearned to have her, to win her, to call her mine—for herself, and for herself alone. She always had exercised over me a sort of cerebral attraction. This attraction had grown and strengthened. It was both intellectual and physical. It was beginning to overwhelm me. I knew that, when the moment came in which we should see each other eye to eye, for the first time in my career I should look upon the face of my undoubted master. I had met my master in my mistress, if the fates would but let me win her for my wife. If but Dame Fortune had that crowning mercy to bestow! The knowledge that she was my master was beginning to fill my veins with a frenzy of desire—we should be so fairly mated.

As I was dressing, the look which I had seen in her glances was haunting me. I told myself that, after dinner, I would put my fortune to the touch, and lose or win it all.

And so I did!

We were a lively lot at dinner—all but Archie. He was black as black could be. Tommy Verulam began chaffing him about his shooting. Tommy himself, I should say, could shoot as well with one end of his gun as with the other. But that did not prevent his being down on Archie. The worse a man is at a thing himself, the more disposed he seems to be to exploit the deficiencies of others, especially if he is a fool of the transcendental sort. Tommy had heard Vicary's remark about the haystack. So he told the tale—with embellishments of his own. I thought Archie would have thrown a plate at his head. There would have been a row royal if the ladies had not been present. Trying to snub Tommy—I expected that Vicary would hear something from headquarters about that little slip of his tongue—Dora endeavoured to extend her sympathies to Archie. But Archie would have none of it. The light had gone out of the world for him.

Directly the ladies' backs were turned the band did begin to play. Leaning his arms on the table, Archie addressed himself to Tommy.

"Mr. Verulam, have you ever had your head punched?"

Tommy gaped.

"What the doose do you mean?"

"What I say. If you haven't, consider your head punched now."

Innes interposed.

"For shame, Beaupré!"

Archie turned on him like a wild cat.

"You mind your own business! Don't you interfere with me!" Evidently, as regards interference, in Archie's estimation what was sauce for the goose was not sauce for the gander. He stood up. "Mr. Verulam, so long as you are in this house you are in sanctuary. On the first occasion on which I meet you outside, I shall kick you."

With that he stalked out of the room—it's a pretty Scotch temper he has of his own!

But I cared neither for his bad taste nor for his bad temper, and as little for Tommy's folly. I went in search of Dora. I peeped into the drawing-room. Mary Porteous was making a noise at the piano, but in spite of the noise she made Mrs. Crashaw was having forty winks upon an easy-chair.

The millionairess was nowhere to be seen, nor was Dora. From the morning-room there was a door leading into the conservatory; entrance to this conservatory was to be gained from the drawing-room as well. I went to the morning-room. I looked into the conservatory. At first I thought it was empty. But, when I went farther into it, there was Dora.

The glass house was a large one. In the centre was a fountain. The water fell into a basin in which were goldfish. Looking into this basin, seated under the shadow of a palm, was Dora.

She was thinking, perhaps, of me. She did not become conscious of my approach until I was close upon her.

"A penny for your thoughts."

She looked up with that odd smile which, to me, seemed to glorify her countenance.

"They ought to be worth more than that to you."

I was silent. I, too, looked into the basin. The goldfish were swimming round and round. The fountain fell into the water with a musical splash. The noise of the piano came from the drawing-room beyond. Now that I was close to her the task seemed harder than I had supposed. My ready tongue seemed to have forsaken me. My pulses were throbbing in my veins like some young lad's.

It was she who broke the silence.

"Your thoughts; are they worth a penny too?"

"Can you not guess them?"

"That is not an answer to my question."

"I have not your gift of prescience. I cannot tell if they are worth a penny to you. To me they are worth more pennies than I am ever likely to possess."

"You place a high value on your own thoughts."

"Shall I tell you what they are?"

"If you like. Though, is it worth the trouble, if you are sure that I can guess?"

"Give me leave to tell you them."

"I give you leave."

"I was thinking what fallible creatures we men are."

"Is that all? Surely that is not worth a penny, even to you."

"Because so small a thing may change all our lives."

"Not worth a penny yet."

"Have you bewitched me?"

"I cannot tell."

"I believe you have."

"You are not bewitched so easily."

"As you say, I am not so easily bewitched. That makes it still more strange."

"I await the penny's worth."

"Will you forgive me, Miss Jardine?"

"For what?"

The words trembled on my lips. And yet, without a struggle, I could not utter them. As I looked into the water, all at once my eyes seemed blinded by its glare.

"For loving you."

She was still. I did not dare to turn to look upon her face, for fear of what there might be there to see.

"You have your methods, Mr. Townsend."

"In what sense, Miss Jardine?"

"I await the penny's worth."

On a sudden a great shame came over me; a sense of overwhelming horror. I sank on my knee. I hid my face in my hands on the basin's edge.

"God help me!"

The cry was wrung from me by something which, for the moment, was stronger than I.

"Hush!"

The word was whispered. Then she, too, was still.

"Begin again." The words seemed to come to me like the words which we hear in a dream. "What is done, is done. You cannot put it behind you altogether. But it is done. It is not yet to do. And, because it is done, therefore, you need not do it again, in the time which is to come. If you have strength—and you have strength, Mr. Townsend—play the man."

I had never thought that any one would have had to bid me play the man. But she had to bid me then. She laid her hand upon my shoulder. Beneath her touch a shudder went all over me. Then I looked up at her.

"You are not for such as I am."

"But you are for such as I am."

I held my breath. I knew not what to do or say. I stared in front of me, not understanding what it was I saw.

"What is it that you say?"

"Are you so deaf? All in an instant have you become so dull? Come, I will do the wooing, since you are afraid to woo me." That ever I should have been told by a woman that I was afraid to woo her! "If you but love me half as I love you, you will fill the world with the fame of the great deeds which you will do for love of me, and leave behind a name which men never shall let die."

"Dora! Dora! My Dora!"

"Well, if I am your's—"

"If? Is it only if?"

"Will you be mine?"

"Body, soul, and spirit. I do believe you have bewitched me. I am going mad for the love of you!"

"I am content."

"Is this a dream of ecstasy from which there will soon be waking?"

"I would that you might wake to something soon."

"What's that?"

"To the fact that I am here."

I woke to it. It was worth while to have lived if only to have woke to what I woke then. For I woke to find that her face was close to mine, that I might take her in my arms, that I was free to smother her with kisses.

Loving is such sweet pain. I learned it then!

And hardly had I loosed her, than some one came upon us. It was Sir Haselton Jardine. I saw his well-regulated eyelids suffered to open to enable him to shoot one of his swift glances. I saw his lips wrinkled by his imitation of a smile. And he said—

"I hope I do not interrupt you. I am but now arrived from town."

Dora, all rosy red, ran into his arms.

"Father!" she cried.

"My dear!" Then to me, "How are you, Townsend? I said I thought it possible that you might have something to say to me before you went away."

"I trust, sir, that I may have."

I believe that I, myself, was blushing like any boy.

While we were standing there—forming, no doubt, a sufficiently awkward group—Tommy Verulam came running in. He seemed to have recovered from the effects of his little episode with Archie. He was quite excited.

"I say, I've just been looking at the London papers. It seems that they've got the chap who murdered the woman at Three Bridges."

I turned to him.

"Indeed! Who may he be?"

"His name is Tennant—Thomas Tennant. I hope they'll hang the brute, upon my soul I do."

Sir Haselton struck in—

"I am briefed by the Treasury to prosecute. If the man's guilty, it will be a positive pleasure to have a hand in sending him to the gallows."

As I was endeavouring to grasp the drift of what it was that they were saying, I saw that Archie Beaupré was staring at us through the drawing-room window.

BOOK III - THE WOMAN.

CHAPTER XXI

THE ADVENTURES OF A NIGHT

To have fallen out of an express train going at full speed! I have had some strange experiences, for a mere woman. But this, I think, beats all.

And to owe it to Thomas Tennant! I will be even with him yet.

I went down to Brighton to spend the Sunday with Lettice Enderby—she was acting at the theatre there. I found her not feeling very well. We spent the day alone together. After dinner I had to make a rush for the train. Who should I find myself shut in with as soon as the train had started, but Tommy Tennant.

It was years and years since we had seen each other. And all the world had happened since we had. But, so far as personal appearance was concerned, he had not changed a bit. He was still the same jack-pudding sort of little man, with round eyes and rosy cheeks. I knew him at sight. What was queerer, he knew me. I take that as a compliment. I flatter myself that I have not changed, except for the better, since those days of long ago. Tommy's prompt recognition was the best testimony to the truth of this fact I could possibly have had.

Although more than seas divided us, and never was a past more dead than his and mine, at the sight of Tommy all my old grudge against him came back again. Perhaps the glass or two of wine I had had with Lettice might have had something to do with it, but directly I saw him I flew into a rage. Tommy Tennant always has been the ideal man I hate. Give me them good or give me them bad, but do give me them one or the other. The irresolute, backboneless, jelly-like sort of man is beyond endurance.

If Thomas Tennant ever had a backbone he lost it in his cradle!

He always used to be afraid of me. In that respect, as in the others, I found he had not changed. He was frightened half out of his life directly he saw who it was. When I began talking to him he started shivering—literally shivering—in a way which made me wild. I do like a man who can hold his own. Talk about conscience making cowards of us all; I like the man of whom nothing can make a coward. He got into such a state of mortal terror that he actually tried to steal out of the carriage and escape from me while the train was going, for all I know, perhaps fifty miles an hour.

That was how the trouble all began. It would have spoiled the sport to have let him go, so I tried to stop him. He had opened the carriage door, and in endeavouring to prevent his going out, I went out instead.

That is the simple truth.

There never was a more astonished woman. I doubt if there ever was one with so much reason for astonishment. How it happened, or exactly what happened, I do not know. There was not time enough to clearly understand. I discovered that I was standing upon nothing, and then that I was flying backwards through the air. After that I suppose I lost my seven senses.

I could not, however, have lost them for long. Perhaps for not more than a minute or so. When I came to I opened my eyes, and looking up saw that the moon was shining in the sky overhead, and that it was almost as light as day. I wondered where I was, and whether the end of the world had come. I found that I was lying among a group of bushes on what seemed a sloping bank, and that something very like a miracle had taken place. Falling out of the train while it was rushing along the top of an embankment, I must have gone, backwards, into a bush, which while it had let me through, had sufficed to break my fall. I must have rolled down the bank, until I was stopped by the clump of bushes amidst which I found myself.

The miracle was that I was unhurt. I was a trifle shaken and a trifle dazed. But not a bone was broken, and I felt that, so far as material damage was concerned, I could get up when I chose and walk off, practically as if nothing had occurred.

But I was a trifle dazed, and it was some moments before my senses quite returned to me. What hastened their return was the fact of my hearing footsteps. I listened. Somebody was walking, and not very far off either. The person, whoever it was, seemed to be quite close at hand. I did not know whereabouts I might be lying. I was only aware that I was somewhere between Brighton and London. I had no notion how far I might be from a station or a town. It struck me that it would be just as well that I should discover who the pedestrian might chance to be.

As I was about to rise, with the intention of prospecting, something heavy falling among the bushes almost on top of me startled me half out of my wits. I sprang to my feet. At the bottom of the bank on the other side of a fence which formed a boundary between the railway and the country beyond, a man stood, staring at me in the moonlight. He was tall, and he wore a long black overcoat and a billycock hat; even then, and in that light, I could see he was a gentleman. But it was the look which was on his face which took me aback. I never saw such a look on a man's face before. He stared at me as if he was staring at a ghost. And just as I was about to accost him, and to request his assistance, at least to the extent of informing me as to my whereabouts, leaping right round, he began to tear across the moonlit field as if Satan was at his heels.

I was going to call and beg him not to leave me, a stranger in the land, alone in the lurch like that, when I was reminded of the something which had fallen among the bushes, and which had first made me conscious of his presence, by kicking against something which felt soft and yielding, and which was lying on the ground.

I stooped down to see what it was.

"Sakes alive! It's a woman!"

It was; a young woman—and she was dead. No wonder he had stared at me as if he had been staring at a ghost. No wonder, as he saw me looking at him from among the bushes, that he had thought that the victim of his handiwork had risen from the dead to look again upon his face. No wonder he had torn for his life across the grass, feeling that she was at his heels.

I seemed to be in for a pretty thing. I have looked upon dead folk many a time; yes, and upon not a few who have come to their death by "accident." I have lived in parts of the world in which life is not held so sacred as it is in England; where not such a fuss is made every time the doctor is forestalled—where the doctor is not the only individual who is licensed to kill; where men shoot now and then at sight, and, when they are pushed to it, women too. I know a girl—and liked her—who shot a man who had insulted her in New Orleans, and left him on the sidewalk. Nobody said a word. She is married now to a rich man, and to a good man, as good men go, and she has a family, and she is highly esteemed. In England that seems odd, but I suppose the fact is that when one is in Rome one does as the Romans do, and that is all about it.

And at that moment I happened to be in England, and I made up my mind there and then that, if I could help it, I would have no finger in the pie. I had no desire to go into the witness-box—I would almost as soon have gone into the dock. Cross-examining counsel have a knack of making mincemeat of a witness. Things come out—the things which one would much rather did not come out. I had not returned to England, a widow, with my big pile, with the intention of coming such a cropper at the outset. Rather than be mixed up in such a mess, I would almost sooner take my passage in the first steamer back to the States, and count the ties out West again.

Please the fates, I had done with scandals—fresh ones, anyhow—for the rest of my days. The woman was dead. She was beyond my help. Let whoever found her hang the man who laid her there. The house in which I lived was too transparent for me to indulge in the luxury of throwing stones.

I gathered myself together. The most miraculous part of the business was that my clothing seemed to have escaped uninjured; falling backwards had been my salvation. I peeped at my face in my handglass. I seemed to be all right—right enough, at any rate, to pass muster at night and in a crowd. I went up the bank to the line. From that altitude I had a good view of the surrounding country. Straight along the line to the left, not so very far away, lights were glimmering. I made up my mind to chance it, to keep along the line and to make for them.

They proved to be the lights of a station. The station was Three Bridges Junction. I managed to enter it to the best of my knowledge and belief, entirely unobserved. I thanked my stars when I felt the platform beneath my feet.

From the mirror in the waiting-room I learned that my handglass had not deceived me. I could pass muster. A woman in the room addressed me—she and I had it to ourselves.

"Excuse me, miss, but do you know your back's all covered with weeds?"

As she brushed them off I thanked her, murmuring something about my having been sitting on the grass.

Going out on to the platform I all but came into collision with the man who had stood staring at me from the other side of the railing. The sight of him fairly took my breath away. He was going from me or he could scarcely have failed to notice the singularity of my demeanour. It was he—there could be no mistake about that. But, lest I might be in error, I resolved to have another glimpse at him. Before I could put my resolution into force he had vanished, into what I discovered to be, as I strolled slowly past it, a refreshment-room.

I should not wonder if he did stand in need of refreshment!

There did not appear to be a seat in the place. English people talk about the discomfort of the American depôts but my experience is that, from the discomfort point of view, the average English station runs the American depôt hard. I sat on one of those square trollies which the porters use for baggage. There I watched and waited for my gentleman to emerge, refreshed. The trolley was close to the refreshment-room. I could see him at the bar. He was not content with one drink. He disposed of two.

Probably he needed them!

Presently he came out. He had had his back towards me while he had been drinking. As he came out of the buffet, turning, he walked in the direction of the trolley on which I was sitting. He moved right past, so close to me that by putting out my foot, I could have tripped him up.

It was he. My first impression had not been wrong. That he had got cured of his fright was plain—certainly he showed no signs of it. He seemed quite at his ease. His hands were in the pockets of his overcoat, an umbrella was under his arm, a cigarette was between his teeth. There might not have been such a thing as a ghost—or the shadow of the shade of a ghost—in all the world.

Back he came. He sailed up to a porter. I heard him asking him when there was a train to town. As the man, having given the information, was making off, I cut in. I put to my gentleman the question which he had put to the porter.

"Can you tell me when the next train starts for London?"

He told me what I asked, adding a word or two on his own account, as I had expected and desired. I responded. He seemed disposed for sociability. Why should I object? We began to talk. The end of it was that we travelled in the same compartment up to town.

It was so funny!

He was that most remarkable product—an English gentleman. Given the real article—and there is no mistaking it when once encountered—there is nothing in the world which can be compared to it. I speak who know. He was tall. He was perfectly dressed. He was handsome—I never saw a more handsome man. And he had that air of infinite, yet unconscious, condescension which the English gentleman, alone of all the creatures of the world, is born with, and which, willy-nilly, he carries with him from the cradle to the grave.

They tell you in the different countries of the world that the Englishman is awkward, shy, ungraceful, seldom at his ease. May be; but not the English gentleman. He is the only man I have known who is always at his ease in every possible situation. But he is not to be found on every bush. Even in his own country he is the rarest of rare birds. Being born a peer, even though he can trace his tree to Noah, does not make a man a gentleman—you bet that it does not. I believe that an English gentleman is a caprice, an accident. He is not to be accounted for by natural laws. And though, for all I know, he may be trusted by his fellows, he is not to be trusted by a woman. He has one code of honour for his own sex and another for ours.

That is so, though it may not be according to the copybooks.

My friend the gentleman was a real smart man. As he lolled back in his seat, enjoying his tobacco, it did you good to see him smile. His voice was typical of his kind, it fell like music on your ears. As you looked at him and listened, you could have sworn that he had not a care upon his mind. He was at peace with himself, and all the world. And it was all so natural; he was to the manner born.

I found him quite delightful. I could see what he was doing—he was reckoning me up. And he was puzzled where to place me. I took him into my real confidence, for reasons of my own, and that puzzled him still more. I told him nothing but the truth. How I had gone out to America, and met poor dear Daniel, and married him. And how he had died and left me a widow, and his pile to comfort me. And how I had come back to England childless and forlorn and all alone. I laid stress upon my loneliness. I think that touched him. When a woman tells a man that she is lonely he takes it that she means that there is not a man anywhere in sight, and that the coast is clear for him, and that does touch him. His manner became quite sympathetic. He was as nice as could be—allusive, as a real smart man can be, with a delicate, intangible directness almost equal to a woman's.

We were almost like old friends by the time that we reached town. He put me into a hansom at Victoria station. I asked him to come and see me, to have consideration for my loneliness. He promised that he would. All the way home, as the cab bore me through the streets, I kept thinking of Mr. Reginald Townsend—that was the name which he had given me—and of the woman he had left, lying by the line, amidst that clump of bushes.

I believe I have written that I like a man to be thorough. It seemed probable that Mr. Townsend was that.

CHAPTER XXII

LOUISE O'DONNEL'S FATHER

Next day Jack Haines came to see me. Mr. Haines promised to be a nuisance.

Jack Haines and Daniel J. Carruth had been partners. I might have married either of them, for the matter of that. I might have married any one in Strikehigh City. Of two evils I chose what seemed to me to be the lesser, which was Daniel. For one thing, he was the boss partner and had the larger share, and for another, he was the older man. I could have twisted either of them round my finger, but it occurred to me that I might manage best with Daniel. So I became Mrs. Daniel J. Carruth, and poor dear Daniel lived just long enough to capitalize his share—he made a better thing of it than we had either of us expected—and then he died. Hardly was he buried than the chief mourner at his funeral, Mr. Haines, wanted me to marry him. He hinted that it would be just as well to keep the partnership alive, which struck me as absurd. Anyhow, I did not seem to see it. I came straight away to England, instead of marrying him, with the intention of getting as much fun out of Daniel's dollars as I possibly could.

What I had not bargained for was his coming after me.

The folks in Strikehigh City had all lived queer lives, but I rather guess that, in some ways, Jack Haines had lived one of the queerest. He had told me about it over and over again, and, whatever I might think of him, I knew that he had told me the truth.

He had been married. He and his wife had lived like cat and dog. She had died. She had left a daughter. He had brought the daughter up—trying to rule her with a heavy hand. There came a time when she objected. There was a disturbance—she left him. That was just before he came to Strikehigh City—in fact, her going sent him there, and he had never seen her since. I could see plainly that he had been more in the wrong than she had. In his way, he loved her. His conscience pricked him all the time. When Daniel died, it began to prick him worse than ever. Finding that I would not have him, he set himself to look for her.

This I learned from his own lips when I met him again in London.

It seemed that, when she had left him the girl had gone on to the stage—attaching herself to a variety show. From that she had passed to a burlesque troupe. The burlesque troupe had gone to England—she went with it. The burlesque troupe returned—she had stayed behind. No doubt for reasons of her own. Jack Haines wanted very much to know what those reasons were, because, no sooner had the troupe gone, and left her, than she vanished. No one seemed to have the faintest notion what had become of her. She had simply disappeared—gone clean out of sight.

The old man had come over to see if he could not succeed where others had failed; if he could not light on the clue which others had missed.

The desire to find the girl had become with him a regular mania. It was like a bee in his bonnet. It occupied his thoughts, to the exclusion of all else, both by night and day. As I have said, the man was becoming a nuisance. I did not want to quarrel with him, but I saw that, without a quarrel, I never should be rid of him. He insisted on making me his confidant. And, although I took care never to give him a chance to say a word outright, I knew that, as soon as he had found the girl, he would renew that hint about the desirability of keeping the partnership alive.

On the day after that little trip to Brighton, he turned up in my drawing-room. I had run over to Kensington High Street for something. When I came back, there he was—and I was not by any means best pleased to see him there.

I should have disliked him for one thing if I had disliked him for nothing else—he was so deadly serious. I do not think I ever saw him smile. Indeed, I doubt if he had a smile left in him. He had no sense of humour, and, to him, a joke was as meaningless as double Dutch. He was bald at the top of his head, his face was as long as one's arm, his eyes generally had an expressionless, fishlike sort of stare, and, since he had assumed the garb of respectability, he was always attired in funeral black. He seemed to be under the impression that that was the only hue in which respectability could appear. As for his temper, it varied from doubtful to bad, and from bad to worse, and when he was in a rage, which he quickly was, he was by no means an agreeable person to have to deal with. He and Daniel were always falling out, and, until I came upon the scene, he used to ride over poor dear Daniel roughshod. But, when I did I let him understand that whoever fell out with Daniel fell out with me.

For my part, I did not wonder so much at his daughter's having run away as at her having lived with him as long as she did.

His hat was on one chair, his umbrella on another, he himself sat, with his hands clasped in front of him, on a little centre table, in an attitude which suggested that he was about to offer prayer. He did not rise as I entered—respectability has not yet worked such havoc with him as that. He stared at me as I went in, solemnly speechless, as if he wondered how I could venture to interrupt the meeting.

"Well, Mr. Haines, any news?"

I did not care if there was any news, but I did object to his sitting and staring at me like that.

"She is dead."

"Dead!—You don't mean it!—How do you know?"

"It was told me last night in a dream."

Among the rest of his little peculiarities, he was one of the most superstitious creatures breathing. In religion, I believe, he called himself a spiritualist. Anyhow, he was always seeing things, and hearing things, and having things revealed to him. Talking to him in some of his moods reminded one of that scene in Richard II. where the poor dear king wants to sit upon a gravestone and talk of epitaphs.

"Is that the only reason why you know that she is dead—because it was told you in a dream?"

"Do not mock at me. The voice which speaks to me in visions does not lie. I saw a coffin lying in an open grave, and 'Louise O'Donnel' was on the coffin-lid."

"You did not happen to see in which particular graveyard that grave might be located."

"I did not. But I know that she is dead. My daughter, oh, my daughter!"

I had to turn aside to smile. I grant that it was not a subject for laughter—but he was so funny!

"And as I looked the coffin-lid was lifted. And, on her breast, there was an open wound."

He rose slowly, painfully, inch by inch. He pointed with his right hand towards the floor.

"Woman, my daughter has been slain."

"Really, Mr. Haines, you are always seeing the most dreadful things in dreams. If I were you I should take less supper."

"It's not the supper. It's the spirit."

"Well, in that case, I should take less of that."

He frowned.

"You know very well what I mean. I am not speaking of the spirit of alcohol, but of the spirit of the soul. Now one task is ended. Another is begun. I will be the avenger of blood. Mine will it be to execute judgment on him who has destroyed my daughter's body, having first of all destroyed her soul."

"Jack Haines, what nonsense you do talk."

"What do you mean, woman?"

"My good man, do you think that you awe me by your persistence in calling me woman? I am a woman; but let me tell you in confidence that you strike me as only being part of a man!"

"You jeer at me. You are always jeering. You know not what you say."

"That is good—from you. Your style of conversation may have been suited to Strikehigh City, where they all were lunatics. But in London it is out of place."

"London!—bah!"

He threw out his arms, as if to put the idea of London clean behind him.

"Precisely. Then if it's London!—bah! Why don't you return to Strikehigh City?"

"I will finish the work which I came to do. Then I will return."

I had sat down on an easy-chair. I had crossed my legs, and was swinging my foot in the air. Old Haines stood glowering down at me, clenching his fists to hold his temper in. I looked him up and down. After all he was, every inch of him, a narrow-minded, cross-grained, hidebound New Englander.

"You are more likely to see the inside of a prison if you don't take care. You know, they manage things differently upon this side. Jack Haines, let me speak to you a word in season—a candid word. It may do you good. You killed your wife; I do not mean legally, but you killed her all the same. A prolonged course of you would be sufficient to kill any wife."

"Woman!"

"You drove your daughter from you. So unwilling was she to have it known that she was connected with you, that she took her mother's name. She called herself Louise O'Donnel. Under that name she came to England. Conscious that, even underneath her mother's name, you might trace her out in England, she has changed her name again. Under that new name she is deliberately hiding herself away from you."

"It is false."

"It may be. It is but a surmise. But, as such, it is at least as much likely to be correct as yours."

"She is dead."

"You have not one jot or tittle of proof that she is anything of the kind."

"I will have proof." He brought down his fist upon my pretty, fragile table with a crash. "I will have proof."

"Don't destroy the furniture."

"Furniture!" He glared at the inoffensive table as if he would have liked to have chopped it into firewood. "You should not anger me. I say that I will have proof. And I will have proof of who it is has murdered her. And I will find him, though he hides himself in the uttermost corners of the earth. And when I have found him I will have a quittance."

"What do you mean by that?"

"Do you not know what I mean? Have you known me so short a time that you should need to ask?"

"Do you mean that, if there is anything in these wild dreams of yours, you will kill the man who has killed your girl?"

He raised his hands above his head in a sort of paroxysm.

"Like a dog."

"Then let me tell you that you are treading the road which leads to the gallows. They manage things in their own way upon this side. Killing's murder here. And the more excuse you think you have the tighter you're likely to fit the rope about your neck."

"The hemp has not been sown which shall hang me on an English gallows. Do you think I am afraid?"

He gave me the creeps. Although it surpassed my powers to adequately explain the thing, I knew that he had a trick of seeing things which had taken place before they became known to other people. I had had unpleasant experience of it more than once. One might begin by laughing at what he called his dreams and his visions, but, in the end, the laugh was apt to be upon the other side.

It was quite possible that his girl was dead. Young, pretty, simple, innocent, alone in a foreign land—what more possible? It was even possible that she had been done to death. Some one might think that no one would miss her. In that case, that some one might as well at once place himself in the hangman's hands as wait to interview Jack Haines.

I was glad to be rid of him. He was not a cheerful companion at the best of times. But since he had got this bee in his bonnet he was more than I could stand.

In the afternoon I went to see Kate Levett. Kate and I had been together in Pfeinmann's "King of the Castle Operatic Combination." We were friends all through. I fancy it was a case of "a fellow-feeling makes us wondrous kind"—after a fashion we were girls of a feather. When the Combination came to eternal grief at Strikehigh City, we went different ways. I stayed where I was, Kate went East. It was at Boston she married Ferdinand Levett. He was touring at that time through the States as acting manager for a famous English comedy company. It was a case of marriage at first sight as it were. It proved to be the best thing Kate had ever done in her life. Levett turned out a regular trump, and they hit it off together to a T. Now they were settled in England, and, although Kate had kept off the boards, they were doing uncommonly well in a modest sort of a way.

When I turned up at their flat on the Thames Embankment, at the back of the Strand, Kate wanted me to stay and dine. So I stayed. After dinner we went to a theatre. Levett was at business—managing the Colosseum, so we went there. To finish up, we went back to supper at the flat.

I had gone originally to Kate with the idea of gleaning a little information. Before I left I had got all that I wanted, and, perhaps, a little more. What I wished to find out was whether Kate knew anything about a Mr. Reginald Townsend. She and her husband knew something about all sorts and conditions of men, and it struck me that my friend, the gentleman, was just the sort of man of whom one or the other of them might have heard.

I did not want to seem too anxious. So I just slipped my question in casually, as if I was indifferent whether I received an answer to it or not. I kept it till after supper. Kate was at the piano strumming through all the latest things in comic songs. I was lolling in a rocker, joining in the chorus whenever there was a chorus. Ferdinand was taking his ease upon a couch. We were all as snug as we could be. Kate had been saying she knew somebody or other, I don't know who, when I struck in.

"Between you, you two seem to know pretty nearly every one."

"Those whom we don't know are not worth knowing."

"Quite right, my dear!"—this from Ferdinand, on the couch.

"Have you ever heard of a Mr. Townsend?"

"What!—Reggie Townsend?"

She spun round on the piano-stool like a catherine-wheel.

"Reginald Townsend—that's it."

She and her husband looked at each other—in that meaning sort of way.

"Fred, have we ever heard of Reginald Townsend?"

Ferdinand laughed. She held out her hands in front of her.

"Why, my dear, there have been times and seasons when we've heard of little else but Reginald Townsend."

"Perhaps your man is not my man. My man's tall."

"So's our man!"

"And dark."

"You couldn't paint our man blacker than he is."

"And very—very swagger, don't you know."

"Our man's the swaggerest man in town. It's impossible that there could be two Reginald Townsends. What do you know of him?"

"Oh, I only met him once. But he rather struck me."

"Take care that he doesn't strike you too much. He's not only the swaggerest, he's also the wickedest man in town. I could tell you tales of him which would shock your innocent ears. He's a terror, isn't he, Fred?"

"He has rather liberal ideas on the subject of the whole duty of man."

"I should rather think he has."

And Kate went off at score. I could see from what she said that my friend the gentleman was all my fancy painted him. When she gave me an opening, I slipped another word in edgeways.

"Is he received in respectable society?"

"That depends, my dearest child, upon what you call respectable society. He's the boon companion of dukes, marquises, and earls, and that kind of thing. He visits the best houses and the best people. But I was raised at Salem, Mass., and our ideas of respectable society were perhaps our own. I haven't found that they obtain to any considerable extent round here."

It was scandalously late when I left for home.

The same thing occupied my thoughts in the cab as on the night before—my friend the gentleman. Whatever could have made him do the thing which he had done? That is, if Kate's Reginald Townsend was mine—of which, by the way, I had no doubt. A man may be all that's bad; he may be worse than a murderer, but he takes particularly good care not, if he can help it, to be the thing itself. What could it be which, in the judgment of a man in his position, had compelled him to place himself within the shadow of the gallows?

The problem occupied my mind. The man had been placed by nature in such a fortunate position. It appeared that he had so much to lose—and he had lost it all! What for? I wondered. What was it which had constrained him to choose between the devil and the deep sea—and then to choose the devil?

As I thought of it, and how handsome he was, and how well bred, and how there was everything to please a woman's taste, and to gratify her eye, a wild notion germinated in my brain—which was watered by circumstances, and grew.

I dismissed the cab at the end of my road. The night, though dark, was fine. The horse was tired. I had no objection to saving the creature's legs by walking the rest of the way. I did not suppose that, at that hour of the night, or, rather, of the morning, there would be any one about.

In supposing that, however, I was wrong.

The street was a pretty long one. When I got about half way along it I perceived that a cab was stopping at a house in front of me. As I reached the cab a man got out of it in a fashion which, to say the least of it, was rather sudden. He plunged on to the pavement, rather than stepped on to it. As his feet touched solid ground, he turned towards me.

It was Tommy Tennant!

For a moment I was frightened half out of my wits. It was such an hour, he was without a hat, he looked wild and dishevelled, his appearance at such a place—within a stone's throw of my own house—at such a moment was so wholly unexpected, that it fairly took my breath away.

But if his appearance startled me, my appearance seemed to have an even more startling effect upon him. He gave one glance at me and tumbled in a heap on to the pavement.

The driver of the hansom leaned down towards me from his perch.

"It's all right, miss; he's only been enjoying of hisself. The cold stones will cool 'is head."

I said nothing; I hurried on.

CHAPTER XXIII

MR. TOWNSEND COMES TO TEA

I have not lived in the world so long as I have done, and seen so much of it, without realising how small a world, after all, it really is, and how full it is of coincidence; but I do think that this beats all the coincidences of which I ever heard.

To think that I should have pitched on the one street in London which Mr. Thomas Tennant has chosen for a residence! It seems that I have. I lay awake for an hour trying to account for his sudden appearance from that cab. At last I hit on something. I sat up in bed with quite a jump.

"Can it be possible that he lives in this street?"

Rest was out of the question till I had made sure. I got out of bed—it was nearer five than four—and I tiptoed my way downstairs. I routed out a directory, and I hunted up the street. Sure enough he did. There was his name, as large as life—"Thomas Tennant." He lived at No. 29. My house was blank—it had been empty at the time the directory had gone to press—but I had taken No. 39.

"Well, this beats everything! To think that I have spent all this money, and come all this way, to plant myself five doors from Mr. Tennant!"

He might be unwilling to have me for a neighbour, but I could assure him that I was equally unwilling to have him. I did not wish the first entry on the fresh leaf which I had turned to be a reminiscence, and especially a reminiscence of that particular friend.

I thought that was strange enough, but stranger things were yet to follow. What a queer little world this is!

Recognising that it was no use addling my brains by puzzling out conundrums at that time of the morning, so soon as, by reading it over and over again in the directory, I had made quite sure that my eyes had not misled me, and that Tommy did reside five doors away, I toddled up to bed again. "There is nothing like leather," says the proverb. I say there is nothing like sleep. Give me plenty of sleep and I am good for anything. As I have always been blessed with a clear conscience—if there is a vacuum where the conscience ought to be it must be clear—and, what is equally to be desired, a good digestion, I have ever found sleep come at my bidding. Once I have my toes well down between the sheets, my head on the pillow, and the blankets well up to my ears, I snooze. I know I did just then. And I never dreamed; none of Jack Haines's lively visions came my way.

I looked at my watch when I awoke. It was past eleven. I just turned over. I had a stretch. I believe that, when you wake in the morning, it does you good to have a stretch; it seems to help you to realise that there is a piece of you between your head and your heels. "What should I do?"

"I'll have some tea."

I had some tea. The girl brought me the letters and the papers. There was nothing in the letters, but in the papers there were ructions!

At first I could not make out what it was all about. Directly I opened the Telegraph these were the words, in big, black letters, staring me in the face: "Murder on the Brighton Line." That was my friend, the gentleman! But at first, as I have said, the more I looked at it the more I couldn't make it out.

A platelayer—whatever that might be in connection with a railway line—going to his work in the morning had seen the body lying among the bushes—in that clump of bushes, I took it, where it had almost fallen on top of me. That was all right. Where I found the puzzle was in what directly followed. The girl had, of course, been murdered in the field, probably within a foot or two of where I had seen Townsend standing. The papers, or the people who inspired the papers, seemed to think that the murder had taken place in a train, and that then the body had been thrown on to the line. What could have made them think such a thing as that?

As I read on the whole thing flashed upon me; it was another coincidence!

It seemed that when the 8.40 train from Brighton had arrived at Victoria—the 8.40? Why, that was the train in which I had travelled with Tommy! My stars and bars!—it was discovered that the window in one of the carriages was shivered to atoms, that the carriage was marked with blood, and that it bore signs of having been the scene of a recent struggle.

Jerusalem! what was coming next? I had to put down the paper and take another drink of tea.

Nothing came next except what they called a "presumption," and if ever there was a piece of real presumption it was that same.

The presumption, according to the papers, was that the railway carriage had been the scene of a hideous tragedy—of a frightful murder, of one of those recurrent crimes, which force us, from time to time, to recognise the dangers which, in England, at any rate, are associated with railway travelling. The identity of one of the dramatis personæ—as poor, dear Daniel used to say, "I'm a-quoting"—was unfortunately, but too evident. There was the woman who had been found lying among the laurels—I wonder if they were laurels?—with her face turned towards the skies. As a matter of fact, she had lain face downwards. It was owing to that I had not seen her face. She was a silent but an eloquent witness—that was touching. The public demanded the prompt production of at least another of the dramatis personæ—"still a-quoting"—of the man—it would not, perhaps, display too much rashness to hazard the prediction that it would prove to be a man—who had hurled her there.

If that did not point to Tommy, I should like to know to whom it pointed.

I began to wonder. What had Tommy done when I had made my exit? Had he done nothing but twiddle his thumbs and stare? It would be characteristic of him if he had. He never did do the right thing at the right time if there was a wrong thing which could be done. The window might have been smashed by the banging of the door. I dare say that there had been signs of a struggle. I could not make out about the blood, but, perhaps, in the midst of his muddle, Tommy's nose had started bleeding. That was just the sort of thing his nose would do. It was quite conceivable, to one who knew him, that Tommy had toddled home without saying a word to any one about the lady who had tumbled out upon the line. If so—

If so, and I kept in the background, it was equally conceivable that, as a glorious climax to the muddle, because of that woman who had been found upon the line, Tommy might find himself in a very awkward fix.

I had to take another drink of tea.

I found what might turn out to be the top brick of the building while I was in the very act of drinking. Tommy himself might think that I was dead. I might have died. From a mere consideration of the odds point of view, I ought to have died. The miracle was that I wasn't dead. Tommy knew nothing about the woman who had been thrown on the top of me. He might think—he was capable of thinking anything, but in the present instance it was natural that he should think—that the body which had been found was mine.

If he did think so?

But he had seen me the night before. The fact rather supported my theories than otherwise. He had glared at me as if I had been a ghost. The sight of me had struck him senseless. According to the cabman, he was drunk. Knowing what he knew, or what he thought he knew, he might very well suppose that I was a creature born of his delirium.

It appeared to me that my cue, for the present, at any rate, was to keep sitting on the fence. I might still be even with Tommy, and that without having to move a finger of either hand. As for my friend, the gentleman—we should see.

Oddly enough, I came across Mr. Reginald Townsend that very afternoon. I had been shopping—shopping was about all there was for me to do; after Strikehigh City I found life pretty dull West Kensington way, but then I had expected it to be dull. As I was strolling homewards, who should I see but Mr. Reginald Townsend. He was a sight for sore eyes—at least, he was a sight for mine. I like to see a man that is a man—handsome, well set up, and dressed as only the thoroughbred man knows how to dress. I am not so particular about a man's morals as about his manners, and his manners were all they ought to be. From his bearing, as he stood there, in front of me, you would have thought I was the very person he had wanted to see and had expected to see. I don't believe that he had supposed that I was within a hundred miles of him. I should not have been surprised to learn that, until my actual presence recalled it to him, he had entirely forgotten my existence.

He was the sort of creature one finds amusing.

After poor, dear Daniel one liked to feel that one was connected with such a picture of a man. One liked to feel that he was doing credit to one's good taste as he was walking by one's side.

I asked him to come and have a cup of tea. He was delighted, or he professed to be. When I remembered the occasion on which I had first encountered him it seemed to me that, in his heart of hearts—or whatever it was that passed for his heart of hearts—he must wish that I was at the bottom of the sea. He could not like being reminded of Three Bridges Junction. But one can never tell. From his manner he might have met me first of all in Queen Victoria's drawing-room, and none but pleasant memories might have been connected with the meeting.

When we got indoors, who should I find in the drawing-room, sitting in solitary state, but Mr. Haines. The look he gave me! And the look he gave my friend, the gentleman! The old nuisance might have been my husband.

Mr. Townsend appeared oblivious of there being anything peculiar in the old worry's demeanour, and, fortunately, the old worry did not stay long, considerably to my surprise. I was afraid that he would make a point of outstaying Mr. Townsend. But it was all the other way. After he had tried to freeze us for about five minutes he disappeared.

"It's very odd," said Mr. Townsend, as soon as he was gone, "but I've either seen that gentleman before or somebody very like him. There's something in his face which positively haunts me."

I shook my head.

"Your imagination plays you a trick; it sometimes is like that. Mr. Haines has only been in England, for the first time in his life, for about a month. He was my late husband's partner. I fancy he is under the impression that I'm a little lonely."

"That is a complaint which may easily be cured."

"The complaint of loneliness?"

"You will be able to make as many friends as you desire."

"It is not so easy for a woman to make friends as you may, perhaps, suppose—that is, of course, friends who are worth the making. You see, I have ambitions."

"Ambitions?"

"Yes, ambitions." He looked as if he would have liked to have asked me what I meant, only he was too civil. "In my position I think I am entitled to have ambitions."

He still seemed puzzled. It did me good to look at him, to know that he was sitting there, to breathe in, as it were, the aroma of his refinement and his high breeding. I have always hungered for those two things in a man, and I have never had them. I could understand a woman's falling in love with my friend, the gentleman. For the first time in my life the idea of a woman being in love with a man became conceivable.

All too soon—for me—he rose to go.

"You will come again?"

"I shall only be too happy."

"Seriously, I mean it, Mr. Townsend."

"And equally seriously I mean it too. Our acquaintance was made in an informal fashion, but I trust that, in course of time, I may be able to induce you to allow the informality to stand excused."

"It will be your fault if you do not."

When he went an appreciable something seemed to have departed with him, and that although his voice, his presence, seemed still to linger in the air. I found myself touching the cup from which he had been drinking, even the chair on which he had been sitting, with quite a curious sensation.

It was very odd.

I believe that if I had been born with a silver spoon in my mouth, and the right sort of man to whom to attach myself, and to become attached to him, I should have been one of the best women in the world. I agree with Becky Sharp, that for a woman five thousand a year is something; but it is nothing, after all, without a man. Love in a cottage is a lunatic absurdity. Love itself may be all stuff. But there is something which, for all I can tell, may be akin to love. If one never knows it, life can never have its fullest savour. Perhaps, after all, for every square peg there may be a square hole somewhere in the world. If, when it meets it—it might; one can conceive that such meetings are—it cannot claim, and obtain possession, it will be hard upon the peg.

I had half a mind to tell the girl to put the cup which he had used aside and keep it free from the contamination of anybody else's lips until he came again. It would seem so silly. And yet—

Somebody came striding into the room. I turned. It was Jack Haines come back again. I almost dropped the cup, which I was holding, from my hand in my surprise. He was looking as black as black could be and his manners proved to be in full accord with his looks.

"Who is that man?"

"What man? What is the matter with you, Mr. Haines? I thought that you had gone."

"You know what man I mean—he who has just left your house."

"I am at a loss to know how it concerns you. That gentleman is a friend of mine."

"He is a thing of evil."

"Mr. Haines!"

"He is a shedder of innocent blood!"

Jack Haines was becoming really charming. I had always known he could be pleasant. I was only just beginning to realise how pleasant he could be when he tried.

"Mr. Haines, are you stark mad?"

"Woman!"

"Sit down."

He was raging like a wild bull about the room.

"Why should I sit down?" He threw up his hands. "I warn you against that man!"

"Sit down!"

I pointed to a chair. He sat down—I knew he would—and he looked as if he would like to eat me for forcing him to do it.

"Now, Mr. Haines, if you feel that you have, to a certain extent, mastered your excitement, perhaps you will be so good as to tell me what is the meaning of your behaviour."

"Nelly—"

"To you, Mr. Haines, I am Mrs. Carruth."

"Nelly, I say!"

In proof of his saying it, he stretched out towards me his clenched fist.

"Even at Strikehigh City, I did not think you capable of insulting an unprotected woman."

"I'm not insulting you."

"If you think not, then your ideas of what an insult is must be your own."

He rubbed his hands slowly up and down his knees. He stared at me hard. He shook his head.

"It's very hard; it's very hard. Between you and the girl, I'm suffering. The lines have fallen on me, and they're cutting right into my vital places." He brought his hands down upon his knees with a sudden thwack. "I asked you first, before even Daniel said a word to you; I laid myself at your feet."

"Was that my fault?"

He looked at me in silence. Then he drew the back of his hand across his brow.

"No; it was not your fault. I'm not blaming you. It was to be. Some men are made for women's feet to spurn." He paused. "Mrs. Carruth—since it is to be—I mean you well."

"Some people's meaning is very badly expressed."

"That's me. That's me all through—yes, right along. I ask you again, Who is that man?"

"Are you referring to the gentleman who has just been kind enough to come and see me? That is Mr. Townsend."

"Then Mr. Townsend is a thing of evil—he is!" He held up his forefinger to me with a warning gesture. I did not interrupt. "When I came near him I knew him for what he was. I saw right through. He is a whited sepulchre. I saw the blood gleaming on his hand. I could not stay where he was. I went outside, and stood on the corner of the street until I saw him go. And when I came back, I found that his presence was still with the house."

For my part I was glad that it was—if it was.

"This sort of talk, coming from you, is very ridiculous. Has your own life been so pure that you should attempt to blacken another man's character merely because he is my friend?"

"Pure? No; no man's life is pure. We are born to evil like the sparks fly upwards. But there's a difference."

"Pray, in what does the difference consist? I presume you have not forgotten that at least a portion of your record is known to me?"

He shook his head with dogged insistence.

"There is a difference. You know there is a difference. There's bad ones and there's bad ones; and Mr. Townsend's the sort of creature that no woman ought to have any truck with. He'll bite you if you do."

I got up from my chair.

"I am sorry this should have happened, Mr. Haines. I fear I shall have to ask you to come and see me more seldom than you have been in the habit of doing. I hope Mr. Townsend will be a frequent visitor. It would be pleasant neither for you nor for me for you to have to meet him, in my house, when you hold the opinions of him which you say you do."

He pressed his lips. He looked, if anything, sourer than ever.

"So Mr. Townsend is going to be a frequent visitor, is he? And how about Daniel?—and about me?"

I laughed.

"About you, Mr. Haines? I hope, Mr. Haines, that you will have a cup of tea."

He had one. And did penance in having it. For he hated tea.

And it was cold.

CHAPTER XXIV

WHAT MRS. CARRUTH SAW

All sorts of things have happened—past all belief. Tommy Tennant has been arrested for murder—for the murder of me! Those wise police! And Reginald Townsend is coming to dine.

But let us proceed in order. Each thing in its place, and one at a time.

To take two or three things to begin with. The muddle they have made about what happened at Three Bridges is, really, in its way, quite marvellous. And it all pans out so clean—or seems to—to those who are looking on. No one is talking of anything else, and some of them talk of it to me. It only wants Mr.

Townsend to favour me with a few remarks, and Tommy to add a postscript, to make me begin to think that I must be dreaming.

They have found the porter who saw me into the train at Brighton, and he has declared that the corpse is me! What a sweet creature that porter man must be! And they have found the porter who saw Tommy get out of the empty, blood-stained carriage at Victoria. But how they have found Tommy himself I don't, as yet, altogether understand. I know they have not found me.

I have had another sight of Tommy since the one on that first night—or, rather, so early in the morning. And, again, the manner of it was curious.

I have been in rather a predicament since I realised that Tommy and I were neighbours. There has been a certain delicacy about the situation. I might tell tales of him—he is married! I have seen his wife—such a pretty woman; but, unless I am mistaken, she wears the breeches! But they would not do him a tithe of the injury his tales would do me. And we women are so handicapped. The justice of the world is so unjust. A man may steal the horse, while we may not look over the hedge. Primitive civilisations are, after all, in certain respects, the best; but then they lack the very things we want!

I'm a widow—bonâ fide. I could put down as much hard cash, dollar for dollar, as many women who are famed for riches. I want to begin again. I have ambitions. I want to ruffle it among the best of them. Why shouldn't I? I have the qualities. So I have taken this highly respectable house in this highly respectable street, and furnished it in a highly respectable manner. I wanted to look about me—to find out where I am. I did not want to start with a splash, or folks would want to know who I was. And there are people who could tell them. For instance, Tommy for one. I want some one to launch me; some one fully equipped with the necessary equipment to give me a good send-off.

Tommy, if he liked, could spoil me. On the thin ice of my perfect respectability, at this stage of the game, I stand or fall; and, if I do fall, I fall right in. If I had known that Tommy and I were neighbours, I should have behaved in a very different fashion when I discovered we were fellow-passengers. I should have shown a spirit of Christian forgiveness; and, in excusing the past, I should have buried the hatchet. Tommy is a good-hearted creature, in his way. I could have easily induced him to hold his tongue, or even to assist me with a helping hand.

Now that boat is burned!

My first impulse, when I discovered that we were neighbours, was to fly before he made the same discovery on his own account. Had he chosen, he might have made my position absolutely untenable. While this mood was on me, I did my little best to conceal the fact. When I went out, I took care not to pass his house, lest he should see me from the windows. And the funny part of it was that the first time I did pass his house, he saw me.

The papers were full of the Three Bridges tragedy. The hue-and-cry was hot against the man who had travelled in that blood-stained carriage. What amazed me was his continued silence. It showed not only abject cowardice, but drivelling idiocy to boot. Anything was better—for him!—than keeping still. It was the Friday night. I had some letters to post. I had a headache. I felt that I must have some fresh air, or a change of air if fresh air was not obtainable; so I took them myself to the pillar-box at the end of the road. Doing so involved passing Tommy's residence. But it was dark; there was more than the suspicion of fog—the risk seemed small.

I went on the opposite side of the street. The fog was so thick that, when I had despatched the letters, it seemed absurd to take precautions.

"I'll stroll back past Tommy's. Why should I be afraid of him?"

I strolled. The fog appeared to be thicker every moment. The houses in the street, externally, were as like as two peas. I really found it difficult to find out exactly whereabouts I was. I was thinking of Tommy, and of how eagerly he was being hunted, and of what a sensation I might make by sending his address to Scotland Yard—when there he was in front of me!

Right close in front of me!

He was standing at the bottom of a flight of steps—his own steps—hatless, his hands in his trousers' pockets, as if, like me, he had come out to get a change of air. Suddenly he became conscious of my presence. He turned my way, and stared. The encounter was more than I had bargained for. It made me feel a trifle awkward. But the effect which it had on him was most astounding. The look which came upon his face actually frightened me—it's a fact! I had not thought that a human countenance could have been capable of an expression of such awful horror. To look at him—and I had to look!—made me go all cold. As I advanced, he went—automatically, I am sure—backwards up the steps, never removing his eyes from off me, the awful something that was on his face intensifying every second. At the bottom of the steps I paused—I had to; something made me. I don't know what he thought; but, as he saw me standing there, he made a convulsive movement backwards, went into the house, and banged the door.

I am cool enough as a rule. It takes something to put me off my balance. But I was off my balance then. The whole thing was so unlooked for, and seemed so strange; it unnerved me. When Tommy had gone I found that I was trembling.

But the incident was not by any means concluded.

When I had gone a few steps further on, I all but cannoned into what seemed to be a crowd of men, who, of malice prepense, were blocking up the pavement. What with the fog and my state of fluster, I did not perceive what they were till I was right upon them.

They were policemen.

My nerves were in such a condition of tension that, when I realised that fact, it was all I could do to prevent myself from screaming.

"I beg your pardon," I mumbled. "I did not see you."

"It's all right, miss," said a voice. "Pass on."

I passed on. But I had not passed on another dozen yards when, it seemed to me, by a sort of inspiration, I guessed what might have brought them there. What might have brought them there? What had?

Be the consequences what they might, I felt that I must stay and see what was about to happen. Turning, I went back a little way; and, keeping as much in the shadow as I could, I stood and watched.

A man, who was dressed in ordinary private clothes, went on in front. The policemen divided in two sections. Two of them followed closely on this man's heels. The rest went out into the road.

Just as I expected, the man in plain clothes passed up Tommy's steps. He hammered with the knocker at Tommy's door. The door was opened. He went in. The two policemen went in with him.

I knew that, even while I was standing watching there, Tommy was being arrested for the murder of me!

The confusion of my ideas filled me with panic terror. He had seen me not a minute back. He had only to tell the policemen so. They would come and find me there. There would be an end to all my dreams.

I rushed home. For the first time in my life I could not sleep. Indeed, I scarcely tried to sleep. All night I lay in agony. A thousand thoughts came crowding on my brain. I lost my self-control. I was half stupefied with fear. I wished that there were a hundred miles between my house and Tommy's. More than once, even in the middle of the night, I nearly made a bolt of it. I was so oppressed by the consciousness that he had only to send these policemen five doors along the street, and there was I.

But I did not lose every fragment of common sense. I did not become an utter fool. When the morning came, I was still there to see it out.

Next day I never moved outside the door. I bought all the evening papers. They were selling them in the streets all day. Tommy filled them all. "Arrest of the Three Bridges Murderer!" "Examination before the Magistrates!" They were shouting the words in the streets all day. It seemed that they had taken him to East Grinstead, wherever that might be, early in the morning, and brought him before the magistrates directly they got him there. To me the whole business was amazing. Why had he not told them at once that he had seen me, and put the police on my track? I was close at hand. They could scarcely have failed to find me. So far as he was concerned, there would have been an end of the affair upon the spot.

But Tommy's ways always were beyond my finding out.

What the newspapers called his examination was of the most perfunctory kind. The police simply said that they had arrested him, and he was remanded for a week.

And on Thursday Mr. Townsend was coming to dine.

CHAPTER XXV

MR. TOWNSEND'S DOUBLE

That Thursday was wet. It drizzled all day long. I was not feeling well. I had had trouble with one of my maids—caught her tampering with a lock, and sent her packing on the spot. Altogether I was feeling run down.

The best of us women get the blues at times!

Things were worrying me, as things will if one is not feeling quite the thing. I was almost disposed to tell myself that I had made a mistake in coming to England. After all, I should have done better by remaining on the other side. Here there were so many things which were against me—in England there is no mercy for the woman that repenteth. And getting myself mixed up in this business was scarcely a promising beginning.

The arrival of my friend, the gentleman, acted as a pick-me-up. It did a poor, nerveless creature good to gaze on so vivid a representative of sunshine and of strength. I was leaning back upon a couch when he came in—somehow his knocking at the door had set all my pulses twittering. It was with an effort I looked up and met his eyes.

He looked so well in evening dress—it was the first time I had seen him in it. When one has lived for years with savages one notices such little things.

"It is good of you to come to cheer me. I am so much in want of being cheered."

He laughed, retaining my hand for a minute in his.

"The want is common to us both. I am in want of being cheered as much as you—we will cheer each other." He sat down on a little easy-chair, which he drew in front of me. "I have only just returned from Devonshire, which is like coming from the sunshine into the night."

"Have you been there alone?"

"I have been staying with a friend—Sir Haselton Jardine."

Sir Haselton Jardine? Where, quite recently, had I heard that name? Of course! It was the name of the famous counsel. I had seen it stated in that day's paper that he was to be retained by the Crown to prosecute Tommy.

I wondered if that item of news had come Mr. Townsend's way.

"Sir Haselton Jardine? Is that the lawyer?"

"Yes. I suppose he's the greatest barrister at the Bar just now."

"Didn't I see that he was going to have something to do with this murder there's all the stir about?"

I had to let it out—I could not help it. So far as any effect which the allusion had upon my visitor was concerned I need not have tried. He never turned a hair. I was watching the white hands, which were resting on his knee. Not a muscle quivered.

He replied to my question without a moment's hesitation, and in his ordinary tone of voice.

"He tells me that he's going to prosecute. He seems rather eager about the business, too. If the chap is guilty I don't fancy Jardine will let him slip."

I was still for a moment. I looked into my visitor's eyes with wonder, and—I don't mind owning it—with admiration. This was the sort of man it was worth one's while to know—he was a man.

"Don't you think the affair is rather an odd one?"

"Very odd, indeed—and not the least odd part of it is that I know this fellow Tennant very well."

"No!" I was startled.

"I do. He's a stockbroker. He's done a good deal of business for me. Unless I am mistaken, he is, or was, almost a neighbour of yours."

"I know. He lives five doors down the street. But fancy your knowing him. It seems so strange."

He made a little movement with his hands.

"In this world it is the strange things which happen."

"That is true."

As I sat there, looking at him, I realised how true it was with a vividness of which he probably had no notion. This man was a study for the gods. His attitude of perfect unconcern was not acting, it was nature.

I felt that, having gone so far, I must go farther.

"Do you think he's guilty?"

"It seems almost incredible. He always struck me as being one of the pleasantest and most inoffensive little chaps alive."

"Every one seems to think he's guilty."

He smiled.

"Every one's an ass."

"Suppose he were to be found guilty, and was hanged, and all the time he was innocent; how dreadful it would be."

Another little movement with his hands.

"It's the way of the world. The innocent are always being hung. Half the time we guilty ones go free."

This was a man. I went still further.

"Do you know that we met each other, for the first time, on the night which the murder happened?"

"Am I likely to forget it?"

"Thank you. It's very kind of you to say so. But do you know that we must have met each other quite close to what they call the scene of the tragedy."

"I believe that we were within half a mile of it."

"And it must just have happened."

"Probably within twenty minutes of our meeting. By all of which you will perceive that our acquaintance in the beginning was cemented with blood."

What did he mean? What kind of creature was he? I really began to wonder.

We went in to dinner, for which, by the way, he already had given me an appetite.

I had seen a good deal of men—of all sorts and conditions of men!—but I never saw a man who came within measurable distance of Mr. Reginald Townsend in the exercise of that very rare, and wholly indescribable gift, the gift of fascination. I should say that he would have been a favourite alike with men and women—I will stake my bottom dollar, as poor, dear Daniel would have said, that he would have been popular with every woman. To me the average "fascinating man" is a monstrosity. He so obviously bears his honours thick upon his brow. He so plainly tries his hardest to live up to them. There was nothing of that sort about Mr. Townsend. The charm was in him; it would come out of him whether he would or he would not. He was not conscious of it. There was no sign of effort. There was no effort. He was always natural, always completely at his ease. He could not help but give you pleasure. You yourself did not notice the glamour of his manner and his presence till, as it were, it had compassed you about.

Nor were his powers of fascination decreased by the fact that he was the best bred, the best dressed, the most graceful, and the handsomest man I ever saw.

This sounds like tall talking. But it is not. I am no tall talkist, especially where men are concerned. It is the simple truth. My friend, the gentleman, was a man in twenty millions; any woman would have been proud to own him.

I felt this very strongly, with a tendency to personal application, before the dinner was through. His conversation did me good. He talked as if he had been brought up in the same cradle with all the leading members of the British aristocracy. There was nobody who was anybody whom he did not seem to know, male and female. To listen to him talking was like reading the Almanach de Gotha and the Court Guide bound up together. Only it was better, and a deal more satisfying.

He began to speak of a particular friend of his, one Lord Archibald Beaupré, in a way which set me all of a tremble.

"I will bring Archie to call on you—if I may."

This Lord Archibald Beaupré was a son of the Duke of Glenlivet, and, so far as blood went, not very distant from the Throne itself.

"I shall be very glad to see him, or, indeed, any of your friends. Is this Sir Haselton Jardine, with whom you have been staying, a married man?"

"He is a widower."

"Has he any family?"

"He has a daughter."

I don't know what there was in his tone, but there was something when he said "He has a daughter" which made it almost seem as if he had slapped my face. I felt almost as if he had taken my breath away. I found myself echoing his words.

"A daughter? I see."

There was silence. Something seemed, all at once, to have taken the heart out of the conversation. It floundered, fell flat; seemed, for a time, to die. I knew very well what that something was just as plainly as if it had been told to me.

It was that daughter of Sir Haselton Jardine.

It may seem odd. I had never seen the girl. I had never heard of her before. But, all the same, I hated her right then. She spoilt my dinner. That's a fact. And, straight on the spot, she made me stand to arms.

I knew he loved her. And it made me feel—well, I had never thought that a little thing like that could have made me feel so queer.

I had meant to talk to him about my plans for the future. To have asked his advice upon points on which I wished him to think I needed it. I wanted to beguile him into showing interest in what I had set my heart upon, until he had drifted, though but a little, into the current of my affairs. But, somehow, after all, I did not seem to care to try. At least, not then. I let him go.

He was very nice. I was conscious that the man was almost like a woman in the quickness of his intuition. That, if it came to shooting I should have to move like lightning to get my shot in first. That he would detect any intended movement towards my gun even before the intention was wholly formed. And instinct told me that he was aware that I had perceived the intonation with which he had said "He has a daughter," and that it rankled. I do believe that for the first time in my life I had given myself away. And to a man. But this man could read the stars. And after dinner, he was particularly nice, because he happened to have read them.

After he was gone I sat for ever so long in the drawing-room forming plans. The first wild notion had come to me before. I gave it form and fashion then. I, too, would buck the tiger. Why not? Who would have more cause than I? It is a peculiarity of my constitution that, whatever the game, I always play better when the stakes are high.

I would win my friend, the gentleman. I would go the limit every time until I did.

In winning him I should win all. Everything my soul desired. At a single coup, the game.

First of all, I should win the man. He was well worth winning—just the man.

Then I should win social recognition. By becoming Mrs. Reginald Townsend I should be spared years of struggling—struggling, too, which might only bring failure at the end. He wanted a clever wife, and he should have her. He wanted a good wife, and he should have her too. He wanted a wife who believed in him; he would never meet one who believed in him more than I did. He wanted a wife with money; probably there was not in England half a dozen possible women who had as much as I had. Given a wife who had all these things I doubted if there was a drawing-room in which he could not make her welcome—from the Queen's own drawing-room, downwards or upwards. Practically he could place Society—with a big S!—at her feet, to do with as she chose.

To think of it! What a realisation of one's dream. What a short and what an easy cut to the Kingdom of the Blest!

Again, in making him the captive of my sword and of my bow, I should be giving one to the daughter of Sir Haselton Jardine. That, also, would be worth the doing. To dislike any one is a mistake. I reminded myself of that over and over again. But I knew I hated her.

As to whether I should be able to win him—on that point I had no shadow of doubt. It was true that the overtures might have to come from me, but they should come. And when they came they should come in a guise which he would find resistless.

Or we should see!

I slept very well that night—soothed by my own fancies. I remember very well that, when I was in my bedroom, just before I got between the sheets, I looked at the hand which he had held in his, and, just where his hand pressed it, I kissed it. It was a silly thing to do, but it did me good.

I wondered if, when he had held her hand in his, she was silly too. But, no doubt, she had freehold rights—or she thought that she had freehold rights—to what was much better worth the kissing.

Never mind! But bide a wee!

Days slipped by. At his next examination before the magistrates things began to look very black indeed against poor Tommy. I suppose the witnesses supposed they spoke the truth—so far as I could see, there was no possible cause for their wishing to do otherwise. But how they lied! Unconsciously, we will hope, and in their haste. It was becoming plainer and plainer that unless something, as yet wholly unsuspected, turned up in his favour, Tommy bade fair to hang.

Well, I have seen a man hung on suspicion of stealing a horse, and directly he was hung the horse in question has turned up underneath the thief that really stole him. As Mr. Townsend observed, sometimes it seems as if the innocent were born to hang. If everything in life were certain, where would be the sport, and what would be the use of betting?

It is the element of chance that makes the game!

One afternoon something happened which struck me as being distinctly curious. It was after lunch. I was thinking of taking the air. I had just gone into the drawing-room for a moment, when there came a knocking at the door.

"Now, who's that, I wonder?" I stopped the servant on her way to answer the door. "Eliza, let me know who it is before you say I'm in."

I knew who it was directly she opened the door. It was no good telling him that I was not in. He did not even ask. He came himself to see. It was old Jack Haines, and with him was a stranger.

It was the stranger who made me open my eyes. I had to stare. For he was—and yet he wasn't—the living, breathing image of my friend, the gentleman. He was Reginald Townsend, with a difference. And the difference—which was all the difference—was this: Reginald Townsend was a gentleman; this man was emphatically quite another kind of thing.

And Jack Haines treated him as if he was quite another kind of thing. He treated him as if he had been nothing but a cur, and the man bore himself as if he was used to being treated like a cur.

Mr. Haines strode into the middle of the room. He pointed to the stranger.

"You see this creature?"

It was an awkward sort of introduction. I scarcely knew what to make of it. The more I looked at him, the more I wondered who the man could be.

"He's a detective—a private detective. That's what he calls himself. If he is, he's the English kind. When first I landed on this darned old island I went to him, like the fool I was, and I said, 'I want to find my girl.' And he said, 'I'm the man to find her.' And I said, 'You are?' And he said, 'You bet. It's only a question of money, that's all it is.' And that's all it has been ever since—a question of money. That's the only time he told the truth. If you knew the amount of money he's had out of me you would laugh. He kept thinking that he's found a clue, and wanting twenty pounds to find out if he'd found it, and every time he got that twenty pounds he found out he hadn't. And now he thinks he's found another clue, and I've brought him along with me in here to find out what sort of clue he thinks he has found."

The man coughed behind his hand. He puffed out his chest. He drew himself upright. He tried to think himself a man.

"You are severe, Mr. Haines, uncommonly severe. Even detectives are but fallible. But, on this occasion I do not only think I have a clue, I am positive—quite positive."

"What's the figure?"

"Figure? Expenses—merely!"

"And what's the clue?"

The man seemed a trifle fidgety.

"I am afraid that I am scarcely in a position at present—"

Mr. Haines cut him uncivilly short.

"Stow that! You don't touch a nickel till you tell me what's the clue."

The man cleared his throat. He looked round and round the room, as though looking for the clue. Mr. Haines's inquisition seemed more than he had bargained for.

"As you are aware, Mr. Haines, I have searched all England for Miss Louise O'Donnel."

"Judging from the amount of money you've had I should think you've searched all Europe."

Again the stranger cleared his throat, as if he deprecated the allusion.

"You probably have it in your recollection that at one time I believed that I had traced her to Liverpool. Circumstances have recently occurred which have brought to me the knowledge that in so believing I was right. She is in Liverpool."

Mr. Haines began to tremble like a leaf. I saw how easily this man, or any other man, could play upon what seemed to have become the dominating passion of his existence.

"Whereabouts in Liverpool? Tell me that!"

"Unfortunately, at this moment, that is beyond the limit of my power. But this I will undertake to do. If you are disposed to expend a further sum of fifty pounds I will undertake to place you in communication with her within, yes, certainly, within fourteen days."

"You swear it?"

The man threw himself into an attitude which he, no doubt, intended to be sublime. "As one gentleman to another I undertake, sir, to do what I have said."

"You shall have your fifty pounds. I will go and get it. Stay here." Mr. Haines turned to me. "Do you mind my leaving him here while I go and cash a cheque? I want to give him the money in your presence, and on conditions which you shall hear."

"I have no objection."

I had not. Indeed, I had been wondering how I might find the opportunity to ask the man a question which should be entirely between ourselves. Whether he was as willing to be left alone with me as I was to be left alone with him, is more than I can say. He ought to have been. Mr. Haines took me at my word. He stamped through the hall and from the house. The stranger and I were tête-à-tête.

He did not seem to be exactly at his ease. Mr. Haines had not offered him a chair. He seemed to think that he would like one. Indeed, he said as much.

"With your permission, madam, I will sit down."

"I would rather you did not."

He was about to act on his own suggestion when my words arrested him. He seemed disconcerted, looking at me as if wondering what it was that I might mean. I went on, "Of course you are lying again?"

The man drew himself up with what he intended to be an air of dignity.

"Lying?—Again?—Madam! May I inquire what you mean?"

"Pray don't put on that sort of air with me. I understand you very well, my man. You are too common a type not to be understood. Of course, you are lying again and of course I shall tell Mr. Haines so when he returns." He looked as if he felt that in exchanging Mr. Haines' society for mine he had made a change for the worse. "Or, rather, I shall tell Mr. Haines unless you give me satisfactory answers to the questions I am about to put to you."

"I assure you, madam, that, as a gentleman—"

"Stop! Confine yourself to answering my questions. On your answers will depend whether or not I shall keep silence. What is your name?"

CHAPTER XXVI

ANNOUNCED!

The man twiddled his hat round and round between his hands, as if he sought inspiration from its brim. I sat and watched him. He was a poor kind of scamp. He was so easily nonplussed.

"My name, madam? Yes." He struck himself with the palm of his hand upon his chest, affably, as it were. "My name is Trevannion—Stewart Trevannion."

"Have you ever heard of Mr. Reginald Townsend?"

Mr. Trevannion went all of a heap. He looked at me like a startled rabbit. He turned, as if to obey an impulse which suggested that he should make a rush from the room. But he thought better of it. Instead, he put his hand up to his chin, appearing, all at once, to be plunged into a sea of contemplation.

"Townsend? Townsend? No! I don't seem to remember the name." He glanced at me out of the corner of his eye. He saw that it would not do. "Stay. I had a client of the name of Townsend—he was a merchant in the West Indies—but his name was John."

"You won't get that fifty pounds."

Again he drew himself up, with an attempt at that air of dignity which he seemed so anxious to assume.

"I haven't the honour, madam, of being acquainted with your name—excuse me, you must permit me to conclude—but I have to assure you that you appear to altogether misunderstand my character."

After all, Mr. Trevannion was amusing. I laughed at him.

"I should be sorry to do that. In proof of it, if you could manage to tell the truth, just once in a way, should it not be too great a strain upon your constitution, I shall be happy to add twenty guineas of my own to Mr. Haines's fifty."

He appeared to be more startled than ever. This time his amazement seemed to be of a pleasurable kind.

"How much?"

"Twenty guineas."

"Honour?"

"Straight."

He adjusted his coat upon his shoulders.

"I'll do it. Hanged if I won't. Why shouldn't I? I'm not afraid of him! He's nothing to me! What is it that you desire to know, madam—for your twenty guineas?"

"Have you heard of Mr. Reginald Townsend?"

"I have."

"I thought you had. What relation is he to you?"

"Relation?" He sought for inspiration from the ceiling. "Cousin."

"Cousin? I see. You're sure he's not your father?"

"Father? No, certainly not! Absolutely not! There's not the slightest ground for any presumption of the kind."

"You won't get the twenty guineas."

"Madam!"

"Lied again."

"I will be candid with you, madam. I will tell you the truth. Why should I conceal it?" Mr. Trevannion shot his cuffs. They were a trifle soiled. "The fact is that, for reasons of his own—what they are I have not the slightest notion! I think it possible that they may not be wholly to his credit! Mr. Reginald Townsend does not appear anxious to advertise the particular degree of consanguinity which binds us to each other—or, rather, which ought to bind us to each other—because, as a matter of fact, so far as he is concerned, with me affection never dies! I never can forget that the same heart nourished us both!—the binding is merely theoretical I'm his brother—his elder brother—and, as such, qualified to take my place beside him in all the salons of the land."

He looked his brother. I had guessed he was a sort of Corsican brother from the first. He was like a caricature—all alive, oh!—of my friend the gentleman; reminding me of nothing so much as a picture I once saw in "Cassell's Popular Educator." It was called "The Child: What shall become of Him?" On the top line they showed you portraits of the child at various periods of his life, as he advanced towards honoured age. While, on the bottom line, were portraits of the child, also at various periods of his life, as he advanced towards the other kind of age. Mr. Trevannion recalled the portraits of the child advanced towards the other kind of age.

While he still continued in the pose which he had done his best to strike, and before either of us had spoken again, Mr. Haines came in.

Mr. Haines made short work of this brother whose affection did not die. He counted nine five-pound notes and five separate sovereigns on the table.

"There are fifty pounds. You mark it?"

"I certainly do observe that there appear to be fifty pounds."

"Appear to be! There are!"

Mr. Haines raised his voice to a roar, which made Mr. Trevannion jump.

"Exactly—as you say—there are."

"You can have that fifty pounds on the understanding that you undertake to place me in communication with my girl within fourteen days. If you don't, next time I find myself in communication with you I'll have value for my fifty pounds. You hear?"

"While you continue, Mr. Haines, to speak so loudly, I can hardly fail to hear."

Mr. Haines covered the money with his hand.

"Swear that you will find my girl for me within fourteen days."

I had noticed Mr. Trevannion's eyes begin to glisten directly the money appeared. He seemed to fear that he might find such an oath a little difficult of digestion. Still he swallowed it.

"I swear."

Mr. Haines turned to me.

"You hear? He says he swears." He removed his hand. "Take the money. If you're lying to me again, when next we meet there'll one of us have fits."

Mr. Trevannion took the money in rather a hurry, as if he feared that, after all, Mr. Haines might change his mind.

"I may truly say, Mr. Haines, that I never saw a father's love which equalled yours. It is a rare, noble spectacle. It will be my pride, as well as my pleasure, to restore, in the shortest possible space of time, your child to her father's arms."

"Mind you do."

Mr. Trevannion had disposed of the money. He turned to me.

"Eh, madam, might I have the pleasure of saying one word to you in private?"

"Certainly not."

He seemed surprised.

"With reference to that little matter—"

I interrupted him.

"Mr. Haines, if you are finished with this person might I ask you to relieve me of his society?"

Jack Haines chose to fly into a rage.

"What the devil, sir, do you mean by wanting to speak in private to a lady who's a friend of mine! Outside!"

Mr. Trevannion went outside, Mr. Haines accompanying him to the door to see him go.

The very next day the Corsican brother obliged me with a call—my friend, the gentleman. He came accompanied by a friend—none other than that Lord Archibald Beaupré, of whom he had spoken.

My lord was long and thin and a little weedy. His hair was sandy, and parted, with mathematical exactness, precisely in the middle. It would not be many years before he went bald. His eyes were light blue—the kind of eyes which not only suggest a bad temper, but a senseless temper too. It is excusable—though foolish—to fly into a fury about something. But people with those sort of eyes are apt, when they feel that way disposed, to get into a rage about nothing at all, and to go blind with passion when they are at it. Milord's manner was very well. Only he struck me as being the least bit condescending—as if he was conscious of what a well-born man he was.

It was very kind of Mr. Townsend to bring him, and so I told him.

By the way, all the time I was looking at Mr. Townsend, I could not help my thoughts travelling to Mr. Stewart Trevannion. How alike they were, and yet how different. How came the two lives to be lived on such different roads? Sometime it might be worth my while to improve my acquaintance with Mr. Trevannion. One might acquire from them a scrap or two of gossip which might prove useful by and by.

Could this man ever be like that man? I doubted it. This had what the other had not—the courage of Old Nick. He would never crouch, whatever else he did.

But, as I was saying, it was very kind of Mr. Townsend to bring his friend. Although there was something about the fashion of his introduction which, instinctively, put my back up. I wondered what he had said to milord before he came. Nothing could exceed Mr. Townsend's courtesy, but I had a kind of suspicion that he was seeking to recommend his friend to my notice as a substitute, as it were, for himself. I almost felt as if he were throwing us, with all the delicacy and grace conceivable, at each other's heads. I could have sworn that he told milord, before he brought him on the scene, that I was a rich American widow, and that he had dropped, perhaps, something stronger than a hint that I was just the sort of woman whom it might be worth his lordship's while to marry.

If he had, he had thrown his hint away. He was trying to travel along the wrong line of rails. That bird would not fight. There was only one man's wife I meant to be, and he was himself that man.

They went away together. When they had gone, somehow or other I felt a trifle sore. I was beginning to get into a funny frame of mind. I was half disposed to feel that I should be willing to get my friend the gentleman—to get just him, and nothing more. I had never thought that I should fool like that for any man; or that I could. It puzzled me.

Things went on worse and worse for Tommy. At the close of his next examination before the magistrates, he looked as much like hanging as any man cared to do. As I read, I could scarcely believe my eyes. I stared and I stared. I almost began myself to believe that he must be guilty—that I must be dead. It just showed that things are not always what they quite seem.

A new witness went into the box. He said his name was Taunton. I soon saw that if Tommy was to be hanged it would be Mr. Taunton who would hang him.

It was Mr. Taunton, after all, who had given the police the office. It was he who had delivered Tommy into their hands. He had travelled in the same train with Tommy from Brighton. He had been in the next compartment. He had heard all the argument. And, from what he said, he must have been listening for all that he was worth.

But there! When I read all that was in the paper, I gasped for breath. In imagination I already saw the rope round Tommy's neck.

Who would have thought that it ever would have come to that?

Two or three days afterwards I received a shock. I was looking through the morning paper when I came upon a paragraph which sent all the blood running out of my finger-ends—or it seemed to. It was in the column of daily gossip. Here it is:—

"An engagement is announced between Mr. Reginald Townsend, one of the best known and most popular society figures, and Dora, daughter and only child of Sir Haselton Jardine. We understand that the marriage will take place very shortly. This announcement will be received with the wider public interest in view of the position of counsel for the Crown which Sir Haselton Jardine will occupy, should Mr. Thomas Tennant have to stand his trial for the Three Bridges murder. It is understood that the trial will be set down for the next Lewes Assizes. In that case the judge will be Mr. Justice Hunter."

When first I saw the thing all that struck me was the bold fact of the engagement—that it was announced. On a re-perusal, it began to occur to me that the announcement was rather oddly worded. It might almost have been done with malicious intent. Beginning with marriage, it ended with murder.

A comfortable juxtaposition!

What was more, there seemed to be more murder in it than marriage. The stress seemed to be laid upon the murder. Certainly the impression likely to be left upon the imagination of the average reader was a combination of blood with orange blossoms.

I wondered who had inspired the paragraph in that peculiar form, and what would be my friend the gentleman's sensations if, as I had done, he should chance to happen on it unexpectedly.

But, still, the engagement was announced.

That thing was sure!

The more I thought of it, the more I went all hot and cold. No wonder I had hated her directly he had told me that such a creature was in the world. Her name was Dora! What a name! It sounded Dolly. It must be her money he was after. He could not care for a woman with a name like that. She must be brainless!

Well, other women had money; and brains as well.

So the newspaper man had been given to understand that the marriage was going to take place very shortly. Was it? A marriage was going to take place very shortly. But not that one. We should see!

I pranced about the room; I worked myself into a rage. I felt that I must have it out with some one.

And I had. I had it out with Tommy's wife!

It was all that paragraph.

The day before a servant had offered herself as a candidate to fill the place of the one I had dismissed. She referred me for her character to her late mistress. When she told me who her late mistress was I stared. It was Mrs. Tennant. It occurred to me, very forcibly, that one of Tommy's servants would hardly do for me. Things might get about, and tales be told. I gave her application scant consideration.

Now, in the middle of my rage, it struck me that here was an opportunity to get rid of some of it—on some one else's head. I might bait Mrs. Tennant. I could pretend to go and ask about the servant's character, and give the servant's mistress one, just by the way. I went and put my hat on, and made myself look as nice as I knew how, and off I trotted there and then.

I thought it more than possible that I should not be admitted—in her position some people would have declined to see strangers on business of any sort or kind. But I was. At the door they asked my name and what I wanted. When I said I had come about a servant's character, I was shown into a sitting-room. And presently in came Tommy's wife.

Directly I saw her I knew I had made a big mistake. I perceived at a glance that she was not anybody in particular—I mean that she was not a lady, or much to look at. She was just a woman. But, all the same, I knew that if I tried to close with her the odds were that I should get a fall.

She was just that kind!

She waited for me to begin. So I began—quite a thrill going through me when I realised that I was actually talking to Tommy's wife.

"I have called about a servant named Jane Parsons." She moved her head—the motion was scarcely equivalent to a bow. "She tells me that she was in your service. She has referred me to you for a character."

"I have nothing to say against the way in which Jane Parsons performed her duties."

Her voice was of that peculiar kind which you never hear issuing from between the lips of any but an Englishwoman, and from but few of them. Sweet, soft, gentle, yet incisive and clear. It may seem ridiculous—one can only speak of one's own experience—but I have never known it to be a possession of any but a good woman. It is apt, when I hear it, to have a most absurd effect upon me—for some occult reason, which I do not pretend to understand, it makes me go ashamed all over.

"May I ask why she left you?"

She flushed, though very slightly; and, perhaps unconsciously, she drew herself up straighter. I saw that, unwittingly, I had rubbed against a raw.

"Did she not tell you?"

Jane Parsons had not told me. I said so, though I did not think it necessary to explain that I had got rid of her before she had had a chance to get as far.

She hesitated, as if mentally selecting the fittest words.

"Jane Parsons left me because I was in trouble."

At once I perceived my opportunity. I saw what it was she meant, though I pretended innocence.

"In trouble? Indeed? Was there illness in the house?"

"There was worse than illness. To do Jane justice, I do not think she would have left me merely because there was illness in the house."

"I am afraid I do not understand."

Mrs. Tennant smiled—very faintly, and not with joy.

"It is immaterial. The point is, I did not discharge the girl. She left me of her own accord. I should have been glad to have kept her. She is sober, clean, honest, and industrious. As good a servant as I should wish to have."

I pretended to look at a little memorandum book which I took from my purse.

"Your name is Tennant—Mrs. Tennant?"

She nodded her head, still faintly smiling.

"My name is Tennant."

"I perceive that the names are similar; but I take it that, in spite of the similarity, you are in no way connected with the Three Bridges murderer?"

The shot sped straight home. She went red all over, then white as a sheet. Her lips trembled. I thought for a moment that she was going to cry. But she didn't.

"I don't know what it matters to you or how it concerns a servant's character; but I am the wife of the Mr. Thomas Tennant who is being wrongfully accused of murder, but who is wholly innocent of any crime." Then, with what was very like a hysterical outburst, she added, "He is the dearest and the best husband in the world."

"Dear me!" I rose from my seat. I went to the door. "I had no notion that you were in any way connected with that dreadful creature, or I certainly should not have troubled you. To think that you can be the wife of such a man! Of course it is altogether out of the question that I could knowingly engage a servant who had lived in such a house as this!"

Without waiting for her to summon a servant to escort me to the door, I showed myself out into the street.

I had given her one. But now that I had done it I was not by any means proud of the gift I had bestowed. Indeed, when I got indoors I could have bit and slapped and scratched and pinched myself—and worse. Women are cats. There is no doubt of it. Especially to each other! I know it, to my sorrow, of my own experience. If there was one thing on which I had always prided myself, it was that—at any rate, in that respect, I was not like other women. Whatever else I was, I was not a cat.

And now I had been the cat of all the cats!

And all because of that stupid paragraph in that stupid paper.

When I thought of that pale-faced woman, with her sweet, true mouth, and brown eyes, and of all the trouble she had to bear, and of how I had gone out of my way to add to the bitterness of it all, and to rub it in, I could have banged my head against the wall.

But there! the thing was done. And when a thing is done—especially a thing like that—it is not the least use being sorry. One may as well pretend that one is glad. And, after all, the engagement was announced. And why did they announce it, if they did not want to drive me into a rage?

Poor Tommy! He bade fair to have the most to suffer. After his next examination before the magistrates, they committed him for trial. According to the newspapers, it would take place almost immediately. Things were moving fast. It was time that I should move as well. It was time that I should come to an understanding with my friend the gentleman.

So I wrote to him to come and see me, putting a touch or two into my note which I knew would bring him.

And he came.

CHAPTER XXVII

MR. TOWNSEND IS MADE TO UNDERSTAND

I wondered if he had an inkling of what it was that I might have to say to him. He showed no signs of it. But one could not tell. I felt, instinctively, that his intuition was every whit as keen as mine. While as for his appearance of perfect ease, it clothed him like a skin.

As he lounged in an easy-chair I drank in, as it were, the atmosphere of his grace and elegance and charm of manner. I felt that I was going to enjoy myself. I believe that the fighting instinct is the strongest instinct that I have. I knew that, at least, for once in a way, I was going to cross swords with a foeman who was worthy of my steel.

I began to play with him, as a preliminary to the earnest which was to follow.

"I hear that I am to congratulate you, Mr. Townsend." He made a slight movement with his hands—it was a pretty little trick he had. "I understand that you are about to make a change in your condition of life. You are about to be married."

"In that respect I do deserve your congratulations, for if ever there was a marriage which, to one of the parties at any rate, promised all that the heart of man could desire, it is that on which I am about to enter. Therefore, Mrs. Carruth, I do solicit your congratulations."

He looked me straight in the face as he said this, a smile peeping from the corners of his lips. The first score had been with him. And I felt he knew it.

"I saw that the engagement was announced."

"I know that it was announced—I believe at the suggestion of Sir Haselton Jardine."

"It was rather an odd announcement, the one I saw."

"Odd? In what way?"

"Perhaps the oddity was also part of Sir Haselton Jardine's suggestion."

"What was there peculiar about the one you saw?"

"Well, there was a little about the marriage, and a good deal about the murder."

"What murder?"

"The Three Bridges murder. It seemed to me to be rather a funny mixture. It was not so much an announcement of the engagement as of Sir Haselton Jardine's connection with the murderer."

"His connection with the murderer?"

"As counsel for the Crown."

"I'm afraid I don't quite follow your meaning."

"No? Really?"

He got up.

"I fear, Mrs. Carruth, I must tear myself away. I have an appointment which I am inclined to think is already overdue."

"You mustn't go. Did I not tell you in my note that I have something which I particularly wished to say to you? Have you forgotten? I am coming to it now."

"I am but too disposed to yield to temptation, Mrs. Carruth, being fully conscious of how good it is of you to say anything to me at all."

He said that kind of thing with an easy assurance and an exquisite grace, which seemed to rob it of its banality. Resuming his seat, he continued to look me straight in the face. He gave me no lead. I had to make one for myself.

"It is about the murder."

"The murder? Every one seems to be talking of that!"

"Are you going to let Mr. Tennant hang?"

To look at him one would not have imagined that he understood me in the least.

"I am afraid that that is an issue which scarcely rests in my hands. I wish the poor chap well. I don't know that there is anything else that I can do for him. Is there any talk of a petition being got up in case he is convicted?"

"You see, I saw you do it."

"You saw me do—what?"

He asked the question as coolly as you please.

"The murder!"

It might have been my fancy, but I thought that a sort of greyness passed for a moment over his face, and that the pupils of his eyes came to a point. But certainly he showed no other signs of discomposure.

"I suppose, Mrs. Carruth, that you are jesting?"

"I have been jesting. I jest no more."

He watched me for some seconds with anxious scrutiny.

"What am I to understand you to mean?"

"You are to understand that I saw you commit the murder with which Mr. Tennant stands charged."

He continued to examine my face. Reading as much of it, I suppose, as he desired to read—which, possibly, was more than I intended. Not the slightest shadow of a change took place in his own. Having concluded his examination, he got up from his chair. He went to the fireplace. Leaning his elbow on the mantelboard, he stood looking down into the burning coals.

To judge from his demeanour, what he had just now heard possessed only the smallest personal interest for him.

"Where were you?"

"I was on the bank. You almost threw the lady upon my head."

"Really?" He positively smiled. "How do you know it was I?"

"I saw you. You stood on the other side of the hedge and stared at me."

He glanced up from the fire.

"Did you rise up, like a sort of accusing spirit, from the middle of the bushes?"

"I did. That kind of thing was enough to make any one rise."

"How very odd! Do you know, I took you for a ghost. You gave me a horrid fright. I took to my heels, and ran for my life."

"I know you did. I saw you start off running."

He laughed softly. He seemed to find the thing amusing in a way which began to strike me as a bit uncanny. His gaze turned to the fire.

"Do you know, I thought that you were that kind of woman from the first?"

"What do you mean? That I was what kind of woman?"

"I mean nothing disagreeable, on my honour. Only I thought that we might be sympathetic."

His words or his manner, or both together, cut me as if he had struck me with a lash. So far he seemed to be doing all the scoring. I was silent. I still would bide my time. He went on—

"By the way, how came you to be upon the bank?"

I hesitated. Should I tell him anything? And, if anything, how much? I knew that he was watching me. I decided to be frank.

"I fell out of the train."

"What train?"

"I was in the same compartment with this Mr. Tennant. We had a discussion. In the course of it I fell out."

"While the train was moving?"

"Yes. It was a miracle I was not killed. As a matter of fact I fell among some bushes, and was not even scratched."

"You say that you fell out. Do you mean that you fell out with Mr. Tennant's help?"

"He had nothing to do with it. It was a pure accident. He may have thought that he had, but he had not."

"Is it possible that he thinks you were killed?"

"It is extremely possible. When that body was found I believe he thought that it was mine."

"This is very curious; but if he saw the body he would know it was not yours."

"Would he see it? Taking it for granted that it was mine, he would not want to see it, and would they compel him to see it against his will?"

His tone was contemplative.

"I suppose they wouldn't—no. So, if he is found guilty, and is sentenced to be hung, he will actually go to the gallows under the impression that he deserves his fate. I never heard of anything so curious."

It occurred to me that not the least curious part of the situation was the fashion in which he appeared to regard it from the point of view of a mere outsider. He continued to gaze at the fire. Presently he smiled again.

"And now may I venture to ask you why you have told me this extremely interesting scrap of news?"

"Because I intend to save the life of an innocent man."

"How?"

"By laying the real facts of the case before the police."

"Unless I do what? I suppose there is something I can do to save myself. Otherwise you would have laid the real facts of the case before the police before."

"There certainly is a way by which you can constrain me to silence."

"Oh, yes; there are several ways of doing that."

Something in his tone caused me to grasp the revolver which I had slipped into my dress pocket. I had not known how he might take what I had to say. I had thought that it might be just as well that I should come prepared.

"You need not fondle that pretty little pistol of yours. I was not thinking of that way, I assure you."

The man's quickness of perception verged upon the supernatural.

"It is a matter of indifference to me whether you were or were not thinking of it. I am not afraid."

"I believe that you are not."

"I am not. You are wrong in saying that there are more ways than one of constraining me to silence. There is but one."

"And that is?"

"You may save yourself from the law by the law, and, so far as I am concerned, only by the law."

"Explain yourself."

"According to the law of England, on a capital charge, a wife may give no evidence against her husband."

Unless I was mistaken, he slightly started. Anyhow, his elbow came off the mantelboard and his arm fell to his side. There was silence.

Presently he returned his elbow to its former place upon the mantelboard.

"I see."

It was an ejaculation, rather than anything else. To the best of my judgment his face was expressionless as a mask. But I could not see his eyes—he kept them flamewards. Next time he spoke he confined himself to the utterance of a monosyllable.

"Well?"

"So far as I am concerned, that is all."

He stood up straight. He faced me, turning his back to the fire.

"May I ask why you wish to marry me?"

"I? It is you who wish to marry me, surely."

He regarded me with unwavering eyes.

"Let us be frank with one another. Why do you wish to marry me?"

"I am not conscious of having expressed any wish of the kind. I merely suggest that if I were your wife, in time, your neck would be saved. Otherwise—"

I allowed the sentence to remain unfinished.

"I am not a prize in the matrimonial market."

"I have not inferred that you were. However, that is a question of the point of view."

"And your point of view is?"

"You have certain things I want."

"As for instance?"

"You have position—I have money."

"What sort of position do you imagine me to have?"

"You have the entrée to the best society in England."

"It does not follow that I can give that entrée to my wife."

"If you have a particular kind of wife, it does."

"And you would be that particular kind of wife?"

"I should. I have sufficient brains, sufficient looks, and sufficient money."

"What is your idea of sufficient money?"

"I can spend, say, between forty and fifty thousand pounds a year, and still economise."

For the first time, he evinced genuine surprise. I thought I had him; but I had not.

"Between forty and fifty thousand pounds a year? No. Then why do you live in such a place as this?"

"If you have any doubts as to the existence of the money, I shall be happy to give you ample proof, not only that my income is considerably over the larger of the two sums which I have mentioned, but also that it is certain to increase."

"Then you are a rich woman, even as riches go. You might have your choice of the best partis in England. You would have no difficulty in marrying a man who really has what I only have in your imagination— family and influence. For instance, there is Archie Beaupré. He has some of the bluest blood in England in his veins. He has just the things you want. Why not marry him?"

"If I did, you would hang."

He smiled. It seemed to me that this time his smile was a little strained.

"Again I am compelled to ask, why do you wish to marry me?—me, in particular?"

"I will hint at a possible reason—one which may commend itself to you. You said, just now, that when first you saw me something told you that we were sympathetic. That something told you aright—we are."

I had hit him at last. Something came into his face and eyes which said I had. It stayed only for a moment. But it stayed long enough to show that, under that expressionless mask, there was a volcano raging.

"You certainly are an unusual type of woman."

"Precisely; and you are an unusual type of man. We approximate."

He laughed out loud. But, to my ear, there was something in his laughter which was scarcely gay.

"But, my dearest lady, you are aware that I am already engaged to be married?"

I shrugged my shoulders.

"I have seen something about it in the papers."

"And now you hear it from me as a fact. There are circumstances as connected with my engagement which render it certain that, if by any overt act of mine, it is ruptured, I shall be ruined, I shall forfeit my reputation; I shall lose, entirely, and for ever, what you say you want—that fragment of a position, which in reality is all that I possess."

I simply tilted my chair backwards, pressed the tips of my fingers together, and smiled at him.

"I have enough money to buy it back again—all that you are likely to lose, and more. I would not allow any consideration of that kind, if I were you, to frighten me. Besides, I think that, perhaps unconsciously, you exaggerate. However, don't let us carry the discussion just now any farther. The great thing is that we understand each other. Should I remain a free agent, or, in other words, should I not be your wife, in time, I shall do my utmost to save the life of an innocent man."

"What do you mean by being my wife in time?"

"Within eight-and-forty hours of the jury bringing in a verdict of guilty against Mr. Tennant."

"Poor wretch! Then, I take it, you do not require a promise from me now?"

"Neither now nor at any other time. From first to last the matter is purely one for your own consideration. It is your affair, not mine. There are such things as special licenses. I believe one can get married within twelve hours. By the way, Mr. Townsend, I want you to do me a favour."

"If I can. What is it?"

"I want you to get me a ticket for the trial."

He started—really! The start was unconcealed. There was no mistake about it.

"The trial? Do you mean for Tennant's trial?"

"I do."

"Do you propose to be present?"

"Certainly."

"What for?"

"It will be so funny."

"Are you meditating active interposition?"

He eyed me as if he would have searched out my inmost soul. His anxiety—obvious at last—amused me.

"My dear Mr. Townsend, you may take my word for it that I shall stand, literally and exactly, to every syllable I have uttered. You need be under no apprehension of my interposing in the trial. I shall do nothing in the business, of any sort or kind, until eight-and-forty hours after Mr. Tennant has been found guilty. What I am to do then rests, as I have explained, with you. You will be able to obtain the ticket I require from your friend, Sir Haselton Jardine."

The keenness of his scrutiny relaxed. Possibly he deemed it wiser to pretend that he was satisfied, even if he was not.

"If I can get you a ticket, you shall have one. I think I have read somewhere that, on a question of taste, there is no room for disputation." He smiled—his natural smile once more. "And now, dear Mrs. Carruth, let me assure you that I am very sensitive of the compliment which you have paid me and of the still greater honour which you would do me. Of my own unworthiness I am but too conscious. But I would ask you to let me tell you frankly—since frankness is the order of the day—that, were it not for the ramifications and complications of my unfortunate position, I should long ere this have been at your feet, upon my knees. I protest that, more than once when in your presence, I have experienced the greatest difficulty in keeping myself upstanding."

I laughed. How the man could lie! With what a grace!

We parted the best of friends.

CHAPTER XXVIII

THE PRISONER COMES INTO COURT

I got the ticket, and I went to the trial.

I travelled in the same train with the judge. At Victoria, as I was standing at the carriage door, a little old gentleman, of the beer-barrel type of architecture, went toddling by. He wore gold spectacles, he had a very red face, a double chin, and big, pursy lips—the sort of old gentleman one would have liked to have smacked on the back.

Another old gentleman was standing near me. He was tall and thin. When the little old gentleman went toddling by this other old gentleman moved his head in the toddler's direction and his arms in mine.

"Judge Hunter."

I was most benign.

"Indeed! Is that Judge Hunter?"

"Going down to Lewes Assizes; been spending a day in town."

That was a Monday. Of course, the day before had been Sunday. But what the man meant is more than I can say.

The thin old gentleman and I shared a compartment. He fed me with scraps of information by the way.

"Good judge, Hunter. He has one qualification which a good judge ought to have."

"What is that?"

"Been a bit of a rogue himself."

"Is that a qualification which goes to the making of a good judge? Then what a number of good judges there must be."

The thin old gentleman smiled.

"I don't mean in a criminal sense, you understand. He's not been in prison, and that kind of thing. But Hunter has not lived exactly the life of a saint. In the case of a judge a fellow-feeling ought to make one wondrous kind."

"I see."

It was a delightful journey. The sun was shining; the air was warm and sweet; the country through which we passed seemed lovely. Perhaps I was in the mood!

As we rattled through Three Bridges Junction the thin old gentleman recommenced his process of feeding me with titbits of information.

"This is where the murder took place."

"Is that so?"

How different it looked in the sunshine!

"Just about there"—he was pointing through the window of the carriage—"is where they found the body."

I wondered if he was right. I, myself, had the vaguest notion. I had not been in a position to make a mental map of my surroundings. It struck me that it must have been a little farther on; to me, at the time, it had seemed to be a good distance from the station. But then I had to allow for the rate at which we were moving. I had walked along the line.

"It was a dreadful thing—dreadful! It makes one's blood boil when one thinks of it. I do hope that, this time, no false sentimentality will be allowed to interfere, and that they will hang the man."

I had become used to hearing that sort of remark. Everybody seemed to be taking it for granted that Tommy was guilty. I could but acquiesce.

Lewes seemed to me to be a charming town—all up-hill and down—though I must confess that there was a little more up-hill than down. And all so old! I do so like a town to be old. Of course one would never dream of living in it, but it is so nice to visit.

The assizes were not to open till the Tuesday. Tommy's trial was not expected to begin till the Wednesday. So I had time upon my hands. I was truly rural. I went to Newhaven—a horrid hole!—and across the road to Seaford—which was much of a muchness. And I lived on the Lewes Downs. What a breeze there was up there! And what a view! And I saw the prison—the outside of it, I mean, not the inside. It was built right on the edge of the downs—rather cool in winter, I should think.

I came on a warder. He was smoking a pipe. I suppose he was taking the air. He was a big man, with a huge red beard and one of the best-humoured faces I ever saw. I wondered what he did with his good-humour when he went inside. I should think it must have been against the prison rules to take it in.

We foregathered. He was affability itself. He pointed out the various parts of the prison.

"That is the debtors' wing, that is; that's where we keep the hard-up 'uns. A chap can't earn five-and-twenty shillings to pay his poor rate, perhaps, so we spend ten pound over locking him up. That's a pretty game, that is. I've never been able to make head or tail of it myself. But, of course, it's no affair of mine. Those are the convicted wards. We haven't got enough prisoners of our own to keep the place properly going, so they send us a few down from town—some of the worst they've got. Nice ones some of them are. That's the chapel. Oh, yes, we have a regular daily service; we couldn't get on without one, could we?—twice on Sunday—Protestant and Catholic. They're very particular, some of 'em, about their religion. We chaps don't do much in the service. All our time's took up in looking after the boys; and the worse a man is, the more he likes his bit of chapel. That's where we keep the prisoners who are awaiting trial—Tennant's in there."

"Indeed! How very interesting! And what sort of a man is he?—I suppose he's a dreadful man?"

The warder began combing his beard with his fingers.

"Not a bit of it; don't you think it. He's as decent and nice a chap as ever you'd wish to meet."

"Don't you think he's guilty?"

"Oh, I don't know nothing at all about that. Some of the very worst murders ever I have known have been done by some of the very nicest chaps ever you met—when you come to talk to 'em, I mean. I don't know how it is, but so it is. He'll be hung—safe to. That's where they'll hang him. You can't see it from where we are, but there's a little yard in there where they build the gallows. I expect I shall have the charge of him in the condemned cell. I generally do have. I've hung 'em before to-day; but it's not a nice job."

Poor, dear Tommy! It made me go queer all over to hear the man talk of him like that. What a funny world it is? Or is it the people in it who are funny?

When the trial began the court was like a theatre. I got in early—for reasons of my own. I wanted a particular place, and succeeded in obtaining the object of my heart's desire.

I had had a peep in at the court on the opening day of the assizes. What I wanted was a position in which I should not face the prisoner. I found that the prisoners were placed in a sort of railed enclosure. Their feet were about on a level with the lawyers' heads. On one side of this enclosure was a kind of pew. So long as the occupants kept their seats it was impossible for any one in the enclosure to even guess at their identity. I soon saw that a seat in this pew was exactly what I wanted. If I wore a thick veil, and made certain changes in my attire, Tommy would never dream that the woman whom he was charged with having murdered was actually sitting within reach of his hand, a spectator of the trial.

When I reached the court the usher—or whoever it was—wanted me to sit on the bench, on a line with the judge and immediately facing the prisoner's dock. He assured me that that part of the court was specially reserved for ladies who were ticket-holders, and that it was quite impossible that they could be allowed to sit anywhere else. This impossibility I rather doubted, and when I presented him with two beautifully bright, new yellow sovereigns he seemed to doubt it too.

"I don't want to be conspicuous," I explained. "I just want to see everything without being seen."

Nothing could have possibly been truer or more reasonable. Possibly those two sovereigns aided that usher to see both the truth and the reason. Anyhow, he showed me into actually the seat I wanted.

Very soon the place was crowded. No end of ladies graced the bench. Some of them must—unlike modest little me!—have come to be seen as well as to see. Certainly they were dressed for show. The court wore quite an air of fashion.

Among the crowd, but not on the bench, was Tommy's wife. She came in with an elderly lady and gentleman, whom I took to be her father and mother, or else Tommy's—I could not make my mind up which—and a younger gentleman, who still was pretty well on in years. I had no doubt that he was Tommy's solicitor. As Mrs. Tennant came in two of the barristers, who were sitting among a heap of others at a table, stood up and shook hands with her. I found out afterwards that, as I suspected at the time, they were Tommy's counsel. Somebody must have known who she was, because, directly she appeared, quite a buzz of whispering went round the court. The women on the bench leaned towards each other, and stared and did everything but point at her. They might have been ladies—gentlewomen, as my old mother used to have it, they were not. She removed her veil and looked at them—just once, and that was all. She looked very sweet and pale and troubled, but grit to the finger-ends.

Other counsel were sitting cheek by jowl with Tommy's counsel. One of them, turning as Mrs. Tennant entered, looked her keenly up and down. He was an ugly, mean-looking, colourless, bloodless little man. His robe, or whatever they called the thing he wore, was different to the others—it was of silk. I wondered what he was.

Suddenly there was a stir in court. Somebody appeared like an undertaker's mute—only he wasn't a mute—from a door at the back.

"The judge."

Everybody rose to their feet. In waddled the fat little fellow I had seen in the train. He reminded me, somehow, of the comic man in the burlesque. He had on an enormous wig, about sixty yards of what, from where I sat, looked like some sort of scarlet blanketing, and—as if that wasn't enough!—fur. He presented a dreadful spectacle. Goodness knows that he had a red enough face of his own! They might have put him in white.

There was some rubbish which I did not understand—and did not want to. It was some time before I could take my eyes off the judge. He was something to stare at. The more I looked at him the more I wondered what they would do if the man was struck with apoplexy. To me the risk of something of the kind, which he seemed to be running, was simply awful.

Then they swore in the jury. Among them were some of the stupidest-looking men I ever saw. If they were married it was a pity they could not have sent their wives, and they themselves have stayed at home. There must have been more sense somewhere in the family.

Then somebody said—

"Bring in Thomas Tennant!"

A hush came over the court. All eyes were turned in one direction. I, alone, did not dare to turn to look. There were movements behind me, then all was still. I noticed that Mrs. Tennant had removed her veil again, and had turned round in her seat and was looking at some one whom I could not see—looking at this some one with a smile.

I knew that she was looking at her husband, and that Tommy was going to be tried for the murder of me.

As I sat there, scarcely daring to breathe, staring straight in front of me, yet seeing nothing, my thick veil obscuring my features, my hands tightly clasping the knob of my umbrella, I was experiencing the most singular sensation I had ever known.

It was worse than stage fright, by a deal.

CHAPTER XXIX

THE TRIAL BEGINS

I am not able to describe all that took place. To begin with, everything that happened seemed to me for some time to be happening in a dream. When, afterwards, I read the account in the newspapers, it came to me with all the force of novelty.

The fact was that, for ever so long, it was all I could do to prevent myself from swooning and making a scene and spoiling it all.

It seems funny that, after having gone so much out of my way, and taken all that trouble, I should have been such a goose; but I was.

When I begun to have my wits about me I found that the mean-looking little man who had so keenly eyed Mrs. Tennant was making a speech. Then I understood, not all at once, but by degrees, that he was counsel for the Crown, that he was opening the case for the prosecution, and that, in short, he was Sir Haselton Jardine.

So this was the father of Mr. Townsend's Dora!

Well, if the daughter in any way resembled the father, I could not say much for Mr. Townsend's taste.

But the thing was out of the question. I was certain that he did care for her, and it was altogether impossible that he could care for a woman who in any way whatever resembled this shapeless, pulseless, mummified little man. I knew my friend, the gentleman, too well. I felt persuaded that, as regards resemblance, or rather want of resemblance, to her father, Dora Jardine was one of nature's eccentricities.

It seemed odd when I did begin to come to myself, to notice how the people hung upon every word which the little man was uttering—and they had to hang if they wished to hear. He seemed to be speaking in a whisper. His voice matched his appearance and his size. After one had listened for awhile, however, one began to realise what a singularly penetrating whisper it was. He never raised his voice; he made not the slightest attempt to produce an effect. He spoke as one could fancy a machine might speak, yet each syllable must have been audible to every person there.

And probably his speech, as a whole, produced a strong impression on every one who heard it. I only heard—to understand—the concluding words, but I know that when he sat down I felt as if the first string of the rope which ultimately was to bury the man behind me had been woven before my eyes.

"Call Samuel Parsons!"

Samuel Parsons proved to be a big, shock-headed man of the navvy type. He was not examined by Sir Haselton Jardine, but by another barrister, who was as big and blustering as Sir Haselton was small and quiet.

Samuel Parsons was a ganger. He had been walking along the up line to his morning's work, when he saw something lying among the bushes about half-way down the bank. It was a woman. She was dead. He described the position in which she lay, and exactly whereabouts he found her.

Tommy's counsel asked no questions.

A policeman followed. He had been informed that a woman had been found dead on the line. Went to see her. Described the position in which she lay. Was informed that she had not been touched before he came. She was quite cold. Was well dressed. Her clothes were wet. It had rained earlier in the morning. There was nothing about her to show who she was. Examined her linen later; there were no initials or marks on it of any kind. Her pocket was empty.

Again Tommy's counsel asked no questions.

A porter came next—Joseph Wilcox. He was examined by Sir Haselton Jardine. Joseph Wilcox was a pleasant-faced young fellow, who gave his evidence with a degree of assurance and an air of conviction which—considering what his evidence was—took me aback. If ever there was a witness who seemed convinced of the truth of his own testimony, Joseph Wilcox was the man. And yet—

Well, this is what his evidence amounted to:—

He was the porter who had shown me into Tommy's carriage when the train left Brighton. I had not noticed him. Indeed, I remembered nothing at all about him. He declared that he had noticed me particularly. He should have known me again if he had seen me anywhere. Asked what had made him notice me, he said because I had come running up just as the train was starting, and—this with something of a blush—because I was so good-looking. I ought to have blushed, but I did not. Asked to describe me, he gave a pretty glib and pretty clear description of a woman who was not in the least like me.

I wondered what impression Joseph Wilcox's ideas of my personal appearance made on Tommy. I guessed that they did impress him, because presently a scrap of paper was handed from the dock to the counsel in front.

Asked if he had seen me since, he said that he had. He had gone to East Grinstead, and had seen me in the mortuary, dead. Had he the slightest doubt that the woman he had seen in the mortuary dead was the same woman he had shown into the carriage?

He had no doubt whatever.

He said this with an air which, I am persuaded, impressed every one who heard him with the conviction that there was no doubt.

I wondered what Mr. Wilcox's feelings would be if he ever came to learn that he had done his utmost to hang a man by the utterance of as great a lie as ever yet was told.

Sir Haselton then asked him if he had noticed if there was any one in the carriage into which he had shown me. There was—a gentleman. He had occasion to notice him because he had been leaning out of the carriage window talking to two other gentlemen who had come, apparently, to see him off.

"Should you know him again?"

"I should." Mr. Wilcox pointed towards the dock. "This is the gentleman."

"You are certain of that?"

"I am quite certain."

As Sir Haselton sat down I felt as if he had woven another strand.

Tommy's counsel rose.

I found out afterwards that his name was Bates, M.P., Q.C. He was tall, well-built, grey-headed. His wig suited him. He had a bold, clear voice, and a trick of standing with one hand under the skirt of his gown and the other pointed towards the witness.

"You appear to have noticed this unfortunate woman very closely, Mr. Wilcox. Can you tell us something else which you noticed about her?"

"In what way?"

"Did you notice, for instance, if she had been drinking?"

"I did not."

"Can you swear that she had not been drinking?"

"There was nothing about her which made me suppose that she had."

Mr. Bates sat down. If Tommy had told him that I had had too much to drink he had told as big a story as was ever told.

"Call George Baxendale!"

Mr. Baxendale was the first gentlemanly-looking witness who had appeared in the box; he was also the one who seemed to be least at his ease. He was a tall, fair, slightly built man, with long, drooping moustache, the ends of which he had a nervous trick of twisting. He glanced towards the dock with what he possibly intended to be a friendly smile. The distortion of his visage, however, which actually took place, more strongly resembled a ghastly grin.

He was examined by Sir Haselton's colleague.

"Are you related to the prisoner?"

"I am related to his wife. I am Mrs. Tennant's cousin."

This explained the ghastly grin.

"Do you remember Sunday, the 8th of November?"

"I do."

"Where were you?"

"I was at Brighton, staying with some friends of mine."

"Did any one come to see you on that day?"

"Yes. Mr. Tennant."

"By what train did he return to town?"

"By the 8.40."

"Have you any particular reason for remembering that it was by that train he returned to town?"

"Well, for one thing, Jack Cooper and I went up to the station to see him off."

"What happened while you were at the station seeing him off?"

Mr. Baxendale told of my getting into Tommy's carriage. He answered the questions which were put to him as if he was desirous of giving as little information as he possibly could, which did not make it better for Tommy. He had not noticed me particularly. Did not think he should know me again. Had seen the body at East Grinstead. Had not recognised it. Could see no likeness. Still, it might be the same woman. Could not swear that it was, or that it was not. Had really not taken sufficient notice of the woman who had got into the train.

His questioner sat down, leaving an impression on the minds of the people that if the witness had not been Mrs. Tennant's cousin some of his questions would have received different answers.

Mr. Bates stood up.

"About this woman of whom we have heard—was there nothing about her which you noticed?"

"There was."

"What was there about her which you did notice?"

"It struck me that she had been drinking." The witness became voluble all of a sudden. "She seemed to be in a state of excitement, which, probably, was induced by drink. She certainly was not a lady. She struck me as being a woman of a certain class. In fact, I was just going to suggest to Tennant that he should get into another compartment, when the train was off."

"Why were you going to make that suggestion to Mr. Tennant?"

"Because I knew that he was a shy, nervous sort of fellow, who easily loses his presence of mind, and I thought that, cooped up in a compartment alone with a woman of that sort, who was in that condition, without a stoppage before he got to town, there might be unpleasantness."

"You thought it probable that she might annoy him?"

"I thought it extremely probable."

When Mr. Bates sat down, the other counsel once more got up. He proceeded to turn Mr. Baxendale inside out.

He could not swear the woman had been drinking. He only surmised it. Could not exactly say what caused him to surmise it. She was excited. That might have been owing to her anxiety to catch the train. Women do get excited when they are flurried. She might have been a lady. Had no groundwork of fact for his suggestion that she was a woman of a certain class. It was quite true that, as he had said in his examination-in-chief, he had not noticed her. Should not like to swear that she was not a teetotaler and a lady of the highest birth and breeding. In fact, he should not like to swear to anything at all. He might get down.

He got down, looking badgered.

I owed him one.

He was followed by the Mr. Cooper with whom he had stayed at Brighton. Mr. Cooper was a short, thick-set man, looking just what he was, a captain in the navy. His manner was self-contained; his answers short and to the point.

He had accompanied Mr. Baxendale to see Tommy off. Had seen me get into his carriage. Had scarcely glanced at me. Should not know me again. Had seen the body at East Grinstead. Could not say if it was the same woman. Was not qualified to express an opinion.

Mr. Bates asked no questions.

Next came a porter, John Norton. He had an anxious, careworn face, and grizzled hair. His manner was tremulous. He kept fidgeting with his cap. More than once he had to be asked to speak up. He was examined by Sir Haselton Jardine.

Was a porter at Victoria Station. Remembered the 8.40 from Brighton coming in on Sunday, November 8th. It was due at Victoria at 10 p.m. Noticed a gentleman sitting alone in a first-class carriage. It was the prisoner. Noticed he was holding a white handkerchief to his cheek. There were red stains on it, as of blood. Was going to open the carriage door when a gentleman jumping out of the next carriage opened it instead. When he passed again the gentleman was standing at the door of the compartment speaking to the prisoner. Prisoner was holding another handkerchief to his face—a silk one. Presently the prisoner and the gentleman went off together. Passed the carriage again immediately afterwards. Saw something lying on the floor. Found it was pieces of glass. Found that the carriage was in disorder. There were stains of blood on the cushions and the carpet. The window, in front of which the prisoner had been sitting, was down. On pulling it up, found that the glass was smashed to pieces. Gave information to the guard. Efforts were made to find the prisoner, but he had left the station. Was certain that the prisoner was the man he had seen sitting in the empty carriage.

Mr. Bates asked no questions. I wondered what was the defence he intended to set up. If he was going to do nothing more to earn his money than he was doing at present, it seemed to me that Tommy might as well have kept it in his pocket. Here was Sir Haselton Jardine twisting the rope tighter and tighter round Tommy's neck, and Mr. Bates seemed to be doing nothing at all to stop him.

I would have asked John Norton questions.

The guard of the train came next. John Norton had called his attention to the broken window. He corroborated what John Norton had said as to the condition of the carriage. He had noticed that the alarm bell appeared untouched. Nothing had attracted his attention on the journey. The compartment in question was in the next coach but one to his, but he had heard nothing. Sounds would have travelled in his direction. Still, it was difficult, when there was a wind, and the train was going at a high speed, to hear what was taking place in the next coach but one; for instance, if there were two persons quarrelling. At the same time, if any one had screamed at all loudly he could scarcely have failed to hear that. His hearing was very good. The compartment looked to him as if somebody had been having a fight in it.

Again no questions from Mr. Bates. So far, Tommy could have managed equally well without his help.

Though it is true that that is saying little.

CHAPTER XXX

MR. TAUNTON'S EVIDENCE

"Call Alexander Taunton!"

He came not, though they called.

Instead there was an interval for refreshment. A buzz of talking rose in the court. With one hand the judge pressed his spectacles more firmly in their place. He took a bird's-eye view of the proceedings.

"I think," he observed, "that before taking the evidence of the next witness, it might be convenient if we were to adjourn for luncheon."

So we adjourned. At least, some of us did. The prisoner was taken away. I heard them removing him behind me. Most of the counsel removed themselves, and some of the people. The greater part of us who stayed set to eating. Sandwiches were produced and other things. Mysterious refreshments were brought in from without. I had my own little store. Everybody chattered. It was quite a festive scene.

"Call Alexander Taunton!"

Proceedings recommenced by a repetition of the words. But again he did not come.

"Alexander Taunton!"

One heard the name shouted by different voices, apparently in different passages and at different doors. Still none answered. The delay ruffled the judge's feelings.

"What does this witness mean by keeping the court waiting? Where is he?"

Sir Haselton Jardine's colleague rose with the apparent intention of personally assisting in the search.

"Here he is," said some one.

And there he was. I almost dropped from my seat.

Who should get into the box but Reginald Townsend's Corsican brother, Jack Haines's private detective, who had told me that his name was Stewart Trevannion.

I could scarcely believe my own eyes at first. But it was the man—if one had seen him once, there was no mistaking him. To me he seemed to be peculiarly ill at ease—an uneasiness which was not by any means concealed by an attempt to carry things off with a flourish. He bowed to the judge, he bowed to the jury; I believe he was going to bow to the lawyers too, only at the last moment he changed his mind. He placed his silk hat on the rail at his side. He took off one of his brand-new gloves. Unbuttoning his overcoat, he opened it so as to display his chest. There was something about him which destroyed the effect he evidently intended to produce—it made the people smile.

The judge was serious enough.

"What do you mean by keeping the court waiting?"

Alexander Taunton—or whatever his name was—pressed the finger-tips of his left hand against his chest.

"I beg your lordship's pardon. I had just that moment stepped outside."

I could have wagered he had stepped outside to drink just another drop to help him to keep his courage up. The more I looked at him the plainer I saw that there was quite a hunted look about his eyes.

The story he told in response to Sir Haselton Jardine's questions filled me with something more than amazement. Of course he was the Taunton whose evidence at the examination before the magistrates one had read in the papers, but I had never for an instant suspected—who would have done?—that the two men were, or could be, one and the same. By the time he had finished he had hammered every nail in Tommy's coffin. And the strangest part about it was that—as none knew better than I—certainly the larger portion of what he said was true.

He had travelled from Brighton in the next compartment to Tommy and I. Think of it! On that fateful Sunday night I had journeyed with one brother half the way and with the other brother the rest of the way to town.

He had heard us having our little discussion. He had heard some of the things we had said to each other—especially some of the very strongest. He had heard the banging of the door as I fell. According to him, the sound had so agitated him that he had not known what to do. He suspected that something had happened, but he had not known what. He owned now that he ought to have given the alarm and stopped the train, but at the moment he lost his presence of mind. On reaching Victoria he found Tommy sitting in the next compartment alone. Blood was flowing from a wound in his cheek. Prisoner's own handkerchief being soaked with blood, witness lent him one of his own—a silk one. On which prisoner threw his bloodstained handkerchief out of the window.

At this point, altogether unexpectedly, Sir Haselton Jardine sat down. Mr. Bates got up. As he did so, the witness looked over his shoulder as if he would have liked to have turned tail and run.

I saw that Mr. Bates was going to do something to earn his money at last.

The witness saw it too.

"My learned brother, Mr. Taunton, has brought your story to a point at which it reminds one of those sensational tales which are to be continued in our next. With your permission we will continue it together. You have told us of your charitable loan of a handkerchief—a silk handkerchief. May I take it that you then communicated with the police?"

"No."

"Then what did you do?"

"I had no actual knowledge that a crime had been committed."

"I ask you, Mr. Taunton, when you had lent the silk handkerchief, what you did."

"I saw the prisoner to a cab."

"Then did you communicate with the police?"

"I did not."

"Then what did you do?"

"I accompanied him a short distance in the cab."

"Did he give you anything when you parted?"

"He gave me his address."

"Did he give you anything else?"

"He gave me a deposit on my silk handkerchief."

"He gave you a deposit on your silk handkerchief. I see. What was the amount of the deposit?"

The witness hesitated.

"Ten shillings."

"Do you swear it was not more than ten shillings?"

"It might have been a pound."

"Do you swear it was not more than a pound?"

"It might have been thirty shillings. I don't exactly remember."

"I see. For the first time your memory begins to fail you. Then did you communicate with the police?"

"I did not."

"What did you do?"

"The next day I called on the prisoner at his office at Austin Friars."

"Yes. And then?"

"I charged him with the murder."

"You charged him with the murder. Of course, then, you did communicate with the police?"

The witness seemed to find the reiteration trying. He looked around him, as if seeking shelter.

"Unfortunately, I did not."

"Unfortunately? I see. Unfortunately, what did you do?"

"At that time I was very pressed for money. I yielded to the pressure of my necessities."

"By which you mean?"

"That I accepted a small loan."

"You accepted a small loan. Did you not levy blackmail? Did you not extort blood-money, sir? Did you not demand a sum of money in exchange for your silence?"

Mr. Bates raised his voice very considerably. The witness quivered.

"I believe I did suggest that a small loan should be made to me."

"And you got it?"

"I did."

"What was the amount of this small loan?"

"A hundred pounds."

"A hundred pounds?" This from the judge.

The witness, "Yes, my lord."

"You call that a small loan? Well, go on."

Mr. Bates went on.

"Then what did you do?"

"I called again at the prisoner's office. When I found he was not there on this Friday I called at his private house."

"On which occasion you found him ill in bed?"

"I found him in bed."

"In the presence of Mrs. Tennant you suggested that another small loan should be made you?"

"I might have done."

"You did not get it?"

"I did not."

"You were shown to the door instead?"

"I left the house, resolving to tamper no more with my conscience."

"Having been refused another small loan?"

"I went at once to the police, and told them everything."

"Including the incident of the small loan?"

"I don't know that I told them about that."

"I think it probable that you did not. Mr. Taunton, what is your profession?"

The witness gripped the rail in front of him.

"I have none."

"May I ask, then, how you earn your living?"

"As best I can."

Mr. Bates turned to the judge.

"I think it possible, my lord, that I may be able to throw a flood of light upon what the witness means by saying that he earns his living as best he can. Mr. Taunton, when did you last come out of gaol?"

Obviously the witness gripped the rail in front of him still tighter. The moisture gleamed upon his forehead.

"That has nothing to do with it."

The judge interposed. "Answer the question, sir."

The witness turned his twitching countenance towards the judge.

"I would respectfully suggest, my lord, that it has nothing to do with the present case."

Mr. Bates struck in.

"With your lordship's permission, I may be able to render the witness material assistance. Mr. Taunton, at York Assizes, five years ago this month, under the name of Arthur Stewart, were you not sentenced to five years' penal servitude by Mr. Justice Hunter?"

The judge pressed his spectacles into their place.

"I thought I had seen the man before. I remember him very well. Was it a case of bigamous intermarriage?"

"The man—this man—was found guilty of having married four women, one after the other, of robbing them of all they had, and then deserting them. Possibly, also, your lordship will remember that no less than three previous convictions were proved against him."

"I remember the case very well. And I remember the man. It was one of the worst cases of the kind I had ever encountered. I believe I said so at the time."

"Your lordship did. Strangely enough, while your lordship was judge, I was for the prosecution. I recognised the man directly he stepped into the box. I have no doubt that he recognised me."

Mr. Bates sat down.

"When did this man come out of prison?"

Some one spoke from the side of the court.

"He was released on ticket-of-leave, my lord. The ticket has just run out."

"Was there any police supervision?"

"I believe not, my lord."

"Then I hope that the police will keep their eyes upon him." He turned to the witness. "According to your own statement, you appear to have been guilty of an offence as heinous as any of your previous ones. Your conduct has been as bad as it could have been. I may consider it to be my duty to recommend your prosecution. As I have said, I hope the police will keep their eyes on you. Go down!"

The witness went down—all the flourish gone clean out of him. He looked more dead than alive.

It may seem queer, but I felt quite sorry for the wretch.

CHAPTER XXXI

THE CASE FOR THE CROWN CONCLUDES

After that the court adjourned till to-morrow. Mr. Alexander Taunton's performance wound up the programme of the day's entertainment, as it appeared to me, with adequate spirit.

At the inn or hotel, or whatever they called it, at which I was stopping, every one was talking of the trial. The chambermaid, who waited on me at dinner, could talk of nothing else. She went gabble, gabble all the time that she was in the room, and it seemed to me that she stopped in the room as much as she possibly could. Her manners, if rustic, were familiar.

She had witnessed Tommy's arrival at the court.

"A more dreadful-looking wretch I never saw. It gave me quite a feeling to look at him. He's got pig's eyes. And cruel! There was cruelty all over him!"

Poor Tommy! She must have had an insufficient view, or she was prejudiced. A milder-mannered man was never charged with having cut a throat, nor, I verily believe, a tenderer-hearted one.

"And they tell me his wife was in court. I never! She must be a one! I'd have drowned myself sooner than let people know I was the wife of a man like that. She must be almost as bad as he is, or she would never have dared to show her face."

Alas for the rarity of Christian charity! Dear, dear, how these Christians do love each other! To think that that sweet-faced, true-hearted woman should have been spoken of like that!

"They're sure to hang him, that's one comfort. I think it's a shame they don't hang him out of hand, without making all this fuss about it. I think such creatures ought to be hung directly they catch 'em."

"Before ascertaining if they are guilty?"

"He's guilty, safe enough. The wretch!"

Well, of course, she knew best. Still, what a funny world it is.

At dinner I ordered a bottle of wine. The landlord brought it up himself, as an excuse for a gossip. He was a shrivelled-up little man, about sixty, not at all like the typical Boniface.

"I thought that I should have been on the jury. But I was on the jury yesterday instead. But there are two cousins of mine who are—got heads screwed on their shoulders both of 'em."

"Indeed? Will you have a glass of wine?"

"Thank you, ma'am, you're very kind. I don't mind if I do." He did not mind.

"I can recommend this port wine. I've had it in my cellars over twenty years. Your very good health, ma'am. Yes." He shook his head. "Neither of them holds with this chap's little games." I had not the faintest notion to what little games he alluded. "I saw you in court, ma'am. Might I ask if you're interested in any of the parties?"

"Not at all. I am an American. While I was staying in England I thought that I would not lose an opportunity of seeing one of your great trials."

"Ay, this is a very great trial, this is. It won't soon be forgotten. Do you think he's guilty?"

"Do you?"

"Well, what I say is just this. I wouldn't be locked up alone with a strange woman in a railway carriage all the way from Brighton to London, not for—not for any amount of money."

"You are flattering."

"I don't mean nothing—not at all. Only, in this case, how are we to say what happened? He seems to be a decent kind of chap. She might have been nasty, there might have been a rumpus, he might have tried to get away from her, she might have fallen out upon the line. How is any one to tell?"

My friend, the landlord, in spite of his somewhat unpromising appearance, seemed to be one of the few sensible persons I had recently encountered. I pressed him to take another glass of wine. He yielded to the pressure.

"Don't you think they'll find him guilty, then?"

"Oh, they'll find him guilty, safe enough, and I daresay they'll hang him, too. That's just the best of it. When a man gets mixed up with a woman in a thing like this they're sure to think the worse of him. But it doesn't follow that he did it, any the more for that. As for that chap Taunton, I'd hang him!"

It seemed that my friend the gentleman had good cause to congratulate himself on the possession of such a relative. He seemed to be held in general esteem.

When the court reopened the next day I changed my seat. I had taken careful stock of the scene of action the day before. The result had been that I came to one or two conclusions. I perceived, for one thing, that one might very easily sit upon the bench and yet preserve one's anonymity. If I wore a cloak, kept my veil down, sat on the back row, and kept myself in the shade, I need fear no recognition from Tommy.

I quite hungered for a sight of the prisoner. I had not dared to turn and look at him from where I sat the day before. The action might not improbably have attracted his attention.

Besides, I wanted to have a good view of what might, not improperly, be described as the closing tableau.

So when I entered the court this time I presented the usher with a sovereign for a seat on the bench. I had a seat on the bench—quite in the shade.

The place was, if anything, more crowded than ever. It was understood that the trial was to conclude in the course of the day. Perhaps that proved an extra attraction. Anyhow, we were uncomfortably crowded on the bench, and the court, everywhere, was as full as it could hold. I wondered how much—in a theatrical sense—the house was worth to a some one—say the usher.

The judge came in. Then Tommy. They let him have a chair. I had a good look at him. He badly wanted shaving; there was a month's growth of hair upon his cheeks and chin. But he looked better than I expected—and braver. His wife sat in front of him, as she had done the day before. She turned as he came in, and greeted him with a smile. Such a brave one! Without a suspicion of a tear! He smiled back at her.

Poor dears! Their smiling days were nearly done.

When he was seated and had recovered from the excitement of his entry, after all, the expression began to creep into his face, which I had expected to see there all along. The expression of stupor, of mental paralysis, of shame, of horror at the position in which he found himself, and at the things which were to come.

Poor, dear Tommy! He looked to me as if there was no fight left in him.

I need not have feared his recognition. He never looked at any one. He just glanced now and then at his wife, and every time he did so there came into his face a something which was a curious commingling of pleasure with pain. But, with the exception of Mrs. Tennant, I doubt if he clearly realised the personality of any other creature there.

The first witness called was a man named Stephen Rodman. He said he was a "tapper," which, I suppose, had something to do with railway work, though I don't know what. Early on the morning of Monday, November 9th, he was walking in the six-foot way of the arrival platform of Victoria Station. He saw a handkerchief lying on the ground. He picked it up. It was soaked with blood, and was still damp. In the corner was a name, "T. Tennant." The 8.40 from Brighton had been drawn up at that platform the night before. Sir Haselton Jardine's colleague, who was examining, handed witness a handkerchief—still unwashed. That was the one he found.

Jane Parsons followed, actually the girl who had been in Mrs. Tennant's service and who had applied for my situation. Certainly the prosecution were fitting the rope round Tommy's neck, as if they did not mean to leave him a loophole of escape. I wondered what she had to say.

Not much. She began by showing an inclination to cry, which inclination she presently gave way to. The tears trickled down her cheeks. She kept dabbling at them with a handkerchief, which she had squeezed into the shape and size of a penny ball.

She was a parlourmaid. Had been, till recently, in Mrs. Tennant's service. Remembered November 8th. Mr. Tennant went to spend the day at Brighton. Mrs. Tennant told her he had gone. Miss Minna was not well, so missus stayed to nurse her. Admitted Mr. Tennant on his return. It was pretty late. After eleven. Mr. Tennant did not seem to be himself at all. He seemed all anyhow—as if he had been fighting. There was a great cut on his cheek. Helped him off with his overcoat. It was all torn and rumpled about the collar. The top button had been torn right off, and a piece of cloth torn with it. It was spotted with blood. Shown an overcoat; recognised it as the overcoat which Mr. Tennant had worn. His collar and tie were disarranged. As a rule he was a most particular gentleman about his clothes.

Mr. Bates asked a question or two.

Had been in Mrs. Tennant's employ more than two years. Mr. Tennant was a very good master—no one could want a better. Lived a quiet, regular life. Was very fond of his wife, and she of him. Made a perfect idol of his little girl.

At this point poor Tommy covered his face with his hands.

She didn't believe he had ever done it, and she never would—she didn't care what nobody said. This statement was volunteered, amidst a burst of sobbing. Mr. Tennant was very nervous. They used to make a joke of it in the kitchen. The least thing put him off. She meant that he was easily flustered. He was a tender and a loving husband and father, a gentle and a kind master, and she didn't believe that, willingly, he would hurt a fly. Jane's tears burst forth afresh.

Mr. Bates sat down.

The detective who had arrested Tommy next appeared. His name was Matthew Holman. He was a sinewy, greybearded, greyheaded, not unkindly-looking man, looking more like a sailor than anything else. His evidence was purely cut and dried, and formal. Prisoner had made no statement on being arrested. All efforts to trace the identity of the dead woman had been unsuccessful. Mr. Bates allowed the witness to depart unquestioned.

The medical evidence which followed revived the flagging interest. It roused Tommy more than anything which had gone before. As well it might.

Two doctors were called. The first was a country doctor. A middle-aged man, with a fatherly sort of manner, and something of the milk of human kindness about his mouth, and in the twinkling of his eyes. His name was Gresham.

Dr. Gresham had examined the body twice. First at the Three Bridges, afterwards in the mortuary at East Grinstead. The first occasion was between nine and ten on the morning of Monday, November 9th. Life had been extinct some hours, probably twelve. The body was that of a well-nourished, healthy young woman, probably under twenty-one years of age.

When he heard this Tommy started. Certainly no doctor could have mistaken me for under one-and-twenty.

She was far advanced in pregnancy.

Tommy started again. I fancied that Mrs. Tennant started too.

The cause of death was strangulation.

Tommy started more and more. Leaning over the rail of the dock, he stared at the witness with all his eyes.

He was sure of it. He had no doubt upon the point whatever. Unfortunately, there was no room for doubt. She had been killed by the pressure of a man's hands and fingers. Great violence must have been used. In fact, extraordinary violence. The skin of the throat was discoloured. Marks of a man's hands and fingers were most distinct. Indeed, so distinct, that when he first saw them they amounted almost to a model. There were slight bruises on the body, such as might have been caused by a fall. There was a livid bruise which ran from shoulder to shoulder across the back. It had probably been caused by pressure. For instance, by pressure against the edge of a carriage seat. His theory was that she had been forced back against the edge of the carriage seat, and in that position strangled. Falling from the train had not been the cause of death. The fall had nothing to do with it.

When Sir Haselton Jardine sat down Tommy and Mr. Bates had quite a long confabulation. Tommy seemed half beside himself with excitement—I very well knew why! It struck me, however, that Mr. Bates did not seem very much impressed.

Still, acting no doubt on his client's strenuous instructions, he subjected the doctor to a rigorous cross-examination.

But it was all in vain.

Poor Tommy!

Mr. Bates first of all suggested, as it were, casually, that the woman was more than one-and-twenty. The doctor did not think it possible. Everything went to show that she was not. Then, after some fencing, he tried to induce the doctor to admit that she might have been strangled after she had fallen from the train. That she might have fallen from the train by accident. Been stupefied by the fall, and, on recovering from her stupor, that some one might have come along and strangled her. The doctor would have none of it, He deemed the thing incredible. Mr. Bates hammered away, but the doctor held his own.

Tommy was done!

He was done still more when it came to the second doctor's turn. He was a Dr. Braithwaite, a great swell from London. He had examined the body at East Grinstead. He corroborated all that Dr. Gresham had had to say, putting things, if anything, a little stronger against poor Tommy. He declined to move a hair's-breadth from his fixed conviction that the woman had been strangled—in the train.

When he left the box every creature in court was aware that, unless something amounting almost to a miracle intervened, Tommy's fate was sealed.

Sir Haselton Jardine, half rising from his seat, announced that that was the case for the Crown.

CHAPTER XXXII

MRS. CARRUTH REMOVES HER VEIL

After luncheon came the speeches.

Sir Haselton Jardine's was as deadly as it very well could have been. He was not a bit of an orator. He reminded one of an automatic figure as much as anything, as if he had been wound up to go. He went quietly on, in the same placid, passionless sort of whisper, but as clear as a bell. One never lost a syllable he uttered. He never faltered or stumbled. The words, as they flowed from him, were exactly adapted to the meaning they were intended to convey. He fitted them together with the dexterity of an artist in mosaic.

One began almost to feel that one was listening to the voice of doom.

He recounted the story. He observed that it did not appear to be disputed that the prisoner had travelled in the same compartment with the woman who was dead. He did not know what the defence would be. But if it was intended to suggest that death had been the result of accident, he asked the attention of the jury to the medical evidence. It was shown by that that death had not been caused by falling from the train. The woman had been strangled—strangled by a man's two hands. The degree of violence which had been used not only inevitably suggested premeditation, but also great resolution in carrying out what had been premeditated. The murderer had resolved to kill, and he did kill.

They could not say with certainty what happened after the train left Brighton. A feature of the case was that the efforts of the police had failed in establishing the dead woman's identity. So far as they could discover she was nameless. No one had come forward to claim her—to say who she was. She seemed to have come from nowhere. No one seemed to have missed her now that she had gone. It was a mystery. He could not say if the prisoner had it in his power to supply them with the key to that mystery. Men live double lives. The witness Taunton had told them that what he had heard had caused him to conclude that the man and woman in the next compartment were acquaintances. That might have been the case. In that connection he would merely remark—that the prisoner was a married man; that the woman was young and pretty; that she was far advanced in pregnancy; that she wore no wedding-ring.

In these facts they might, possibly, find a motive for the crime.

A great crime had been committed. A young woman, scarcely more than a girl, who would shortly have become a mother, had been done to death. So far as one could perceive, there were no palliating circumstances. It was the other way. The crime was the act of a coward, as well as of a criminal. He did not desire to press the case unduly against the prisoner. It was his duty to ask them, as jurymen, if the facts which had been presented were not adequate to bring the crime home to him. If they deemed them inadequate, then, without showing fear or favour, it was their duty to say so.

Sir Haselton Jardine sat down.

And Mr. Bates got up.

Mr. Bates began by remarking that he did not propose to call any witnesses for the defence.

Then, in that case, in view of the body of evidence which had been called for the other side, Tommy's goose was cooked, and he was done for. Mr. Bates might have as well kept still. A general movement which took place in the court seemed to be a voiceless expression of this consensus of opinion.

Mr. Bates said that, in taking this course, he was almost overwhelmed by a sense of responsibility. That was chiefly owing to the fact that the law of England was still in such a state that the prisoner could not go into the box and testify. He was exceedingly anxious to give his testimony, but it could not be received as evidence. If he had spoken out at first he might not, and probably would not, have been in the position which he was occupying now. But he had shrunk from the course which a wiser man would have pursued—shrunk from it for reasons which were natural enough, but which still, he was bound to say, were insufficient. Now it was too late. His voice could not be heard.

It was his duty, as the prisoner's advocate, to lay before the jury the prisoner's story.

Then Mr. Bates told what had really happened, and told it very well indeed. His story was literally accurate. I did not detect a single discrepancy. I think I should have done! He was frank almost to a fault. He nothing extenuated, nothing set down in malice. Nothing was omitted—even the dotting of the i's.

And yet I doubt if a soul in court, with the exception, perhaps, of Tommy's wife, believed a word he said.

To me, listening up there, the thing was inconceivably funny.

The chief difficulty which Mr. Bates had to contend with, as he owned, and as one perceived without his owning it, was the medical evidence. He admitted that it was difficult to reconcile it with the prisoner's story. The prisoner declared that he did not understand it; that it had come upon him with the force of a surprise.

His theory was that the woman had been stunned by her fall from the train. As she was unconscious, or before she had recovered, some straggling vagabond had found her lying on the bank. He had robbed her. To effect his purpose he had had to add murder to robbery. The prosecution had not laid stress upon the point, but she evidently had been robbed. There was not the slightest tittle of evidence to connect the prisoner with the robbery, so counsel for the Crown had been wise not to dwell upon it. On the other hand there was complete absence of motive, and the fact that nothing of any sort could have belonged to the dead woman had been found in the possession of the prisoner.

He admitted that the suggestion that murder had been committed after the fall from the carriage was well worthy the attention of the jury.

The prisoner made a mistake—which however, he submitted, was the mistake which we might naturally have expected from a constitutionally nervous man—in not giving the alarm immediately the accident took place. He ought to have spoken when they reached Victoria. He ought not to have allowed himself to be frightened by the blackmailing Taunton. But, after all, these were all mistakes which a perfectly innocent man, of his constitution, in his position, might have made. We none of us could absolutely rely upon having our wits about us when we most wanted them.

The prisoner had made mistakes. He owned it. But he begged the jury to consider that the law did not permit him to put the prisoner into the witness-box, and that the prisoner was convinced that, if he only might be suffered to tell his tale his innocence would be established. Above all, he entreated them not to send a fellow-creature to an ignominious death because he had yielded to the promptings of a timorous constitution and had not played the man.

When Mr. Bates sat down the judge summed up.

And he did it very briefly.

He pooh-poohed Mr. Bates's story altogether. He told the jury that they were at liberty to believe it, if they could. But it was not supported by a shred of evidence. It was disproved in several essential particulars, and it was his duty to inform them that it was contrary to every principle of English law that an ex parte statement which was without any sort of corroboration should be allowed to weigh, for an instant, against a large and authenticated body of evidence which had been sworn to by credible and impartial witnesses. At the same time, if there was any doubt in their minds, let the prisoner have the benefit of it; though, so far as he was concerned, he had not the least doubt in his own mind that the man was guilty, and, if they did their duty, they would say so.

Of course this was not exactly what he did say, and of course he said a good deal more than this, but this is the gist of what his saying amounted to. Certainly the judge's summing-up was every whit as damning as Sir Haselton's speech had been. Mr. Justice Hunter had evidently himself no doubt upon the matter, and, by inference, he took it for granted that no one else could have any either.

The jury followed the judge's lead. They never left their places. They whispered together for a few moments. Then one of them announced that they were prepared with their verdict.

"Do you find the prisoner guilty or not guilty?"

"Guilty."

Some one told the prisoner to stand up. He stood up.

"Have you anything to say, prisoner, why sentence should not be pronounced against you?"

The prisoner had something to say—just a word or two.

He was very white. He was clinging to the rail in front of him. His throat seemed parched. It seemed all that he could do to speak.

I noticed that his wife was looking at him with upturned face, and that her eyes were streaming with tears.

"I am innocent. I did not do it. I did not kill her. I never touched her. There is something I do not understand."

That was all he had to say—and that was not enough.

As the judge very soon made him comprehend.

He took a black thing out of a tin box which was at his side and perched it on the top of his wig, and he sentenced Tommy to be hanged; and, in sentencing him, he gave it to him hot.

He told him that instead of exhibiting any signs of remorse for the dreadful thing he had done he had just uttered an infamous lie to add to the rest of his crimes. That lie had extinguished any spark of pity which he might have felt. Tommy had been guilty of as wicked, as cruel, and as cowardly a murder as had ever come within the range of the judge's experience. He might not hope for mercy. There was no circumstance of extenuation. He had behaved more like a devil than a man. He was a disgrace to his class and to his station, and he had brought shame upon our common manhood; and the sentence of the court was that he should be taken to the place from whence he came, and there be hanged by the neck till he was dead; and might God have mercy on his soul!

And that was the end of it—or it might have been, if it had not been for me.

I don't know how it was; I don't know whether the devil prompted me or not. But the idea came to me, all at once, with a force which was beyond my powers of resistance.

And I did it!

I dropped my cloak, I removed my veil, and I stood up where I knew that Tommy would see me. And he did see me. He looked my way, and he saw me, and he knew me too!

And I smiled at him.

And with sudden, instant recognition he stretched out his arms towards me in a kind of frenzy; and he tried to speak, or shout, or do something, but he couldn't. And before he could get a word out edgeways the warder bustled him down the stairs below.

BOOK IV - THE CRIMINAL.

CHAPTER XXXIII

MR. TENNANT SPEAKS

"I saw her! I saw her!"

"None of that now. You'd better come quietly."

Mr Tennant looked at the warder who spoke. With the assistance of his colleague the man was hurrying him along in a fashion which, even at that moment of amazement and of horror, in some subtle way reminded him of his school days.

"I saw her!" he repeated.

"So you might have done; nobody says you didn't. Only don't let's have any fuss."

The man spoke as one might speak, not ill-naturedly, but with the superior wisdom of a senior to a fractious child. Mr. Tennant knew that he was not understood; that it was no use to attempt to make himself understood. His mind was in a chaos. What was he to do?

It had come to him in a flash of revelation that he had been made the subject of some hideous mockery, the victim of some malevolent plot; that he had been racked and re-racked for nothing at all; that he had stood his trial for the murder of a woman, who, all the time, was actually alive; that the law had committed some grotesque blunder; that he had been condemned to be hung for another person's crime.

What was he to do?

He did nothing till he was back again in gaol. In the condemned cell this time. Nobody had told him, but he knew what it was. He knew that here a long line of murderers had awaited their fate, that here he would be kept until he was hung.

A natural shudder shook him as he realised that they were about to thrust him into this last abiding-place of the damned. He felt that if he did not speak so as to make himself understood before they had him fast in there he would never have a chance to speak at all: That if that door clanged upon his silence, hope, for him, would have died with its clangour.

He turned to the warder.

"I wish to see the governor."

"You can't see the governor now."

"I must. Listen to me." He tried to restrain his emotion, to hold himself in hand. "Some extraordinary error has taken place. Just as I was leaving the court I saw the woman whom I am charged with having killed."

The warder stared, as if inclined to laugh.

"I am not mad, nor am I dreaming; nor did I see a ghost. I saw this woman. She was as much alive as you or I. She was among a number of other women on the bench near the judge. She stood up and she stared at me. I saw her as plainly as I see you. There has been some astounding mistake. Tell the governor that I must see him at once or it will be too late. If you do not tell him my blood may be upon your head."

"All right."

The warder clanged the door, and went.

Mr. Tennant was left alone in that abode of the haunted.

Would the man tell him? Would the governor come? Would he listen if he came? Would they stir a finger? Would they believe him? Would they pay the slightest attention to anything that he said?

It would have been hard enough to hang believing her dead, although he had not killed her, but now that he had seen her standing up and looking at him, and smiling at his agony—!

This explained the two ghostly visitations. It was not a ghost, it was herself he had seen. All this time he had been suffering the agonies of the damned, and she had been laughing in her sleeve. How she must have enjoyed the play! Oh, what a fool he had been!

What was that? Was that footsteps ringing on the stone pavement along the vaulted corridor? He listened. It was somebody going, not coming.

Suppose the governor would not come?

There was a bell. Should he ring it and make a scene and in that way emphasise the expression of his desire? If he could succeed in no other way, he would try that. It was time that was precious. Every moment that passed made his task the harder. If they had only given him an opportunity to proclaim the woman's identity! If they only had! If he could only get back into the court even now and stop her before again she vanished into air!

Would the governor not come?

Then he would ring the bell and wake the echoes of the prison, and keep on ringing until they either disconnected the bell or put him into irons. He would not hang without a struggle now. He would ring at once.

Ah! There was some one coming.

Two persons. He could hear two separate tramp tramps, one falling a little behind the other as they came along the flagstones.

The door was opened. It was the governor.

"You wish to see me?"

"I do, sir."

Again Mr. Tennant tried to master himself, to hold himself in hand. He realised to the full, and very late in the day, how much might hinge upon his being able to preserve his presence of mind.

"What do you wish to say?"

"I wish to say that the woman whom I am charged with having murdered was actually in the court."

"Nonsense."

"It is not nonsense. It is the simple truth. I saw her as plainly as I see you."

The governor eyed him with what, for him, was a look of ferocity—unofficially, he was one of the softest-hearted creatures breathing.

"Man, don't tell such tales to me."

"I am telling you the absolute, literal truth. I have felt all along that there was something about the medical evidence which I did not understand. The woman they described was not the woman who fell out of the train. Now I understand how it was. That woman is not dead. I saw her, just now, alive, in court."

"Why did you not interrupt the proceedings to say so?"

"I did not see her before sentence was pronounced. When I did see her I was so astonished that, before I had recovered sufficiently from my astonishment to be able to speak the warders removed me from the court. I told the warders who it was that I had seen."

The governor observed the prisoner, as it was, reflectively. Certainly Mr. Tennant had become on a sudden a different man. He had lost his awkwardness. He was no longer ill at ease. He held himself erect. His eyes were clear, his glance unwavering. His bearing was simple—the simplicity of the man was what struck one first of all—yet assured. He spoke with a calmness, and even with a dignity which, considering that sentence of ignominious death had just been pronounced upon him, could scarcely fail to be impressive.

"Tennant, so far as it concerns your fate, whatever you may have to say will be without effect. For you in this world there is no hope. You had better prepare yourself for the world which is to come. Do not buoy yourself up with any hopes that anything you may say will prevent the sentence which has been pronounced upon you being executed. That sentence will certainly be carried out."

The condemned man would have spoken, but the governor went on.

"But the warder has just told me what you told him, and in discharge of what I hold to be my duty I have requested the detective who has been in charge of the case to come and hear what you may have to say. Here he is."

And there he was—Matthew Holman, the man who looked so like a sailor.

"Well, Tennant, what cock-and-bull story have you to tell us now?"

"None. I have to tell you the truth."

"It is time."

Mr. Holman's tone was biting, his glance was keen.

Mr. Tennant re-told the story of his famous journey. The detective seemed not so much to be listening to the words he uttered as searching for what might be behind them.

"So you did know her? What was her name?"

"I knew her as Ellen Howth. But she may have had half a dozen names before I knew her and since."

The detective made a note in his pocket-book.

"Where did she live?"

"I have no notion. As I have told you before that night I had not seen or heard of her for years."

"Describe her."

Mr. Tennant described her.

"You understand that, until I heard the medical evidence, I supposed that she had been killed by the fall from the carriage. When I heard what the doctors had to say I began to wonder. It became clearer and clearer to me that they could not be talking of Ellen Howth. The two descriptions did not tally. I did not believe that she was pregnant. I knew that she was over thirty, and it seemed inconceivable that a medical man could mistake a woman of considerably over thirty for a girl under twenty-one. When I saw Ellen Howth standing up there and smiling at me, in an instant it was all made plain."

"What was all made plain?"

"Many things. For one, it explained what seemed to me to be the discrepancies between the evidence and what I knew to be the facts—the facts, that is, so far as they concerned myself."

"Where was the woman whom you say you saw standing—tell me exactly."

Mr. Tennant paused to think. The detective's eyes were on him, and the governor's and the warder's at the back.

"She was on the bench. She was on the last row of seats. She sat either second or third from the judge, to his right. When he had pronounced sentence I noticed her rising and I noticed her remove her veil, and she looked at me, I have no doubt with the deliberate design of attracting my attention."

"I believe I noticed the woman to whom you refer."

This was the governor. The detective said nothing. He continued to look at the prisoner for a moment or two in silence. Then from a pocket in his coat he took an envelope.

"There is a portrait of Ellen Howth."

He handed a photograph to Mr. Tennant.

"This is not Ellen Howth."

"Then that is."

He passed the prisoner a second photograph.

"Nor is this. Neither of these photographs in the least resembles Ellen Howth. Not in any one particular. I have never seen the woman whose portrait this purports to be. Of that I am sure."

"It beats me, my lad, to think how a man circumstanced as you are, can lie so glibly. You know as well as I do, and indeed better, that you are holding in your hands portraits of the poor young woman whose life you took."

"That is not so. Neither of these portraits at all resembles the woman, Ellen Howth, with whom I travelled from Brighton. If they are photographs of the woman who was found dead, then it is certain that I had no hand whatever in killing her."

"You have seen those portraits before."

"Never!"

"Do you mean to tell me that no one, neither your counsel nor your solicitor, nor any one else showed you them?"

"I do. You appear surprised."

"It is not a question of surprise. I don't believe you."

"You can soon ascertain for yourself that what I tell you is a fact. You must remember that from the first I told my solicitor the actual facts. I took it for granted that the woman who had been found dead was Ellen Howth. Under those circumstances there was no reason why I should be shown or why I should wish to be shown her photograph. I have not seen that portrait before. The woman whose portrait it is is a complete stranger to me. Were she here she would tell you that I am equally a stranger to her. There is some mystery which, at present, I do not profess to understand. But of one thing I am certain, that the woman, Ellen Howth, whom I supposed was dead, is as much alive as you are or as I am."

"Give me those portraits. It strikes me that you are one of those men who will go even to face their God with a lie upon their lips. I don't believe a word that you have said."

"Then you wrong me cruelly. I hope, for your sake, as well as for my own, that you will learn that you do, before it is too late."

The detective made no reply. He went out of the cell without a word. The governor followed him. The door was clanged. The condemned man was left alone to get himself, if he could, into a mood in which he should be able to look the gallows squarely and without flinching in the face.

The governor spoke to the detective as they walked side by side.

"What do you think of it?"

"Queer-street."

"I certainly noticed myself the woman of whom he speaks. I wonder you didn't. Her action was most marked. She certainly did cast at him what seemed to me to be a glance of exultant recognition, while the sight of her seemed to fill him with stupefied amazement. I wondered when I saw it what the scene might mean."

"What was she like?"

"He describes her very fairly."

"If she's still in Lewes I'll leave no stone unturned to find her."

"And if she isn't?"

"You know, sir, that if you give him a chance, a man in his position can always pitch some sort of a tale to save his neck. And the worse they are the more they lie like the truth."

"That's true enough."

The governor sighed.

"If ever a man was found guilty on the evidence this man was. If he's not guilty, then I'll never again put my trust in evidence; and so far I've generally found evidence that will stand sifting quite good enough for me. Still, as I say, I'll leave no stone unturned to find the woman of whom he speaks."

"And of whom I speak."

The governor spoke with a little smile.

"Yes, sir, and of whom you speak too."

CHAPTER XXXIV

MR. HOLMAN AT HOME

But they looked for her in vain. They did not find her. And the following night Mr. Holman was in the bosom of his family.

Mr. Holman's home was in a street off Leicester Square. His family consisted of his wife. Of her he was wont to make a confidant, as he did on the present occasion.

Mr. Holman had come up by an afternoon train from Lewes. Mrs. Holman had prepared a meat tea for him on his arrival. He had commenced his attack upon the viands before she began to question him.

"So they're going to hang him?"

"It would seem as though they were."

Mrs. Holman detected something in her husband's tone.

"What do you mean? Aren't they going to hang him?"

"Did I say they weren't going to hang him? Didn't I say it seems as though they were. Don't you understand Queen's English?"

Mrs. Holman was silent for a second or two.

"Surely they're not getting up a petition to let him off?"

"I've heard nothing at all about it, if they are. But perhaps you've heard more than me. You do sometimes, don't you?"

"You don't mean to say that you don't believe he did it. I thought you were sure that he was guilty."

"I've been sure of a good many things in my time, and been sorry for it afterwards. I'm not the only leather-headed fool there is about, as perhaps you know."

Mrs. Holman was skilled in the inflections of her husband's voice. She perceived that it would be wiser, temporarily, to keep her curiosity in her pocket, and to allow him to finish his meal in peace, which she did and obtained her reward.

When the lady's lord and master had eaten and drunk to his heart's content he wiped his lips and he looked at his wife.

"What do you think he says?"

"I haven't the least idea."

"He says that the woman who was found is not the woman who was with him in the train."

"A man like him would say anything."

"How clever you women are. You know everything. As it happens, it seems to me that he's just the sort of man who would not say anything, and I ought to be a pretty good judge of that kind of thing if any one is." Mr. Holman was regarding the two portraits which he had submitted to Mr. Tennant for inspection. "I don't half like it. I can swear that this is a good likeness of the woman that was found. He says that it's not the least like the woman who was with him in the train.

"Fiddlededee!"

"Of course it's fiddlededee. And if he was hung, and it came out afterwards that what he said was true, it would look like fiddlededee, wouldn't it? I should feel as if I'd murdered him."

"Matthew!"

"Somehow the tale which he tells sounds true, and the queer part of it is that he says that the woman whom he travelled with in the train from Brighton was actually present in the court during the trial."

"It isn't possible."

"Oh, dear no! Of course not. If you say so, it couldn't be. It seems funny though that the governor should be of a different opinion."

"What governor?"

"What governor! The governor of Lewes gaol—stupid! Considering how clever you set yourself up to be, it's queer what a lot of explanation you seem to want. The governor noticed this woman of whom Tennant speaks, and something about her goings-on struck him as being queer. I've been looking for her in Lewes all this blessed day. She's not there. But I'll find her if she's anywhere. I'm not going to have a man hung for a woman that's alive if I can help it. I'm going to make my report in the morning, and if I'm not told off to hunt her up I'll be surprised."

A ring was heard.

"Go and see what idiot that is ringing the bell. If it's any one to see me let me know who it is before you show him in."

Mrs. Holman went to see what idiot it was. She returned and reported.

"It's that American who has lost his daughter, Mr. Haines his name is."

"Confound Mr. Haines! What's he come humbugging about? Show him in. I'll make short work of Mr. Haines."

Mr. Haines was shown in, tall and thin, Yankee writ large all over him. Uninvited, he seated himself. He crossed his legs. He balanced his hat upon his knees. He looked at Mr. Holman without speaking a word. Mr. Holman, without any show of deference, looked back at him, nor was his manner when he spoke marked by a superfluity of courtesy.

For some moments the silence remained unbroken—a fact which seemed to arouse the detective's irascibility.

"Is that all you have to say? If so, perhaps you will excuse me. My time happens to be of value."

Mr. Haines opened his lips.

"That creature has buncoed me again."

"What creature?"

"Private detective Stewart Trevannion."

"When a man calls himself a private detective, nine times out of ten yon may safely write him down a scoundrel. The tenth time, perhaps, he is something worse."

"A scoundrel. That's what he is. And next time we chance to meet I'll write the thing on him in good bold letters in my very plainest hand. He raised another fifty out of me. He undertook to place me in communication with my girl if I let him have it. He has placed me in communication neither with my girl nor with himself since he raised that fifty."

Mr. Holman leaned against the side of the table on which he had just been having tea. He regarded his visitor with something like a twinkle in his eye.

"Governor, do you mind my speaking a little plainly?"

"I do not."

"Take my tip, book a berth in the next boat, and go back where you came from. You'll be more at home like over there."

"Not till I have looked upon her grave if she is dead, or on her face if she is living."

"Ah, then, I shouldn't be surprised if you were to stay this side some time. You'll settle here."

"Aren't the resources of civilisation sufficient to enable me to find my girl?"

"The resources of civilisation aren't interested. You drove her away, it's for you to fetch her back again. What it strikes me is that she don't want to come, and she don't mean to, either."

"She is dead."

"How are you going to prove it?"

"I want you to help me."

"How am I going to help you any more than I have done? I'm a public servant. I receive instructions from my superiors, and I have to obey them. How am I going to devote myself to you? I don't know what good I should do if I could. Thousands of girls are missing; they leave home because they're sick of it, and they set up on their own hook. How do you think you're going to find 'em if they don't mean to be found? It may be easy in the stories, but it isn't out of them."

Rising from his chair, Mr. Haines paced slowly across the room. Mr. Holman watched him. He noticed his air of extreme depression.

"You do as I say, take my tip, and go back by the next ship. You'll be able to look for her as well there as over here—yes, and better. You say she knows what address will find you. You'll hear from her safe enough when she's had about enough of it.

"Not me."

"How can you tell that."

"Because she's dead."

Mr. Holman moved from the table with a gesture of impatience. Not impossibly he would have terminated the interview then and there. He looked as if language of even unusual strength was trembling on his lips. He was prevented, however, from giving it utterance by the unannounced entrance of a second visitor.

The visitor was in the shape of a girl—a young girl. She was pretty, with a prettiness which more than suggested the theatre. She had an amazing array of short, fair hair. It shrined her face like a sort of coronal. The big hat was perched on the top of her hair. There was a hint of kohl about her pretty eyes. And though her plump cheeks were clean enough and tempting enough just then, one could have sworn that they had long been familiar with rouge.

She came into the room with a complete absence of ceremony, as if she was perfectly at home.

"Well, uncle, so you're back again."

Mr. Holman looked her up and down without saying a word. Planting herself right in front of him she clasped her hands behind her back—impudently demure. "You can look at me."

"So you have dyed your hair."

"I have."

"And cut it off."

"And cut it off."

"And fluffed it?"

"Fluffed it? Crimped it, I suppose you mean. My dear uncle, if anybody offered to double your salary on condition that you dyed your hair, you'd dye it all the colours of the rainbow." Mr. Holman turned away. "Aren't you going to kiss me? You'd not only dye, you'd give your hair to kiss me if you weren't my uncle. How nice it is to have relations!"

Mrs. Holman appeared at the door.

"Never mind him, Hetty. He's come back in a bad temper."

"Of course he's come back in a bad temper. Did you ever know him when he hadn't come back in a bad temper? He's the worst-tempered man I ever knew, and that's saying something."

Mr. Holman seated himself in an arm-chair by the fire. The young lady sat on one of the arms. She smoothed her uncle's hair.

"Dear uncle, how well you're looking."

Mr. Holman shook his head, as if to remove it from the reach of her embrace.

"Don't touch me."

"And what a nice, kind look you've got in your eyes."

"Hetty, I'm ashamed of you."

"Oh, no, you're not. You're not half such a goose as you pretend to be."

"I tell you that I am."

"You're what? A goose. Dear uncle, I would never let any one call you a goose except yourself. Won't you kiss me?"

The fair young face stooped down. The man's weather-beaten face looked up. The lips met.

The kiss was interrupted by a series of exclamations which came from the back of the room. So unexpected and so startling a series of exclamations that Mr. Holman rose from his chair with such suddenness as almost to overturn his niece.

"What's up now?" he asked.

A good deal seemed to be up, at any rate with Mr. Haines. That gentleman was standing on the other side of the table staring at something which he was holding in his hand, giving vent to a variety of observations which were scarcely parliamentary.

"It's Loo! Blamed if it ain't! It's my girl! It's Loo!"

Throwing down what he was holding, he rushed at the detective like some wild animal.

"Damn you!" he yelled. "It's Loo!"

CHAPTER XXXV

THE WOMAN OF THE PORTRAIT

The detective easily avoided the man's blind rush, the result of which was that Mr. Haines all but cannoned into Mr. Holman's niece.

Miss Hetty Johnson, however—the young lady's name was Johnson—seemed in no way disconcerted.

"That's right. Knock me down and trample on me. I don't mind. I've done nothing to nobody. But it's all the same as if I had."

Brought back by the young lady's words to a sense of reality, Mr. Haines spluttered out an apology.

"I beg your pardon. It was an accident." Then he raved at Mr. Holman. "You—you devil! You've been having me, tricking me, doing me. You cursed slippery British hound, I feel like killing you!"

He looked as he said he felt. His tall figure was drawn upright, his long arms were stretched out in front of him, his fists were clenched as in a paroxysm of rage.

Mr. Holman stared at him with stolid imperturbability.

"Perhaps, when you've quite finished, you'll tell us what's wrong."

"You know. Don't you try to play it any more off on to me, or the presence of a woman shan't save you."

"What's the matter with the man?" asked Mrs. Holman.

"Don't you hear me asking him?" chimed in her lord. "But it doesn't seem as if he cared to tell us."

As if one was not sufficient, Mr. Haines began shaking both his fists at the detective.

"You said you knew nothing about her; you told me you could not help me; you advised me to go back by the next ship. I could not make it out. Now I do catch on. You had her portrait all the time."

"Whose portrait?"

"Loo's!"

"Who's Loo?"

"My girl!"

The words came from Mr. Haines with a roar.

The detective looked at him as if he was beginning to suspect that, after all, there might be some method in his madness.

"See here, Mr. Haines, I don't know if you are or are not mad, but just try to behave as if you weren't. I've no notion what you're talking about. I tell you I know no more about your girl than I know about the man in the moon."

"You tell me that, and expect me to believe it, when you have her portrait?"

"I have her portrait! Where?"

"Here!" Striding forward, he snatched up one of the two portraits which were lying on the table. As he did so, he perceived the second. "Why, here's another! There are two! You have two portraits of my girl, and you tell me that you know nothing of her."

Although the detective's face remained impassive, a speck of light seemed all at once to come into his eyes. The pupils dilated. There was something in them which suggested that the whole man had become, upon a sudden, alert and eager.

"I would ask you, Mr. Haines, to consider carefully what you are saying. More may depend upon your words than you imagine. Do I understand you to say that you know the original of that photograph?"

"Know the original! Of course I do. It's my girl, my Loo!"

"Are you prepared to swear it?"

"I am, before God and man."

"May I ask if there is anything in particular in which the likeness consists?"

"Don't you think a father knows his daughter when he sees her in a picture? Don't talk back to me. I tell you it's my girl, my Loo! Where is she?"

"I will tell you everything in a moment, Mr. Haines. Look at those photographs closely. Don't you notice anything about them which is peculiar?"

Mr. Haines did as he was told. He peered closely at the portraits.

"She is looking pretty sick."

"Well she might do. Those photographs were taken after death?"

"After death?"

"Have you heard of the Three Bridges Tragedy?"

"The Three Bridges Tragedy? Yes."

"That is the portrait of the victim."

"The victim? So! She is dead. She was done to death. I knew it."

"The man who has been found guilty of the crime is now lying in gaol under sentence of death."

"They shan't hang him?"

"It looks uncommonly as if they would."

"I say they shan't. Not if I have to tear down the prison walls with my hands and nails to get at him. Do you think I've come all these thousands of miles to let them strangers pay the man that killed my girl? You bet I've not!"

Mr. Haines glanced at the detective as if he defied his contradiction.

The detective looked at him, in return, as if he doubted what to make of him.

While the two men were thus, as it were, taking each other's measure, Miss Hetty Johnson advanced to the table on which Mr. Haines had, perhaps unconsciously, replaced the photographs. She picked them up.

"Is this the poor girl who was murdered?" She glanced at them. As she did so she uttered a startled exclamation, "Why, it—it's Milly!" She turned to Mr. Holman all in a tremor of excitement. "Uncle, this is Milly!"

Her uncle turned to her with what almost amounted to a savage start.

"Who do you say it is? You don't mean to say that you know the original? Hanged if I don't believe everybody does except me. And here, all this time, we've been hunting the whole world to find out."

Miss Johnson was not at all affected by her uncle's display of temper. She repeated her previous assertion, and that with more emphasis than before.

"This is Milly Carroll who was with me at the theatre. I am sure of it. Aunt, you've heard me talk of Milly Carroll?"

"Often," said her aunt. "Now, Hetty, don't you let your fancy run away with you. It may be like her, and yet it mayn't be her. Remember the mischief you might do. You think before you speak."

"My dear aunt, there is not the slightest necessity for you to talk to me like that. I am sure that this is Milly Carroll. Heaps of girls at the theatre will tell you so if you ask them. It doesn't do her justice, and she looks as if she were dead, but it's her." She dropped her hand to her side, as if a startling reflection had all at once occurred to her. "I wonder if that explains it?"

"Explains what?"

"Her silence. I wondered why she had never replied to my last letter. All the time, perhaps, she was dead. And I was telling every one how unkind she was. To think of it!"

"Do you know where she lived?"

"When I last heard from her she was living at Brighton."

"Brighton? Then he did do it. What an artistic liar that man must be!"

"She left the stage for good. She was going to be married."

"Going to be married, was she? Then it's her. What was her future husband's name?"

"I never heard his name. We always took him for some big swell, she kept his name so close. She used to call him Reggie."

"Reggie? Oh! Not Tommy?"

"No, Reggie. I knew him very well by sight."

"What do you mean—you knew him very well by sight?"

"Well, I spoke to him two or three times, and, of course, he spoke to me. And I used often to see her with him. And then he was always at the theatre. He used to give her everything she wanted, and made no end of a fuss of her. The girls all envied her good luck."

"It looks as if they had cause to. What sort of party was this swell of hers to look at?"

"He was tall, and dark, and very handsome, and he had most beautiful hands, and one of the nicest-speaking voices I ever heard—and such a smile! And he dressed awfully well—he was an awful swell. Milly told me he was awfully rich, but I could see that without her telling me."

Mr. Holman had listened to the girl's description with some appearance of surprise.

"Of course you could. You girls can see anything. That's how it is so many of you come to grief—you think you see so much. You're sure you haven't made a mistake about this swell of hers? You're sure he wasn't short, and plump, and rosy?"

"He wasn't a scrap like that. He was exactly as I've told you. Short, and plump, and rosy? Indeed! I should think he wasn't."

"Would you recognise him if you saw him again?"

"Rather! I should think I should. I should know him anywhere. If you saw him once, you would never be likely to forget him, he was too good-looking."

"Was he indeed? You seem to have been more than half in love with him yourself. You girls always do fall in love with the right sort of men. Have you any of this young woman's writing?"

"I've some of her letters which she sent me."

Mr. Haines, advancing, laid his hand gently on Miss Johnson's arm.

"Will you let me see her letters—my girl's, my Loo's?"

"Of course I will. You can come round and look at them now if you like. There's time before I'm due at the theatre." The young girl looked up at the old man with a curious interest. "She was an American. She used to talk to me about a place called Colorado."

"She was raised in Colorado. And that is where she left me. So you were her friend—my girl's friend?"

"Well, we were pals."

"Pals? Yes. You were pals."

Mr. Haines looked at Miss Johnson inquiringly, searchingly, as if he was endeavouring to ascertain, by force of visual inspection, what sort of girl she was.

Mr. Holman interposed.

"When you two have done palavering, perhaps Miss Hetty Johnson will be good enough to tell me what was this young woman's address at Brighton—that is, if she happens to remember it."

"I remember it perfectly."

Miss Hetty proved that she did by unhesitatingly furnishing her uncle with the information required. Her uncle entered the address she gave him in his pocket-book. He looked at his watch.

"It's twenty minutes past seven. There's a train from Victoria to Brighton at 7.50. If I got a decent cab I ought to have time to catch it, and to spare. If I do catch it, I ought to be able to get all the information I want in time to catch the last train back to town. If I don't, I'll wire." This was to his wife. He turned to his niece. "You keep a still tongue in your head, if you can, and don't go chattering at the theatre. And don't let anything that was that young woman's pass out of your hands to any one—do you hear?"

"I hear. But, uncle, I don't, and I can't, believe that Milly's sweetheart had anything to do with killing her."

"No one asks you for what you believe. I've been asking you for what you know. And that's all I'm likely to ask you for. You mark what I say, and don't you give a scrap of her writing to any one. I'm off."

He was off, catching up the portraits from the table as he went.

As soon as her uncle had gone Miss Johnson turned to Mr. Haines.

"If you want to see those letters, you'll have to come now. I have to be at the theatre soon after eight."

The young girl and the old man went away together. Miss Johnson led the way through Coventry Street. Suddenly stopping, she caught Mr. Haines by the arm.

"Oh! There he is!"

"Who?"

"Milly's sweetheart."

"Where?"

Miss Johnson pointed to a tall man who was standing on the pavement talking to the driver of a hansom cab. Mr. Haines started. His companion felt that he was trembling. He spoke as if he were short of breath.

"Are you sure?"

"Quite sure—certain."

Mr. Haines went forward without a word. Miss Johnson stood still and watched, fearing she knew not what.

But she need have feared nothing, for nothing happened.

By the time that Mr. Haines had reached the cab the man in question had seated himself inside. Mr. Haines had a good look at him before the cab moved off.

"It's he! Her aristocrat! I knew that he smelt of blood first time I saw him, but if I'd known that the blood was hers—"

He raised his hands above his head, as if by way of a wind-up to his unfinished sentence.

The passers-by stared at the old man talking to himself and gesticulating on the pavement, wondering, perhaps, if he was drunk or if he was merely mad.

CHAPTER XXXVI

THE VARIOUS MOODS OF A GENTLEMAN OF FASHION

Mr. Townsend was shaving himself. Advancing his face an inch or two nearer his shaving-glass, with his fingers he smoothed his chin.

"Very awkward," he said. "Very!"

The allusion could scarcely have been to the process in which he was engaged. Everything had gone with smoothness. Not even a scratch had marred the perfect peace.

Mr. Townsend concluded that his chin was as clean shaven as it possibly could be. He put his razor down. He took up a cigarette. He lighted it.

"Exceedingly awkward!"

As he murmured the iteration, seating himself in an armchair, he selected an open letter from among a heap of others which lay on a little table at his side. The letter he had selected was unmistakably a feminine production. It was written in a large, bold, running hand, on paper which was as stiff as cardboard.

"MY DEAREST REGGIE,—You must come and see me! At once! I shall expect you this morning!

"Whatever you have done, it it quite impossible that I shall let you go—you are mine!

"You understand that I am waiting for you, and that you are to come to me as soon as you possibly can.

"You are to tell the bearer when I shall see you!

"YOUR DORA."

That was what the letter said. The italics and the notes of exclamation were the lady's own. As he puffed his cigarette Mr. Townsend read the letter carefully through and smiled. Removing his cigarette, he pressed the letter to his lips. Then, carefully folding the letter between his fingers, he laid it down.

"As I said I would go, I shall have to go—it's uncommonly awkward. Had she been wise, she would have taken what I wrote as the final word, and left it so."

Rising, he continued his toilet, humming to himself, now and then, snatches of a popular comic song. Going to the fireplace, he began pushing about, with the toe of his shoes, the pieces of burning coal.

"It's odd how I love her—very! After my experience. And this time, as the man says in the play, it is love. Well, she has called the stakes. It is for me to win. If I don't, I can but lose."

He returned to the table on which the letters were. He picked up another, also unmistakably the production of a feminine hand. It contained but a line or two. It was without prefix or signature. And this time the writing was small and fine and clear:—

"I have heard nothing from you. The eight-and-forty hours will be up this afternoon at five. After that time I shall feel it my duty to do my utmost at once to save the life of an innocent man. I shall be at home to you till five."

Mr. Townsend read this epistle also with a smile, but he did not press it to his lips when read. Instead, he commented on it with a curious sort of humour.

"You pretty dear! You are the dangerous sort that always smiles. I have heard and read a good deal about women being cleverer than men, but till I met you I never met my match."

Tearing the letter into pieces, he dropped the fragments among the burning coals. As he adjusted his necktie before a looking-glass he indulged himself with further snatches of that comic song. Having completed his toilet, he went into the adjoining room. In response to his ring breakfast was brought in. And, with every appearance of the satisfaction of the man whose conscience is perfectly at ease, Mr. Townsend sat down to the discussion of his morning meal.

As he was finishing, a manservant opened the door.

"Lord Archibald Beaupré, sir, wishes to see you."

"Show him in here."

Presently there entered a tall, thin, and rather weedy-looking young man. His scanty hair was of that colourless fairness which is almost peculiar to a certain type of Scotchman. He would not have been bad-looking, in spite of his being slightly freckled, if it had not been for three things: first, he had obviously at least his share of the pride for which his countrymen are proverbial; second, he was obviously more than sufficiently weak; and third, he was equally obviously bad tempered.

On this occasion he did not seem to be by any means in the most agreeable frame of mind. Taking no sort of notice of Mr. Townsend's nodded greeting, he marched straight to an easy-chair, and, sitting down on it, he rested his hands on the handle of his stick, and his chin on his hands. He looked straight in front of him with about as sour a visage as he could well have worn. Mr. Townsend continued his breakfast as if there was nothing at all peculiar in his visitor's demeanour, and as he ate he smiled.

After a while he leaned back on his chair.

"Well, Archie, any news?"

"News be damned!"

Mr. Townsend still smiled.

"By all means if you wish it. It is the same to me."

"You know very well what I have come for."

"I take it that you have come to bestow on me for a short period the charm of your society." The visitor scowled. His host but smiled the more. "Have anything to eat?"

"I'll have something to drink."

"You'll find all the ingredients on the sideboard. Help yourself, dear boy."

The visitor helped himself. As he stood at the sideboard pouring the liquor out into a glass his host sat watching him with amusement which was wholly unconcealed. The contrast between the two men was striking. It would have forced itself on to the attention of the most casual spectator. The one weak, irritable almost to the point of peevishness; the other strong, unruffled, self-contained. The one with, in his whole bearing, that suggestion of self-assertion which is often but the child of shyness, but which none the less repels; the other with that easy, graceful, seemingly unconscious, personal magnetism which, in spite of oneself, attracts. One could understand how the one might be forgiven till seventy times seven, while the other would be condemned, without benefit of clergy, for his first offence.

Lord Archibald Beaupré returned to the easy-chair, armed with a tumbler of whisky and soda. He took a considerable drink. And then he spoke—morosely.

"It's the meeting of that cursed club to-night."

Mr. Townsend had watched his every movement, particularly seeming to note the quantity he had drunk—and still he smiled.

"So it is."

The other burst into a torrent of words.

"I wish I had never heard of it! I wish I had never had anything to do with it! I wish I had never had anything to do with any one of you! I wish—"

His emotions proved too much for him; he prematurely stopped.

"Wish it out." Mr. Townsend was lighting a cigarette. "And when you've wished it out, what then?"

"Damn you. You do nothing else but jibe and jeer at me."

"My dear Archie, your manners are not good."

"Curse my manners!"

"By all means, if you wish it. Only I am inclined to think there won't be very much to curse."

Lord Archibald ground out an oath between his teeth, and he groaned. Mr. Townsend went on; he was enjoying his cigarette.

"By the way, have you done anything for the Honour of the Club?"

His visitor half rose from his seat, then sank back into it again.

"No! You know I haven't! Don't talk of it! No!"

"I have no desire to talk of it. It is scarcely a question of talk. It is rather a question of do."

His hearer covered his face with his hands and shuddered. There was something in his host's eyes, as he smilingly regarded him, which suggested possibilities—and also limitations—of a distinctly curious sort. He kept his glance fixed on his companion, and, as he spoke again, he expelled through his nostrils the smoke of his cigarette.

"On the whole, perhaps, your policy of postponement may turn out fortunately for both of us. You will remember that under certain circumstances I reserved the right to nominate a candidate—a candidate, that is, for your attention. The circumstances which I thought might arise have arisen."

"Townsend!"

"Archie!"

Lord Archibald removed his hands from his face. The two men looked at each other—the one face ghastly, haggard, frightened; the other easy, careless, smiling.

"Do you mean it?"

Lord Archibald's voice was husky. Mr. Townsend flicked the ash from his cigarette.

"I am in the habit, in matters of moment, of meaning what I say, although that may not be the case with you."

The airily-suggested insinuation stung. The other burst into a sudden blaze of passion.

"What do you mean by that?"

The host met his visitor's furious gaze with a smile which seemed to convey a fulness of meaning which was sufficient to subdue the other's wrath.

"What did you mean by asking me if I meant what I said? Didn't you know?"

Lord Archibald turned his face away. Taking up the tumbler of soda and whisky he drained it of its contents. Getting up from his chair, he went to the sideboard to replenish. While he was in the act of doing so, and his back towards his host, he asked a question.

"Who is it?"

"A woman."

Lord Archibald spun round like a teetotum, a decanter in one hand, a tumbler in the other.

"A woman? Reggie? You—you don't mean Miss Jardine?"

Mr. Townsend's lips curled. In some subtle way his countenance was transfigured. The ease and the carelessness vanished. He became all bitterness and gall.

"Beaupré, I am inclined to think that you are the most consummate ass of my acquaintance. Why will you perpetually harp upon a single string? You are so utterly inept that the wonder is I have borne with you so long. Might I ask you not eternally to play the fool?"

Lord Archibald put down the decanter and the glass. The muscles of his face quivered as if he was about to be afflicted by an attack of St. Vitus' Dance.

"If anybody but you had spoken to me like that, at the very least he should never speak to me again."

The only effect which his visitor's fury had on Mr. Townsend was to make him still more scornful.

"Don't gas to me, my good fellow. Reserve that sort of thing for some other of your acquaintance. I regret that you should have rendered it necessary for me to remind you that you are under a considerable obligation to me, and I regret still more that you should have compelled me to ask if it is your intention to fulfil that obligation. I believe that even Scotchmen do occasionally fulfil their obligations."

His listener's face was a sickly yellow. Rage had made him calm.

"Mr. Townsend, be so good as to tell me who this woman is."

Thus requested, Mr. Townsend, scribbling something on a scrap of paper, tossed the scrap of paper across the table to his guest.

"There is her name and her address. I took you with me once to call on her. Probably you remember the occasion and the lady. Your business with her must be transacted before five o'clock this afternoon. If you are a quarter of an hour after that time you may as well postpone the fulfilment of your obligation to a future day. For my purpose you will be too late."

The other scanned what was written on the scrap of paper. He folded the paper up; he placed it in his waistcoat-pocket.

"You shall have the literal letter of your bond. Afterwards, Mr. Townsend, I will deal with you."

Without another word Lord Archibald Beaupré left the room.

Left to himself, Mr. Townsend threw the end of his cigarette into the fire. Thrusting his hands into his trouser-pockets, stretching out his legs in front of him, he stared at the flame and he smiled—not pleasantly.

"What a fool the fellow is! I have had about as much of him as I can stand. Indeed, I have had more. I hope they'll hang him. It will be a happy despatch. Or perhaps, after he has done the deed, he will turn, as a relief, to suicide. It's just the sort of thing he would do."

Something tickled him. He laughed.

"What a game of touch and go I'm playing."

He stood up.

"To think that he should have supposed that I meant Dora. My Dora!"

A panel photograph was on the mantelboard. It was the portrait of a young girl. Mr. Townsend apostrophised it as if it had been a living thing.

"My darling! If you had only come into my life before, how different it might all have been! If fortune had but let you come my way, evil should not have been my good. There is the making of a man in me, somewhere, that I swear. If I could but get out of it all and shake myself free and begin again, I'd quickly prove it."

Taking the photograph into his hand, he kissed it. It was strange how tender his voice had suddenly become.

"My love! What thing is this which I have been consorting with all this time, and supposing it was love? That's not love. Bah! I have learnt my lesson rather late in the day, but I have learnt it, sweet. You have taught me what is love."

He put the portrait back. He sat down again. But he still looked at the face which was on the mantelboard.

"The place in which I am is such a tight one. You had been wiser, dear, had you believed me when I wrote that I was not fit for you, and so straightway have let me go. Again I'll endeavour to persuade you. But if you'll not be persuaded I will win you, and I will hold you, and I will keep you if I can, though to do so I have to plunge deeper in the mire. It may be, indeed, that that way atonement lies. Who knows?"

CHAPTER XXXVII

"CALL ME DORA."

Mr. Townsend's rooms were at Albert Gate. Miss Jardine's home was in Sloane Gardens. From Albert Gate to Sloane Gardens is not very far. It was a clear, brisk morning. Mr. Townsend decided to walk.

Just as he had crossed the road some one touched his arm from behind, and a voice said—

"Excuse me—might I speak to you for a moment?"

Mr. Townsend turned. He supposed it was a beggar. The speaker looked like one. The man—it was a man—had on a top hat which was battered and bruised out of all semblance of its original shape. His overcoat, which was trimmed with imitation astrachan, was torn in half a dozen places and covered with mud, as if it had been rolled in the gutter with its owner inside it, but it was buttoned right up to his chin in a manner which suggested a not unnatural anxiety to conceal material deficiencies in the rest of his attire. His countenance bore evidence of having been recently subjected to serious ill-usage. One eye was ornamented by a purple patch, the skin of his right cheek was bruised and broken as by a blow from a fist, and his mouth was so badly cut as to say, the least, to render it highly inconvenient for him to be compelled to open his lips.

The sorry spectacle was Stewart Trevannion, alias Alexander Taunton, alias Mr. Arthur Stewart, alias a dozen other names—the immaculate Mr. Townsend's brother. A striking contrast the two brothers presented as they stood there.

Alexander was rubbing his hands over each other. He seemed to experience a difficulty in holding himself straight up. He shivered as if in pain.

"Reginald," he muttered.

Possibly Alexander was in a sensitive frame of mind. He seemed to shrink from the look of mingled amusement and scorn with which his brother regarded him.

"You!" Mr. Townsend's voice rang with laughter. "Well, my man, what do you want with me—charity?"

Alexander put up his hand, as if to hide his injured mouth.

"It isn't only that."

"No? What else is it then?"

"It's a word I want to say to you—a word of warning."

"Of warning? Against what?"

"Do you know a man named Haines—an American?"

"Haines?" Mr. Townsend reflected. "Well, what of Mr. Haines?"

"You've been doing something to his daughter—you best know what. He's found it out, and he's looking for you. If he gets a chance he'll kill you. He's almost done for me."

Mr. Townsend made a significant gesture in the direction of his brother.

"Is this his handiwork?"

"It's no laughing matter. I tell you he means murder. If you take my advice you'll clear. He left me as good as dead last night. He wouldn't have cared if he had left me quite. I don't believe I've a whole bone in my body. It's as much as I can do to stand." Alexander put his hand to his back and groaned. His tone became a whine. "You couldn't oblige me with the loan of a shilling or two?"

"With pleasure. I'll oblige you with the loan of a whole sovereign. If you take my advice you'll spend part of it on plaster. I'll think of what you've said. Good-day."

As he walked away Mr. Townsend swung his cane. He seemed amused. Alexander, clutching the sovereign tightly in his hand, stared after him. He did not seem to be at all amused.

"You may laugh now, but you won't laugh then. You've been up to some devil's trick, and this time you've caught the devil. If he does find you, one of you'll be missing."

As he pursued his way down Sloane Street, Mr. Townsend did not appear himself to regard his situation in such a serious light. The idea that there could be anything serious about it appeared to afford him nothing but amusement.

"Haines? Haines? I fancy that that's the name of Mrs. Carruth's Yankee friend. The dissenting parson sort of looking individual. I take it that Alexander, as usual, has the wrong end of the stick—from the look of him he appears to have felt both ends of it, and the middle too. If Mr. Haines has done me the honour to object to my behaviour, I imagine that it is because he supposes that I have poached on his preserve. I assure him he need be under no apprehension. If he only knew!"

Mr. Townsend laughed—then checked himself. He struck the ferrule of his stick against the pavement.

"Now, what am I to say to Dora? Its awkward—very!"

It was awkward. Especially as he had not made up his mind what to say to Dora, even when he found himself at Sir Haselton Jardine's.

He was shown at once into Miss Jardine's own sitting-room, and there he found the lady.

Miss Jardine was short and slight. Although she was not handsome, she certainly was not bad-looking. Her appearance, her bearing, her movements suggested buoyancy, activity, health. Her eyes were her most characteristic possession. They affected different people in different ways. They were blue eyes. Their chief peculiarity was that they were light—some people said unnaturally light. But, as also they were beautiful eyes, that saying may be set down to malice. Somehow one felt as one looked at Miss Jardine that she would never cry.

She held out her hand to Mr. Townsend.

"Reggie!"

Mr. Townsend made no attempt to touch the outstretched hand. He merely bowed.

"Miss Jardine!"

Miss Jardine was not at all disconcerted. She laughed.

"So it's that way!" She assumed an air of mock dignity, which became her very well. "Mr. Townsend, may I offer you a chair?"

"With your permission I will stand."

Mr. Townsend spoke with an air of decorous propriety which approached the severe. The lady did not fall into his mood at all. She looked up at him with her sunny eyes.

"Stand! Why stand?"

Mr. Townsend returned the young lady's smiling glance, without evincing any inclination to smile in return.

"You have sent for me. I have come."

Going to the fireplace, Miss Jardine stood with one foot upon the kerb. Her hands were behind her back. Her face was inclined a little upwards. She reminded one somehow of a bird—a resemblance which owed something, perhaps, to the brightness of her eyes.

"I have one or two questions which I wish to ask you. You must answer them. First, Do you love me?"

"You must forgive my suggesting that that is scarcely the first question which you should ask me. The man in the street may love you. It does not follow that he is worthy."

"But if I love him?"

Mr. Townsend made a slight movement with his hands. He was standing in what, to the average Englishman, is a rather trying position—in the centre of the room, away from any article of furniture, with his arms hanging loosely at his sides; and yet he looked well.

"He may love you. You may love him. And yet any connection with him may bring you, at the best, unhappiness."

"You have not answered my question. Do you love me?"

"You know that I do."

"As you say, I know that you do. You know also that I love you. My second question, Are you married?"

"I am not."

"Then why should you not marry me? Stay! Let me explain my position."

His eyes became, if anything, brighter. Something came over her which made one forget how physically small she was. One realised that the girl, like the man she was addressing, had a magnetic personality of her own.

"I am, in a measure, Reggie—I am going to call you Reggie—what it is the fashion to call a pessimist. It is my father's dower. I am afraid that, in a sense, from the men of my acquaintance, I always expect the worst. I believe most of them do, in their youth, many things which they ought not to do—and for which, in their age, they are sorry. I take this for granted. And I believe that, in spite of this being so, some of them make good husbands and good fathers. I think it possible that your temptations have been greater than is the case with the average man, and that, therefore, your misdoings have been more. But I am convinced that, as regards real strength, you are stronger than the average man, and that you can, if you like, put these things behind you for ever—and, on the stepping-stones of your dead self, rise to higher things. And I believe that you will like, because you love me—and because, also, I love you."

"Unfortunately, Miss Jardine—"

She made an imperious gesture with her hand.

"Call me Dora. With you, now, it shall not be Miss Jardine."

"Unfortunately"—there was an almost imperceptible pause, and then there came very softly the Christian name—"Dora, there are things which, when they are once done, we cannot put away. They meet us at Philippi."

"If in your life there are such ghosts, why did you ask me to marry you?"

"I ought not to have done. When I did I hoped that I should be able to lay the ghosts, and that for me there would be no Philippi."

"But is there no hope now?" He seemed to hesitate. She went on with, in her voice, a sudden tremor. "Consider! Think well before you speak! Reggie, I wonder if you know how much the spoiling of your life will mean the spoiling of mine?"

Her voice, or her manner, or her words—or all three combined—affected Mr. Townsend strangely. There seemed to be something in her glance which he found himself unable to encounter. He turned away. Going to him, she touched him softly on the arm. A shudder went all over him. The muscles of his face seemed to stiffen; his expression became a little set. His voice also became, as it were, a little rigid.

"There may be hope."

"There may be? Reggie!" She paused—as if breathless. "Of laying the ghosts—for ever?"

"For ever."

She was still again. Her articulation seemed to be actually impeded.

"When will you know—for sure?"

"This afternoon, at five."

"Reggie!" His words appeared to take her by surprise. "Do you mean it—really?"

"I do."

He turned and looked at her. Their glances met. She shrank away from him. The hot blood flowed into her cheeks. Her emotion was so great, it made her beautiful. His name came from her lips, with a catching of her breath, and in a whisper. She was visibly trembling.

"Reggie!"

CHAPTER XXXVIII

ON THE THRESHOLD

It was plain that Mrs. Carruth was impatient. Nor was the thing made less evident by her attempts to conceal it from herself. She lounged on a couch. A pile of books and magazines was at her side. She pretended to read—or, rather, it would be more correct to write that she tried not to pretend to read. But it would not do. It was nothing but pretence. And she knew that it was nothing but pretence. She took up a book. She turned a page or two. She put it down again. She exchanged it for a magazine—a magazine with pictures. She tried to look at the pictures. The pictures palled. She essayed a magazine without pictures.

That was as great a failure as the other. In her present mood the ministrations of print and pictures alike were ineffectual.

No wonder she had become impatient. She had been on tenterhooks all day—waiting! waiting! All the morning she had expected to receive some sort of communication—some acknowledgment of the expressive line or two which she had sent. But when lunch came, and there still was nothing, she was quite sure that, during the afternoon the gentleman would come himself.

She was ready for him by two. She did not think it likely that he would come quite so early. Still, it would be well that she should not be taken unawares. So she made herself even unwontedly charming. She put on a brand-new dress, which suited her to perfection. It really did make her look uncommonly nice! It fitted her so well that it displayed her long, lithe, and yet by no means unbecomingly bony figure, to the best advantage. She took astonishing pains with her hair. She even went in for unusual splendour in the way of shoes and stockings. And the effect produced by the few touches which she bestowed upon her countenance was wonderful.

In spite of all she was ready by two. And still—he cometh not, she said. The silvery chimes of the exquisite little clock which stood on the top of the overmantel announced that it was three-quarters after three. She looked at her own watch to see if it really was so late. The thing was true enough. Her watch was in complete agreement with the clock—it was a quarter to four.

She put down the last of the magazines with, in her manner, an appearance of finality. She rose from the couch. She went to the window. She stood there with her fingertips drumming idly and noiselessly against the pane. The only creature in sight was a milkman, who, by way of killing two birds with one stone, was serving a customer across the road, and flirting with the maid. Mrs. Carruth watched the flirtation proceed to its conclusion, and, when the milkman, springing into his cart, had disappeared with the inevitable clatter, Mrs. Carruth, turning away from the window, came back into the room.

She stood at a little centre table. She laughed to herself.

"If, after all, he shouldn't come—what fun it would be!"

She was very far from being an ill-looking woman, as she stood there, with smiles puckering her lips and peeping from her eyes.

"If he should suppose that I am not in earnest! His experience may teach him that many women never are in earnest. If he should imagine that I am one of the many!"

Raising her right hand, she began daintily pinching her lower lip between her finger and her thumb.

"It would be a pity for both of us." She made a little impatient movement with her head. "And yet, I can't believe that a man with his experience could suppose that I am one of the many. If he did, it would be his fault—not mine."

The little clock struck four.

"An hour more, my friend—an hour more. And then—well, I do hope you'll come before the hour's out, for your sake, as well as mine. I wonder if, in this little matter, I've been counting my chickens before they're hatched. I, of all women, should have known better. And, with such a hand faced on the board, one might be excused for supposing that it would take the pool. A straight flush cannot be beaten."

She laughed again, this time not quite so lightly.

"It reminds me of some of the games which I have seen played. You can't show a hand to beat a straight, but you can fight to save the pool. I wonder if he means fighting. If he does, it'll be against all the odds. He has neither gun nor bow. When I start shooting, he's bound to drop. Sure."

The merriment passed from her face, the laughter from her eyes—an expression of anxiety came into them instead; a look which suggested hunger, a something which made her, all at once, seem actually old.

"Perhaps he takes it that a victory, on these lines, may mean more than a defeat. And he counts on that. It would, too. It would mean farewell—a long farewell, an actual farewell—to another of my dreams. And the brightest of them all. But I don't care. It would mean death to him. Death! And such a death! And, after all, it would only mean a stumble to me. From the practice I have had, I have become so used to stumbles that surely one other wouldn't count."

She began moving about the room restlessly, touching here a table, there a chair, to the window, and back again, as if a spirit possessed her which made her not know what it was she wanted to be at. She approached a corner of the room, as if she were about to take refuge in it, like some naughty child. As she went, clenching her fists, as if she were pressing her finger-nails into her palms, she gave a little cry.

"Oh, I'd give—I'd give, what wouldn't I give?—if he'd come into the room, now—without keeping me waiting any longer, now!—and speak to me as I would have him speak! Why doesn't he come? He has everything to gain, he has nothing to lose!"

She swept right round, with a swish of her skirts, in a sort of frenzy, echoing her own question as she swung out her arms in front of her.

"Why doesn't he come?"

Even as the words were on her lips, at the hall door there came a knocking. She went red and white, despite the aids of beauty! She caught at a chair, as if desirous of having something to lean against.

"Thank God!"

Then, as if conscious of the incongruity of such words upon her lips, she put her hands up to her face.

"Oh, I'm so glad he's come!"

Some one outside had hold of the handle of the door. She uncovered her face. She touched her hair. She touched the bosom of her dress. She dropped into the chair by which she was standing. In an instant she was the picture of composure.

The door opened to admit Mr. Haines.

His appearance was a shock to Mrs. Carruth. She looked negligently round, as if indifferent who the new-comer might be, and then—she stared.

"You!"

There was something in the lady's intonation which was very far from being complimentary. She stood up, quivering with disappointment and with rage.

"I thought I gave instructions that this afternoon I was not at home to visitors."

Mr. Haines did not seem to be at all nonplussed.

"That's what the young lady who opened the door told me. I said I would wait until you were. I will."

Mr. Haines sat down—with every appearance of having come to stay. Mrs. Carruth looked at the clock, then at her watch, then at the gentleman upon the chair. The gentleman in question, with his head thrown back, was staring at the ceiling, as if quite unconscious of her neighbourhood. It seemed to be as much as the lady could do to retain her self-control.

"I am sure, Mr. Haines, that you cannot wish to be rude. I have an appointment this afternoon which I regret will prevent my having the pleasure of receiving you."

"I'm going to have my say. I'll say it afterwards, or I'll say it now. It's all the same to me."

"What do you mean by you're going to have your say?"

"If you're ready, I'll let it out. But don't mind me. Don't let me spoil your appointment. Keep anything you've got to keep."

Mrs. Carruth seemed to be at a loss to know what to do. Her looks were eloquent witnesses as to what she would have done if she could. But, apparently, she did not see her way to do it. She temporised.

"If there is anything of importance, Mr. Haines, which you wished to say to me, perhaps you will be so good as to say it as briefly as you can, now. Possibly it will not detain you, at the utmost, more than a quarter of an hour."

"Possibly it will not. I rather reckon you'll have a word to say in that. It won't all be for me." Mr. Haines brought his eyes down to the level of the lady's face. He spread out his hands upon his knees. He looked at her very straight. "What I have to say may be said in about two words. It's just this—I've found my girl."

Mrs. Carruth did not display any great amount of interest, but she did seem to be surprised.

"Indeed! I am glad to hear it. I hope that she is well."

"She is well. She's better than many of us ever will be. She's at rest."

"At rest? How?"

"As it was told to me. She is dead."

"Dead! Mr. Haines?"

"Yes, murdered. As I saw it in the vision, so it is."

Mrs. Carruth looked at Mr. Haines as if she felt that he had a somewhat singular method of imparting information—especially of such a peculiar kind.

"If what you say is correct, you have such a queer way of putting things. I never can quite make you out. I need not tell you how sorry I am."

"You have cause for sorrow. The grief is about half yours."

"Half mine? What do you mean?"

"I have loved you, true and faithful, since the first time I set eyes on you. Before ever Daniel did."

The sudden change of subject seemed, not unnaturally, to take the lady aback.

"What nonsense are you talking? What did you mean by saying the grief's half mine?"

"I'm coming to it, in time. I want to put to you this question. Will you have me, now, just as I am?"

"I will not; neither now or ever. How many more times am I to tell you that? Jack Haines, I do believe you're more than half insane."

"I may be. So'll you be before I'm through." Raising the big forefinger of his right hand, he wagged it at her solemnly. "There's some one come between us. Yes. That aristocrat."

"Aristocrat? What do you mean?"

"You know what I mean. Yes. The blood-stained Townsend. I knew he was stained with blood when first I saw him inside this room. But I did not know with whose blood he was stained, or I would have called him to his account right there and then. I did not know he was stained with the blood of my girl."

"Jack!"

The name came from her with an unconscious recurrence to the days which were gone.

"Yes. This is the man who has stolen what ought by rights to have been mine—the slayer of my girl."

"It's not true! You coward! You know you lie!"

"I do not lie."

"You do lie! What proof have you?"

"Enough and to spare—for him, for me, and for you."

"Out with it, then. Let's hear what some of it's like."

Mrs. Carruth was standing by the little centre table. Rising from his chair, Mr. Haines went and stood at the other side of it. Resting his hands on the edges, he leaned over it towards her.

"Have you heard of the Three Bridges tragedy?"

She looked at him just once. In that one look she saw something, on his face or in his eyes, which, to use an expressive idiom, seemed to take the stiffening all out of her. She dropped into a chair as if he had knocked her into it. She caught at the arms. Her complexion assumed a curious tinge of yellow. There was a moment's pause. Then, from between her rigid lips, there came one word.

"Yes."

"The woman who was killed was Loo—my Loo."

She shuddered, as if attacked by sudden ague.

"It's a lie!"

"It's not a lie. It's gospel truth. And Townsend killed her."

Her rejoinder, under ordinary circumstances, might have struck him as an odd one.

"You can't prove it."

"I can prove it. And the police can prove it, too."

Half rising from her chair, she turned to him, every muscle in her body seemed to be quivering with excitement.

"The police? Do they know it?"

"They do. To-morrow the whole world will know it. They've laid hold of the wrong man. They've found it out just before it's a bit too late. They hope to have hold of your friend Townsend soon. They're hoping wrong. His first reckoning will be with me. When that is through, neither he nor I will care who has what's left. Since I have loved you, true and faithful, all these years, I calculated I would come and ask you if, when all is done, you'd give me my reward. We might make a happy ending of it, you and me together, over on the other side. But if you won't, you won't. So I'm through. I've only one word left— good-bye."

He held out his hand to her. So far as she was concerned, it went unheeded. Indeed, it would seem, from the eager question which she asked, that most of what he had been saying had gone unheeded too.

"Are you sure the police are after him? Are you sure?"

He looked at her from under the shadow of his bushy, overhanging eyebrows, in silence, for a moment. Then he said, more in sorrow than in anger—

"So your last thought is of him? Well, I'm sorry!"

Without anymore elaborate leave-taking than was comprised in these few words. Mr. Haines went from the room and from the house.

Mrs. Carruth seemed scarcely conscious of the fact of his departure. All her faculties and all her thoughts seemed far away. Indeed, it was only after a lapse of some seconds that, looking about her, with a start, she appeared to recognise that she was alone. Getting up, she began to pace feverishly about the room, as if only rapid movement could enable her to control the fires which were mounting in her blood.

"I wonder if it's true! I wonder if it is! Perhaps that explains why it is he hasn't come. I may have been misjudging him. Perhaps he can't come. Suppose he is arrested. Perhaps he doesn't know what it is the police have discovered. He's nearly certain not to know. Who's to tell him? I will go and tell him! This instant! Now! I will warn him against the police and against Jack Haines. I will save him yet, yet. He shall owe it all to me."

With her hands she brushed her hair from her brow—the hair which she had so carefully arranged.

"After all I have longed for, after all I have lived through, I do believe that for him I should esteem the world well lost."

She ran upstairs—literally ran. She put on a coat and hat in a space of time which, for shortness, considering that a pretty woman was concerned, was simply marvellous. And having put them on, she ran down the stairs. She hurried through the hall. She opened the hall door.

And as she did so something or some one bounded up the steps—rather than mounted them in an ordinary fashion. There was a flash of something in the air. Mrs. Carruth was borne backwards.

A second afterwards she was lying half on her face, with the lifeblood streaming from her on to the floor.

CHAPTER XXXIX

THE LAST MEETING OF THE CLUB

Horseferry Road. A hazy though a cloudless night. A house, the windows of which showed no lights. Up two flights of stairs.

The rendezvous of that agreeable social institution, the Murder Club.

The Club was to hold a session. The gentleman who, if he was not the actual source of inspiration, was, at any rate, the founder, the promoter, the organiser, the backbone of the Club, was making ready for the members coming. A man about the middle height, somewhat slightly built, in evening dress, with an orchid in his buttonhole—Mr. Cecil Pendarvon. Mr. Pendarvon was not bad-looking. He had a long, fair beard, which he had a trick of pulling with both his hands. His eyes were certainly not ugly, but to the close observer they conveyed an odd impression. As one watched them, one began to wonder if they were the man's real eyes which one saw, or if the real eyes were behind them. Perhaps one had this feeling of wonder, because, although there always was the light of laughter in Mr. Pendarvon's eyes, their real expression was one of such cold, passionless, unrelenting cruelty.

For some reason Mr. Pendarvon seemed ill at ease. One hand was resting on the large oval table which occupied the greater portion of the room, with the other he tugged at his beard, while he stared at a manuscript volume, bound in a beautiful scarlet binding, which lay open in front of him. A cackling sound was emitted from his throat, which was, possibly, intended for a chuckle.

"His signature! His sign manual! An elegant example, too! With his own hand—tied tight. If I remember rightly, he did say something about his practically committing suicide by affixing his signature to such a declaration. How often is truth spoken in a jest. What fools men are!"

His statement—which was very far from being an original statement—of the folly of humanity, seemed to afford him a large amount of satisfaction. He combed his beard with the fingers of both his hands. He kept on chuckling to himself as if he had given utterance to one of the best jokes that ever was heard.

"What's that?"

It was queer to notice how, in an instant, all signs of amusement fled. He gripped the rim of the massive table, as if seeking its support. He cast a stealthy glance about him. He stood and listened, seeming to hold his breath to enable him to do it better. The man's real self peeped from his eyes. His whole bearing suggested fear.

There was a perfect silence for some moments. Then he drew a long breath.

"It's nothing." He began again to tug at his beard, as if mechanically. "What a little upsets a man if he is in the mood." He glanced at his watch, seeming, as he did so, to make a mental calculation. "It's time that some of them were here." He paused, the remainder of his speech apparently referring to some other theme. "I hope that one can rely upon them sometimes—that one may take it that the guardians of law and order do not always blunder. I suppose that we are shadowed. I suppose, too, that they will make no movement until they have received ocular demonstration of the fact that all of them are here. What's that?"

Again there was a sudden, startling change in Mr. Pendarvon's outward bearing. Obviously his every faculty was strained in the act of listening. So far as an ordinary observer would have been able to judge there did not appear to be a sound. Yet it is not improbable that something had made itself audible to Mr. Pendarvon's unusually keen sense of hearing, because presently a slight click was heard, as it seemed, within the wall itself upon his right.

"Number one!"

Mr. Pendarvon's state of tension seemed to slightly decrease. The wall upon his right was panelled from floor to ceiling. One of the panels Mr. Pendarvon slipped aside, and, in doing so, revealed a dial-plate of peculiar construction, which apparently had some connection with electricity. On it was a prominent figure 2. Beneath it a needle made three separate strokes. A large 1 appeared. Then three more separate strokes. Then another prominent 2. On the appearance of the second 2, on Mr. Pendarvon's touching an ivory button, the whole thing performed a complete revolution, and a sound as of a gong was heard.

While the gong still continued to vibrate, a voice was heard outside the door exclaiming "Reginald!"

The announcement of the name seemed to precipitate Mr. Pendarvon back into his former condition of uneasiness.

"The man himself," he muttered. Then, by way of an afterthought, with a smile which by no means suggested mirth, "I wonder if they saw him come."

He seemed to hesitate, then, with an effort, to pull himself together.

"The honourable member should not be kept waiting."

As he made this observation to himself, with another mirthless grin, he pressed a second button, which was on the other side of the dial. Immediately the door without swung open.

In another moment Mr. Reginald Townsend appeared upon the threshold of the door.

"A trifle slow to-night, Pendarvon—eh?"

Mr. Pendarvon admitted the soft impeachment.

"I'm afraid that this time, perhaps, I am. You've caught me napping. I was just putting the things in order when you came."

"Putting the things in order! I see. The things want putting in order, Pendarvon—eh?"

"There is a certain amount of work which has to be done, which, of course, by virtue of my office"—this with a sneer which, perhaps, the speaker found it impossible to suppress—"I have to do."

"By virtue of your office; yes." Mr. Pendarvon looked up at Mr. Townsend, only, as it were, by accident and for a moment; then his glance went back again. "It would be a fine night if it were not for the mist which is in the air. One now and then can get peeps at the stars beyond. But this mist gives me a chill."

"It's warm enough in here."

"Oh, yes, it's sufficiently warm in here."

In each man's manner there was something which was distinctly out of the ordinary, and the strangest part of it was that, though each was, as a rule, as keen an observer as one might easily meet, neither seemed to realise that there was anything unusual in the bearing of the other. Mr. Pendarvon was restless, fidgety, fussy, continually on the watch for something to happen, not in the room, but out of it. He was like a person who has an appointment of the first importance, and who is devoured with anxiety lest the individual with whom he has the appointment should fail to keep it. Mr. Townsend's mood, on the other hand, seemed almost transcendental. His physical beauty, uncommon both in type and in degree, seemed to-night to have positively increased. It was almost startling. He seemed, too, to have increased in height. He bore himself with an unconscious grace which displayed his splendid figure to singular advantage. His head was thrown a little back from his shoulders, and in his eyes and in the whole expression of his face there was something which suggested rapturous calm. One felt that, whatever happened, this man's mind would be at ease. He recalled the soldier who, having volunteered for a forlorn hope, advances to meet death, and worse than death, with a smile.

It is probably when our soldiers have been in just that mood that they have done the deeds which have seemed to the world to be miracles of valour. It is when one cares for nothing that, sometimes, one can do anything.

Each of these men, however, seemed to be so preoccupied in his affairs that he noticed nothing uncommon in the other. Mr. Pendarvon fidgeted about the room. He set the chairs straight, the decanters on the table. He occupied himself with a dozen trifling things which scarcely seemed to stand in need of his attention. Mr. Townsend stood in front of the huge, old-fashioned fireplace paying no sort of heed to the other's fussiness, seeming indeed to be in a condition of mind which, psychologically, approximated to a waking dream.

Although he took no notice of the fit of fidgets with which Mr. Pendarvon seemed to be afflicted, his very calmness caused that gentleman to seem still more ill at ease. More than once he seemed to be on the point of saying something and then to stop short as if for want of being able to find something appropriate to say.

At last he did hit upon a sufficiently apposite remark.

"They're late to-night."

The sound of his voice seemed to rouse Mr. Townsend to the fact of Mr. Pendarvon's presence.

"They are a little late to-night, Pendarvon." He looked at his watch. "Indeed! Is it possible that they may have neglected to make a note of the occasion?"

Mr. Pendarvon laughed—again not merrily.

"I don't think there is much fear of that. They're sure to come, if only for their own safety's sake." Again the cheerless grin. "Possibly they're trying to get their spirits up by putting the spirits down upon the way. Hark! there's some one coming now."

There was a silence as the two men listened, with their eyes upon the dial-plate which Mr. Pendarvon had left exposed. It repeated the performance with which it had announced Mr. Townsend's arrival.

"You have good ears, Pendarvon. I heard nothing."

Mr. Pendarvon admitted that it was so.

"I have good ears."

He spoke with a dryness which seemed to be unnecessarily significant. He sounded the gong. There was a voice without.

"Henry!"

"Dear Mr. Shepherd. You may let him in."

The door swung open. There entered a tall man, with long grey hair, clad in the attire of a superior mechanic. He had a silent face—the face of a man who can be silent in very many tongues—and the eyes of a man who sees visions. He vouchsafed no sort of greeting, but at once sat down on one of the chairs which stood around the table.

Mr. Townsend looked at him as one looks at an object which one finds an interesting study.

"I trust, Mr. Shepherd, that you may have fortune in drawing the lot to-night."

Mr. Shepherd opened his lips, which hitherto he had kept hermetically closed. He spoke with a nasal twang which suggested a certain type of prayer-meeting.

"Not to-night: my hour is not yet."

"Indeed! May I ask when your hour is likely to be?"

"I seek not to inquire."

The hint which Mr. Shepherd intended to convey was unmistakable. Mr. Pendarvon laughed. Mr. Townsend stared. Before the latter could speak again the dial-plate repeated its previous performances. This time two voices answered to the summons of the gong.

The door opened to admit Mr. Teddy Hibbard and his inseparable friend, Mr. Eugene Silvester.

They were both of them boys, rather than men, and were obviously members of that class which, in a more advanced stage of social organisation, will probably, during its salad days, be detained in some kindly institution, the inmates of which will be gently, yet firmly, persuaded to do themselves as little injury as they conveniently can. They grow out of it, some of these young men, in time. But one had only to look at this particular two to see that, with them, that time was scarcely yet.

The bell, being started, was kept rolling. One after the other the members of the Club came in. A heterogeneous gathering they were. One wondered what some of them did in such a galley. They seemed to be so oddly out of place.

At last, with two exceptions, all the members were assembled. One of the exceptions was Lord Archibald Beaupré. His absence was the cause, not only of comment, but, as time went on, and still he did not come, of obvious uneasiness to some of those who had arrived. Tell-tale looks came on their faces. They eyed each other, as it were, askance. They not only inquired of one another why it was he did not come, but they made the same inquiry of themselves with still more emphasis. The appearance of indifference with which, at first, they had treated the absent member's tardiness became less and less convincing. It was he who last had drawn the lot. It was he who had to do something for the Honour of the Club.

What was it which had detained him?

Mr. Pendarvon, who, plainly, was not the least uneasy of those who were present in the room, addressed an inquiry to Mr. Townsend.

"You are Beaupré's fidus achates, Townsend. When did you see him last?"

Mr. Townsend had evidently shown an indifference to the fact of Lord Archibald Beaupré's non-arrival which evidently in his case was not assumed. He looked at Mr. Pendarvon a moment before he answered, and when he did answer his manner, although completely courteous, was hardly genial.

"For information of Lord Archibald Beaupré I must refer you—to Lord Archibald Beaupré."

Mr. Pendarvon seemed to relish neither the look with which he had been favoured nor the answer. Indeed, Mr. Townsend's manner, even more than his answer, seemed to increase the general feeling of uneasiness which was beginning to dominate the room.

Suddenly there was the sound of a click. With a rapidity which, in its way, was comic, all eyes were fixed upon the dial-plate. Its mechanism had been set in motion. The familiar movements followed.

"There he is!" exclaimed a voice.

Mr. Silvester added, with a show of hilarity which was slightly forced, "Better late than never!"

Mr. Pendarvon sounded the gong, seemingly in a state of fevered agitation.

"Stephen!" exclaimed a voice.

A blank look came on some of the faces.

"It isn't Beaupré; it's Kendrick!"

Colonel Kendrick was the other member who had not yet put in an appearance. His absence had gone almost unnoticed. He had to do nothing for the Honour of the Club—as yet.

Colonel Kendrick came into the room. He was a thickset, soldierly-looking man, with a slight grey moustache and a pair of bold, unflinching eyes. He bowed as he came in, speaking in that short, crisp, staccato tone of voice which is apt to mark the man who has been accustomed to command.

"Gentlemen, I have to apologise to you for my delay." He turned to Mr. Townsend. "I have to inform you, Mr. Townsend, that Mr. Pendarvon has set the police upon your track."

CHAPTER XL

MR. TOWNSEND REACHES HOME

The members, for the most part, stared at the Colonel. Then they stared at one another. They did not seem to understand. Mr. Townsend looked at the Colonel, then at Mr. Pendarvon. Mr. Pendarvon, with twitching lips and dilated eyes, was leaning, as if for support, against the dial-plate.

"Pendarvon, I am waiting for you to contradict what Kendrick has said."

Mr. Pendarvon was making an effort to control his faculty of speech.

"It's false."

Mr. Townsend turned to the Colonel.

"You hear what he says?"

The Colonel pointed at Mr. Pendarvon.

"And you see how he says it." They did see. The disclosure of his treachery, being premature, had taken Mr. Pendarvon unawares. It had, unfortunately, caused him to lose his nerve. He stood crouching against the wall, trembling, like a cur, in terror of what might be to come.

The man's guilt was self-confessed. They perceived that it was so with a stupefaction which made them dumb.

Colonel Kendrick went on.

"I have a cousin at Scotland Yard. He has just now told me that, this morning, they received information of the existence of an organisation called the Murder Club. They had been told that the individual who was actually responsible for the Three Bridges Tragedy was a member of the Club. His name was Reginald Townsend. I asked who was their informant. I was told that it was a man named Cecil Pendarvon. So, gentlemen, the person who is responsible for the position in which we find ourselves is the one who has given us away."

One or two of the members made a half-unconscious movement forward. Mr. Pendarvon seemed to endeavour to huddle himself closer to the dial-plate.

"My cousin informed me that the club was to meet tonight, and that a coup was to be made while the members were in actual assembly. I have hurried straight from my cousin here. I have some acquaintance with the personnel of Scotland Yard. As I approached these premises I recognised one or two individuals whom I knew by sight. Mr. Townsend, the police are at the door waiting to receive the signal to effect your capture."

Of all those present Mr. Townsend seemed the least affected by the Colonel's communication. It was the humorous side of the situation which seemed to strike him first.

"It is the unexpected happens, my dear Kendrick. I do believe that all the wisdom of the world is contained in that one phrase. The blow has come from the quarter from which I least expected it. Mr. Pendarvon, I presume that you are acquainted with the rule which you yourself framed, and which lays down the measure which is to be meted out to traitors."

Mr. Townsend moved towards Mr. Pendarvon. Snatching a revolver from his pocket, Mr. Pendarvon pointed it in the face of the man he had betrayed. In an instant Colonel Kendrick had struck it from his hand. One barrel was discharged harmlessly as it fell. Immediately a dozen weapons were in a dozen hands. Mr. Townsend retained his appearance of perfect ease. Standing in front of Mr. Pendarvon, he regarded that gentleman with courteous contempt which caused him, literally, to seem to wither.

"Well done!"

The tranquil scorn of Mr. Townsend's tone seemed to affect Mr. Pendarvon as if it had been vitriol. He writhed.

"You—you hound!" he spluttered.

Mr. Townsend merely repeated his former commendation, which the other received as if it had been a scorpion's lash.

"Well done!"

There was a click. Mr. Pendarvon's body was obscuring the dial-plate. With scant ceremony, the Colonel thrust him aside. The dial had made a new departure. It displayed the figure 3.

The Colonel spoke.

"I fancy we may take it that that is the signal which Mr. Pendarvon has arranged with his policemen friends. It is they who have given it, being now outside the door. I imagine, gentlemen, that, so far as we are concerned, we have but little to fear. Be so good, some one, as to tear that book and to burn it."

The Colonel pointed to the manuscript book in the beautiful crimson cover. Some one snatched it up. In a moment it was in pieces and the pieces were in flames. Mr. Pendarvon made a movement as if he would have done something to check the destruction of so important a witness. The Colonel checked him with a word.

"Stand still!" And Mr. Pendarvon was still. The Colonel turned to Mr. Townsend. "It is you who have most to fear. Can you suggest how you may be able to effect your escape?"

"Unless Mr. Pendarvon has romanced, he has not only provided the trap, but also the means of escape from the trap which he has baited—unless, I say, he has romanced. We shall see. Good-bye, Pendarvon."

With a gesture of careless insolence, with his open palm, Mr. Townsend struck Mr. Pendarvon lightly across the face. That was too much even for Mr. Pendarvon. He sprang at Mr. Townsend. Mr. Townsend knocked him down. Being down, he seemed to deem it wiser, on the whole, to stay there.

A voice was heard without—a peremptory voice, an official voice.

"Open this door immediately, or we shall break it down!"

Mr. Townsend gave a mocking rejoinder.

"Break it down; by all means, break it down!" He went to the fireplace; he stood within it. He turned to the assembled company. "We shall meet again—at Philippi!"

He grasped the first two stanchions and was immediately out of sight.

"Count twelve," he told himself as he climbed. "This is the twelfth. Put out your hand to the right, and you will feel a bolt. This does feel like a bolt, and a door. After all, Pendarvon, you're not such a liar as you might have been."

Scrambling through the door which he had thrust open, Mr. Townsend found himself standing on what was evidently thereof. It was flat just there. In front of him was a high brick wall, which served as a base for a stack of chimneys.

He stood for some seconds listening. He could distinctly hear voices ascending from the room below.

"I wonder what they will do to our friend Pendarvon, and how long they will keep those dear policemen out—if I shall have time to do what I have to do. Keep moving, sir! The moments are all that you can call your own."

He went forward, keeping the stack of chimneys on his left.

"Hallo! There's the edge of the roof! Yes, and here's a rail and a bridge—all spoken of by our friend Pendarvon. To essay the great act of crossing the bridge!"

He stepped on to the plank. It quivered beneath his weight.

"This bridge is of somewhat rickety construction and the rail unsteady."

When about half-way across he paused. The plank seemed to be bending double. He peered into the depths below.

"It occurs to me that it would not be a difficult business to smash this bridge into two clean halves as I stand here. That might be an easy way to end it all. But it will not serve. There is that which I must do."

He moved on more rapidly. The frail planking shuddered and shook; it swung in the air. More than once it seemed as if the tall, quickly-moving figure was supported upon nothing. But the bridge became firmer as he approached the opposite side. He put out his hand to the left, feeling for what Mr. Pendarvon told him he would find there.

"The ladder! As he said, straight against the wall. Bravo! Now, if the house is only empty, the thing is done!"

The house was empty, and the thing was done. It all happened as Mr. Pendarvon had said it would. He ascended the ladder, raised the unlatched window frame, struck a light, passed through the empty house, and into the street beyond. He found a cab, and, ere long, he was at Albert Gate.

As he stepped out of the cab some one touched him on the shoulder from behind. He turned sharply round, thinking, perhaps, that he had but escaped from one pitfall to fall at once into another.

But it was not so. The person whom he found himself confronting was that recalcitrant member of the Murder Club, Lord Archibald Beaupré.

"You! Well?"

This was Mr. Townsend's greeting. Lord Archibald's response was a little delayed. When it did come it came in a hoarse whisper from between tremulous lips.

"Why did you do it?"

"Do what?"

Lord Archibald, leaning forward, whispered something into Mr. Townsend's ear.

"I was afraid, my dear Archie, that you might be a quarter of an hour too late." Mr. Townsend paused, looking at, without seeming to notice, the other's ashen countenance. "Is she dead?"

"No."

"Will she die?"

"No."

There was silence. Then Lord Archibald went on, rendered almost voiceless by contending emotions, "I was there in time; you should have waited."

"As I tell you, my dear Archie, it was a question of a quarter of an hour."

"When I got there the house was in commotion. They had found her lying in the hall, as you had left her. She was regaining consciousness as I arrived. When she saw me she made me stoop down and she whispered to me. She told me that it was you who had done it, and that you did it just as she was starting to save you."

"She has, perhaps, her own notions of salvation."

"I think she meant it. She said she was coming to warn you against a man named Haines."

"Haines? Indeed! That is the second time I have been warned against a man named Haines. By the way, I have just come from Horseferry Road. Pendarvon has given the show away."

"Pendarvon?"

"Yes, Pendarvon. He has, what I believe old-fashioned thieves used to call, blown the gaff. The place is in the hands of the police. I escaped up the chimney. I expect that the gentlemen in blue will soon be here. I have no doubt that already they have missed me and are hot upon my trail."

"Reggie!"

In Lord Archibald's voice there was something which sounded very like a sob.

"Don't worry about me, dear boy. For me, anyhow, all things are over. You'll be all right. After all, it was lucky for you that I was first upon the scene." Having paused, he added, "Tell her, when she is all right again, as you seem to think she will be, that I am sorry I did it. She should have left me a wider option."

"I don't believe she means to give you away. When the policemen asked her who had done it she said that the man was a stranger to her. She had never seen him in her life before."

"Did she, indeed? How very odd! They tell you not to trust a woman. My experience teaches me not to trust a man. One thing I do regret. I should have liked to have killed Pendarvon. Archie, I want you to do me a favour—to take a message."

"To whom?"

"To Miss Jardine. Will you do it?"

"Yes."

The speaker's voice was even more husky than before.

Mr. Townsend scribbled a few words on a page of his pocket-book. Tearing out the leaf, he handed it to Lord Archibald Beaupré.

"Give her that. Not necessarily at once, but some time when the thing's all over. And tell her—" He stopped; then, with a smile, went on, "Yes, tell her that I loved her, but that already, when my love for her was born, it was too late."

"I'll tell her. What are you going to do yourself?"

"Do? Wait; they'll soon be here. I have one or two matters which will occupy me till they come. Good-bye."

He held out his hand. The other grasped it in his own.

"By —, Reggie, I had almost sooner that it had been I."

"Don't be an ass, dear boy. Slip across the water till the wind has blown a little of the dust away."

He nodded, moved quickly across the pavement, and disappeared into the house. Lord Archibald Beaupré was left standing in the street, clutching the sheet of paper tightly in his hand.

As Mr. Townsend entered a woman came forward to greet him. She wore an air of considerable concern.

"Oh, Mr. Townsend, sir, I'm so glad it's you. Burton's out, and something has happened which has quite upset me.

"I'm very sorry, Mrs. Lane, that you should have been upset. What has upset you?"

"There's been a man who wanted to see you—leastways, he didn't look as if he was a gentleman, and he didn't behave like one. I told him you weren't in, but he wouldn't take no for an answer. He pushed right past me and marched straight into your room, and said he'd wait until you came. He's been there an hour or more; and I just went in to say that I really didn't think it was any use his waiting when I was taken quite aback to find that the room was empty and that he wasn't there."

"That, probably, was because he had gone. Let us trust that the spoons have not gone too!"

"Oh, sir, I do trust they haven't. But what makes it seem so queer to me is that I have been watching all the time, and haven't seen a creature leave the room."

"Possibly, Mrs. Lane, he has vanished into air."

Laughing at her as he passed, Mr. Townsend went into his room.

CHAPTER XLI

TAKING LEAVE

It was a handsome room, that in which Mr. Townsend, when at home, passed the larger portion of his waking hours—large, lofty, well-proportioned. The walls were wainscoted. Here and there was a piece of tapestry. Curtains suggested, rather than screened, an occasional recess. Veiled, too, were entrances to rooms beyond. A window, running from floor to ceiling, extended on one side of the room, almost from wall to wall. Had it been daytime, one would have seen that it overlooked Hyde Park.

On his entrance Mr. Townsend went immediately to the portrait of the girl which stood up on his mantelboard. He looked at it long and earnestly. He took it out of its frame. He kissed it, not once or twice, but a dozen times at least. He regarded it with something of the veneration which the religious Russian peasant regards his Icon.

"Dora!" he murmured. "Dora!" Then, with a smile, "What might have been!"

Gripping the portrait with both his hands, he began to tear it into two; then stopped.

"It seems almost like sacrilege." He kissed the face again. "It would be a sacrilege to let it fall into their hands as evidence that she had endured the contamination of my acquaintance."

He tore the portrait, not only into halves, but into fragments, and the fragments he cast upon the fire. As the flames consumed them he made a little gesture towards them with his hands.

"Good-bye!"

He picked up several knick-knacks which were about the room and examined them, as if he were considering what ought to be their fate. Some of them, which bore unmistakable traces of feminine handiwork and taste, he threw, after the portrait, into the fire. He opened a large despatch-box which stood upon a table at one side. From among its varied contents he took all sorts of things—a glove, a knot of ribbon, a menu card, some programmes of dances, a chocolate bonbon, a variety of trivial impedimenta with which one would hardly have thought such a man would have cared to be troubled. Last of all he took out four or five envelopes addressed to himself in what was evidently a woman's hand.

"My love letters!—love letters! I doubt if there was a word of love in one of them, except that which came to me this morning. In our courtship hitherto love letters have scarcely entered. There has been no opportunity. It is another case of what might have been—and yet these are my love letters, for they were written by her hand, and these are my love tokens, because they are tokens of certain passages which she has had with me. Nor must they become their spoil. These sort of tales find their way into so many sorts of papers that, for her sake, it is well that I have had time enough to destroy what might tend to show that I ever was engaged—save the mark!—to marry Miss Jardine."

He threw the letters and the various trivialities together into the fire, breaking up the coals to enable them to burn the faster. He stood watching their destruction. When they were entirely consumed he turned away, the finger of his right hand in his waistcoat pocket, apparently feeling for something which was there.

"I think that that is all; now I'm ready."

"That, young man, is just as well, because so am I."

The voice came from behind his back. Mr. Townsend showed no sign of being startled, nor did he evince any anxiety to turn and inquire into the speaker's personality. He stood, for a moment, as if he was endeavouring to recall to his memory the tones of the speaker's voice. He turned at last, at his leisure, and with a smile—

"Mr. Haines?"

It was Mr. Haines. His sudden appearance was explained by the fact that he had obviously just stepped from behind a pair of curtains which concealed the entrance to an inner room. He still held one of the curtains in his hand. He eyed Mr. Townsend in silence, one hand being in suggestive proximity to the hip pocket in his trousers in which the Westerner is apt to keep his gun.

"Yes, I am Mr. Haines."

"I am glad to have the pleasure of seeing you, Mr. Haines. Might I ask you to be good enough to select your own chair?"

Mr. Haines took no notice of Mr. Townsend's gesture of almost exaggerated courtesy. Manner and tone alike were dogged.

"I've been watching you."

"I am gratified to think that any action of mine should have been esteemed worthy your attention."

"The woman said that you weren't in. I said I'd wait. I knew you'd come. She fidgeted. So I stepped behind the curtains. I thought trouble might be saved."

"It was very thoughtful, Mr. Haines, of you, indeed."

Mr. Haines moved away from the curtains. He came farther into the room, his hand still in the neighbourhood of his pistol pocket, his eyes never wandering from Mr. Townsend's face.

"Last night I reckoned with your brother."

"My brother?"

"He says he is your brother. He let it out as I was laying into him. And he's about your style all over. He calls himself Stewart Trevannion, and he's a thief, but not near such a thief as you."

"Is that so? May I inquire, Mr. Haines, what I have done that you should say I am a thief?"

"You've stole my girl."

"Your girl?" Mr. Townsend raised his eyebrows slightly, but still sufficiently for the movement to be perceptible. "Are you alluding to Mrs. Carruth?"

"Mrs. Carruth? No, young man, I am not alluding, as you call it, to Mrs. Carruth."

"I thought that Mrs. Carruth could hardly be adequately described as a girl."

"Is it sneering at Mrs. Carruth you are?"

Mr. Haines's idiom, on the sudden, became flavoured with, as it were, a reminiscence of Ireland.

"I trust that I never, Mr. Haines, shall be guilty of so heinous a crime as sneering at a lady. I believe that I am merely asserting a fact in venturing to express an opinion that Mrs. Carruth can hardly be adequately described as a girl."

Mr. Townsend's exaggeration of courtesy, suggesting more than it expressed, seemed to be something for which Mr. Haines was unprepared. He hesitated, as if in doubt; then repeated his previous assertion.

"You've stole my girl, and I've come to call you to account."

"I am unconscious of having conveyed from you any property of the kind. Of whom are you speaking as your girl?"

"My Loo."

"Your—" Mr. Townsend obviously started, regaining his self-possession only after a momentary pause. "I am still, Mr. Haines, so unfortunate as to be unable to follow you."

"Whether she was known to you as Louisa Haines, or Louise O'Donnel, or Milly Carroll, she was my girl. You stole her. You killed her. I am here to kill you for it."

There was silence. The two men eyed each other. Mr. Haines with that sullen, dogged look upon his face which it was used to wear; Mr. Townsend with the natural expression of the man who has just been told a sudden startling, wholly unexpected piece of news. He seemed to find it so startling a piece of news as to be almost incredible.

"Is it possible, Mr. Haines, that the lady whom I knew as Louise O'Donnel was your child?"

"She was: my only child—my one ewe lamb. You took her life. What have you to say why I shouldn't have your life for hers?"

"Only that it is the unexpected happens. I may tell you, twice I have been advised to beware of you. I had no notion what was your cause of quarrel. Now that I do know, I admit its perfect justice."

"Put up your hands."

Mr. Haines flashed a revolver in the air. Mr. Townsend remained unmoved; he simply looked at Mr. Haines and smiled.

"I am afraid that I must decline to obey you, literally, Mr. Haines. We do not do it quite that way this side. To an English taste the method seems a little bizarre. But I will undertake to offer no resistance. Nor to move. So far as I am concerned, you may shoot. I'm ready."

Mr. Haines moved a step or two forward. He pointed his revolver at Mr. Townsend's head, pointed it with a hand which did not tremble. There was an interval of silence. They steadfastly regarded each other, neither moving so much as an eyelash.

"You've grit. Which is what your brother'd like to swallow."

"It pleases you to say so. I would not wish to put you to inconvenience, but if you will permit me to advise you you will shoot and waste no time. Time is precious. I happen to know that, if you waste it, others may cheat you of your prey."

Mr. Haines lowered his revolver.

"I reckoned to shoot you on sight. It's not because you've grit I don't. Don't you think it. I've seen men like you before. A few. Some of them with grit enough to dare the devil to do his level worst when he gets them down to hell. Grit's just an accident. It don't count with me neither one way nor the other. Young man, I'm going to make you an offer."

"Make it."

"There are two things I've had to live for. Just two. No more. You've robbed me of them both. My girl, and the heart which I reckoned to have one day for mine."

"If, as I presume, this time it is Mrs. Carruth to whom you are referring, I do protest with all my heart that you are welcome to her heart, Mr. Haines."

"It's not your consent I should be asking. No. It's hers. I've asked for it. In vain. I reckon that with nothing to live for living isn't worth it. I've another gun in here." Mr. Haines produced a second revolver from one of his tail pockets. Mr. Townsend smiled. "What are you laughing at, young man?"

"You must forgive me. You reminded me for a moment of a pirate king of whom I used to read in my boyish days, whose habit it was to carry an arsenal about with him wherever he might go."

"Laugh on. One of these guns is for you, the other gun's for me. We are going to shoot each other."

"Excuse me, we are not."

"I say we are." Mr. Townsend slightly shrugged his shoulders. The gesture seemed to anger Mr. Haines. He went still closer to him. "You are going to put the muzzle of one gun to my forehead, and I'm going to put the muzzle of the other gun to yours, and we're going to fire together on the word."

"I beg ten thousand pardons for being constrained to contradict you, but—we are not."

"I say we are." Again the only response was a movement of Mr. Townsend's shoulders. "Take hold of the gun."

Mr. Haines endeavoured to thrust one of the revolvers into Mr. Townsend's hand.

"Not I."

"Take hold of the gun!"

Mr. Haines, on Mr. Townsend's betraying an inclination to remove himself from too near neighbourhood, caught him by the shoulder.

"Remove your hand, sir. I have no objection to your shooting me. But to your touching me while I am still alive I have."

"You hearken to what I say, young man. Take hold of this gun!"

Mr. Haines endeavoured to subject Mr. Townsend to what, in the nursery, is called a shaking.

"If you attempt to do that again, Mr. Haines, I shall be under the disagreeable necessity of knocking you down—before the shooting."

Mr. Haines attempted to do it again. Mr. Townsend tried to knock Mr. Haines down. Mr. Haines was not to be easily felled. Bursting into sudden passion, he seized Mr. Townsend by both shoulders. His two "guns" fell, unnoticed, to the ground. With commendable promptness Mr. Townsend returned the compliment which had been accorded him by clutching Mr. Haines. They clenched, struggled, and together fell to the floor.

On the floor they continued to discuss to the best of their ability the side issue which Mr. Haines had raised.

So engrossed were they with their own proceedings that they failed to notice the sudden opening of the door, followed by the unannounced entrance into the room of four or five men. One of them moved quickly to where the two combatants were contending on the floor. He placed his hand on Mr. Townsend's shoulder.

"You are my prisoner, Mr. Townsend. I arrest you on the charge of murder."

The sound of Mr. Holman's voice—for Matthew Holman was the speaker—did produce a diversion of the interest. The two men ceased to struggle. Then, being suffered to do so by Mr. Haines, Mr. Townsend rose to his feet. As he did so, some one who had come into the room with the police broke into laughter as he pointed at him with his finger. It was Mr. Pendarvon.

"Yes, officer, that's your man. That's Townsend, the Three Bridges murderer."

Mr. Pendarvon's merriment seemed out of place. He had cause to exchange it for something else a moment afterwards.

Mr. Townsend turned to Mr. Holman.

"As this person says, I am the man you want. And—" He paused; before they had a notion of what it was he intended to do, rushing forward, he had caught Mr. Pendarvon in his arms and borne him completely from his feet. "You are just the man I want."

Mr. Townsend's movements were so rapid that, before they could do anything to stop him, he had carried his victim right across the room, and, brushing aside the curtains, with a tremendous splintering of glass, had crashed with him through the closed windows into the night beyond.

"All right," cried Mr. Holman, as, too late to check his progress, the constables rushed after him. "There are some of the other chaps out there. They'll have him."

From Mr. Holman's point of view it proved to be all right. The drop from the window was only six or seven feet. By the time Mr. Holman had reached it Mr. Townsend was already again in the hands of the police. The detective shouted his instructions through the shattered pane.

"Put the handcuffs on him."

A voice replied from below—

"They are on him. He has almost killed this other man."

Mr. Townsend was heard speaking with a most pronounced drawl.

"Almost! Not quite! That's a pity. Still, 'twill serve. Officer, will you allow me to use my handkerchief; my mouth is bleeding?"

He succeeded, in spite of his handcuffed wrists, in withdrawing a handkerchief from an inner pocket of his coat. He pressed it, for a moment, to his lips. When he removed it, he tossed something into the air.

"Done you!" he cried. "Hurrah!"

There was an exclamation from the officer who was in charge of him.

"He has taken something. I can smell it."

"Yes," said Mr. Townsend, "I have taken leave." There was a small commotion. Mr. Townsend, reeling, would have fallen to the ground had he not been supported by the sergeant's arms. The man leaned over him to smell his breath. He, probably, was something of a chemist. "Hydrocyanic acid!" he exclaimed. "He is dead."

CHAPTER XLII

HAND IN HAND

Mrs. Tennant had obtained permission to see her husband in prison once before he was hung to say good-bye. She was starting upon the errand now—alone.

She had resolved to go alone. She had battled out the question with herself, upon her knees, in prayer, and it seemed to her that, of many alternatives, she had not chosen the worst. She would have with her neither his mother, nor hers, nor any of their kith and kin. The horror of the memory of that parting should be hers alone.

Nor would she take their little child, their Minna. That was for the child's sake. The father might, perhaps, be glad to see, once more, his darling, even though it was through iron bars. But the child must be considered. The picture of that last parting might, and probably would, be impinged upon the retina of the child's brain, never to be obliterated. It might haunt her through the years, colour the whole of her life.

When Mrs. Tennant was ready to start, while she was still in the privacy of her own room, she knelt upon the floor and drew the little child into her arms.

"Minna, I am going to see papa. Shall I tell him that you send your love?"

A small, pleading face looked into hers.

"Can't I come with you? I want to see him too."

"I cannot take you with me, Minna, but I will take your love. I think it would please papa to know you sent it."

"Of course you are to tell papa I love him. He knows I do. And, mamma, you're to give him that." The child kissed her mother. "And you're to tell him that he is to come back soon."

Mrs. Tennant went with the little one downstairs, not daring to trust herself in further speech. Her mother came to receive the child, and to put to her a last inquiry.

"Are you quite sure, Lucy, that you would not like to have me with you—nor any one—even as far as Lewes? Consider, dear, all you are undertaking, and think before you speak." Mrs. Tennant's answer was quietly conclusive. "I would rather go quite alone, mother, thanking you." There was a knocking at the hall door. Since bad news had come crowding so fast upon the household, every fresh knock had seemed to be the precursor of more ill-tidings. The two women looked at each other with frightened faces, a question in their very silence. While they still were looking there came, bursting into the room, no less a personage than that eminent counsel, Bates, Q.C., who had defended Mr. Tennant at his trial.

Mr. Bates seemed to be in a condition of very unlawyerlike excitement.

"Mrs. Tennant, I bring you good news!"

Mrs. Tennant shrunk back.

"Good news! For me!"

"The best of all possible news. I have only just heard it. I have come rushing off at once to tell you. Your husband is pardoned!"

"Pardoned! Do you mean that his sentence is commuted?"

"Nothing of the sort! He is a free man—as free as air! He has told us all along the absolute truth. He had nothing to do with the woman falling out of the carriage—she isn't even dead! It's an extraordinary story, and you shall hear all the details another time; but he had no more to do with the death of the poor girl who actually was murdered than you or I. Mrs. Tennant, your husband is a hardly used and a deeply injured man."

Mrs. Tennant had sunk into a chair. She was crying. Mr. Bates blew his nose; he wiped his eyes.

"Don't cry madam, don't cry! This isn't a case for tears! I am told that a Queen's messenger is taking the official pardon to Lewes by the next train. If you make haste, you'll be able to travel with him. And I'll come with you if you like!"

"Thank you, Mr. Bates, I will go alone."

And, practically, she went alone. In the same compartment of the train was the official messenger, but they did not exchange half a dozen words. Sitting in a corner of the railway carriage, with her veil down, she cried all the way to Lewes, smiling through her tears. They had a carriage from the station up to the prison on the hill. And Mrs. Tennant was suffered to be the bearer of the glad tidings to her husband.

In the condemned cell, locked in each other's arms, the man and woman cried as if their hearts would break.

And very shortly the prison gates closed after them, as, out of the valley of the shadow of death, they passed to face the world again, the husband and the wife, together, hand in hand.

Richard Marsh – A Short Biography

Richard Bernard Heldmann was born on 12th October 1857, in St Johns Wood, North London, to parents Joseph Heldmann and Emma Marsh.

Shortly after his birth his father became ensnared in a bankruptcy proceedings which enforced the abandonment of a career as a merchant for that of a schoolmaster at a school in Hammersmith, West London.

By his early 20's the young Heldmann, showing a talent for writing, began publishing fiction. In 1880, he began to publish works of boys' school and adventure stories for the myriad magazine publications all eager for good well-written content. The most important of these was Union Jack, one of the better quality boys' weekly magazine associated with the popular authors G. A. Henty and W.H.G. Kingston.

Heldmann was promoted to co-editor in October 1882, but his association with the publication ended suddenly in June 1883. After this, Heldmann published no further fiction under that name.

The reason at the time was not immediately apparent but in April 1884 Heldmann was sentenced to 18 months of hard labour for issuing a series of cheques, all forged, in France and Britain the year before.

In order to be well away from the scandal and damage this had caused to his reputation Heldmann adopted a pseudonym on his release from jail. Shortly thereafter the name 'Richard Marsh' began to appear in the literary periodicals. The use of his mother's maiden name seems both a release from the criminal record now associated with his given name and a lifeline to a fresh beginning.

A stroke of very good fortune arrived when his novel The Beetle was published in 1897. There had been more than a few previous publications of his works but The Beetle would turn out to be his greatest commercial success and added some much-needed gravitas to his literary reputation. The story concerns a mysterious oriental person who follows a British politician to London, and then wreaks havoc with his powers of hypnosis and shape-shifting. The Beetle has some similar aspects to certain other novels of the period, including those such as Bram Stoker's Dracula, George du Maurier's Trilby, and Sax Rohmer's many Fu Manchu novels. Like Dracula, and also the sensation novels written by Wilkie Collins and others during the 1860s, The Beetle is narrated from the various viewpoints of multiple characters to create suspense. The novel is also layered with many themes and issues of the Victorian era including women's rights, unemployment, urban poverty, radical politics, homosexuality, science, and Britain's imperial adventures, particularly in regard to Egypt and the Sudan. The Beetle sold out upon its initial print run and thereafter sold well for the next several decades. After Marsh's early death the novel's story was made into a film and adapted for the London stage, both in the 1920's.

It should also be noted that in the year of its first publication it outsold Dracula, then also in its first year of publication. In hindsight a remarkable achievement.

Marsh was a prolific writer and wrote almost 80 volumes of fiction as well as many short stories, across several genres from horror and crime to romance and humour.

However, at horror he was particularly adept. Works such as The Goddess: A Demon (1900), in which an Indian sacrificial idol comes to life with murderous resolve, and The Joss: A Reversion (1901), whose central premise is that of an Englishman who transforms himself into a hideous oriental idol are prime examples.

An important element of many of Marsh's novels is the investigation of the mystery. Several of his novels are centered on the crime and its subsequent detection. In the novel Philip Bennion's Death (1897) a bachelor is discovered dead the day after discussing Thomas De Quincey's essay on murder as a fine art, and his neighbour and friend begin efforts to solve his death. In The Datchet Diamonds (1898) a young man who has lost a fortune on the stock market mistakenly swaps bags with a diamond thief, and then find himself pursued by both the thieves and police. In A Spoiler of Men (1905), Marsh puts together crime and science-fiction; the gentleman-criminal villain renders people slaves to his will by a chemical injection.

As with many authors success with popular fiction was never quite enough. He also wanted to be regarded as a serious author. His novel A Second Coming (1900) imagines Christ's return to an early-20th century London and is his most well-handled attempt in that pursuit.

His prolific output of short stories ensured his being published in a plethora of magazines including Household Words, Cornhill Magazine, The Strand Magazine, and Belgravia, as well as in a number of short story book collections. These collections; The Seen and the Unseen (1900), Marvels and Mysteries (1900), Both Sides of the Veil (1901) and Between the Dark and the Daylight (1902) all feature an eclectic mix of humour, crime, romance and the occult.

He also published several serial short stories. Here he was able to develop characters whose adventures could be related in discrete stories across numerous editions of a magazine. An example is Mr. Pugh and Mr. Tress of Curios (1898). They are rival collectors between whom pass a series of bizarre and disturbing objects–poisoned rings, pipes which seem to come to life, a phonograph record on which a murdered woman seems to speak from the dead, and the severed hand of a 13th-century aristocrat.

During his career he sometimes came up with characters or stories ahead of their time. His character Miss Judith Lee, a young teacher of deaf pupils whose lip-reading ability involves her with mysteries that she solves by acting as a detective was very pro-active in this regard.

Richard Marsh died from heart disease in Haywards Heath in Sussex on 9th August 1915.

Several of his novels were published posthumously.

Richard Marsh – A Concise Bibliography

As Bernard Heldmann
Boxall School: A Tale of Schoolboy Life (1881)
Dorrincourt [Union Jack, April-September 1881]
Expelled: Being the Story of a Young Gentleman (1882)
Daintree (1883)

As Richard Marsh
Capturing a Convict (Strand Magazine 1893)
The Devil's Diamond (1893)
The Mahatma's Pupil (1893)
The Strange Wooing of Mary Bowler (1895)
Mrs Musgrave—and her Husband (1895)
The Mystery of Philip Bennion's Death (1897)
The Crime and the Criminal (1897)
The Duke and the Damsel (1897)
The Beetle: A Mystery (1897)
The House of Mystery (1898)

Under One Cover: Eleven Stories by S. Baring-Gould, Richard Marsh, Ernest G. Henham, Fergus Hume, Andrew Merry and A. St John Adcock (1898)
Curios: Some Strange Adventures of Two Bachelors (1898)
Tom Ossington's Ghost (1898)
The Datchet Diamonds (1898)
The Woman with One Hand and Mr Ely's Engagement (1899)
In Full Cry (1899)
Frivolities: Especially Addressed to Those Who Are Tired of Being Serious (1899)
The Purse Which Was Found
For One Night Only
Returning a Verdict
The Chancellor's Ward
A Honeymoon Trip
The Burglar's Blunder
Ninepence
A Battlefield Up-to-date
Mr. Harland's Pupils
A Burglar Alarm
A Lesson in Sculling
Outside
The Chase of the Ruby (1900)
An Aristocratic Detective (1900)
A Hero of Romance (1900)
The Seen and the Unseen (1900)
The Goddess: A Demon (1900)
Ada Vernham, Actress (1900)
A Second Coming (1900)
Marvels and Mysteries (1900)
The Long Arm of Coincidence
The Mask
An Experience
Pourquoipas
By Suggestion
A Silent Witness
To Be Used Against Him
The Words of a Little Child
How He Passed!
The Joss: A Reversion (1901)
Both Sides of the Veil (1901)
Amusement Only (1901)
The Twickenham Peerage (1902)
Between the Dark and the Daylight (1902)
The Adventures of Augustus Short: Things Which I Have Done for Others and Wish I Hadn't (1902)
A Metamorphosis (1903)
The Death Whistle (1903)
The Magnetic Girl (1903)
Miss Arnott's Marriage (1904)
Garnered (1904)

A Duel (1904)
A Spoiler of Men (1905)
The Marquis of Putney (1905)
The Confessions of a Young Lady (1905)
Under One Flag (1906)
In the Service of Love (1906)
The Garden of Mystery (1906)
A Woman Perfected (1907)
The Romance of a Maid of Honour (1907)
The Girl and the Miracle (1907)
The Surprising Husband (1908)
The Coward behind the Curtain (1908)
That Master of Ours (1908)
A Royal Indiscretion (1909)
The Interrupted Kiss (1909)
The Girl in the Blue Dress (1909)
The Lovely Mrs Blake (1910)
Live Men's Shoes (1910)
The Twin Sisters (1911)
A Drama of the Telephone (1911)
Violet Forster's Lover (1912)
Sam Briggs: His Book (1912)
Judith Lee: Some Pages from her Life (1912)
The Master of Deception (1913)
Justice—Suspended (1913)
If It Please You (1913)
The Woman in the Car (1914)
Molly's Husband (1914)
Margot—and her Judges (1914)
The Man with Nine Lives (1915)
Love in Fetters (1915)
His Love or his Life (1915)
The Flying Girl (1915)
Violet Forster's Lover (1916)
The Adventures of Judith Lee (1916)
Sam Briggs, V.C. (1916)
Coming of Age (1916)
The Great Temptation (1916)
The Deacon's Daughter (1917)
On the Jury (1918)
Orders to Marry ([1918)
Outwitted (1919)
Apron-Strings (1920)

Periodicals

For Debt, Windsor Magazine (January 1902)

Returning a Verdict, Cornhill Magazine (January 1896)

The Lost Duchess, Cornhill Magazine (January 1895)

Mrs Riddles Daughter, All the Year Round (17 March 1894)

An Episcopal Scandal, Cornhill Magazine (February 1894)

A Rubber or Two, All the Year Round (16 September 1893)

A First Night, Cornhill Magazine (April 1893)

The Mystery of Philip Bennion's Death, Household Words (3/10/17/24/31 December 1892)

The Princess Margaretta, Household Words (3 December 1892)

The Puzzle, Cornhill Magazine (November 1892)

A Victim to Art, All the Year Round (2 July 1892)

The Burglar's Blunder, Derby Mercury (24 June 1891)

Pourquoipas, All the Year Round (9/16 May 1891)

The Pipe, Cornhill Magazine (March 1891)

When Greek Joined Greek, Household Words (6 September 1890)

His First Experiment, Cornhill Magazine (September 1890)

"Mignonette", All the Year Round (9 August 1890)

The Long Arm of Coincidence, Household Words (24 May 1890)

The Match of the Season, Cornhill Magazine (May 1890)

A Set of Chessmen, Cornhill Magazine (April 1890)

A Dream of Diamonds, Household Words (7 December 1889)

My Uncle's Flirtation, Household Words (16 November 1889)

"Em", Household Words (2 November 1889)

The Barnes Mystery: An Adventure of Judith Lee, Strand Magazine (October 1916)

"Scandalous!", Strand Magazine (August 1916)

What Fell on her Hat, Strand Magazine (April 1916)

The Adventures of Sam Briggs: On the Film, Strand Magazine (March 1916)

A Set of Chessmen, Cassell's Magazine of Fiction and Popular Literature (Dec 1915)

Sam Briggs Becomes a Soldier: A Fighting Man, Strand Magazine (December 1915)

Sam Briggs Becomes a Soldier: On the Way Home, Strand Magazine (November 1915)

Sam Briggs Becomes a Soldier: An Official Mistake, Strand Magazine (October 1915)

Sam Briggs Becomes a Soldier: In their Own Gas, Strand Magazine (September 1915)

Sam Briggs Becomes a Soldier: Sanctuary, Strand Magazine (August 1915)

Sam Briggs Becomes a Soldier: In the Nick of Time, Strand Magazine (July 1915)

Sam Briggs Becomes a Soldier: A Night Surprise for the Germans, Strand Magazine (June 1915)

Sam Briggs Becomes a Soldier: In the Trenches, Strand Magazine (May 1915)

Sam Briggs Becomes a Soldier: Baptism of Fire, Strand Magazine (April 1915)

Sam Briggs Becomes a Soldier: Two Stripes, Strand Magazine (March 1915)

Life in the King's New Army: Jack Carpenter's True Story, VI: Career for our Boys, Daily Mail (27 February 1915)

Life in the King's New Army: Jack Carpenter's True Story, V: The Tailor and the Man, Daily Mail (26 February 1915)

Life in the King's New Army: Jack Carpenter's True Story, IV: Hutments', Daily Mail (25 February 1915)

Life in the King's New Army: Jack Carpenter's True Story, III: First-Rate Fighting Men', Daily Mail (24 February 1915)

Life in the King's New Army: Jack Carpenter's True Story, II: The Berwick Borderers, Daily Mail (23 February 1915)

Life in the King's New Army: Jack Carpenter's True Story, I: Crossed Swords, Daily Mail (22 February 1915)

Sam Briggs Becomes a Soldier: A Man in the Making, Strand Magazine (February 1915)

Sam Briggs Becomes a Soldier: Sam Briggs Becomes a Soldier, Strand Magazine (January 1915)

The Amazing Visitor, Strand Magazine (December 1914)

Looping the Loop: An Adventure of Sam Briggs, Strand Magazine (August 1914)

The Torch, Strand Magazine (October 1913)

"Gaiety" Abroad, Strand Magazine (September 1913), 274-82

A Self-Appointed Guardian, English Illustrated Magazine (August 1913)

For the Cause, Strand Magazine (April 1913)

The Adventures of Judith Lee: The Affair of the Montagu Diamonds, Strand Magazine (February 1913)

The Adventures of Judith Lee: Mandragora, Strand Magazine (August 1912)

The Adventures of Judith Lee: "8 Elm Grove—Back Entrance", Strand Magazine (July 1912)

The Adventures of Judith Lee: The Restaurant Napolitain, Strand Magazine (June 1912)

The Adventures of Judith Lee: Uncle Jack, Strand Magazine (May 1912)

The Adventures of Judith Lee: Was It by Chance Only? Strand Magazine (April 1912)

The Adventures of Judith Lee: Isolda, Strand Magazine (March 1912)

The Adventures of Judith Lee: "Auld Lang Syne", Strand Magazine (January 1912)

The Adventures of Judith Lee: The Miracle, Strand Magazine (December 1911)

The Adventures of Judith Lee: Matched

The Burglary in Berkeley Square, Pearson's Magazine (December 1908)

The River of Light, Strand Magazine (December 1908)

The Girl in the Light Blue Dress, Strand Magazine (October 1908)

O'Rourke of the Saucy Sixth, Grand Magazine (June 1908)

The Adventures of Sam Briggs: The Limerick, Strand Magazine (February 1908)

The Adventures of Sam Briggs: The Star of Romance, Strand Magazine (July 1907)

The Adventures of Sam Briggs: A Social Evening, Strand Magazine (April 1907)

My Best Story and Why I Think So No. 21: The Strange Occurrences in Canterstone Gaol, Grand Magazine (October 1906)

The Adventures of Sam Briggs: That Hansom, Strand Magazine (May 1906)

The Adventures of Sam Briggs: Her Fourth, Strand Magazine (December 1905)

The Adventures of Sam Briggs: A Modest Half-Crown, Strand Magazine (November 1905)

The Adventures of Sam Briggs: The Gift Horse, Strand Magazine (March 1905)

My Wedding Day, Strand Magazine (January 1905)

The Adventures of Sam Briggs: The Girl on the Sands, Strand Magazine (October 1904)

The Parson, the Soldier, and the Child, London Magazine (November 1903)

The Girl and the Boy, London Magazine (October 1903)

By Whose Hand? New Short Novel by Richard Marsh, Answers (1 August – 31 October 1903)

A Girl Who Couldn't, Strand Magazine (January 1903)

The Kit-Bag, Windsor Magazine, 17 (January 1903), 298-309

Their Reasons: Two Hitherto Unreported Conversations, House Annual (1902)

At Large: Being the Strange Perils and Experiences of George Otway, Suspect, Answers (12 July - 27 December 1902)

The Handwriting, Strand Magazine (June 1902)

La Haute Finance, Windsor Magazine (March 1902)

A Wonderful Girl, Strand Magazine (March 1902)

Skittles, English Illustrated Magazine, (February/March 1902)

Breaking the Ice, Strand Magazine (February 1902)

My Aunt's Excursion, Windsor Magazine (January 1902)

The Haunted Chair: The Story of a Strange Mystery, Harmsworth London Magazine (January 1902)

Miss Donne's Great Gamble, Strand Magazine (November 1901)

The Man in the Glass Cage; or The Strange Story of the Twickenham Peerage, Manchester Times, (6 September – 27 December 1901

The Adventures of Augustus Short: Things Which I Have Done for Others, and Wish I Hadn't: The Address Which I Gave for Rudman, Cassell's Magazine (November 1901)

The Adventures of Augustus Short: Things Which I Have Done for Others, and Wish I Hadn't: Jones's Love Affair, Cassell's Magazine (October 1901)

The Adventures of Augustus Short: Things Which I Have Done for Others, and Wish I Hadn't: The Duel I Fought of Jarvis, Cassell's Magazine (September 1901)

The Adventures of Augustus Short: Things Which I Have Done for Others, and Wish I Hadn't: Griffin's Offspring, Cassell's Magazine (August 1901)

The Adventures of Augustus Short: Things Which I Have Done for Others, and Wish I Hadn't: McCulloch's Shoes, Cassell's Magazine (July 1901)

The Adventures of Augustus Short: Things Which I Have Done for Others, and Wish I Hadn't: The Fitzroy-Jenkinsons' Rooms, Cassell's Magazine (June 1901)

Staggers, Windsor Magazine (April 1901)

How I Drove a Motor Car for Randal, Strand Magazine (April 1901)

The Disappearance of Mrs Macrecham: The Amazing Story of a Strange Cat, Harmsworth Monthly Pictorial Magazine (March 1901)

The Irregularity of the Juryman, Strand Magazine (December 1900)

The Strange Fortune of Pollie Blythe: The Story of a Chinese "God", Manchester Times (12 October 1900 – 8 February 1901)

Pugh's Poisoned Ring, Harmsworth Monthly Pictorial Magazine (October 1900)

Willyum, Penny Illustrated Paper and Illustrated Times, (26 May 1900)

Willyum, Hampshire Telegraph and Naval Chronicle (26 May 1900)

The Goddess: A Demon, Manchester Times (12 January – 30 March 1900)

The Stolen Treaty, Manchester Times (27 October 1899)

For One Night Only, Answers (8 April 1899)

In Full Cry, Manchester Times (3 March – 9 June 1899)

The Colonel's Cane, Cassell's Magazine (February 1899)

The Burglary at Azalea Villa, Manchester Times, (13 January 1899)

The Burglary at Azalea Villa, Newcastle Weekly Courant (14 January 1899)

Our Christmas Burglar, Answers (17 December 1898)

Something to his Advantage, Manchester Times (7 October – 4 November 1898)

A Lesson in Sculling, Newcastle Weekly Courant (October 1898)

That Five Hundred Pound Price, Harmsworth Monthly Pictorial Magazine (September 1898)

The Chancellor's Ward, Harmsworth Monthly Pictorial Magazine (August 1898)

The Ossington Mystery, Ipswich Journal (1 April – 17 June 1898)

The Duchess of Datchet's Diamonds, New Zealand Graphic and Ladies' Journal (New Zealand) (7 May – 25 June 1898)

The Peril of Paul Lessingham: The Story of a Haunted Man, Answers (13 March – 19 June 1897)

The Purse Which Was Found, Answers (17 April 1897)

The Rector and the Curate, Answers (19 December 1896)

An Illustration of Modern Science, Pall Mall Magazine (November 1896)

A Battlefield Up-to-Date, Idler Magazine (August 1896)

Twins, Idler Magazine (January 1896)

Lady Wishaw's Hand, Leeds Mercury (January 1895)
Young George, St Nicholas (March 1894)
Exchange Is Robbery, Idler Magazine (December 1893 - January 1894)
The Tipster: An Impossible Story, Home Chimes (December 1893)
The Influence of Women, Home Chimes (November 1893)
By Deputy: A Reminiscence of Travel, Home Chimes (October 1893)
Rivals, Home Chimes (September 1893)
Capturing a Convict, Strand Magazine (August 1893)
A Burglar Alarm, Home Chimes (June 1893)
Music Halls and Theatres, Home Chimes (March 1893)
A Strange Bride, Manchester Times (6/13 January 1893)
The Mask, Gentleman's Magazine (December 1892)
A Vision of the Night, Strand Magazine (December 1892)
Nelly, Home Chimes (November 1892)
A Prophet: A Story, New England Magazine (October - November 1892)
Mr Harland's Pupils, Home Chimes (August 1892)
The Brothers in Grey, Home Chimes (April 1892)
The Half-Back, Derby Mercury (March 1892)
The Half-Back, Home Chimes (February 1892)
The Violin, Home Chimes (December 1891)
The Short Story, Home Chimes (August 1891)
Magical Music, Gentleman's Magazine (May 1891)
A Honeymoon Trip, Home Chimes (April 1891)
Mitwaterstraand, Time (September 1890)
A Pack of Cards, Longman's Magazine (August 1890)
The Burglar's Blunder, Ladies' Journal (Canada) (1 July 1890)
The Strange Occurrences in Canterstone Jail, Blackwood's Edinburgh Magazine (June 1890)
A Substitute: The Story of My Last Cricket-Match, Longman's Magazine (June 1890)
The Burglar's Blunder, Gentleman's Magazine (May 1890)
A Silent Witness, Belgravia (October 1889)
A Bed for the Night, Belgravia (Summer 1889)
Payment for a Life, Belgravia (Summer 1888)

www.ingramcontent.com/pod-product-compliance
Lightning Source LLC
Chambersburg PA
CBHW060550260626
47161CB00003B/1139